A GOLDEN CORNISH SUMMER

Emma loved her life in the seaside village of Silver Cove. But when the discovery of sunken treasure ignited a feud between her family and that of Luke, her first love, everything fell apart. Heartbroken and betrayed, she fled.

Now, as she wades into the sparkling surf for the first time in fifteen years, she remembers everything she loved about this beautiful place. Then a huge wave knocks her off her feet. Wet and dripping, Emma is rescued by none other than Luke — who is, to her dismay, even more handsome than ever.

Emma starts to wonder if returning home was a huge mistake — or if the real treasure could have been waiting here for her all along . . .

PHILLIPA ASHLEY

---◆---

A GOLDEN CORNISH SUMMER

Complete and Unabridged

CHARNWOOD
Leicester

First published in Great Britain in 2022 by
HarperCollins*Publishers*
London

First Charnwood Edition
published 2022
by arrangement with
HarperCollins*Publishers*
London

This novel is entirely a work of fiction. The names,
characters and incidents portrayed in it are the work of the
author's imagination. Any resemblance to actual persons,
living or dead, events or localities is entirely coincidental.

*A catalogue record for this book is available
from the British Library.*

ISBN 978–1–4448–4946–2

Published by
Ulverscroft Limited
Anstey, Leicestershire

Printed and bound in Great Britain by
TJ Books Ltd., Padstow, Cornwall

This book is printed on acid-free paper

For John, ILY x

1

How could the sea possibly be this bloody *cold?*

Carrying her kitten heels by their straps, Emma Pelistry resisted the urge to run out of the sea onto the sand of Silver Cove. With the afternoon sun shining down, her suit had made her uncomfortably hot, which was why she'd decided to cool off in the water.

Partly why she'd decided to go in the water.

Like so many times before, she couldn't resist the lure of the sea, lapping the shore like liquid mercury and painting the rocks a silvery hue. Despite having been away so long, it was as enticing as ever.

Letting her toes sink into the sand, she tried to enjoy the sensation of the cold water. Years ago, she'd have thought nothing of dashing right in wearing her bikini, shrieking and laughing with Luke. The tide was coming in, about to wash away the heart in the sand that had been drawn by some deluded soul. If only the past could be erased so easily.

Had it really been fifteen years since she'd last set foot here?

Silver Cove had barely changed apart from the café in the dunes where several couples were basking in the late May sun.

There were a few people scattered over the sand including a small group with sticks and sacks, poking around the tideline. They were probably beach-cleaners or beachcombers. 'Eco-warriors,' her dad would have called them.

At the thought of him curling his lip in disdain, tears

1

stung the backs of her eyes. It had been two months since his passing and she still couldn't believe it.

With the water nipping at her ankles, her gaze rested on the building at the edge of the beach that had once been her home. The Old Chapel was still there, of course, and probably would be for another two hundred years.

Her parents had had to move away from Cornwall not long after she'd gone to university. They'd insisted to everyone that they'd wanted to 'downsize' and move further north but none of the locals had been fooled. Everyone knew the real reason.

As for her father, he'd never recovered from the crushing disappointment of having to leave Silver Cove all those years ago.

Two years after moving out of the Old Chapel, her parents had divorced. Emma had been at university and, afterwards, had been busy in her first job as an artist with a greeting card firm. With the family scattered, it had been difficult to keep in touch, especially with her father who'd made no real effort to meet up. It was as if he'd withdrawn from not only her mum, but from Emma too.

She'd done her best to try and talk to him but, eventually, they'd drifted apart, to the point where she'd seen him only a few times in the intervening twelve years. The last had been the previous spring in a pub in Oxford, the city where Emma now lived. She'd been shocked at the state of him. He was haggard and sinking whisky like it was going out of fashion but all her questions about his health had been met with a curt dismissal.

Less than a year later, her mother rang to break the news that he'd died.

Despite their estrangement, Emma had still been shocked at how much she'd wept at the funeral, and the heart-squeezing grief that had caused her to cling onto her ex, Theo, as the service had ended. Only the cold bite of the water around her ankles stopped her from bursting into tears again now.

A wave splashed her legs, spattering her skirt with droplets. She felt ridiculous paddling in a suit, but she hadn't been thinking straight when she'd grabbed it from the hanger first thing that morning. She'd had an early meeting with the solicitor's in Oxford, before heading straight to Cornwall and apart from her dad's funeral and today, it had stayed in the wardrobe.

She'd no need for formal clothes in her job as a freelance illustrator, preferring jeans or a comfy jersey dress and well-worn plimsolls. Never mind. She could change as soon as she reached Maxi's.

When her old school friend had heard Emma needed somewhere to live for the summer, she'd very kindly invited her to stay at her home outside Falford. Emma had just landed a dream commission: the illustrations for a gorgeous book about the coast for a high-end publisher.

They wanted a series of drawings and paintings to accompany the text and, when her agent had secured her the job just a few days before, she'd jumped at the chance. It was the one bright spot after a very dark few months. However, the project came with a very tight deadline and she'd decided she needed to focus on it for the next few months away from the city.

Sadly, her father's funeral had also sounded the death knell for her relationship with Theo.

Oh, he'd been kind enough, offering tissues and making soothing noises, but on the way home from

3

the wake it had become clear that he expected her grief to be a temporary blip. He'd told her he couldn't understand why she was 'quite so upset' given she'd hardly seen her father over the years.

She'd found it impossible to explain then realised she shouldn't have to explain . . . Theo should surely have understood? The alarm bells might have rung then but it was a week later that the axe had fallen. He'd phoned her from a business trip — he couldn't even face her in person — to say he'd accepted a new job in Dublin and was leaving.

'I was going to tell you, but I kept putting it off and then your dad passed away and it didn't seem right,' he'd said hastily, clearly desperate to get off the line. 'I'm so sorry but I can't miss this opportunity. It's head of marketing and I might never get the chance again.

'Obviously, I can't possibly expect you to move to another country.' Well, obviously, Emma had thought. In other words, he didn't want her to move with him. Emma didn't want to uproot her life either, but it still hurt not to even be asked.

The killer blow was when Theo had added, 'Your heart wasn't really in our relationship, anyway, was it?'

'What do you mean?' Emma had said.

'I never felt you thinking of us as long-term. Be honest, Emma, neither of us could see us sitting by the fire with a brood of grandkids on our golden wedding anniversary. You always seem to be somewhere else.'

She'd cut off the call, too choked with shock to try to express how hurt she was. She hadn't heard from him after that, and she didn't expect to, but his words had harried her ever since. Your heart wasn't really in our relationship. Did he mean just her and Theo, or any relationship?

The chill of the water around her calves had begun to bite. That was it, she was getting out before the blood supply to her feet was cut off. She was also worried by the audience she'd attracted. The beach-cleaners were gathered in a huddle nearby. They seemed to be looking at something in the tangle of weed and rubbish on the tideline. God knows what — or why.

'Oh God!'

One of her shoes slipped from her hand into the surf.

'No!'

It bobbed a few feet away but, amazingly, was still afloat. Gritting her teeth against the cold, Emma waded towards it. The water was around her thighs now and absolutely freezing. Yet still the shoe bobbed agonisingly, just out of reach . . . She took another step before a wave picked it up and swept it a few yards further out. Another wave broke just ahead of her, spattering her with chilly droplets.

'Owww!'

She threw her other shoe up the beach out of reach of the surf and turned around again. Her shoe was about to be carried further off. Knowing she could hardly get much wetter, she hitched her skirt high around her waist. It meant people would be able to see her knickers but she had to get that shoe. She'd treated herself to the pair after landing her most recent contract. She'd never owned shoes that expensive: never spent that much on an item of clothing.

The shoe floated slightly closer, borne by the wave. She turned to face it, wading against the current, waist-deep. The cold ripped the breath from her lungs, but she was in too deep now to turn back. Abandoning any attempt to keep her clothes dry, she lunged for it as it started to sink.

Her fingers closed around the strap. 'Yes!'

There was a swoosh and Emma glanced to her side in time to see a foamy crest thundering down on her. She tried to take a huge step but found herself suddenly chest-deep in a hollow scoured out by the waves.

'Oh!' She let out a shriek.

Another wave rolled in, smacking her in the face, stinging her eyes and filling her mouth with salty water. Coughing, she stumbled again, her feet finding not firm sand, but water. She went under and panic seized her. It was like being in a washing machine from hell. Her heavy suit weighed her down and she was so *cold*. Which way was up? Where was the shore?

'OK. OK. I've got you.'

Two arms lifted her up, hauling her from the depths. 'Stay calm. You'll be OK.'

Thank God. She was in shallower water now, her feet on the firm sand. Coughing and spluttering, she staggered away from her rescuer, towards the beach-cleaners. She didn't look round or thank him, she was too ashamed. Desperate to escape, she marched away across the beach but some of the beach-cleaners had other ideas.

'Don't worry! We'll save you!' a young woman shrieked, blocking Emma's path.

'I d-don't need s-saving,' Emma cried, wiping her eyes and snotty nose. 'I w-was only trying to get my shoe.'

They clearly didn't believe her.

'Are you OK, love? Here, have this to keep you

warm.' A very tall, thin man was unzipping his fleece by her side.

Emma had to stop as three people formed a semi-circle in front of her as if they were about to tackle her to the ground. None of them sounded like her rescuer, not that Emma cared because her only object was to get the hell away from them before she died of embarrassment. 'No. I'm f-fine.'

He held out the fleece. 'Here, my love, put this round you.'

'No, really, *thank you.*'

'It's never worth it, love,' he said softly. 'Shall we call an ambulance?'

'Don't you dare!' Emma was filled with shame at the idea of the emergency services being called out over a lost shoe.

The lanky man held up his hands. 'OK. OK.'

'My dear young woman, we won't do anything you don't want us to,' a pink-haired woman in a linen kaftan said haughtily. 'However, may I suggest that no item of footwear is worth risking drowning or hypothermia.'

'Now, Ursula, give the girl some credit,' the gangly man replied, still clutching his fleece. 'I expect those shoes were worth a week's wages.'

Ursula and her hair seemed to visibly rise up, like the crest of an angry parrot. 'I absolutely have no idea about the cost of designer footwear, Marvin. It holds not the slightest interest for me.'

Ursula squinted at Emma, a puzzled look on her face as if she was staring at a painting. A painting she didn't like very much and wasn't sure was authentic.

However, Emma knew instantly that Ursula was the real deal.

Ursula Bowen was her old art teacher and the two of them had had a thorny relationship at best. Nothing Emma ever did seemed to impress Ms Bowen and Emma had reacted by dismissing most of her 'advice,' even when she might have agreed with it. She thought it was a miracle she'd got the top grade at A level. Had she recognised her? Emma prayed not.

Marvin was also vaguely familiar and his name was too distinctive to be a coincidence. Still reed-thin, though now almost bald, he'd been a talented high-jumper at the school and was the son of a local undertaker. However, he'd been four years above her so she doubted he'd even registered her existence. Emma had never met the younger woman, who had long blonde hair in a plait like Rapunzel, and was gawping at her.

They were all kindly, concerned — apart from Ursula whose mouth was set in a disgusted line — and they clearly thought she'd been about to do away with herself.

'Look,' she said, with what she hoped was a winning smile. It wasn't easy to sound calm and collected when your teeth were chattering away and you couldn't stop shivering. 'I *really* only went in to get my shoe and I slipped and fell. Really, I am f-fine. A little chilly but absolutely *fine*. Now, I th-think I'll go back to my car and put on some dry clothes. I have some in the boot in my suitcase.'

Without waiting for an answer, Emma stomped off, as much as you could stomp when your whole body was turning into a popsicle and your frozen feet were sinking into the sand. She was half worried that the gang, led by the bloke who'd hauled her out of the sea might run after her. She didn't know where the bloke who'd pulled her out was, and she wasn't going to linger to find out in case he was on his phone at this moment calling 999, despite the others saying they'd leave her alone.

Her shoe had been given up as a bad loss, and was now the least of her worries, the biggest of which being that if this bunch of do-gooders called for an ambulance to cart her off somewhere, she'd have to answer a load of awkward questions.

'Wait! Emma.'

At the mention of her name, she turned instinctively. That was a voice she recognised.

Her rescuer, as dripping wet as she was, was a few paces behind her, following her up the beach. He was also tall, though any resemblance with Marvin ended there. He had thick, curly chestnut hair and a blue T-shirt that was plastered to his broad shoulders and chest. Now she finally dared to look at him, her heart missed a beat. His Cornish accent placed him firmly where he was born, barely a mile from this very beach.

Yet this man was a fantasy, cover-model version of the wiry boy she'd fallen in love with fifteen years before. The lad who'd caused her so much pain, ruined her family's livelihood — and who she thought she'd never see again.

She spoke one word. '*Luke.*'

'Hello, Emma.' The blue eyes were hesitant as he held her soggy footwear by its heel. 'Here's your shoe.'

Emma didn't care about the shoe. Every atom was focused on the man in front of her. In a heartbeat, fifteen years vanished and she was back in her bedroom at the Old Chapel on a sultry summer's afternoon, a textbook in her lap and Luke Kerr by her side.

2

'Good grief, was that Emma Pelistry?' Ursula said as Luke loaded the last sack of rubbish into the pickup truck. 'You know, I think it must have been!' she went on. 'I've left my damn glasses in the car and she looked so different in that suit when you fished her out of the water. Silly girl!'

Only half-listening, Luke was still reeling from finding Emma in Cornwall, let alone having plucked her from the waves of Silver Cove.

'Luke?' Ursula was right under his nose, glaring at him.

'Yes, it was,' he muttered.

She whistled. 'Well, well. I wonder why she's washed up here after all this time?'

'I've no idea. Sorry, Ursula, I have to go. I've got to take this to the recycling place on my way to the dive centre and I'm already running late.'

'No wonder after that palaver. Risking drowning to chase after a shoe! Mind you, it's typical Emma, isn't it? Headstrong, does what she pleases and damn everyone else.'

Without replying, Luke opened the truck door and started the engine.

'Luke!' she called through the window.

'Sorry, I'm late for work.'

He roared off, wheels spinning on the sand that had blown onto the beach road. Emma was back, after fifteen years. The last time he'd seen her, they'd been hurling accusations at each other. There had been tears and anger, and not only on her side.

Yet, seeing her today, it was another moment that stuck in his mind. A moment when everything in their young lives had changed forever.

Driving back past the gates of the Old Chapel, he recalled a heady afternoon in her bedroom many years ago, before the storm broke.

Emma had been drawing him but he'd found it uncomfortable to be the subject of such scrutiny, even by her. He'd fidgeted and kept looking through the window, but he remembered the conversation as clearly as if he were there now.

'Don't you think it's weird to have dead people for neighbours?' he'd asked.

She'd glanced up at him, her frown of concentration still in place. 'What kind of a question is that?'

'The kind of question you ask someone who lives in an old chapel with a graveyard in the garden.'

Her frown had melted into amusement. 'I'm used to it,' she said, going back to her sketchbook and tucking her hair behind her ear, exposing a smooth cheek, dappled with freckles. 'Now shut up and keep still.'

'Can I smile?' Luke asked.

'No. Don't move a muscle. I need you to look mean and moody.'

'Why?'

'Because . . . it's more interesting.'

More interesting than what, Luke wanted to ask. Was he boring as himself? As for looking 'moody', Luke thought that Emma was the one whose moods changed at the drop of a hat these days. Sometimes, he felt as if he was the most important person in her life: the only one to make her eyes light up with real delight. At other times, she seemed distant, as if he

11

were someone to be tolerated. Occasionally, she could be impatient and cutting, almost as if she was trying to push him away. He never knew where he stood.

However, today, he was happy to go along with her demand that he let her draw him, though he'd no idea what she saw that was worth so much effort to commit to paper.

She rapped him on the arm with her pencil. 'Keep still,' she ordered.

He rearranged his face into the expression he adopted most of the time at school: shutters down and hoping no one would notice him. Meanwhile, her pencil darted over the sketchpad, her eyes constantly glancing up at him, her fingers capturing him on the paper.

Looking her as she sat cross-legged on the bed with sunlight gleaming on her red hair, Luke had thought she was more beautiful than ever, though he'd never have told her. Besides, she must surely be aware of it? Most of the lads at school thought so, and would have given a lot to be in his position. They'd have been amazed he was dating the 'Ice Maiden', though not as amazed as Luke himself.

He'd come over to her house after school and before her parents came home. They were supposed to be revising A level biology together, with their exams coming up that summer.

As usual, Emma was more interested in sketching him and Luke was far more interested in the real biology happening to his body than the theoretical stuff in the book. He was fascinated by the way her hair brushed the pages as she leaned lower, tongue stuck out in concentration.

She lifted her head and frowned at him. 'Why are

12

you looking at me like that?'

'I'm not. I'm looking mean and moody.'

'No, you were staring at me and smiling. I can't finish this unless you take it seriously. Don't gawp at me: look over my shoulder at something.'

Luke tore his gaze from Emma's face to the view through the window of her room. The sash was open a few centimetres, allowing the cooling sea breeze in.

A former Methodist church, the Old Chapel had been built right on the edge of Silver Cove. On a day like today, sapphire waters rolled gently onto the flat sands, where the rocks were gilded with the sunlight. Luke used to think that was how the cove had got its name: from the way the smooth, black rocks reflected the light. The real reason was that a famous wreck had gone down two centuries before spilling a cargo of silver into the sea.

The story had always fascinated him and, even now, it was powerful enough to draw his thoughts briefly away from Emma. The *Minerva* was a Dutch merchantman ship, laden with coins, which the Royal Navy had captured in a sea battle in 1805. The navy were sailing her back to England when she'd been blown onto a reef off Silver Cove. Everyone locally knew about the story and the legend was that some of the coins had been taken off the ship before it had sunk.

His dad, Harvey, was obsessed with it — as was Emma's father, Robin. Once, they'd almost come to blows in the local pub over it. Robin's ancestors had been distantly related to the commander of the Royal Navy ship that had captured the *Minerva*. He was convinced the silver had been hidden near the chapel, possibly in a grave.

13

Harvey had laughed at him, saying Robin was naïve and that the coins would have been spirited away by looters years ago. Privately, however, Harvey had told Luke he thought the booty might have been buried somewhere near the cove.

'Who knows? One day maybe you'll find a piece of silver washed up on the beach, son,' he'd said.

For a few weeks after that, Luke had expected every flash of light on every walk to be a coin but had found only ring-pulls or chocolate wrappers, though he hadn't given up hope. In fact, it was one of the reasons he wanted to join the navy when he'd finished school. He'd already looked into becoming a naval diver, and maybe, one day, finding wrecks of his own. As he'd grown up, however, he'd come to dismiss his father's claims as yet another daydream, one of many his dad liked to cling to instead of actually knuckling down to some real work.

'Right! I can't do any more or I'll spoil you.'

Emma brought him back to the moment, holding up her sketchpad, a frown on her face. 'There you go.'

Luke stared at the picture. 'Is that me?'

'Well it's not Santa Claus, is it?' Emma rolled her eyes again.

'I look . . . very serious.'

'That's because you are very serious.' She smirked. 'I'd prefer to call it intense and brooding.'

'Brooding? Don't chickens do that?' he said.

Emma let out a peal of laughter. 'You are so funny, Luke.'

'Funny? I thought I was meant to be serious.'

She tore the sheet from the book. 'I can chuck it in the bin if you want.'

'No! No, don't do that.'

14

She held the sheet out of his reach and Luke tried to grab it. She danced off around the room, teasing him with it.

'Come and get it!'

Any reply was cut off by the sound of a car engine from below the open sash window.

Emma froze, the sketch in her hand. 'Oh God, it's Mum and Dad. They weren't supposed to be home until six.'

Abandoning the picture on the bed, she flew to the window. Luke followed, careful to keep out of sight. Hester Pelistry was walking around to the back door, towards Emma's window on the ground floor of the chapel. She had a tray of plants in her arms. He couldn't see Robin but he was probably on his way too.

'Jesus. You have to go,' Emma cried.

'Now? It's going to chuck it down. Look at those clouds over the cove.'

'Sorry. They'll kill me.' She let out a squeak of panic. 'Oh my God, Mum's coming inside. You can't go out of the window. One of them will see you.'

'Why don't you just tell them we're revising?'

'No! They won't believe us.'

'I can't vanish,' Luke protested.

Emma glanced around her as if a wizard might appear and magic Luke away. 'Look. You can go in there.'

'Where?'

'Into the void. Come on!'

At one end of the room was a painted panel like a trapdoor, secured by a metal catch.

'In there? It's tiny.'

'No, it's much bigger than it looks. It's like a loft

15

space where there's loads of junk. You can almost stand up in it and there's a little window. You'll be fine, I promise, and you can come out in a minute when we know Mum's not coming back.'

He was about to refuse when she kissed him. He reeled. He pulled her to him. Her tanned, slender body, the scent of her hair from that coconut shampoo.

'Why are you ashamed of me?' he said. 'Why do they think I'm not good enough for you? Or is it you that don't think I'm good enough?'

'What? I — d-do think you're good enough. It's just . . . them. Bloody parents. They're . . . well, they don't understand. Please, do as I ask?' She sounded desperate.

'I'm sick of all these secret meetings. We shouldn't have to hide away. We should be happy to let everyone know we're together.'

Emma's expression darkened then she kissed him again. 'If one of us had a car, we wouldn't have to hide away. We could meet anywhere we wanted . . . But we don't, so please, Luke, if you care about me, get up there.'

With a groan of exasperation, Luke did as he was told. He felt as if he were contraband she'd been caught with and had to get rid of, like the smugglers who'd had to hide their brandy and baccy from the customs men in days gone by.

He undid the catch and pushed at the trapdoor. At first it wouldn't budge, clearly not having been opened for ages and sticking in the damp, but he shoved at it, wobbling the chair.

'Be careful!'

'I'm doing my best.' He gave the trapdoor one last

16

shove and it shot open with a crack, showering him with flakes of paint. Emma pushed him up and he wriggled through the opening, scraping one of his shins as he clambered into the roof space.

His leg throbbed but there was no time to think about it because Emma was below, shoving his backpack into the air. Luke pulled it up after him, still coughing and blinking dust from his eyes.

'It's skanky as hell in here.'

'It'll be fine. Please, Luke. Quick! Mum's coming. Shut the trapdoor!' Her voice was so full of desperation that he gave in.

Gradually his eyes adjusted and shapes in the gloom appeared. There was a window in the end of the space, though it was coated in grime. It wasn't big enough to stand but he could sit upright. He rubbed his leg; he'd scraped his shin on the edge of the attic door and the skin was grazed. It stung like hell.

He coughed again, then remembered the Coke bottle in his backpack. Listening for the sound of Mrs Pelistry entering the room — and hopefully leaving again — he delved in his pack for the drink.

Scrabbling noises told him there were mice around. That was fine, they had mice at his home at Roseberry Farm — rats too — though he didn't fancy any of those keeping him company. The whole place reminded him of a tomb and gave him the creeps.

Through the trapdoor, he heard a slightly muffled but heated conversation.

'Emma. Didn't you hear us arrive?'

'No, I was studying.'

'You must have been concentrating very hard. Your window was open and I called hello. Didn't you hear at all?' Mrs Pelistry complained.

17

'Like, I said, I was engrossed in my biology.'

Luke suppressed a snigger. They certainly had been engrossed in biology studies half an hour before.

'You do look rather frazzled. Your eyes are red. I think you should take a break.'

'I'm fine. I need to finish this chapter on human evolution.'

'No, I think you should have a break. Besides, Daddy and I have something to tell you.'

'What is it? Can't you just tell me?'

'No, you need to come downstairs now. We want to tell you together.'

'Oh God, you're not getting a divorce, are you?' Emma sounded panicky.

'A divorce?' Mrs Pelistry shrieked. 'Why on earth would you think that? Now, come on. Daddy's waiting outside.'

Luke sat down on an old beanbag, which rewarded him with a massive puff of dust and sent him reaching for his Coke again. Emma had sounded desperate and Luke didn't blame her. If she left, he'd be trapped in here. She'd also sounded genuinely worried that her parents might announce they were splitting up. Or perhaps she was winding her mum up. Strange thing to say, though.

As far as he knew, Hester and Robin were joined at the hip. They were both snobs and they both clearly loathed the idea of him and Emma being together. He really didn't like them much either so the feeling was mutual. Parents could be mystifying. He found it impossible to imagine they'd ever been teenagers themselves once, otherwise why would they make life so difficult for their kids?

There was a brief further exchange between Emma

and her mother before he heard her say, 'OK. I can spare a few minutes then I *must* get back to work.'

This was followed by footsteps then silence. He realised he was holding his breath and had to let it out as quietly as he could.

The tension of worrying he'd be caught was soon replaced by irritation that he was trapped in the attic at all. They hadn't been doing anything wrong — they were eighteen, two years past the age of consent, old enough to vote, or die for their country . . .

Emma's comment about them not having transport had also rankled. His dad was a mechanic and ran his business from home. Luke had asked time and again about having his own car. He'd passed his test months ago in his mum's Polo, but so far his dad had always been 'too busy' to sort out some wheels for his own son.

None of that helped Luke now, though. All he could do was to sit tight and wait until Emma gave him the all-clear, so he could slip out of her bedroom window and go home.

After silencing his phone, he took a better look at his surroundings. There was an old cot at the far end, along with a couple of farmhouse chairs. A broken rocking horse lay on its side, one rocker snapped in two. There were also lots of books spilling out of packing cases. Luke delved into the nearest and had to stifle a laugh.

There were old romance novels with crazy titles and cartoon drawings of men in suits who, frankly, looked like serial killers. Surely Emma didn't read this stuff? He picked one up: *Taken by the Sheikh*. No way. Another: *Master of Her Fate* showed a long-haired bloke with bad skin snogging a woman in a mini-skirt. He was hardly able to believe anyone had kept this stuff. He took out a few more, openly sniggering.

Three layers of paperbacks down, there was another larger softback with the kind of plastic jacket you saw on library books. It was also a romance, but a pretty racy one with a vampire about to sink his fangs into some poor girl's neck. It was titled *Blood Lust* and Luke almost choked with laughter. He opened it, knowing it was going to be hilariously bad.

But then he saw the jacket was actually wrapped around another book. Not a romance, nor even a printed book, but an old notebook. It seemed as if the vampire jacket had been wrapped around the journal to protect it — or conceal it.

Maybe it was Emma's. Now, that would be worth reading. Luke slipped the jacket off to see if there was a title on the cover but there was nothing.

The binding might have been brown once but was now yellowing and faded. It was clear it hadn't been opened for a very long time and it was no teenage diary, having been written long before Emma was born; and before her parents' time too, if the elaborate handwriting on the first page was anything to go by. The curls and flourishes came from a bygone era, and read:

Journal of
The Reverend Saul Tresize
Falford Methodist Chapel

Luke turned over the next page, his heart beating a little faster as he began to unravel the meaning in the labyrinthine script.

October 1805

Dreadful storm. By the grace of our lord, the chapel roof is in one piece. Not so the seven poor souls on the beach. A ship had foundered on the reef a hundred yards off the cove.

We found several drowned sailors on the sand, all beyond earthly help. Their bodies had been battered by the storm and some had already fallen prey to sea creatures. With difficulty, we were able to put them on the seaweed collectors' cart and bring the lost souls to the chapel for a Christian burial. The villagers had to go to their work so I said the burial service and a solitary grave-digger helped me lower the coffins into graves and cover them with earth. A pauper's grave seemed an ignominious end for them but it was the best that chapel funds would afford.

We found nothing on the bodies to identify them tho' two seem gentlemanly and, from what remains of their uniforms, that pair appear to be officers. I shall make endeavours to find their names and those of the ordinary seamen too.

I prayed for them, as did our founder, John Wesley, when he was in a terrible storm on his way to America. It may be wrong of me but I can't help thinking that he was saved but these souls were not. Let us hope they are at rest now.

While Luke read, he sipped his Coke to moisten his dry throat. He hoped he didn't have to make it last long. If Emma didn't reappear very soon, he was going to text her and he didn't care what questions were asked by her parents.

He returned to the journal. Disappointingly, the

following pages contained no more word about the shipwreck, only pages of trivia about parish business, collections, the weather, the harvest . . .

It seemed strange there was no more about the shipwreck. He was about to shove the journal back in the packing case when he came across another entry, dated a year later, though he barely recognised the spidery scrawl it was written in. It was clearly written by someone in a hurry — or in a bad way.

> I have read my previous journal entry with a degree of shame that disturbs me. I wish I could say I was at rest like the drowned sailors but I am haunted by what happened that day on the beach. I must unburden myself here, and pray for forgiveness. I should never have taken what was not mine to keep.
>
> At least I have given it a Christian burial, though not on sacred land. I had no choice. I can only hope that God will forgive me.

After these words, all the pages were blank.

Luke sat back, the book open in his lap, sipping his Coke and wondering. The journal had gripped him and then it had ended like a TV series cancelled half-way through, leaving the characters in limbo forever.

What had the minister done to make him feel so bad? What had he taken? Jewellery from the bodies? Money? He'd said he'd given a 'Christian burial, as best he could' to 'seven poor souls on the beach.' He'd also admitted he'd 'taken what was not mine to keep' and given it a 'Christian burial, though not on sacred land'.

Could it be? Was the chaplain referring to the loss of the *Minerva*?

22

Luke's pulse spiked. This might be something.

'Oh my God . . .' he exclaimed, forgetting he was supposed to be quiet.

He had to reread the journal again to make sure he wasn't dreaming. Reverend Tresize's account of the shipwreck read like an old adventure novel yet it had *really* happened. He wondered if he'd missed something that would give him a clue to what its contents meant.

'No!'

The bottle slipped from his hand, spraying Coke all over the journal. Dabbing at the cover with the hem of his T-shirt, Luke swore silently, over and over. The old book was stained and some of its fragile pages were stuck together. There was no way that Coke stain would come out and he needed to dry the pages.

He could hide it, of course, pretend he'd never even seen it, shove it under a pile of junk or in a chest with the other books. No one would ever know apart from him, but he'd have to tell Emma. She'd want to read the journal anyway and for her to do that he'd have to come clean about damaging it. Maybe she knew it was up there — if so, she'd never mentioned it to him. Were her parents aware of it? They'd go apeshit if they found out he'd been in their attic and damaged a valuable old book.

There was only one thing to do: take it home, dry it out and confess to Emma. Together, they'd come up with a solution.

He shoved the jacket and journal in his backpack and made a decision. Somehow, he had to get out of there. No longer afraid of making a noise, he tugged at the trapdoor but it was stuck tight back in the frame.

Panic stirring, he crawled over to the round window

23

and peered through it. Relief flooded him. It wasn't as high as he thought. The chapel was built on a slope and, at the rear, the ground had been excavated to fit the chapel onto the plot. If he was careful, he could wriggle out of the window and drop down onto the grass.

It wouldn't do Emma any harm to worry about him for a while, or to imagine him locked up in her attic. If she wasn't prepared to brave her parents' disapproval, then stuff it.

He managed to get the window open and threw the backpack down onto the slope before wriggling out as the rain began to fall. It wasn't a moment too soon because he heard the low rumble of the car already turning into the parking area. Grabbing his backpack, he scrambled up the grass slope, then squeezed through a gap in the fence and into the lane.

★ ★ ★

'*Jesus Christ!*'

Luke shouted as the sign for the dive centre loomed at the side of the road. He barely had time to check the mirror before turning sharply down the track that led to the quay.

His heart thumped. He'd been so fixated on the past that he'd driven from the cove on autopilot and totally forgotten to stop at the recycling centre en route. The beach rubbish was still in the back of the truck. Well, it couldn't be helped. It would have to stay there, stinking, until after work. He had to get a grip and give his full focus to the job, or he'd be unsafe to dive himself, let alone supervise a bunch of clients.

24

He parked outside the dive centre and slammed the door, cursing the moment he'd ever opened the Reverend Tresize's journal and read what was inside.

3

'What in God's name happened to you?'

Maxi's jaw was on the floor. Fair enough, Emma thought. She was, after all, dripping all over the welcome mat on her friend's doorstep.

'I slipped and fell in the sea,' she said sheepishly.

'The sea? What on earth were you doing in the sea in your best clothes?'

'I was paddling and I dropped my shoe and then I fell over.'

'Oh, Emma. What are we going to do with you?' Maxi stuck her hands on her hips. She was wearing faded denim dungarees and a Breton top, her dark curls caught up in a silk scarf. She looked effortlessly stylish and glowing, yet the glint in her eye hinted that mischief might be just around the corner.

'May I suggest you let me have a hot shower then tuck me up in front of the wood burner with a nice hot toddy?' Emma gave a rueful smile, one of the first grins she'd managed since the funeral. 'Maybe even let me in the house first?'

Maxi sighed. 'Not a bad suggestion.'

Emma stepped inside. 'You'll forgive me if I don't hug you just yet,' she said, starting to shiver.

'Fair enough. Come on, shut the door behind you and tell me all about it.'

Maxi found Emma a warm towel from the laundry room and ushered her up to the shower, while she put the kettle on. Despite Emma's assertions to the beach-cleaners, she hadn't changed in the car. She'd

26

chucked a couple of plastic bags on the driver's seat before haring off to Maxi's. Dressed in jeans and a hoodie and with her hair roughly dried with Maxi's high-speed dryer, she was now finally able to feel all her limbs again.

She had to pinch herself to believe she was finally at Maxi's house. It was a rambling granite place outside Falford village. Maxi had said it needed 'a ton of work doing' and had shared many online photos with Emma while it was being renovated. It had been transformed into a wonderful home, cosy yet airy, set in wooded grounds with a stream babbling to the distant estuary.

Emma and Maxi had been friends in the sixth form and continued on to Penryn University together. While Emma had pursued her art, Maxi had completed her teacher training and begun work in a school in the Midlands before eventually returning to Cornwall where she'd married Andy Sinclair, joint owner of the Falford Yacht Club. They had two young children, who Maxi said were currently playing at a friend's.

Emma and Maxi went into the conservatory, which was warmed by the sunshine. There were bright rag rugs on the tiles and throws on the sofa. Emma recognised some of the vibrant modern artwork on the walls as being by Nike Davies-Okundaye and Tola Wewe — favourites of Maxi, whose parents had emigrated from Nigeria when they were young.

The prints hung alongside watercolours of local scenes by, Emma presumed, local Cornish artists. There was something soothing about the works. They transported her into other worlds and among other people, reminding her of her own insignificance while connecting her with their lives.

'Make yourself at home,' Maxi said. 'That's the sunshiny seat.' She urged Emma to sit in the chair in a pool of sunlight and placed steaming mugs of tea and a tray of saffron buns on the coffee table.

'Lovely . . .' Emma lowered herself into the chair. 'Ouch!'

She picked something hard and pointy from under her bottom.

Maxi pulled a face. 'Lego,' she said. 'I ought to warn you not to wander around barefoot.'

Emma put the Lego brick on the coffee table. 'It'll keep me on my toes!'

Maxi laughed and handed Emma a mug. 'Bit early for a toddy,' she said. 'Though when the kids are back from their play date, we both might need it.'

Emma relished the comforting warmth of the mug in her hands. 'I can't wait to see them again.'

'They've been so excited about you staying. They've insisted on helping me get the lodge ready.'

'It's really good of you to have me! I'm excited too.'

Maxi's eyes filled with pleasure. 'We'll go and see it in a little while.'

'You could have let it out for the summer,' Emma said.

'Maybe but we still need to do a bit of work on it.'

'At least let me give you some rent.'

Maxi nodded. 'You know we don't want any but, if it makes you feel better, we can come to an arrangement.'

'It does and we will,' said Emma, with relief.

'Wait and see what you think first,' Maxi said.

Through the steam from her mug, Emma rested her eyes on the garden. It was wooded at one end, where a haze of azure bluebells popped with colour amid the

28

dark green of nettles and grasses. A rope swing hung from an old apple tree. Emma thought she could glimpse a wooden building beyond the bluebells, next to a tiny creek. It was no more than a baby stream, overhung with weeping willows, gurgling its way into the Falford estuary. She longed to explore it later but, for now, she was only too happy to be dry and warm and enjoying one of the saffron buns, whose billowy softness reminded her of her childhood.

'These are delicious,' she said. 'When I was smaller, Mum often used to buy saffron buns from Falford bakery on a Saturday morning. We'd walk there if it was fine.'

'That's a lovely memory. You've never mentioned it before,' Maxi said gently. 'Did your dad go with you?'

'God, no. He was working in his study or too busy with historical 'research'.'

'Into the shipwrecks? I remember him giving a talk once at the village hall.'

Emma did too; she had operated the slide projector. 'He was always saying he'd love to write a book, if he wasn't too busy with earning a living. He worked so hard to buy the chapel and that bloody Rolls-Royce.'

The Rolls . . . a token of guilt, not love, Emma thought.

Her heart squeezed with regret at some of the things that had passed between herself and her family when she was a teenager. 'I guess I never understood how hard it must have been for him. I never realised how much pressure they were under.'

'I'm sure they had a lot of things going on that they didn't want to worry you about,' Maxi said. 'I understand now what it's like to want to shield your kids from the bad stuff.'

29

'Yes, there was probably a lot I never knew . . .' Emma sipped her tea, thinking back to an afternoon at the chapel when she'd come home early from school and seen something she wasn't meant to. Something she'd never told anyone about, not Maxi or Luke . . . nor her parents. 'And I still don't,' she added.

'Remember when we swung above the creek and the rope broke?' It was a welcome relief when Maxi cut into her thoughts, reminding Emma of happier events, not the darker one she'd witnessed that day.

She laughed, cloaking the bad memory with humour. 'How could I ever forget? I was caked in stinky mud and Mum hit the roof.'

Luke had been there that day too, Emma thought.

'What made you stop at Silver Cove before coming here?' Maxi said.

'I'm not sure. Memories, I suppose, good and bad. Losing my dad has brought back such a lot of stuff. Emotions . . . things I don't want to think about but probably should.'

'I don't think there's a 'should' when it comes to grief. When I lost Mum, the old norms went out of the window. I was angry at her, sometimes relieved that she was at rest, and I didn't have to watch her slip away piece by piece.' Maxi patted her arm. 'It takes a long time and you never really 'get over it', nor should you try. It was sudden with your dad, too. No time to prepare.'

'Not that sudden. The heart attack was unexpected . . . but with the amount he was drinking lately maybe I shouldn't have been so shocked. Mum said he started boozing before they split, and I think I realised how bad things had got but didn't know how to help or probably didn't want to face it.'

30

Emma thought back to the divorce, over twelve years ago now. She was certain the break-up hadn't been the main cause of her father turning to the bottle for comfort. He'd never been the same since the discovery of the *Minerva* treasure.

She sipped her tea, before broaching the subject of Luke. 'Maxi . . . I saw the beach-cleaning bunch before I fell in the sea. They clearly thought I was round the bend.'

'No wonder, if you were swimming in your smart suit.'

'Swimming wasn't the word I'd have used. Flailing about under a monster wave is more accurate . . . Ursula Bowen was there and she was loving it all.'

Maxi laughed. 'She's OK when you get to know her. She's a sea glass artist now.'

'Is she? I only remember everything I did not being good enough for her. She was a dragon even then.'

'Mmm . . . I seem to remember you two didn't hit it off.'

Emma laughed at Maxi's understatement. 'She told me I was getting too big for my boots and, while undoubtedly I had a degree of natural artistic talent, I also had a lot to learn. I almost gave up A level art because of her, always carping at me and criticising. God knows how I passed, let alone got an A. I'm delighted to hear she's retired. What a loss to education, though.' Emma giggled, and she hadn't done that for a long time. 'Do you remember we used to call her Miss Trunchbull — not that she looked like her, just that she was scary!'

'We were a horrible lot, but have you forgotten what I do for a living now?' Maxi pointed out.

31

'Sorry, Maxi, I'm sure all your students adore you.'

'I can assure you they don't and Miss Trunchbull is one of the mildest insults I've heard.'

'Oh my God. How awful.'

Maxi shrugged. 'I've a hide like a rhino these days. Now, I'm sorry your little . . . bathe was witnessed by Ursula. She can be a bit abrasive, but I find her bark's worse than her bite.'

'You make her sound like an angry pug.'

'Sometimes she is.' Maxi smiled. 'She's been here a long time so most of us have got used to her.'

Emma softened. She felt Maxi was about to tell her to 'Be Kind', like the notice with a hand-drawn rainbow she'd seen stuck on the door from the hall to the sitting room.

'It's weird coming back, seeing people from a past I thought I'd left behind. I suppose they view me as the newcomer now; the stranger,' she said.

'A few might but plenty of others will remember you. Some might never even know you've been away. You'll always be Proper Cornish.'

Emma wriggled her toes, feeling life returning to them at last. 'I don't feel it. I'm not sure I want to be. I feel like a city girl. I like being a city girl. It stifled me here but, now I've landed this coastal book commission, it feels right to get away to the seaside. Immerse myself in the environment and all that.'

'Is that the only reason?'

'No. There are too many memories of Theo in the flat. Even though he hadn't moved in, I keep finding his stuff.' She sighed. 'I took his jazz vinyl and his precious cashmere jumper to the charity shop, along with those awful manga comics. If he wasn't willing to come back to collect them, I figured they were fair game.'

'Good on you! He was never a keeper, hun. Anyone who didn't understand your grief isn't a functioning adult. Still, you chose to come home to Cornwall rather than try pastures new?'

'I'm not sure whether *this* is home any longer. Apart from leaving, I don't have the energy to make any long-term decisions, but I thought this place might soothe me after the past few months, plus the thought of spending time with you was just irresistible.'

Maxi's face lit up. 'Ditto. We're delighted to provide some kind of sanctuary if that's what you need. You can spend as much or little time with us as you need. Just say if we're all getting too much.'

'You won't be. I just need to work out what I need. This might sound pathetic but I can't even decide what to wear when I wake up most mornings. My brain's so foggy, I look at the wardrobe and think: what does it matter? I'd been to the solicitor's about the estate before I came here. That's why I was wearing that bloody suit. Even though I hate it and all the memories it brings back. I never thought I'd wear it again — and I never will!'

'Good choice. It's not the Emma I know,' Maxi said. 'And I understand the brain fog, the numbness, the utter inability to even know what to eat, or that you *should* eat. When Mum died, I was the same. Andy had to physically scoop me out of a chair, put my socks on, remind me to drink. It's called grief, my love, and it's like a toxin, it paralyses you, mind, body and spirit.'

'I am so sorry about your mum,' Emma said. 'With Dad, it's different because we'd grown apart lately. I bawled at the funeral, but now I feel numb, to

33

everything. That doesn't feel right when he's gone.'

'On top of the split with Theo, you've had a rough time, darling.'

Emma nodded, was reminded of her ex's comment — that her heart hadn't been in the relationship — and felt fresh anger.

'You *are* here, though, and this is your home town.' Maxi said soothingly. 'You *have* made a decision, even if it's only to 'run away', as you put it. You've decided to be kind to yourself, and to take some time to heal. That's good, my love. Did you find a tenant for your flat?'

'Yes, a German academic. She seems delighted with it so I can't go back for a while even if I wanted to.'

Emma hesitated, afraid of betraying the full extent of her shock at being dragged out of the sea by Luke, even to her old friend.

'You know the weirdest thing about earlier?' she said eventually. 'At the beach?'

'Yes?' Maxi prompted.

'The weirdest thing was that Luke Kerr was with them.'

'Ah.' There wasn't a hint of surprise in Maxi's response. 'I suppose he would be.'

'Why 'suppose'?' Emma blurted out. 'You never mentioned he was back here in Falford?'

'I didn't think to,' Maxi said patiently. 'I join the Beachcombers myself occasionally. That's where all the Lego came from . . .' She retrieved a yellow plastic figure from the carpet. 'A container ship ran aground not long after you left. It spilled thousands of bits into the sea years back and it still washes up.'

Emma looked at the Lego. 'That's strange after all this time.'

'In a way, yes, but not if you know anything about the currents and tides. Which you do, Emma, having lived here.'

'I only know the basics. I'm not an expert,' Emma said. Luke was though, she realised. He'd been fascinated even at school and if he'd gone on to be a professional diver, which seemed likely, he must know the underwater landscape inside out.

'Well, we try to collect all the rubbish that washes up. I say 'we' but I only drop in once a month. Luke and the other Beachcombers are there twice a week at Silver Cove. It's their territory.'

The image of the Beachcombers bearing down on her, brandishing their litter-pickers, flooded back. 'Territorial's a good word for them. Luke's their leader, is he?'

'I wouldn't say that. He runs a local diving school and he gets involved with the marine wildlife rescue. He's into the environment and keeping the beach clean and safe for everyone so it's not that surprising he joined the group.'

'Hmm . . .' Emma muttered.

'His involvement has nothing to do with the treasure, if that's what you're thinking.'

'The thought hadn't even crossed my mind.' It had though, if Emma was being honest. 'Have you ever found anything else from the *Minerva*?' she asked, as casually as she could manage.

'No chance. Mind you, I think a couple of coins from different eras have washed up. Not when I've been helping, though, worse luck! Most of the finds are rubbish, plastic pollution — unbelievable amounts of it.'

Feeling a little ashamed of being cynical, Emma

35

nodded. 'I've seen reports about plastic pollution on the TV. It's awful and I can see how it affects the marine ecosystem and plant life. It's fantastic that you're trying to make a difference.'

'I'm no eco-warrior but it gets me out of the house, and the kids off their screens. I sometimes take my class and my own two for a nature walk with the Beachcombers. They love it and they learn so much. I do too.' Maxi laughed. 'We paint pictures and make collages. You might be impressed by what the kids can produce when they're engaged.'

'I bet.' A smile covered Emma's frustration that her friend had held back Luke's return from her.

'Maybe you could join me and the kids one day when you're ready? I'm in dire need of some fresh creative spirit.'

'Me too.' She was already thinking of the marine and coastal plants she used to love drawing. Bladder wrack, sea pinks, anemones, coral weed . . . 'I definitely want to do some of my own work too while I'm here if I can find the time. I've a couple of commissions as well as the book. A magazine wants some illustrations for an editorial on coastal foraging.'

'There you go, then.' Maxi seemed much happier to see Emma in a more positive mood. She broke off a large piece of bun and popped it in her mouth.

'Max, I've got to admit, it was a huge shock seeing Luke so unexpectedly and so soon after the funeral. I came back to lay all the past to rest. I had no idea he'd be here.'

'He wasn't here at all until last summer,' Maxi replied after she'd taken another bite of her bun. 'Apparently he left the navy and came back to run the dive school with Ran Larsen. He's a Norwegian guy

36

from London who's living with Bo from the Boatyard Café.'

'I remember Bo from school. I liked her.'

'Well, so did Ran, clearly.' Maxi smiled wickedly. 'Luke worked there for a few months before going into partnership with him.'

'So, he plans on staying long-term?' Emma was still computing the fact.

'Emma, there's something else you need to know.' Maxi's voice cut into her thoughts, her hesitant tone setting off the jangle of alarm bells. 'I was going to tell you a while back but, what with your dad's death and the bust-up with Theo, I thought you had enough on your plate.'

The chill of the sea returned, even as the sun flooded the conservatory. 'What?'

'Luke's moved into the Old Chapel. He's bought it.'

4

Emma's mouth went dry. It was a few seconds before she could ask:

'Luke bought *our* house?'

Maxi spoke gently — and was that a hint of guilt in her voice? 'I would have told you sooner, but you'd lost your dad and Theo had been such a git, so I didn't want to add to your troubles. I'm sorry if it's come as a shock but I really thought it was better to break the news face to face, though I was dreading you might find out on the grapevine.'

'I wouldn't have. I don't have any contact with anyone here apart from you,' Emma said mechanically.

'Yes, but these things have a habit of seeping out. Hun, are you OK?' Maxi was leaning forward, her hand on Emma's arm.

'Yes, yes, I understand why you didn't tell me.' She scraped up a kind smile for her friend, while reeling inside. 'And it's not my house now. It hasn't been for almost fifteen years.

It's none of my business . . .' She hesitated, still processing the fact Luke was walking through the hallway, sitting by the fire, sleeping in the bedroom of a home that held so many memories, sweet and bitter. 'Do you know any more about why he bought it?'

'Not totally. He's been renting a flat in Falford since he left the navy last year, then the next thing you know, he moved into the chapel. I never even noticed a 'For Sale' board. And one day when I was out with the Beachcombers, Marvin or Ursula — can't quite remember which — remarked on it and Luke admitted he was the buyer.'

'I — I see.' Except Emma didn't see anything. Seeing involved understanding, having clarity about a situation, and she didn't. She also sensed Maxi knew more than she was letting on.

'It must seem weird to you that he's living in your old place,' Maxi said.

'It's more than weird, but what can I do about it? The owners were entitled to sell it to whoever they wanted.'

Maxi hesitated a little too long. 'Look, if it makes you feel any better, I think there was the chance that it could have been worse than Luke buying it.'

'How?'

'I heard a rumour that developers were sniffing around. They didn't have planning permission but wanted to apply for it. The story going about is that the vendors decided to sell to Luke instead of the builders but, honestly, I'm not sure why.'

'He probably offered more money,' Emma said, longing to ask exactly how much the Old Chapel had gone for. She could always check on the Land Registry, of course, but it seemed churlish and petty. She really didn't care about the price, it was the emotional cost that hurt her. She wondered if her own father had known a Kerr had bought his beloved house. She hoped he hadn't found out.

'So, Luke's definitely planning on sticking around in Falford now?' she added.

'Well, it seems like it. He jointly owns the dive centre.'

'Does he?' Emma was still trying to take in the news of Luke moving into the chapel.

39

Maxi had clearly noticed her discomfort. 'Tell you what,' she said brightly. 'How about we go see *your* new home?'

'Yes.' Emma forced a smile. Whether Luke was living in her old house or on the moon, it shouldn't affect her plans an iota. 'I'd love that.'

After collecting Emma's stuff from the hallway, they made their way down the garden to the timber lodge which had been painted pale green. It was set on the edge of the wooded glade behind the house, and stood out against the purple foxgloves and yellow oxeye daises, nodding their heads in shafts of sunlight piercing through the trees. Nature and the weather had already made their mark, mellowing the wooden exterior with lichen.

'Oh, it's gorgeous!' Emma cried, bumping her case over the grass. 'I'm dying to do a picture of it! Is *all* the woodland yours?'

Maxi had her arms full with Emma's portfolio and materials. 'I wish! Only the small part that runs down to the creek belongs to us. There's a wire fence on the right-hand side that marks the boundary with a nature reserve.'

Emma passed the rope swing and a small tepee made of sticks set amid a carpet of bluebells. 'I bet the children love it.'

'They do. Arlo's always building dens and Daisy likes damming the stream and catching 'kweetures'.'

'Are there many 'kweetures' around?' Emma asked, picturing the little ones at play. Maybe they weren't so little. It had been six months since she'd seen them on a visit to Oxford in the Christmas holidays.

'There's nothing dangerous — as far as I know,' Maxi said with a laugh. 'Though you'll hear plenty of

40

rustlings. We've seen badgers and foxes and you get tawny owls to-whit-to-whooing.'

'We had barn owls living in an outbuilding at the chapel. Their screeches used to freak me out when I was small.'

'Like, I said, there's plenty of inspiration here. Let's go inside.' Maxi led the way up the wooden steps to the timber decking where two steamer chairs were already a home to lichen. 'They need a good strip and repaint. We were going to tackle it this weekend, to be honest. I thought they were looking too shabby for guests.'

'No. I love the lichen. Used to think it was like a woolly coat. It adds character.' Emma was already itching to capture its hues. So many colours in such a tiny plant.

'I'll leave it as it is, then.'

'Did you really build the lodge yourselves?'

'By and large. We had the local sparks in to fix the electrics, but we did the rest.' She pushed the door open as it wasn't locked. 'In we go. It's not huge but it should have everything you need.'

Maxi stepped back so that Emma could walk ahead of her into the heart of an open-plan living/dining space. A squidgy grey sofa had been brightened with an eclectic mix of cushions and throws in shades of lemon and green to reflect the surroundings and another Tole Wewe print hung on the wall.

'We tried to make it cheerful but not lurid,' Maxi said. 'Though I don't have an artist's eye.'

'It's perfect,' Emma said. 'So in keeping with the woodland setting. I love it.' Her gaze alighted on a jar of bluebells and twigs on the counter of the galley kitchen. 'Those are so sweet!'

'The kids picked them. They were all for leaving you some rather disgusting larvae in a jar too, but I persuaded them not to.'

Emma laughed, touched by the gesture but relieved she had no invertebrates to care for. 'I'll thank them when I see them.'

'Andy will collect them from their friend's soon.'

'Can't wait to see them again. I loved buying them those tree decorations at the Oxford Christmas market. I can see why you wanted to move here. Falford's a great place for children.'

'You still think so?'

'I always did . . . Just because I took against it doesn't mean I can't see why other people love it.' Emma sat on the sofa.

'If you don't feel you can stay, after what you've found out today, I'll understand. We all will, if you want to go back to Oxford again?'

Emma nodded. She'd been asking herself the same question ever since Luke had handed over her sodden shoe. Seeing him again had been enough of a shock, without learning he'd moved into — or taken over — the home she'd once loved, a home that had since become tainted with bitter memories.

'Thanks. I'll definitely stay for a couple of months so I can get some work done on this book project. My flat's rented out until then anyway and I don't *have* to see Luke. I can hold off on what to do next.'

'Sounds like a very good plan,' Maxi said. 'Now, let's finish the tour.'

She showed Emma the rest of the lodge. 'There's not much room for entertaining, but it's OK, I hope.'

Emma surveyed the galley kitchen, with its bright red kettle and quirky china. It was so very Maxi and it

42

made her smile. 'It's more than OK and I don't plan on doing much entertaining.'

It wasn't huge but it had everything she could need. The scent of cedar still hung in the air.

'There's a wood burner for fun and underfloor heating too. I've had it on to make sure it's not damp.'

Emma was very touched. Her friend's kindness, coming so soon after the funeral and her shock encounter with Luke, brought her to the very edge of tears. 'Thanks,' she said. 'It means a lot to me.'

'You're welcome, my love,' said Maxi. 'I'll let you settle in, then, if you feel up to it and can bear the onslaught, come up to the house for dinner. I think we can allow ourselves a G&T too.'

'I'd love to.'

'Half-five OK?'

'Perfect.'

Maxi left, and Emma was alone again in strange surroundings. Unable to stay still, she busied herself unpacking her clothes and artists' materials. The table by the double doors to the deck had plenty of light for painting and she could work outside on fine days. The peace and quiet was perfect, an artist's dream.

Below the open kitchen window, the stream tinkled by on its way into the creek, and eventually into the Falford estuary. The wind sighed in the willows and oaks surrounding the lodge. Emma could hear birds landing on the roof, gulls squabbling: such a rich vein of inspiration even without being able to hear the sea, a mile distant.

The sound of the sea was always present at the Old Chapel, on calm days and stormy ones. She wondered if Luke was there now, listening to the crashing waves. What bedroom would he have chosen? Her parents' room in the mezzanine above the chapel sitting room was the obvious choice.

Not hers, surely, in the annexe at the side. Not in her bed, the one they'd had sex in during the still of the hot May afternoon before the storm broke.

She laughed at herself. Of course, her bed would be long gone. The previous owners would have chucked it out and Luke would have brought his own. Yet he *was* living in her house.

Fifteen years of living away from Cornwall had severed all the ties and associations and *should* have given her a mature and sensible perspective on what had happened — or what she thought had happened. Even so, no matter how hard she tried, she still thought of the Old Chapel as 'home' and it stung to imagine his name on the deeds.

She'd always been convinced Luke was the reason Harvey had found the *Minerva* hoard. She'd certainly let Luke know that. The memory of some of the accusations she'd hurled at him were crystal clear in her mind.

He'd texted, asking her to meet him at the cove the night after the news had got round the village that Harvey had dug up the treasure. Emma's own father had heard only a few hours before and had locked himself in his study. Her mother had been banging on the door, asking him if he was OK. She'd screamed at Emma, asking her why she'd had anything to do with 'that awful family!'

Emma had defended Luke and, unable to stand the terrible atmosphere, agreed to meet him on the beach. She'd never forget his face when she'd seen him walking towards her in the dunes. He'd been white as a sheet.

That's when he'd told her he'd found the journal in the attic and taken it home. He'd admitted he'd mentioned seeing it to his father but sworn he hadn't actually shown it to Harvey. He claimed his father must have found it in his school bag and somehow have worked out the treasure was at Roseberry Farm. He said Harvey must have put it back in his bag behind Luke's back.

Red-faced, he'd handed it over to her but Emma had been so stunned, she'd flown into a rage.

'You took this home! Why? You could have left it and told me but you took it. I don't believe this story about your father taking it.'

'It's not a story. It's the truth.'

'What else should I have expected from your family?' she'd shouted. 'You chose them before me, didn't you? You wanted that treasure even though you knew what it meant to my dad. Harvey's always wanted to get one over him. You let him do that.'

'No. No . . . No . . .'

'Can you deny your dad hates mine and this is the ultimate way to get to him?'

Luke couldn't speak. He'd stood there shaking his head, his eyes glittering with hurt. Yet all Emma could think about was her father cowering in his study and her mother screaming — and Luke having kept such a secret from her.

'I never meant any of this to happen. You have to believe me, Emma. I love you.'

'Well, I don't. I don't believe you and — and — I don't love you. How can I after this?'

He'd flinched as if she'd struck him.

'Then there's nothing I can do. Goodbye, Emma.'

He'd left her alone, the journal still in her hands.

It was ages before she could look at its fading pages and she knew she could never show her parents. It would break them. Even then, a thought had niggled at her: she'd kept a secret too. Her own father was by no means innocent; he'd been deceiving his own family and Harvey's.

In the years since, she'd come to realise she'd deceived herself too. She'd been eager to believe Luke had betrayed her and given his father the journal, to cover up the real reason she needed to break up with him.

5

'There's the Pelistry girl again.'

Ursula's words jolted Luke from his thoughts — or rather lack of them. He'd been intent on scouring the tideline for rubbish, picking up what he could with his litter-picker and gathering any larger items in a small pile which he'd bag up later. He found the act of focusing on tiny things took him away from worrying about other stuff like the business, his family, the past and the future. If he was making a small contribution to the environment he lived and worked in, so much the better.

He whipped round to find Emma sitting on a rock ten metres away.

She had a pencil in her hand and a sketchpad on her lap. Now she wasn't drenched, he could take her in properly. Her red hair was caught up in a ponytail and the suit had been replaced by a dress and denim jacket. Her feet were bare, flip-flops lying on the sand beside a large jute bag that he presumed was full of artists' materials. She was glancing up and down from the pad, seemingly oblivious to both him and Ursula.

The sight of her made the hairs on his arms stand on end and gave him that fluttering feeling in his stomach he hadn't experienced since he was a teenager. So much had changed, but then, Emma Pelistry was still as beautiful as ever to him, if not more so. As he looked at her sitting there, he could imagine the past fifteen years hadn't happened. The way his pulse quickened at the sight of her, and his inability to string a coherent sentence together, hadn't changed.

'Luke?'

Ursula was at his side. 'Gossip's all over the village, you know.'

Luke feigned intense interest in a plastic bottle at his feet. 'Is it?'

'Yes. Even you must have heard some of it. Surely your mother's said something?'

'I've heard nothing, Ursula.'

'She was hardly brimming with gratitude for us helping her, was she? Spiky as ever.'

'I expect we didn't catch her at her best.'

Ursula snorted in derision. 'Well, I have no idea what her best is, that one, after teaching her in her final year. It's safe to say we didn't hit it off.'

Though not in the sunniest of moods, Luke allowed himself an inner smile, knowing full well that Ursula and Emma had had 'creative differences'.

Ursula planted her hands on her hips. 'Still, I suppose it hasn't done her any harm, going her own way. She got top grades. She's done well, making a living from her art. I've seen her website. She has a fancy London agent and works for all kinds of publications.'

'Oh?' Luke said casually, retrieving a piece of old rope from the strandline.

'Yes. She's a professional illustrator . . . does a lot of work for big publishers and magazines.' Ursula opened her larger bag and Luke popped the rope into it. 'Don't say you haven't stalked her on the web, by now?'

'No, I haven't stalked her,' he said, trying to laugh off Ursula's comment. 'I've had other things to do.'

'And yet you bought her old home?' The older woman's eyes met his, as keen as a hawk's. He wanted

48

to be annoyed with Ursula, and sometimes was sure she wanted to annoy him, but this time he refused to be baited.

'I have, if you look at it that way,' he said neutrally. 'Then again, Emma's family left the chapel a long time ago. The estate agent told me two other purchasers have had it in the meantime.'

'Even so, it must be hard on her to see you living there. Do you even think she knows yet?'

Luke followed Ursula's gaze to Emma, who was now standing with her back to them, ankle-deep in a rock pool.

'I have absolutely no idea,' he said truthfully.

'She must do,' Ursula said. 'Has to. She's staying at Maxi Sinclair's. Bosom buddies, those two.'

'Yeah, I remember.' With a monumental effort, Luke dragged his eyes away from Emma and a saviour in the form of treasure caught in a small piece of frayed netting came to him.

'Ursula. There's some sea glass here.'

'Oh, where!' Ursula skipped over, everything else forgotten.

Crouching down, Luke untangled the glass from the rope, trying not to disturb the sandhoppers resting among the fibres. 'Looks very nice,' he said.

'Nice?' Ursula sounded outraged. 'It's beautiful. Look at those rich colours.' She held out her hand, and Luke deposited the half-dozen pieces in her hand. There was amber, jade, white and even a turquoise piece. 'So many colours in one place. There must be more. Come on, let's go hunting.'

'You hunt,' he said. 'I'll keep collecting the plastic and rope.'

'Do you mind?' she said. 'It's not often I come across

a find like this.' Her eyes were gleaming in delight.

'Not at all,' Luke said, relieved. 'Let me know if you need any help.'

He continued to pick out the rubbish from the tideline. The usual suspects: wet wipes, flip-flops, old beach toys, rusty cans, bottle caps. Mercifully, today, they'd come across no marine life tangled in nets or ropes.

'Luke!' Ursula was a few metres behind him though closer to the tideline. 'Did you see this?' She trotted up, barefoot, holding out a plastic food container. 'You must have walked right over it.'

'What? The food container? Sorry, I don't remember seeing it. God knows how.'

'Not the food container. I brought that with me. This.' She pointed to a brown disc in the bottom of the container. 'You must have trodden on it. I saw it glinting in the dried weed and I thought . . . well I thought it might be part of an old can but then I took a closer look. I'm glad I did.'

Luke's pulse spiked. 'It's not a silver dollar?'

'No. Too small. I need to get it home and have a proper look but I think it's a Victorian crown.'

'Ah. Not gold then.' Luke smiled.

'Not quite. Could be worth twenty quid if it cleans up. I'll have a look under my magnifier in the workshop and I might put it on eBay. It would help to swell the funds.'

The Beachcombers operated as a charity and, while Luke had made several donations, he didn't like to play Lord Bountiful too often. Everyone liked to do their bit, raising money from their occasional minor finds.

'Great idea. Let me know more when you find out,

will you?'

'Of course, and maybe one day we will find some real silver or gold.' Ursula gazed out over the waves with a wistful look that surprised Luke. She didn't refer to the discovery of the *Minerva* coins directly and he hadn't expected her to. She was long past the stage of bringing up an event from years earlier that had only really mattered to the Kerrs and the Pelistrys. It might have changed their lives and created gossip for a while but it was history to most of the locals. Anyone who'd moved in since wouldn't have even been aware of the story at all. For most of that time, Luke had been on the other side of the world, anyway.

After he'd left school, he'd gone straight into the navy. His career had consumed him and it had been nigh on impossible to form long-lasting relationships while he was travelling all over the globe. He'd had a few brief flings, one with a colleague, Anna, but they'd both agreed it wasn't going anywhere and that they were wedded to the navy. They'd parted on good terms and still kept in touch. She was commander of a warship now.

Then, there'd been a nurse from Plymouth. A bright, caring person, pretty and fun to be with, but open about the fact she wanted Luke to leave the navy or take a shore posting and have a family. He'd been in his late twenties at the time and the relationship had lingered on for six months before he'd been confronted with signing up for another three years. It had been the navy versus his relationship.

The navy had won.

Or had it been past memories that had won? Had he always been looking to recreate that intense, passionate youthful relationship? The heady days of first love?

'I think we should call it a day.' Ursula broke into his memories. 'You've had enough by the look of you.' She frowned. 'Have you been sleeping properly?'

'If I look rough, it's because I've been up until late at the dive centre. Ran and I were filing the VAT. The quarter comes round faster than a spring tide.'

Ursula tutted. 'You could never look 'rough', young man, as you well know, but you do work too hard. I know you only came out here with me today because you thought I wanted the company.'

'This is a break for me. You know I'd rather collect a ton of plastic crap in the open air than be stuck in the office.'

'And I'm glad you did because it's been a day for treasure, even among the dross.'

Pleased to see her happy, Luke turned his attention to the 'dross', which had now filled several large rubbish bags. He encouraged Ursula to go back to her studio with her finds, while he loaded up his pickup with the stuff. He would take it back to one of the lock-up storerooms at Falford village hall later where it would be sorted into different categories. Fishing gear could be reunited with local fishermen. The plastic buckets and spades had to go to recycling, though the better specimens were given to charity shops or sold on the Beachcombers' stall at local fetes and markets. Ursula was taking the sea glass home and was probably already mentally planning out designs for her jewellery.

Luke returned to the beach to collect a couple of supermarket carrier bags full of picnic food which someone had 'helpfully' left by the overflowing litter bin. His pulse quickened when he saw Emma still sitting on the rock.

This time, there were no friends around him. It was just him and her, alone together with no place to hide and the lure of walking over to her was impossible to resist.

'Emma,' he said. None of the normal greetings; a 'Hi' or 'Hello' didn't seem remotely adequate to express how he felt at being so close to her again.

Her lips parted in shock. 'You're here again,' she said, as if he was an imposter in his own backyard.

'We had a dive cancelled and cleaning the beach appealed more than catching up with admin.' He put the rubbish bags on the sand.

Her hair blew across her eyes, a strand catching in her lip gloss. 'I can understand that,' she said.

Close up, he was struck by how youthful she still was: she'd barely aged from when they were teenagers. She was still as slender too, yet with a poise, rather than the coltishness he remembered. He still felt lumbering and awkward around her: a battleship to her sleek yacht.

'What's the matter?' She glared at him, chin tilted, defensive as hell.

'Nothing. I saw you sketching.'

'Oh.' She glanced at the pad. He could see whirls and swirls, fronds and leaves on the page. He remembered her drawing him on that stuffy afternoon, just before he found the diary.

'*You are so funny, Luke.*'

'Remember that picture you drew of me . . .?' he said, voicing his thoughts out loud without meaning to.

'I drew a lot of pictures of a lot of stuff.' Her green

53

eyes glittered with defiance and she held the sketch-pad to her chest.

'Yeah. I suppose so. I'll leave you to your work.' Cursing himself for even approaching her, Luke turned away.

'Luke!' Emma's call came after him before he'd gone a few steps.

She was standing next to the rock, still clutching her sketchpad like a shield. He thought twice about going back to her but relented, drawn like filings to a magnet.

'I only wanted to say, thanks for fishing me out yesterday. I'm sorry if I seemed rude to you and your friends,' she said, most grudgingly.

'I don't need your gratitude.'

'I'm not offering gratitude, it's common courtesy.'

'Fine.' Luke squashed his irritation. It was pointless engaging with her. 'Have a good day,' he managed through gritted teeth.

'This is no good.' Her voice was brittle with tension.

'What do you mean, 'no good'?'

'Me coming back here,' she said. 'I'd never have dreamed of it if I'd known you were back in Falford, only I have a commission to do and Maxi offered to have me after . . .'

Hearing the distress in her voice, Luke softened. 'I heard about your dad,' he said as gently as he could. 'I'm truly sorry for your loss.'

'Sorry?' To his surprise, she laughed, yet it was a sound that grated like bone on bone. 'I'll be sure to pass your condolences on to my mum.'

'Thanks,' he murmured, sensing that the conversation was about to blow up at any moment. 'How long

54

are you staying?'

'Couple of months. Like I said, I came back to research a job. That's the only reason I came back. Work.' She lifted her chin as if daring him to contradict her.

Luke despaired. Emma was as prickly as gorse and he himself was finding it hard to stay civil. 'I'll leave you to it, then.'

'Yes, I'm sure you're desperate to get *home*,' she shot back.

Barely able to believe he'd heard those specific words and the emphasis on 'home', Luke couldn't rein in his frustration any longer. 'Sorry? What do you mean?'

Her mouth opened, closed then opened again. 'I know you bought the Old Chapel. Maxi told me when I got back from my unscheduled dip in the sea.'

So, *this* was what she was so upset about: him buying the chapel. His heart sank, but he was also infuriated.

'Oh, really?' he said sarcastically. 'I'm surprised she hadn't mentioned it to you before.'

'She — she didn't think it was the right time. On top of my dad and all that.'

Emma's voice faltered and Luke's stomach contracted. He sensed she was on the verge of tears again and he had no idea how to react. He also wondered what the 'all that' was.

'Why the Old Chapel? Of all the places in Falford. Why did you have to buy that?'

Luke felt a dam had burst and there would be no stopping a confrontation now. He wished he'd never even approached her.

'Because — because it came up for sale . . . and I'd no idea you'd ever come back.' He wasn't sure why he even added that part.

'Would you have still bought it if you had known?'

'Probably,' he said quietly but firmly. 'Unless you'd wanted it.'

'Of course I wouldn't and I couldn't have afforded it *but* . . .' The pain in her eyes made him wince. 'I just don't understand why — why you thought it was OK to move in after what happened between our families.'

'Why he thought it was OK?' Anger stirred along with guilt, then anger — because he had nothing to be guilty about. Not about buying the chapel, that was for sure. He had very good reasons for having bought it. He wouldn't be goaded into feeling bad or examining his motives by anyone, even Emma.

'Emma,' he said as calmly as he could. 'Let's get something straight. I wish I'd never seen that journal and that my dad had never dug up those coins, but it was fifteen years ago. I told you then what had happened and I've nothing more to say now.'

'You told me *some* of it. Not all.'

Her eyes accused him. They were as full of pain and anger as they had been when he'd gone round to the chapel after his father had found the treasure at Roseberry Farm. He'd tried to tell her he'd never meant to take the journal . . . or set in motion a chain of events that had led to Emma and her family leaving Cornwall.

He'd done his best to explain what had happened and that he'd never intended to bring such chaos and misery into her family's life and his own, but how could he confess the complete truth?

He could no more tell her how weak he'd been today than he could when he'd been a confused teenager, devastated to have betrayed the girl he loved;

56

torn between loyalty to her and loyalty to his family.

He picked up the two supermarket bags. 'If you'll excuse me, I've work to do, clearing up other people's mess.'

He strode off, refusing every temptation to look back at her, run back to her and beg her forgiveness. It wasn't his fault that the treasure had been buried on Kerr land but, there was no denying it, it was his fault that it had been found.

And if he'd ever thought there might be any reconciliation between him and Emma now they were meant to be mature adults, he'd been very badly mistaken.

6

'Argh. I wish I'd never come back.'

Standing on one leg, Emma pulled off her sandal with such force it bounced off the tiles and then hit the wall. 'Damn. Sorry! Bloody Beachcombers. Bloody Luke.' And bloody herself, Emma thought, for even engaging with him.

'Wow.' Maxi stood, hands on hips, in the hallway.

'What?' Emma growled.

'You remind me of the kids.'

'Are you saying I'm having a tantrum?' Emma removed her other sandal more carefully.

'Not a tantrum exactly . . .' Maxi said.

'Well, Luke Kerr is enough to make anyone revert to being a toddler!'

'Or a stroppy teenager?' Maxi said archly.

'I'm not a stroppy teenager! I'm an adult. It's . . .' She was already regretting the bitter words she'd hurled at Luke, and she was rocked by how emotional the encounter had been. Grief, anger, hurt. It had all come out in an uncontrollable torrent. 'It's Luke who needs to grow up.'

'Wow,' Maxi said again. She picked up the sandal and held it out.

'Thanks. Sorry about that. I don't think it's marked the wall.'

'If it had, no one would notice among all the crayon marks and paint chips. Come in and sit down and tell me all about it.'

In the haven of the sitting room, Emma flopped

down on the sofa with a sigh. 'Damn. I didn't mean to offload on you.'

'No need. I can see you're royally pissed off and you probably have just cause. It would be nice to know exactly what Luke has done to make you so teasy?'

'*Teasy*? Oh my God, I haven't heard that for a very long time.'

Maxi arched an eyebrow. 'Would it help if I sent you into the garden for some quiet time?'

Emma burst out laughing, something she'd have thought impossible a minute ago.

Maxi sat opposite Emma. 'Hun, what exactly happened between the two of you all those years ago to make things so painful for you now? I know the basics but we've always largely avoided talking about it, and I've never really been sure. Forgive me if I'm raking up the past but perhaps it would be better to have everything out in the open between us? If only so I don't go putting my big foot in it when I'm talking to Luke, or we're all in the same place together?'

Emma pressed her lips together.

'Of course, you could also tell me to mind my own business?' Maxi smiled.

'None of this is your fault, and you're right. I should be able to share it with you.' She heaved a sigh. 'You know some of it already but there's no point starting in the middle. I suppose it first kicked off the day Dad bought that bloody ridiculous car.'

Though in truth, her heart reminded her, that wasn't the real start of the problems between her and Luke . . .

Maxi nodded. 'The Rolls? I remember him dropping you off at school in it.'

'I almost died of shame. I was so embarrassed. I

59

hated it and we couldn't afford it. He had to sell it when he lost his job and we had to move out of the chapel. After Harvey found the hoard, Dad was so angry and depressed. You know he'd always wanted to be a historian. He'd often told us there was 'no money in academia' and that's why he'd gone into finance.'

And, Emma thought, her dad had been reasonably successful, gaining his clients' trust and doing well at selling them insurance policies and investments, but she'd always known his heart wasn't in it. She'd felt sorry for him and his disappointment had made her all the more determined to follow a career she loved, not one that might lead to security or wealth.

'It's so sad that his world had collapsed after the discovery of the coins,' Maxi said.

Emma sighed. 'He took it very personally, and not only because of his family connections to the ship-wreck,' she said. 'Poor Dad. He wasn't perfect. He was a snob — so was Mum — and they were so over-protective that I hated them at times. But since he died, I've thought more about the pressures he was under. He'd been so good at his job until then but he fell apart almost overnight after Harvey found the hoard at Roseberry Farm. He took so much time off and he stopped caring about meeting their sales targets. His bonuses dried up and we couldn't pay the mortgage or the loan on the car.'

'I don't think I'd realised the treasure meant so much to him,' Maxi said. 'I'd forgotten he was related to the captain of the navy ship that captured the *Minerva*.'

'I was young and so preoccupied with my own life, I hadn't taken his obsession seriously enough,' Emma said. She'd also been obsessed herself — but with

Luke. 'I suppose he'd wanted to find the silver for as long as I can remember. He did tons of research but he came to the conclusion it had been spirited away long before. How wrong he was . . .' Emma paused, transported back to that thundery day at the chapel. 'When he brought the Rolls home for the first time, Luke was hiding in the attic space next to my bedroom.'

Maxi raised an eyebrow. 'Oh my God, I never knew that.'

'I never told anyone about it before but seeing Luke on the beach today, and knowing he's living there, brought all the memories back.'

'And all the regrets too?'

'Yes. That day, we'd been having sex . . .' It was impossible not to think of that part of the afternoon without pleasure, though even that whole period of her life was now tinged with bittersweet regret. 'We were young, it was intense and wonderful and I knew I was in love.'

'Oh, Emma. I know you were. I thought you'd get married one day.'

'Did you?'

'I was young too,' Maxi said gently. 'I had romantic notions. I thought you'd find a way to be together forever.'

'So did I — but I wasn't sure how. We were living for the moment. I was supposed to be revising my biology because Mum and Dad wanted me to be a scientist.'

Maxi laughed and Emma smiled, but then her memories darkened.

'Instead, I'd been drawing Luke, but Mum and Dad came home unexpectedly. I flew into such a panic.

61

You know how much they hated the Kerrs and they'd have gone apeshit if they'd found Luke in my room. So, I had the bright idea of making him hide in the attic.'

'The attic!'

'Yeah, I know. It was a horrible place and he was pissed off — I don't blame him — but agreed. Unfortunately, the door locked from the outside, and then Mum practically dragged me out for a ride in the new car and he was trapped.'

'Oh God. Poor Luke.'

'Yes, but he managed to climb out of the window and, when I finally got home, he was gone.' Emma paused, pulling a thread on a cushion. The panic she'd felt when her mother had forced her to go on the drive had never left her. 'A week later, you know what happened.'

'How can I forget? I still remember your face at school the next morning. You refused to talk about it, even to me, so I knew it was bad.'

'Yeah. Dad had heard from a mate at the golf club. He came home and I've never seen him so shocked. His face was white, he went into his study and closed the door. Mum told me not to go near him. He didn't come out until the next morning. I heard them arguing until late and Mum eventually told me what had happened.' Emma swallowed. 'He was never the same again.'

'And you blamed Luke for everything?'

'Yes. I did. I — it seems ridiculous now, but I did. As soon as Harvey found the hoard, he went to the Ferryman, got pissed and started boasting about it. Obviously word got out and Dad heard and locked himself away. That same evening, Luke called me, begging me to meet him at the beach. He was almost in tears . . .' The memory of his distraught face had never left her. She thought he was going to say one of his parents had died. She'd run to him and held him, soothing him, saying he could tell her anything.

'And he said he'd found a journal in the attic.'

'A *journal*?' Maxi said slowly. 'What journal? You've never mentioned it before.'

'No one knows about it apart from me and Luke — and Harvey Kerr. Luke admitted he'd found it when he was hiding and taken it home. He'd been reading some of it because he was bored while he waited for me to let him out. It turned out to be the chaplain's journal and it basically said the treasure was hidden somewhere near the chapel.'

'Oh my God, Emma. You mean Luke stole it?'

'Not *stole* it, exactly. He said he spilled Coke on it while he was reading it and shoved it into his back-pack in a panic.'

Maxi covered her mouth with her hand. 'You've kept this to yourself all these years.'

'Yes, because, although I was angry and upset that he'd taken it, I still didn't want to get Luke into trouble . . . Anyway, the chaplain confessed in the journal that he'd found the bodies on the beach and, we assume, taken the coins too. The diary's very vague but Harvey must have worked out that the chaplain had spirited them away. The minister was wracked with guilt, so we think that, eventually, he buried them under the gate at the farm. Or someone did.'

'And Harvey knew all this because Luke showed him the journal?'

'Luke says not. He claimed he'd hidden the jour-nal and only told his dad he'd *seen* it in our house but sometimes I wonder . . .' Emma broke off. It had seemed strange to her that Harvey had worked out specifically where to find the coins. 'I think Harvey must have got hold of it, without telling Luke. How else could he have *known* exactly where to find the treasure? The journal mentioned the coins had had 'a Christian burial' so Harvey guessed it meant the Celtic cross used for the farm gate. He put two and two together and got lucky.'

'Oh God. So your poor dad had been looking for it for years and the clue was on his own property all the time. And then to discover the treasure was on Harvey's land, the man he loathed . . . At the time, I thought it was pure luck it was on Luke's farm. No wonder it sent your father over the edge.'

Maxi's words, while honest, summed up a brutal truth for Emma. She was on the verge of tears.

'Luke must have been devastated too,' Maxi said.

'Yes. He was beside himself when his father dug up the hoard. Or said he was.'

'I can understand that.'

'I've accepted it wasn't Luke's fault that he *saw* the journal. I was just — so hurt that he didn't tell me he'd taken it straight away.'

'But — why didn't he?' Maxi asked.

'Harvey begged him not to say he'd taken it. Threatened him. He told Luke that if he had the journal in his possession, he'd be accused of stealing it. Apparently, Harvey had always been joking about a family legend that there was treasure on the land but Luke dismissed it as his dad fantasising.'

'Poor Luke.'

'Yes, but you can see why I was so upset and angry? He could have phoned me and told me he'd taken it by mistake. It was my fault in a way. I had locked him in and abandoned him. I could have phoned him to apologise but, when I got home and found he'd escaped and not told me, I was angry too.'

'So it was more than a teenage tiff?' Maxi said.

'More like a feud.' Emma thought of all the history between their two families: an animosity that was rooted in more than a dispute over the treasure.

'Our families had never been friendly. I know the Kerrs thought we were snobs and my parents thought they were feckless. It ate Dad up that he hadn't found the coins himself. Harvey 'stole' all the glory and the money. Harvey boasted about it.'

'I know. I'm so sorry.'

'I wish Harvey had won the lottery instead or found the Holy Grail. *Anything* but that bloody Silver Cove hoard. Despite his faults, I loved Dad, and I didn't care about the money. Mum didn't either. She tried to understand why he was so upset but he spiralled down. They split up and he ended up living on his own ever since. I suppose I've always blamed the treasure and the disappointment for him dying early.'

'I'm amazed Harvey could keep the news about this journal to himself.'

'Me too, but I think he was worried that people would think he'd broken in to get it — or that Luke had stolen it. He preferred people to think he'd just happened to be repairing that gate and come across it by chance.'

'Even if your dad had found that journal, the treasure would still have been on Harvey's land,' Maxi said.

'Yes, but he thought he could have made a case for sharing it. As the finder.'

'Harvey would never have given him permission.'

'Who knows? He would still have been the person who located it. If he'd been the one to find the journal, he'd probably have kept the knowledge to himself and tried to buy the farm. Mum told me that he ranted on about what might have been, what he could and should have done.'

'So, you haven't forgiven Luke, either?'

'I — I ought to have done, and he didn't do anything wrong or illegal, but I can't disconnect him from his family and the consequences. My dad had been searching for it all his whole life. He was the authority on it. Mum told me at the funeral that's why he bought the chapel. She said they almost bankrupted themselves buying it. He was convinced the cargo — he refused to call it treasure — was somewhere on the land. When he bought it he ripped the place apart looking for it. It was an obsession, and many times she begged him to give it up. He wouldn't.'

'Why did he never find this journal before?' Maxi asked.

'Luke said it was hidden inside another book. There were a load of old novels up there when we moved in. Dad told Mum to sort through them in case there was anything interesting but she said there wasn't. Dad said he'd put them on a bonfire but Mum told him she would 'never see any book burned' and would take them to the charity shop. She never got round to it though. The attic filled up and then we hardly ever went in there until . . .'

Emma broke off. 'Until Luke went in there that afternoon. Dad was convinced that it had something to do with Luke — maybe he even blamed me for bringing Luke to the house.' She stopped. 'Whatever I believe makes no difference now.'

Maxi got up and crossed over to Emma's sofa, enfolding her in her arms. 'I am so sorry, my love. Sorry about your dad, about everything.' She leaned back and sighed. 'And I can now understand why you might blame Luke for what happened. Do you believe he didn't steal the book or show it to his dad on purpose?'

'I don't know. Maybe. That's what truly caused the split between us. I refused to trust his word and I never forgave him. Mum and Dad forbade me have anything to do with him again, of course, but we could have carried on seeing each other. We were eighteen and leaving home anyway, but they were so upset after the treasure was found, how could I hurt them even more? So, I had to choose between them and him. I couldn't pile on further misery when Dad was falling apart. So I ended it. I know Luke's dad would have loved that. It would have played right into his hands: the snooty Pelistrys rejecting his son.'

'I remember how devastated you were but I thought you'd just decided to end it after the row between the families. I'd no idea of the real reasons.'

'No one did. How could I tell anyone without revealing that Luke had taken the journal? I'd never have accused him of stealing it. I knew it was a mistake to come back,' Emma cried out in frustration.

'Yet you are here, my love. I can understand if you want to go back but, for what it's worth, might it not be better to try and make your peace with him? Or at least try to ignore him?'

'I don't know if I can.' Emma sighed. 'But I can't go home, even if I wanted to. I've let the flat for three months.'

'Then you've no choice but to stick it out and try to

live with him being here.'

Emma nodded. 'Yes, that would be the grown-up thing to do. Trouble is, I don't feel very grown-up right now.'

'Being grown-up can be very overrated. Give yourself time to grieve, be kind to yourself and, if you can bear to, to Luke. He's a sensitive soul and I'm sure he's as full of regrets as you.'

'Perhaps. Trust you to be so wise,' Emma said with a smile.

'It's easy to be reasonable when you're not in the thick of the situation,' Maxi said.

A short while later, Emma walked back to the lodge, breathing in the flower-scented air, trying to calm herself. Sharing some of her secrets of the past with her best friend had felt like an unburdening but had also caused painful memories to resurface.

And she hadn't told Maxi everything. One secret about the past would be locked in her heart forever.

7

Normally when he was on a dive, Luke could forget everything but the moment and the environment he was in. Yet here he was, forty feet below the surface, thinking about Emma. Ever since she'd turned up, she'd taken up residence in his thoughts and haunted his dreams.

She was angry with him — unjustifiably so, he thought — and yet he could understand why she was upset. Having only recently lost her father, she must be raw with grief and it would have been a huge shock to find him living in Falford at their family home. Despite it all, the sight of her had made his heart beat faster and stopped him in his tracks. She might be older but, to him, she was as beautiful as ever. He'd loved the way the sunlight brought out the coppery tones in her hair. He'd even loved seeing her footprints in the sand, so delicate and small compared to his own.

A fellow diver caught his attention, pointing furiously at the sea bed near the wreck where they were diving. Luke dragged himself back to the present, reminding himself that his own and, more importantly, other people's lives depended on his concentration. Before responding, he checked the depth and time they could safely stay underwater on his wristwatch dive computer before finning over to his diving buddy.

They descended a few more metres to investigate a rusty object embedded in the sand and removed it from the place it had lain for over two centuries. Then he gave the OK sign and pointed upwards. It was time to ascend and go back to the real world . . . trouble was, any world he was in now seemed to be occupied by Emma.

The skipper piloted the boat back to the dive centre while Luke and the others in the party speculated on the find they'd brought up from the sea bed. His experience on salvage dives after leaving the navy made him pretty sure it was a cannonball. Luke had lost count of the number he'd salvaged over the years, but the excitement among the clients still hadn't abated when they unloaded at the quay.

After the others had gone to the centre to shower and change, Ran spoke to Luke while he pulled off his drysuit on the quayside.

'Looks like a good dive,' Ran said, full of smiles. 'Customers are happy they found some 'treasure'.'

'Yeah. It's always exciting to them to find something that old from a wreck.'

'I'll do the report on the find for *The Receiver*,' Ran said.

'Thanks, buddy.' Luke quietly thanked the day he'd found a business partner as efficient and great to work with as Ran. It meant he wouldn't have to do the paperwork for the government department that monitored salvages from wrecks.

'You're welcome.' Ran's grin faded. 'Oh, you had a call while you were out.'

'Who?' Luke retrieved the suit from the ground.

'Your dad.'

Luke swore quietly.

Ran grimaced. 'Sorry, mate. Is it bad news?'

'Old news,' Luke said wearily. 'Don't worry. I'll sort it. I'm going to get changed.'

After work, he took the cannonball back to the chapel. Rusty and misshapen, it was barely recognisable after two centuries on the sea bed. It certainly had nothing to do with the *Minerva*, which had gone down forty miles away on the other side of the Lizard.

Even so, with his mind full of Emma and his father's call — which he hadn't returned — Luke was catapulted back to the moment his father had first found the treasure on the farm.

He took a beer out into the garden, intending to enjoy the sun sinking over the cove and remind himself that he'd every right to be there. However, all he could think of was that day he'd escaped from the attic, with the journal in his backpack.

He'd been soaked by the time he'd reached home. In the mood he'd been in, excited about the journal and disappointed at being hidden away by Emma, he'd thought the contrast between the chapel and Roseberry Farm seemed greater than ever.

Roseberry was several centuries older and, while the chapel was a grand if austere building, the farm was a tumbledown house with crumbling outhouses. It was a metaphor of the neglect Luke himself felt where his dad was concerned: Harvey couldn't be bothered to keep his own home from falling down around his ears.

Roseberry hadn't been a farm for a long time, but the old barn was just about standing and was where his dad worked when the weather was bad. The grounds were a graveyard for defunct vehicles, complete with rusting car shells, agricultural relics and a campervan that was green with slime.

The lights had been on in the kitchen windows and his mum's Polo was parked at the side, with his father's tow truck in front of the barn. Any hope of sneaking in unnoticed was gone.

Luke stopped by the gate. It had been open for as long as he could remember, hanging off hinges that had once fixed it to the granite post that, according to his dad, was originally the shaft of a Celtic cross. Luke remembered him saying: 'In those days, son, our ancestors used anything they could get their hands on to get by. They were resourceful people.' His dad was always going on about their 'ancestors' and his 'heritage', as if the Kerrs were a special breed.

Bracing himself for a grilling over his lateness, Luke walked through the back door into the kitchen where his mum was washing up.

She gasped when she saw him. 'Luke! Where have you been? I've been worried sick. Look at the state of you!'

'I got caught in the rain.'

'Your backpack's soaking! Are your school books in there?'

Luke clutched the backpack tighter. 'Yes, but they'll be better drying out in the airing cupboard upstairs. I'll sort them out.'

'Make sure you do.' His mother glared at him. 'Why didn't you answer your phone?'

He remembered it had been switched off so he could ignore Emma and teach her a lesson. That seemed a mad decision now.

'My battery died,' he said, knowing his mum wouldn't believe he'd actively chosen to turn it off.

'No wonder.' She pursed her lips. 'You're always on it. Surprised it hasn't melted.'

Luke grunted in reply, which at least would sound authentic to his mum.

72

'If you'd had your phone on, you'd have known that I'd called you to see if you wanted a lift home.'

'Sorry. If I had my own car, I could have driven.'

Her lips twisted. Luke felt guilty. 'I was joking, Mum.'

'I'm not.' She heaved a sigh. 'Your dad really ought to do up an old banger for you.'

'Yeah . . .' Luke had heard this before but now he was seeing Emma the need for his own transport had never felt more urgent. 'I could help him.'

'I know.' His mum smiled and rubbed his arm. 'I'll ask him again.'

'Thanks, Mum, but don't waste your breath.'

'Oh, Luke. He's not that bad.'

Luke shrugged, but decided not to push this contentious issue further. Obviously, he'd have loved his own car. He hated catching the bus, or walking to school, or relying on lifts, or borrowing the car from his mum. She needed it for her own commute to work at a different school. He'd only passed his test thanks to driving lessons from her. He also knew his dad could have found him an old car and they could have made it roadworthy.

'You'd better put those wet clothes in the machine.'

'I'm not stripping off here in the kitchen.'

'OK, don't get your hair off.' She smiled, this time in amusement. 'But don't soak the carpets or your bed. Here,' she shoved a bin bag at him, 'get changed in the bathroom and put them in this and bring it down when you're decent.'

He nodded and exited the kitchen, taking the stairs two at a time, figuring the least time spent dripping water on the carpet, the better.

'And make sure you dry out those books!'

Showered and changed, Luke put his backpack in the airing cupboard and went outside to find his dad in the barn. The rain had stopped but water was still dripping through the hole in the roof into a tin bucket.

His dad had a wrench in his hand, staring at an ancient Ford Escort with the bonnet up. It seemed beyond repair to Luke, with fist-sized holes eaten by rust. Maybe Harvey was breaking it up for the parts. Luke hung back, torn between trying to communicate with his father or sloping off. He never knew what kind of mood his dad would be in.

Harvey was an unpredictable character, full of bonhomie and promises one minute — morose and sarcastic the next. He'd a chip on his shoulder the size of a battleship — Luke had heard his mum throw that at Harvey, along with 'You think the world owes you a living but you won't do anything to make your own way.'

When he spotted Luke, he grinned, which gave Luke a glimmer of hope he was in a good mood. 'Hello son. Your mum says you got caught in the rain.'

'Yeah,' Luke said, unwilling to invite any further comment.

'She's been on at me to get you a car . . . can't have a strapping young lad having to walk home and get a soaking, can we?'

If it was meant to be a joke, Luke wasn't amused. He turned to traipse out of the barn again.

'I've told her, if you're going to join the navy, what use will you have for it?' his dad said.

Stung into a response, Luke turned round. 'I've still got the summer here and I'll need it when I come home.'

'Home?' his dad snorted. 'To this dump? After travelling the world? You'll never want to see us again.'

74

'I will, and it's not a dump . . .'

'Sure.' His dad's smirk faded into a hard stare. 'Your mother says you were a long time walking home.'

'The footpaths were underwater so I had to walk along the lanes.'

'Even so, half past six? School ends at half past three. Did you stop off on the way by any chance?'

'No!'

'Not for a cider with your mates in the dunes? A crafty smoke of something naughty?'

'In this weather!' Luke snorted in disgust. 'Don't be stupid.'

'I meant indoors, and I may be a lot of things but I'm definitely not stupid, son.'

'I know.' Desperate to avoid a conflict, Luke rolled his eyes but his dad's bored into him. The smirk was back. 'Hold on . . . the Old Chapel's on your way home, isn't it? Did you stop off there?'

'Dad . . .' Luke turned away, not wanting his father to see his guilty expression.

He gave a short laugh. 'I might have guessed. Were the Pelistrys at home?'

'I have no idea.'

'Would have thought Emma's dad would have given you a lift home if he'd seen the rain. Though he's probably too tight. He's always showing off, making out that he's better than the rest of us and acting like the village squire. He lives in that draughty old pile that's mortgaged to the hilt and needs a packet spending on it. Anyone would think he was Lord Muck but he's no time for people like us, has Robin.'

Luke couldn't disagree with his father's assessment of the state of parts of the Old Chapel, although the farm was in a far worse condition.

His dad turned back to the car. 'Bet he wasn't impressed to find you there with his precious princess.' The comment was laced with sarcasm that stung Luke.

'You shut up about Emma!'

Harvey laughed. 'Oh, touched a raw nerve, have I? You were there, then.'

Luke rounded on his dad, finally goaded beyond all restraint. 'OK, if you must know, not that it's any of your business, I walked Emma home from school then I left!'

'Sure, you did, son. Of course.'

Luke marched away.

'Wait! Luke!'

His father's hand was on his shoulder. 'I didn't mean to embarrass you but Emma Pelistry — well, her old man doesn't think we're good enough. She's a nice girl, I'm sure, but the apple doesn't fall far from the tree.'

'What does that even mean?' Luke said.

'That she's a chip off the old block. An ice maiden. She might be interested in you now but she'll never stay with the likes of you — of us. You'll only get hurt, son.'

Luke shook off his hand. 'I don't give a toss what you think.'

Harvey flinched, raising his palms in conciliation. 'OK. It's a sensitive subject. I shouldn't have put my size tens in your love life. I'm sorry.'

Luke curled his lip in disbelief. 'Yeah. Course you are.'

'Hey. I was joking but not everyone appreciates my humour sometimes. I don't want the Pelistrys to come between us, boy. That's the last thing I want . . . only

76

I don't want you to get hurt. If Robin's chucked you out and made you walk home in this downpour, I'll be having words with him myself.'

'He hasn't chucked me out. I chose to leave when Emma's parents came home. It was — I wanted to leave. They don't even know I was there.' Luke cursed himself, already having revealed far more about his relationship with the Pelistrys than he'd ever intended or wanted to. He had to walk away now, before his dad probed any more.

Luke glanced at the rusting and dilapidated vehicles, the gate hanging by its hinges, the campervan that was a home for so many species of algae, it ought to have protected status.

'Doesn't look much, does it,' his father said. 'but that's history there. All around us. This place is much older than the Pelistrys' place. 'Old' Chapel, my arse.' He bracketed his fingers around the word 'old' and affected a posh voice like Robin's.

'Of course, the building is one of the finest examples of Methodist architecture in the south-west. They say Wesley himself visited the spot to preach and declared that a chapel should be built right here on the edge of the sea.' His father laughed. 'All while our ancestors had lived round here since before the Conqueror came over.'

Luke had heard it all before. How his relatives were 'real Cornish' and went back a thousand years. 'There's a lot of history in the chapel too,' he muttered.

'Oh, really?' His dad sneered.

Luke was goaded into mutiny. 'Yeah. The *Minerva* treasure ... how do you know it's not buried at the chapel?' He knew mention of the hoard would push

77

his father's buttons. Harvey was convinced it had been hidden somewhere around Silver Cove, just waiting to be found. Yet Luke was now wondering if the 'Christian burial' mentioned by the Reverend meant it had been hidden in the chapel graveyard.

'The *Minerva* treasure?' He snorted. 'Ha! Robin would like it to be. If it was, he'd have given it to some bleddy museum by now and be asking for his OBE.'

'Well, maybe he's got good reason to think it's there!' Luke threw back.

His dad laughed. 'Don't be ridiculous. There's no chance.'

'You think?' Luke was infuriated by his father's sneering tone. 'You don't know everything, Dad.'

Harvey's smirk faded into a frown. 'What's Robin been saying?'

'I haven't spoken to Robin. I didn't need to. I found out another way! One that would shut you up, that's for sure!'

Sure enough, his father was dumbfounded. His eyes bored into Luke. 'What do you mean?'

Luke wished he could take back his words but it was too late. His dad was like a hound that had scented a rabbit and wasn't going to let the trail go for anything.

'What would 'shut me up'?' His father's voice was silky and his eyes were still on Luke. 'Is it to do with the hoard?' He leered. 'Has Emma been doing some pillow talk?'

'No! She bloody hasn't!' Luke exploded. 'Emma knows nothing about it! I found it myself!'

The moment he blurted out the words, he could have bitten his tongue out. He'd only made things worse. Much worse.

His father took a step closer. 'You found 'it'? What

have you found, boy? Something at the chapel?'

Luke shrugged. 'Nothing. I was winding you up.'

'Doesn't sound like it to me. You look too worked up for that.'

Luke's stomach turned over. 'It was only an old journal thing I saw in the attic. It probably means nothing.'

Harvey's frown deepened and he advanced on Luke. Momentarily, Luke thought he might be about to grab him but instead his father laughed softly.

'Look, son. We all have our secrets and, whether you tell me or not, I don't really care.' He put his arm around Luke. 'I don't mind if you've been snooping round the Pelistrys' place or what you've been up to.'

'I wasn't snooping!' he protested and was about to add that he'd been forced into the attic but stopped just in time. The hole he'd already dug for himself was impossible to get out of.

His father's arm tightened around his shoulders. 'All that matters is that we don't argue over it,' he said smoothly. 'You know, your mum's been going on at me about getting you some wheels. She's right for once. If your dad can't do that for you, well, it's a pretty bad thing, right?'

Luke inclined his head with the smallest of nods. 'Suppose,' he muttered, wary of this sudden change in mood and longing to run away. He'd no idea if his dad's offer was genuine or just talk.

'This is my fault in one way,' his father said. 'You shouldn't be walking miles in the rain when your old man's a mechanic.' He grinned. 'Doesn't make sense, does it? Especially when you've passed your test.'

Despite his trepidation, Luke's ears pricked up.

'About the car,' his dad went on. 'I had a customer

today wanting to sell a Corsa. It's not bad. Not too many miles and, with a bit of work, it might suit.'

Luke didn't want to get his hopes up, yet it was too late not to fan the flames of excitement. With a car he'd be free. Free to take Emma to remote beaches, to the pub, much further away from Falford and prying eyes. There'd be no need to hide in a dusty attic . . .

'Yeah?' he said, as casually as he could muster.

'Don't sound so enthusiastic.' Harvey gave a grin. 'You're growing up. Already grown up. When you go in the navy, your mum and I will miss you. Despite my little joke earlier, I want to make the time we have left good. I'll see the bloke first thing and if the car's sound, I'll buy it. Come here. Let's have a beer before our dinner and have a chat about this car.'

A few days later, Luke had driven out of the farm gates on his way to meet Emma at Silver Cove car park. He could barely believe his dad had kept his promise. Wait until Emma saw it. Then he glanced in the rear-view mirror to see his father walking towards the gatepost, carrying a pickaxe and a spade.

He hadn't realised what part he had played, back then . . .

Sitting in the garden of the Old Chapel, beer in hand, Luke's pulse rocketed. His phone was buzzing insistently in his pocket. He snatched it up and swore when he saw the name on the screen.

Dad.

The ringtone echoed off the walls and gravestones. It was as if his father had read his thoughts and chosen this moment to remind Luke that he could make his son's life a misery from many hundreds of miles away, and after so many years.

Cursing out loud, Luke stabbed the red button and

turned the phone off.

Why had he been so stupid all those years before? Why had he made the biggest mistake of his life, one that haunted him even now?

Harvey hadn't found the journal in his backpack, as Luke had sworn to Emma. Luke had shown it to him. Admittedly under some coercion, but he'd still revealed its existence and let his father see it. Then, when he'd gone to Emma to try to explain, he hadn't dared tell her he'd actually let his father have it after he'd been lured by the promise of car.

God knows, it wasn't that simple.

He hadn't betrayed her for a car but because, for once in his life, he had his father's full attention. He'd tried to buy his father's love and approval with the journal and even though his dad had found the treasure, it still hadn't been enough.

Harvey had left Luke and his mother. Maybe he wouldn't if he hadn't got the money.

All he knew for certain that whatever he did for his father would never be enough.

8

The day after her encounter with Luke at Silver Cove, Emma joined Maxi and the children for lunch, where Arlo and Daisy proceeded to cheer her up and reminded her there was more to life than looking back in anger and grief. There was important stuff like finding 'kweetures', balancing spaghetti on your nose and making rude noises until your mum threw up her hands in despair.

After helping Maxi clear away, Emma went back to the lodge to do some work. She dipped her brush in the purple paint, excited and nervous about applying it to the paper. Just the perfect amount to capture the beauty of the of the violet sea snail she'd seen in Silver Cove that morning. To think, hundreds of feet walked over the creature every week, unknowing.

The empty shell was tiny but exquisite, a perfect spiral of mauve beauty. She'd taken mobile phone pictures, made sketches then proceeded to do a water-colour of it.

The painting would be perfect for a feature on beachcombing she was producing for a high-end countryside magazine. She'd received the commission the day before, a rush job with a very tight deadline, as usual.

'What could be more perfect, darling!' her agent had said, phoning her.

Emma flicked through her other sketches and photos of beach and rock-pool life, deciding which to create in pen and ink and which were suitable for watercolour. She liked to travel light on an outing, taking a few colours so she wasn't overwhelmed with choice. There were faint marks in the tops of the pages from where she'd clipped them back with a bulldog clip to stop them blowing open all the time.

After tea, she started work on a cover for a memoir about an eighty-year-old woman's journey by kayak around the British Isles. Emma had read the draft manuscript before her father died, and found it incredibly moving then. The woman had lost her husband and taken off in the kayak because she 'couldn't bear to be still any longer'.

Emma couldn't reread it now — it was too raw — but she could lose herself in the drawing for the cover. She'd done an illustration showing the woman and kayak alone in a huge sea, with cliffs towering above her and a gull wheeling overhead. It was in shades of inky blue and jade green and was meant to show the author battling against the elements and her grief.

She'd waited with bated breath for the verdict from the publisher on the initial proposal — and more importantly the author. Most of the feedback she received was positive and filtered through the publisher so she didn't get an author's or agent's raw reaction. You never knew, though, and it was part of the job to take feedback professionally and tweak, and re-tweak the design or sometimes go straight back to the drawing board.

She shook her head at the ways of the business she was in, so different to the path her parents had planned for her. They'd finally accepted she was never going to be a biologist when she'd got her first job. Now, as a freelance creative, Emma herself had also accepted that she would always be either too busy or broke. She was happy simply to be able to make a living in such a competitive field, and to be well regarded was a huge achievement in itself.

She didn't want to think too hard about the other aspects of life — partner, family . . . Coming back and finding Luke in her former home had made her think about those things again. She didn't really know why . . .

A tear plopped onto the work desk, terrifyingly close to her picture.

'No!'

She leaped back, grabbing a piece of blue paper towel to wipe her eye, then the desk. She hadn't even known she was crying.

She let out a litany of swearwords.

'Emma? Can I come in?' Maxi called through the open door of the lodge.

Emma checked her face in the mirror and met a beaming Maxi in the doorway. She was brandishing an old-fashioned bottle with a stopper top.

'I brought some homemade mint lemonade.' She peered at Emma. 'Everything OK?'

'Yeah. Fine. Just had my head down all afternoon. Eyes on stalks.' She licked her lips. 'Yum. That looks delicious.'

'Kids helped me make it. It is actually rather nice. Lemons from Falford Country Stores. Mint from the garden.'

'Come in.'

'I won't stay. You seem busy.'

'Yeah . . . I needed to get back to work. My brain was so woolly I couldn't get going until now. It was rusty but coming here has started the gears again. My

84

clients are understanding to a point but there's no safety net for the freelance. Besides, I need to escape into it.'

'I'm happy to see you at work again.' Maxi handed over the lemonade but didn't sit down. 'While I'm here, I wanted to ask if you wanted to come to the beach market at the weekend? It's held on the field behind Silver Cove. It's fun. Some lovely food from local producers and some local craftspeople. Which you may find a mixed blessing, so absolutely no obligation if you want to hide away.'

Emma laughed.

'Tip from me: don't tell anyone what you do for a living if you don't want to be kept chatting about your job all day.'

'I'll say I'm an accountant.'

Maxi squeaked in mock horror. 'Prepare to be asked for free financial advice then.'

'Maybe I'll admit to being an artist after all. Besides, I can't squirrel myself away here forever in my little woodland cabin like an elf.'

'I love the idea of having an elf in the cabin ... I'm happy you're coming, but I thought I'd forewarn you that there will be people from Falford and some of them might be from the Beachcombers.'

'You mean Luke?' Emma hadn't thought of that, but it was too late to back out now.

'Well, yes. I think it's more than likely he'll be there. Last time I was with them, they were talking about having a stall to promote their work.'

Emma felt a fresh pang of embarrassment for her 'tantrum' the previous day. Maxi deserved another grown-up in the house.

'I can see they mean well and they're doing a good

job. I promise I'll be nice. It will be a chance to show them I'm normal.'

Maxi gave a squeal of mock horror. "Normal' is so boring. Being you is more than enough. You don't owe them anything.' She beamed. 'I'll tell the kids. They'll be ecstatic when they find out Auntie Emma's coming.'

Now it was Emma's turn to squeak in horror, genuine this time. 'I'm not an auntie! Oh no, please don't make them call me that. Emma is fine.'

Maxi laughed. 'I'm winding you up. We should set off early. I'll have to take the car. The kids can't walk that far and back.'

'OK. Tell you what. I'll drive.'

'Excellent. I can sample some of the gin stall's wares in that case. I've been dying to try the clotted cream one for ages. You can take the kids to the ice cream stand.'

'Can't wait,' Emma said, wondering if she could hang around the ice cream van all day and not go near the Beachcombers' stand.

Maxi left and Emma returned to her almost-finished cover illustration, with its great swirl of a wave, whose foamy crest might, at any moment, crash down on the kayak or miss it by inches.

Her brush hovered over the paper yet she didn't dare apply the wash to the paper. Her hands weren't steady enough. Her drawing was meant to be about the woman who'd written the book but it was exactly how she felt herself: at the mercy of forces beyond her; staring at a tsunami racing towards her, about to sweep her world away.

It was how she'd felt that day she'd come home early from school a few weeks before the discovery of the treasure and found her father's car unexpectedly parked in the courtyard. She'd been surprised but thought he'd had an appointment cancelled and walked into the hall, ready to say hello.

It was then she'd heard voices, her father's and a woman's, coming from his study. She'd thought he was on his speakerphone to a client but then realised the voice was familiar, and the conversation was anything but businesslike. The next words were etched on her mind forever.

'*No one must find out, Robin. Harvey would kill us both.*'

'*They won't. Stop worrying. Live for the moment, while we can. I love you, Sue. I can't exist without you.*'

The silence that followed was punctuated by sighs and murmured endearments, but Emma could bear no more. She'd rushed out of the house, not stopping until she reached the cove, breathless with shock and running.

She'd flung herself down on the sand in the dunes, sobbing and trying to blot out what she'd heard. No matter how she tried to un-hear those words, or pretend she'd misheard, it was impossible to deny it. Her father, the ultimate family man, had been having an affair with Luke's mum.

That was shocking enough. How could she have faced Luke himself now their secret had become hers? How could she possibly have shared it with him, knowing he might tell Harvey and blow everyone's lives apart?

And yet, how could she conceal it? How could they have carried on seeing each other, knowing what had been — still was — going on between their parents?

9

Emma woke in her bed at the lodge to a balmy Saturday morning, with a haze that would clear as the sun rose in the sky. No one could dream of being swamped by huge waves on a morning such as this . . . even if she still carried the burden she'd discovered all those years ago, and never shared with anyone, not even Luke.

He'd be at the market today for sure.

Nothing she could do about it except show she'd moved on, even if the memories pecked at her like crows.

With a sigh, she took her breakfast coffee and toast onto the deck. Sinking into the willow chair, she admired the way the dew sparkled like tears.

'The grass is crying,' she'd heard Daisy say the other morning.

The image had given Emma some ideas, which she'd stored away, hoping they'd emerge when she was in need of inspiration. She might even do a quick sketch and file it, rather than relying on her memory alone. Anything that distracted her from dwelling on what she'd heard that day at the chapel was a good thing.

Over the years she'd tried to blot it out. But returning to Falford and finding Luke living in the house had triggered it all over again. Looking back, she wondered if Harvey had known about the affair and that's why he'd been so hellbent on making her father suffer when he'd found the treasure. It was certainly the ultimate revenge on her father. Emma still didn't know if her mum had been aware of it, she'd never dared ask.

As for Luke . . . Emma had never told him. He'd have been horrified and upset. She'd been terrified that it might cause them to split up — and how could she burden him with knowledge like that? He might have felt he should tell his father.

Emma finished her breakfast and tried to look forward to the day ahead. Immediately her spirits were lifted when she walked into the house to find Maxi trying to squirt sun cream onto two excited four- and six-year-olds. It was like trying to catch the wind and Emma had a hard time suppressing her giggles. The kids reminded her of the fun, innocent times of childhood before the burden of adulthood encroached.

'Urgh! I don't want it on me!' Daisy wailed.

'Please keep still. You don't want a burned nose!' Maxi caught Daisy and rubbed at the splodge of cream on her nose.

Meanwhile Arlo grabbed the sun-cream bottle, ran up behind his sister and squirted it on her hair.

'Arlo!' Maxi shouted. 'Stop that now!'

Daisy squealed. 'Mumm-eee! My hair!'

Emma dived in. 'Arlo. Can I have the sun-cream squirter, please?'

Without waiting for an answer, she grabbed it and he giggled. She brandished it. 'You want a taste of your own medicine?'

'Noooo!'

'Then fetch a towel for your sister's hair, please.'

'Or you won't be going to the market,' Maxi added, keeping hold of Daisy. 'Emma will take Daisy and you can help me weed the veg patch.'

Arlo put his hands on his hips and did an impression of Maxi rolling her eyes. 'Oh, if you in-sist, Mummy!' he declared and stomped off to the towel rail.

Twenty minutes later, with Daisy's hair still damp and Arlo still eyeing the sun-cream gun with envy, they were on their way to the beach. The market had been set up on a field next to the car park behind the beach, although some of the stands were pitched on the sand itself.

It was ten a.m. and the market had only just opened but scores of people were already milling around the stalls. The kids spilled out of the car, hyper, and Maxi had a job to keep them from running headlong into the ice cream stall.

Emma took Arlo's hand while Maxi kept hold of Daisy.

There were dozens of stalls and food vans selling everything from artisan cheese and wooden crafts to beach sarongs and second-hand books. The aroma of pasties competed with the scent of handmade soaps. One area was given over to traditional fairground attractions with a wooden helter-skelter towering over the car park.

The kids made a beeline for it.

After their spells on the fairground, they wandered around the market for a while. Emma left Maxi at a plant stall with the children, while she browsed one selling fused glass. Maxi's birthday was coming up so she chose a framed plaque of a gold starfish on turquoise glass and popped it into her backpack. She'd already decided to make a card of her own to go with it, perhaps of the house.

A few metres away, she saw the Beachcombers' stall, where Ursula and Luke were behind the table.

Adorned with buckets and spades, fishing nets, buoys and posters of marine life, it sported a banner reading: 'Falford Beachcombers — Join us to help keep our beaches clean and safe for all'.

Both Luke and Ursula caught her eye and Emma felt she could hardly walk off. She felt obliged to acknowledge their presence at least, though Luke in particular was the last person she wanted to talk to at this moment.

She went over, ready with a 'Hello, goodbye. I must go back to Maxi and the kids', etc.

A sign declared: 'All the items on this stall were collected from local beaches in just one month. They represent a fraction of the items discarded or washed up on Cornwall's sands every day.'

There were photos and stories of some of the other rubbish found — and its effects on local wildlife.

Today, Ursula had a pink tint on her white hair. The candy floss had been tamed and tied back with a black velvet ribbon. Ursula was in linen again — a grey smock and trousers — with a screen-printed silk scarf draped around her neck and sunglasses on a chain.

Her hair and clothes had changed little since they were at school. Fifteen years had obviously added lines around her eyes, nose and mouth, and yet her tanned skin was still smooth. She was probably in her early sixties and it occurred to Emma that Ursula could only have been in her forties when she'd taught Emma — an age that had seemed ancient to an eighteen-year-old, but relatively young to Emma now.

She was chatting to a family who bought a bucket and spade, then she registered Emma's presence.

'Hello,' Ursula said. 'Didn't expect to see you here.'

91

'Maxi and the kids invited me,' Emma said, wondering what Ursula meant by the comment. Biting back a retort, she decided to move on to more neutral territory. Anything would do so she picked up a Kilner jar.

'What are all these tiny coloured shards?' Emma asked.

Ursula wrinkled her nose. 'This is plastic swarf; it's the waste from drilling plastic.'

'But how does it end up in the sea?'

'Most of it comes from domestic and commercial landfill sites. It gets blown into rivers or sewers.' Ursula let out a sigh. 'And hey presto, it finds its way to the oceans and our beaches. Aren't we lucky?'

For once, Emma empathised with Ursula's exasperation. 'I don't remember this much pollution on the beaches when I lived here,' she said.

'There's far more plastic waste now. It's an absolute nightmare.'

'Can you do anything with it?' Emma grimaced at the jar packed with coloured pieces, imagining where they might end up.

'I keep the prettiest and turn them into bracelets.'

'Really? That sounds a very clever thing to do.'

'I don't know about clever,' Ursula said, rather haughtily. 'It satisfies me to make something beautiful out of something ugly. To turn the ugliness of man's sins into a positive thing . . . If that doesn't sound too hippy-dippy and twee.'

'Twee is the last word I'd have used,' Emma said with a wry smile and without adding 'about you'.

'Amazing what treasures we find, isn't it, Luke?' Ursula said.

'I wouldn't go so far as to call it *treasure*,' he said hastily, avoiding Emma's eye.

'Depends what your definition of treasure is,' Ursula went on. 'I'll admit the pieces of eight and pearls have so far eluded us, but most things can be repurposed, found new homes or reunited with their owners,' she said.

'You find things that people have lost?' Emma said.

'We try.'

'Rarely,' Luke cut in. 'Sometimes we find a fisherman's gear we can reunite with its owner.'

Emma thought he seemed troubled by Ursula's comment.

'You know, if you'd really like to learn more about the issues we're facing, you should join us,' Ursula added frostily.

'Me?' Emma couldn't hide her astonishment — and horror.

'Why not? You're staying around for a while, aren't you? We need the help and you'd find plenty of inspiration.'

'Thanks for the offer but I need to focus on my work. I'm up against a very tight deadline for this commission.' She glanced over at the plant stall where a very bored-looking Arlo was trying to drag Maxi away. 'I'd better go back to the children. We've promised them a barbecue for tea and I want to buy some sausages from the butcher's van.'

Unfortunately at that moment, Arlo also spotted Emma — or rather, Luke.

'Luuuuu-ke!'

He hurtled up to the Beachcombers' stand.

'Have you found any treasure?' Arlo demanded.

Daisy joined him, standing on tiptoes to see better. 'Any kweetures?' she asked, so mournfully that Emma had to laugh.

Luke laughed. 'No treasure,' he said. 'Some creatures though.'

'What creatures?' Arlo and Daisy chorused as Maxi arrived.

'Oh God, I hope he doesn't share too many horror stories . . .' Maxi whispered.

'A seal,' Luke said.

Arlo was back in a flash. 'Was it dead? There was a dead baby seal on the beach at Christmas.'

'It wasn't dead. It was asleep!' Daisy cried.

Maxi exchanged a grimace with Emma. 'Dead,' she mouthed.

'This seal wasn't dead,' Luke said. 'It was poorly though, so the seal rescuers came for it.'

'Is it in the seal hospital?' Daisy asked.

'It was but I think they've been able to release it,' Luke replied.

'Dad says that he saw a dolphin chopped up by a boat,' Arlo said.

'That's quite enough, thank you.' Maxi glared at Arlo.

'Sad things do happen,' Luke explained. 'But we do our best to help any animal we come across. Some of them don't survive but others do.'

He was great with the kids, Emma had to admit, appreciating his honesty with them. She shivered. She'd seen plenty of dead seals and birds in her time, even a stranded whale once.

'Terrible, isn't it?' Maxi said, shaking her head at a picture of a gannet tangled in a rope.

'Horrible. Poor bird. Did it survive?'

'That one did,' Luke said in a low voice while Daisy picked up a Croc covered in barnacles. Arlo was flicking through a plastic folder of some of the strandings

94

and marine rescues. 'But hundreds don't.'

'What do you do with them these days? Is there still a seabird hospital at Falmouth?'

'Yes, we do take some there. They come out at all hours if one of the volunteers can't safely transport the bird themselves.'

'Luke's in the Marine Divers Wildlife Rescue,' Maxi said.

'Oh?' Emma's interest was piqued. 'Are you?'

'I'm a newbie. I only joined when I came back to Cornwall. I help out from time to time. My business partner, Ran, is involved too.'

How quickly Luke had become reabsorbed into the community, Emma thought. She was anything but ready to rejoin Falford life. In fact, she'd had every intention of keeping her distance and yet here she was, chatting away at the local market within a few days of returning.

'It must be fascinating,' she said, feeling seal rescue was a safe topic on which they could both agree.

'Daisy!' Maxi called to the little girl, who had now got hold of some kind of animal jaw and was chasing Arlo round the stall with it.

Daisy ran back but Arlo was clearly hiding.

While Maxi went off to coax him out, Luke spoke to Emma. 'It is, though it can also be soul-destroying. We see some really distressing sights.'

'I can imagine . . . I remember that stranded whale up the coast. The marine sanctuary people went to try and refloat it but it died. I cried for the rest of the day.'

'I remember that. You did a drawing of it . . .'

'Of the way I wanted it to end. I drew it swimming off out to sea. I couldn't bear to think of it dead on

95

the beach, gasping its last.'

'It can be pretty awful. I've seen grown men cry after days of trying to save a creature like that. Strandings can happen naturally, though. It's the casualties caused by human action that hurt the most. Gannets caught in ropes, dolphins cut by propellors, and don't get me started on the plastic.'

'I saw some of the rubbish at the cove. I'd nothing to put it in so I made a little pile and carted what I could to the bin . . .' It sounded rather pathetic, Emma thought, and as if she was trying to please him. 'Don't worry, I'm not asking for a gold star,' she added quickly.

'If everyone did that we'd not have a litter-picking problem — only an ocean full of plastic to deal with.'

Emma nodded and for a few minutes, they kept up a conversation about the sights the Beachcombers saw and what could be done about it, both avoiding anything that could remotely be connected to events of the past. However, eventually Luke subsided into silence, leaving Emma unsure of how the conversation should go next, or if it should go anywhere at all.

However, the dilemma was solved by Maxi grabbing Emma's arm. She held Daisy tightly by the other hand and her face was panic-stricken.

'Emma!' she cried. 'Have you seen Arlo? He's gone.'

10

Emma's stomach turned over. 'What do you mean, 'gone'? Has he wandered off?'

'He must have. He was playing behind the stall and then I got talking to Ursula for a minute or two. When I called him again, he wasn't there!' Maxi clasped her hands tightly.

'He can't have been gone long,' Luke said. 'You've only been here ten minutes.'

'Yes, but you know Arlo. He's a little demon when something catches his attention.'

Maxi was trembling. Emma put her arm around her. 'We'll find him. I promise.'

'Y-yes. I'm probably overreacting . . . That's what I'd say to a parent in the same situation but . . .' She lowered her voice. 'Oh, Em, what if someone's taken him?'

Emma rubbed her back. 'They haven't. He's off on one of his adventures. We'll find him. You stay here with Daisy.'

Picking up on the adults' anxiety, Daisy's bottom lip began to tremble. 'Where's Arlo?' she said in a tiny voice.

'He'll be back in a minute, darling.'

Luke tapped into his phone. 'I've got all the Beachcombers on the alert and the market organiser is on the way. We'll get each person to search a specific area of the market. Can you let us have a photo of Arlo, please?'

'Yes. Yes. Oh God.' Maxi pulled out her phone and

97

dropped it immediately. 'Oh God, the screen!'

The glass was cracked.

'Don't worry about your phone now. I'll send a picture,' Emma said. 'Luke, can I have your number?'

Without hesitation, Luke gave his number calmly and clearly to Emma. It took all she had to punch it in first time but, within half a minute, the photo of Arlo with a sunflower was on Luke's phone and in circulation to the rest of the Beachcombers, as well as the market organiser and her helpers.

'Stay here, in case he comes back,' Luke said.

'I want to look for him myself.'

'Yes, but Luke's right. You and Daisy stay here because he knows this stall and this is the most likely place for him to come back.'

'I'll stay with you,' Ursula offered.

Daisy had started to cry. 'Where's Arlo?' she said again.

'He's probably exploring,' Ursula said with a sympathetic glance at Maxi. 'He'll be back soon. Daisy, why don't you sit behind the stall and help us look after it while Mummy waits for him. I can show you some of the things we found on the beach.'

Daisy looked to Maxi for reassurance.

'Y-yes, darling. You do that with Ursula.'

Emma hugged her. 'We're checking by the swing boats and carousel. He'll turn up any moment with everyone searching. I promise.'

Luke checked his watch. 'You say he's been gone around six minutes? We'll give it fifteen.' He gave Emma a reassuring half-smile. 'I promise you we'll find him way before then.'

Luke and Emma left Maxi talking to the market organiser who had just arrived, while Ursula was showing Daisy one of the flip-flop animals.

Once they were out of earshot, Emma voiced her true fears. 'Should we call the police now?' Even saying the words made her feel sick.

'I'd hang on another ten minutes but no longer.' Luke checked his watch. 'The market organiser has protocols for this kind of thing. I've helped in searches before; usually for vessels at sea but aboard ship too. Was there anything Arlo was particularly drawn to?'

'Everything,' Emma said desperately. 'He's like a magpie, anything might have taken his fancy. The beach toy stall, the fairground rides, the ice cream van.'

Luke nodded. 'Those are being covered by Marvin and Zoey. We'll look around the food area.'

They split up, each taking a path around the half-a-dozen stalls selling everything from crepes to gin, asking each stallholder if they'd seen a little boy and showing photos to some of the queueing customers. Emma was almost breathless with panic, aware that every moment time was ticking by.

'Do you think he'd have wandered far from the market itself?' Luke asked, when they met at the end of the line of stalls.

'I doubt it. There are too many exciting things here . . .' Emma was staring over to the beach where a couple of stalls had pennants flying. She put her hand to her face.

'What?' Luke demanded.

'I suppose he might have gone to the beach café. He was pestering Maxi for a milkshake earlier but that means he'd have had to cross the road.' She watched a large white Transit rumble past towards the traders' parking area and felt sick. 'Oh God, what if he's been in an accident?'

'We'd know by now,' Luke said briskly. 'And anyway, it's unlikely because the road is closed to all but market traffic. Are you sure there's nothing he's particularly obsessed with?'

Emma wracked her brains then recalled her first encounter with the Lego pieces. 'Tractors. He loves tractors. And JCBs, diggers, the bigger the better. But that's no use here on a beach.' Her spirits plunged further.

Luke frowned. 'Never mind, why don't we head onto the beach to see if anyone at the café has seen him?'

Glad of any thread of hope, however slender, Emma was already on her way. 'OK. I'll ask at the café, you take a look around the beach?'

She ran up to the serving hatch, ignoring the annoyed glances from the long queue. 'Have you seen a little boy? He has dark curly hair and he's six, but he looks a year older. He's wandered off from the market.'

Sympathetic noises replaced the annoyed mutterings and the woman at the hatch called the owner, who went inside and asked the staff and customers.

'Wanna take a look around the back? There's a generator shed and our customer toilets,' she said.

Emma went with her, though her tiny spark of optimism was fading fast. It had been over ten minutes since Arlo had gone and there was no message from Maxi or Luke to say he'd been spotted. What if he hadn't simply wandered off? What if someone had taken him? She had to hold onto the door of the café toilets, feeling faint with fear.

'Are you OK, love?' the owner asked.

'Not really. I'm not his mum and I'm petrified. I can't imagine what's going through Maxi's mind.'

'Oh, he's Maxi's lad, is he? My grandkids go to school with him. Look, let's have a dekko around the trade bins. Kids can get everywhere, trust me!'

Emma ran with the café owner to the bins, but there was no sign.

'Have you tried the lifeguards' hut?' the woman offered.

'It's unmanned at the moment but the kids love to play on the deck.'

Emma saw the shuttered hut, a hundred metres away in the dunes above Silver Cove. It was a long way from the café, even further than the market. Surely Arlo hadn't gone that far?

'Thanks. I will,' she said.

'Call us if you can't find him. We'll help with the search,' the owner said, with her hand on Emma's shoulder.

With the world weighing on her shoulders, Emma dashed off. It had been over a quarter of an hour since Arlo's absence had been noticed. They would have to call the police. Her stomach lurched. Oh, poor, poor Maxi.

In the distance Luke was bending over something by the lifeguards' hut. Emma almost passed out. What if Arlo was injured?

Then Luke turned and waved both arms above his head, beckoning her.

She took off like a rocket, launching herself across the sand. Luke immediately disappeared around the side of the hut. Oh God, what if there'd been an accident? Lungs fit to burst, she hurtled round the side to find Luke standing over a yellow toy digger.

101

'Here you go,' Luke said.

Its driver, a ginger-haired boy, was making chugging noises as he lifted the scoop of the digger higher.

'That's not Arlo!' she said.

'Whoosh!' the boy shouted, dropping a load of sand onto the ground.

There was a shriek and then a dark curly head emerged from the pile of sand under the scoop.

'No. Ow.'

'Arlo!'

Emma flew over, almost tripping over in her haste to scoop him up in her arms.

Arlo pushed himself out of a boy-shaped hole in the sand, brushing sand from his hair and ears.

'Arlo! What are you doing out here? Everyone's looking for you.'

'Oliver was burying me,' he said, pointing to the digger driver.

The driver laughed maniacally and made a rumbling noise, steering his digger straight for Arlo and Emma.

'It's time to go back to your mum,' Luke said, sounding hugely relieved himself. 'I'll call her now to let her know you're all right.'

Luke was soon on the phone to Maxi, reassuring her, and Emma could hear the screams of delight down the phone. She uttered a silent prayer that she'd found the little boy — and a silent thanks to have had Luke's calm support in a moment of crisis.

A few metres away, sitting on the sand in the shade of the hut, half-a-dozen people with a couple of buggies were in animated conversation.

'Does Oliver's mum and dad know you're here?' Emma said.

Arlo scrunched up his face. It was clear that this question had never even entered his head — nor the ginger boy's.

'Dunno,' Arlo said. 'Bye-bye, Oliver.'

Oliver replied with another loud rumble and said, 'See ya!' before starting to excavate another hole.

Emma grasped Arlo's hand, more tightly than he probably liked, and spoke to the group as she passed by them. 'Just so you know, there's a boy digging a second channel tunnel behind this hut. In case he belongs to you. Did you cross the road?' she asked Arlo as they walked back to the market.

'No. I only walked on the sand,' he said, pointing at the road.

Luke exchanged a relieved grimace with her over Arlo's head. They could both see that the car wheels had thrown up so much sand over the tarmac that it might as well have been beach. To a boy intent on finding a yellow digger, it must have all looked the same. Arlo just hadn't noticed anything or realised that his mum was missing. Emma shivered, realising how easy it was to lose someone — just like that. She'd been terrified over the past fifteen minutes, so goodness knows how Maxi had felt.

In half a minute, Arlo was reunited with his mum and sister. Maxi was trying not to cry and made sensible noises, warning him not to wander off again without alarming him. Emma was in awe at her restraint; she'd have bawled and was having difficulty not doing so now.

Maxi then turned to Emma, hugging her until she could barely breathe.

'Luke found him, actually,' she said.

Maxi threw her arms around Luke, hugging him

too. His eyes filled with delight. 'It was Emma's idea about the digger that did it. I saw the other boy by the hut and that led me to him.'

'You are both the best people in the whole wide world and at the absolute top of my Christmas list forever,' Maxi cried.

Luke laughed. 'I'll settle for finding Arlo.'

He beamed with delight at Emma and she smiled back in sheer relief. No matter what had happened between them, they'd both instinctively understood and shared the panic their own mothers would have felt if they'd gone missing.

'Alleluia, the wanderer returns!' Ursula said to Arlo, who shrank against his mum. The attention was clearly more than he could bear.

'Can we have an ice cream?' Daisy asked, adding, with some shrewd insight for a four year old, 'Cos *I* didn't run away.'

Gathering her brood close, Maxi laughed with relief. 'Yes, we can all have an ice cream. If we all stay close *together*.'

Ursula mentioned she knew the farmer who ran the artisan ice cream stall and recommended the strawberry clotted cream flavour, which was met with universal approval.

'I'll join you in a moment,' Emma said to Maxi.

Maxi walked off, both children's hands held tightly in her own. In her relief and the mayhem at finding Arlo, Emma realised she hadn't thanked Luke properly herself and he appeared to have melted away in the past minute.

'Do you know where Luke's gone?' Emma asked Ursula, who was behind the stall again.

'I don't,' Ursula said, adding, 'I'm so happy you

found little Arlo. I know how it feels to lose someone.'

The unexpected words temporarily froze any reply, until Emma managed to mumble, 'Thanks.'

Still thinking of Ursula's sympathy and how it had affected her, Emma scanned the throng, which had thickened considerably since half an hour ago. She couldn't see Luke and she was mindful she'd promised to join Maxi at the ice cream stall, but it suddenly became the most important thing in the world to make sure Luke didn't think she was ungrateful.

She couldn't bear it and pushed away into the crowd, desperate for a sight of those broad shoulders, the head of tousled chestnut hair.

Wait. What was she doing, chasing after Luke? The rollercoaster of emotions of the past half an hour had overcome her. She needed to be with Maxi and the kids. She could thank Luke later. He'd soon be back at the Beachcombers' stall and she could drop by before she left the market.

With that thought partly easing her guilt, she joined Maxi and the kids at the ice cream truck, which had been converted from an old horse box. The day's drama had been forgotten by the children already, though not by Maxi or Emma, who had eagle eyes on them both while they ate their ice creams and as they went around the rest of the market. It was getting even busier so Maxi took the children to the carousel, where it was slightly less crowded, while Emma took her chance to seek out Luke on the pretext of browsing.

After a few minutes, she found him by the dive centre van in deep conversation with a tall, blond man. Not wanting to interrupt, she hung back; however, Luke spotted her, said something that made his friend laugh, and came over.

'Sorry, I've interrupted your conversation. Was that a potential customer?' she asked.

'No, that's Ran, my business partner. I was just catching up on how he was getting on, seeing if he needed any help, but he's fine.'

'You must be busy, between the dive business and the Beachcombers' stall — and chasing after lost boys.'

'We're taking it in turns to volunteer on the stall and, like I said, Ran can handle the dive van.' He held Emma's gaze with his own direct one. His eyes held a fire that drew her closer to its warmth, exactly like when they were teenagers. Except, he was now very much a man. The way he held himself upright, the confidence compared to the diffident teenager. The difference in his physique was obvious too. She was so close to him, a flush of heat blooming inside her.

'Um, I won't keep you, anyway. I only wanted to say thank you for helping us find Arlo. I know Maxi is incredibly grateful and, um, so am I. Arlo's my godson and he's the closest to a nephew I'll ever have. Even if I haven't seen the kids and Maxi so much lately . . .'

As she added the final comment, she realised how much she regretted not seeing more of them all. She'd convinced herself she was too busy, but she'd also used that as an excuse for not visiting Cornwall.

'They're great kids.' He grinned. 'Even if Arlo put us all through the mill for a while, he was only having an adventure. We all need those from time to time.'

Emma smiled, wondering if Luke was referring to himself, having joined the navy. Or maybe he meant *her*.

'True. Coming back to Cornwall has been a kind of adventure . . .' she murmured.

106

'More than you bargained for?' His reply was so soft, she hardly heard it, and before she could frame an answer, he went on: 'Emma, like I said at the beach the other day, I'm genuinely sorry for what happened to your dad. I saw my mum the other day and she asked me to pass on her condolences.'

Her condolences? Sue would have been upset by her father's passing . . . of course. She was certainly in love with him at one time. Did she still have feelings for him? Would their affair have ended at some point . . . or would it have broken up Emma's parents' marriage? She'd never know and neither would Luke.

His sympathy and the reminder of the shock of discovering the affair, brought the threat of tears again. She must not cry. She had to leave but she was determined not to betray her emotions to him.

'That's kind of her,' she said stiffly, then softened. 'I'm sorry too, for being — for the way I spoke to you at the beach the other day,' she added briskly. 'I'd better go now. Maxi's anxious to go home and have a chill-out after the drama and I need to finish a commission.'

'You're definitely staying at Maxi's for a while then?'

'Yes. In her garden lodge.' Emma hesitated. 'For a few weeks, at least,' she added, not wanting to let on she would be there for much of the summer due to her own place being rented out. 'I can't stay too long though because Maxi was planning to rent it out as a holiday let.'

'I've seen it from a distance. She and Andy have done a great job with it.'

'It's very comfortable and in a lovely spot. The light is beautiful under the trees and the stream is right alongside.' Emma didn't know what else to say.

'It must be a good place to work in,' he said, seemingly unwilling to let her leave just yet. 'Peaceful.'

'Yes. It's a contrast with the city. I've a big book commission related to the sea and I need to immerse myself by it, if that doesn't sound mad . . .' she stopped, aware she might be revealing too much about herself.

'Not mad at all. I've seen some of your work. I'm no artist but I think it's beautiful.'

'Oh?' Emma was stopped in her tracks.

'I saw your website. I'm really happy you went for your dreams.'

It was impossible not to smile in pleasure and surprise. Luke had been looking her up on the Internet. She'd never expected that.

'Thank you,' she said, with real warmth in her voice. 'Though the truth is, I couldn't do anything else.'

She had to tear her gaze from those blue eyes, unwilling to read too much in them, or have him read too much in hers. He still had the power to throw her off kilter and send shivers through her body. 'I'm sure I'll see you around. It'll be impossible not to.'

Without looking back, she walked off, glad to melt into the anonymity of the crowds. Yet his gaze seared into her back, as if he could still see her and inside her soul. Dangerous thoughts, Emma decided, parking them in a corner of her mind while she sought out Maxi.

* * *

On Sunday morning, calm of a sort descended on the household after Arlo's 'adventure', though 'calm' was a relative word, with the kids zooming round the garden and splashing in their paddling pool.

108

Emma heard them from the deck but their shouts soon melted away as she lost herself in her work on the book. She enjoyed painting the delicate pinks and pale oranges of shells, checking out her sketches and trawling the Internet for references. The varied colours and textures were beautiful and she was reminded once again of how her work had saved her: all her focus had to be on the artwork. It was exacting and tiring but completely absorbing.

When she broke for a cool drink on the deck, however, Luke flooded back into her mind. Any unkind hope she might once have nurtured that he might have become boring and unattractive had been blown out of the water.

Yet he was still the same person who'd set off a chain of events that had resulted in her family losing their home and her father imploding. Luke being handsome and helpful didn't redress the balance of his past sins, did it?

If he'd sinned at all, of course.

What a thought that was . . . that she might, possibly, have misjudged him. It was too disturbing to contemplate so she parked it in the shadows, along with so many other memories and regrets.

Luke claimed he hadn't shown his father the journal and that Harvey must have got hold of it by stealth. However, could there be another explanation he hadn't admitted to? Harvey might well have coerced his son into showing it to him. God knew, Harvey would certainly have borne a huge grudge against her father if he'd known about Sue's affair.

Emma didn't know the whole truth and she probably never would now.

By late afternoon, a fresh breeze was blowing inland off the sea; the cool Cornish evening reminding her that it was still only May, albeit the final day. Summer proper still stretched ahead of her, with all its promise and uncertainty. Wrapped up warmly, Emma joined the family for a barbecue in the garden.

Maxi was trying to act casually around the kids, but Emma could see she hardly ever took her eyes off them, and overheard her urging Andy to watch them. A scare like yesterday's was bound to take its toll for some time, perhaps forever.

With the children finally packed off to bed later than Maxi had wanted, Emma stayed for a quick drink then went back to the chalet. Maxi and Andy looked exhausted and Emma guessed they needed some time to finally relax and chill out.

That night, Emma found herself lying awake, listening to the wind in the trees and the owls hooting, knowing she'd set her alarm early so she could be up early to catch the low tide at the beach.

* * *

She woke to a moody Monday morning, chilly when the clouds covered the sun, with a brisk breeze from the sea.

She had her sketchbook and pencils in her backpack and headed from the car park to the opposite side of the beach from the Old Chapel. There were a series of flat rocks which were perfect to perch on and rest her gear. The tide had uncovered some glorious rock pools and gullies between the rocks, thick with purply mussels and ruby sea anemones.

However, she was working in pencil today, so the textures, shapes and shadows were as intriguing to her as the colours. The whitewashed walls of the Old Chapel were as far away as possible, sunlight glinting from the windows. At one point, she saw two figures emerging from the steps that led from the chapel graveyard and onto the sands, toting sacks and their litter-pickers.

Even from a distance, she knew they were Luke and Ursula.

She could pack up and go but why should she? The light was so beautiful. The clouds scudded across a huge sky and she experienced that sense of being a small speck in a huge universe that was both comforting and overwhelming. She thought of her father walking over these sands, playing with her in the rock pools — happier, innocent times before she'd become aware of the tensions underlying her family idyll, like underwater currents waiting to pull her down.

Before she knew it, two hours had flown by and the tide had retreated beyond her rocky perch. It must almost be on the turn, she thought, looking at the wet rocks exposed nearer the surf. The sun had given them their trademark coat of silver. Emma took her flask from her bag and sipped the fruit tea she'd brought with her. She peeled a banana and ate it, wondering how drawing could make her so hungry. All that creative energy perhaps.

She left the peel on the rock next to her sketch-book, deciding to investigate a nearby rock pool. She would take some photos with her phone before the tide flooded the gullies and draw anything interesting later in the comfort of the lodge.

'Hello.'

Her phone almost slipped into a pool.

Luke was now standing next to the rock where she'd left her sketchbook.

She walked over to him. 'Oh my God. You startled me!'

'Sorry. I didn't mean to.' He seemed about to move away. 'I won't disturb you.'

'No!' She surprised herself with how eager she was for him to stay. 'I mean yes, you're disturbing me, but that's fine. I needed a break.'

He picked up her sketchbook.

She put out a hand. 'No, please don't.'

11

Too late.

Luke had seen the pages and was stunned. Amid the shells and seaweed there were rough pencil sketches of the Beachcombers in the distance, stick figures reflected in flat pools of water. Ursula crouching on the strandline in her clogs, long hair brushing the sand, fingers curled around some invisible treasure . . . and *him*.

He had his hands on his hips, a frown on his face, intent on something on the horizon.

It was as if Emma could see inside his head. As if she *knew* he'd been thinking of her.

'Please . . .' She sounded desperate then her tone changed to one of studied indifference. 'They're only doodles,' she said, with a shrug.

So, she was acting as if she didn't care he'd seen them. Which meant she very much did.

Resisting the urge to keep the sketchbook and see what else — who else — she'd captured, Luke handed it to her. She kept hold of it, as if he might try to walk off with it.

'You say they're doodles but they look great to me. So lifelike.'

'I was messing about. I should be finding references for the job in hand.'

'The coastal book?'

She seemed surprised he'd remembered. 'Yes, and they'll all be useful for future commissions . . . when I'm back home in Oxford.'

So, she was keen to let him know she was only here for work and planned on leaving again soon. It was no more than he should have expected and yet it disturbed him.

He decided to fill the gap with a safer topic. 'How's Arlo after his adventure?' he asked.

A smile lit up her face. 'Blissfully unaware of the trauma he put us all through.'

'Probably a good thing.'

Emma laid the open sketchbook back on the flat rock. 'I don't think Maxi will get over it so quickly, though. She won't let them out of her sight at the moment.'

'I can understand that.'

Further conversation was ended by Ursula bounding up. 'Ah, Emma.' Her eyes darted to the sketchbook. 'Oh, my word. Is that me?'

Luke exchanged a glance with Emma. He grimaced and she wrinkled her nose. They might have been back in school, rolling their eyes about a bossy teacher.

Hands on hips, Ursula stood over the sketchbook. 'Gosh. There's no hiding place, is there? Got me in all my dishevelled, bent glory. My hair's like a witch's.'

'Oh no, it's more like a mermaid's,' Emma said.

'There's no need to soften the blow. I admire the honesty in your work, and Luke — you seem to have the weight of the world on those young shoulders. What on earth were you thinking of?'

'When I'm going to find the time to refurbish the toilets at the dive school?' Luke suggested with a grin. 'The drains are blocked again and it's already too close to the season to start the work.'

Emma giggled; a sound that filled him with childish pleasure.

Ursula pulled a face. 'Hmm. Sounds like a noxious state of affairs. Remind me to cancel that lesson I'd booked with you.'

'*You* dive?' Emma said, openly incredulous.

'No, I'm ripping the piss out of you, to use the modern parlance, and I know you both think I'm a bossy old trout. Once a teacher, always a teacher.' She fixed them both with a gimlet stare.

'In that case, we won't dare to contradict you,' Emma said archly.

Ursula raised her eyebrows. 'Touché.'

'I think we should get on with the beach-clean,' Luke cut in, alarmed at the resumption of the sparring between the two women. He wasn't ready to referee a fencing match, Ursula with the foil and Emma with a sabre.

'Yes, and I think Emma should join us.' Ursula smirked. 'Though I suspect she'd rather be anywhere but here now.'

Emma's hackles rose visibly. 'Actually, Ursula, Luke mentioned I'd be welcome on your next group outing. I've decided to take him up on the offer.'

Luke swallowed down a gasp of amazement just in time. Ursula made no attempt to hide her astonishment.

'Well, well, I didn't expect that. His powers of persuasion are obviously greater than mine. Though that's hardly a surprise . . .' Her gaze scythed through them. 'I look forward to it. And now, *I* shall get on with the job.'

Leaving them together, she marched off down the beach.

Luke didn't follow, still reeling from Emma's offer to join the group.

'That woman! She brings out the worst in me. I think I've become a mature and sensible adult and she plunges me back to being a stroppy teenager. Gah!' Emma stamped her sandal, before glaring at Luke. 'And what are you smiling at?'

His shoulders shook. 'Nothing.' He set his face in a serious expression that lasted all of half a second before the laughter broke through again. 'You and Ursula. You're right. She hasn't changed. Neither have you — neither have any of us. We only think we've matured but I think that it's an illusion that we're all in control.'

'Oh, I think you have more than an illusion of being in control,' she murmured. 'Thanks for not dropping me in it with Ursula by the way. I know you didn't invite me but I was so mad at her. I feel a bit guilty now at baiting her.'

Luke took a risk. 'Well, if you want to prove her wrong, you'll have to come to the beach-clean, won't you?'

Emma hesitated a second too long. 'Yeah, I suppose so.' She sounded as if she'd rather have her teeth pulled. 'When is it?'

'Next Sunday morning. Eight o'clock.'

'Eight!'

He grinned. She'd never liked getting up for school and had often been late, or squeaked into class at the last minute. 'It has to be that time because it's low tide at nine and we want to be off the beach before it gets too crowded. Of course, if it's too *early* for you, we'll understand.'

'No. No. It's not too early.'

'See you next Sunday, then?'

She nodded. 'Sure you will.'

Leaving her to her sketching, Luke walked off, trying to act casually and not, under any circumstances, look back.

As for the chances of Emma actually turning up? He thought they were as slim as finding a silver dollar in the cove, but you never knew. One thing that hadn't changed about Emma was her ability to surprise him.

12

What on earth was she doing?

On a hazy Sunday morning, Emma pulled up at the beach to find a group of half-a-dozen Beachcombers already at the car park including Luke, Zoey and Marvin.

If she'd intended to keep a low profile in Falford, it hadn't worked. First, visiting the market, and now joining in the Beachcombers. The thought jolted her. She was enjoying herself so much more than she had been in Oxford and she hadn't thought about Theo for . . . well, it must have been a few days at least. She'd stopped looking at his Facebook page too.

The one person who didn't appear to be there was Ursula, which filled Emma with an odd mix of relief and disappointment.

Luke greeted her when she got out of the car. In cargo shorts, flip-flops and a faded polo shirt, he looked so handsome — so 'grown-up' — that she felt lost for words. How would she concentrate on litter-picking?

'You're here,' he said, almost in wonder.

'I said I would be.' Emma was unable to resist being amused. 'Don't sound so amazed.'

'I'm not.'

'Fibber.' She smiled. 'To be honest, I wasn't quite sure until this morning. The rain and wind were epic last night and I didn't fancy coming out in those conditions, but it's a lovely day and I'm looking forward to what we might find.'

'I hope you're not disappointed, although the storm might have blown some interesting stuff in. Come on, I'll introduce you and find you a bag and grabber.'

He handed her a jute collecting sack and a litter-picker. Much to her relief, they didn't make her wear a hi-vis jacket or she'd have had to draw the line, and, she thought with a smile, Ursula must have refused one too.

Bracing herself, Emma finally had a proper introduction to her fellow Beachcombers. They'd been there when Luke had rescued her from the sea, but she'd hardly been in the socialising mood then.

Zoey stared at her wide-eyed. 'Oh, gosh. You're the last person I ever expected to join us after the first time we met you!'

'Well, I haven't joined yet,' Emma said, feeling embarrassed but determined to be polite to Zoey. 'I thought I'd find out more about what you do.'

'That's *very* brave of you.' Zoey's kindly expression made Emma cringe. 'It can't be easy after . . . you know what.'

Luke came to her aid. 'Emma was brought up around here,' he said. 'She wants to help out.'

'Oh, of course.' Zoey nodded. 'I had heard you used to live here. Must be soooo weird to be back.'

Wondering how much Zoey had heard about her past, Emma flashed her a smile before turning to Marvin, the undertaker's son.

'How's the high-jumping going?' she joked, keen to keep things light.

'Oh, I had to give that up. Bad back,' he said gloomily. 'I've taken over my dad's business now and it's going really well. I'll give you my card when we get back to the car in case you ever need it.'

119

'Shall we get going?' Luke muttered, seemingly embarrassed by what Marvin had said. 'Emma, I'll brief you on our safety protocols on the way to the beach.'

She knew instinctively that Luke didn't want to talk about health and safety. 'Sorry about Marvin,' he said as they walked off together. 'He doesn't know you recently lost your dad.'

'Don't worry. Why would he know?'

'Yeah, but offering you his business card when he's only just met you again.'

'Well, it's a safe bet I'm going to need it one day,' Emma said drily.

Luke gave a little sigh mixed with a wry smile.

'Where's Ursula?' she asked.

'She said she'd join us later.'

'Does she know I'm coming?'

'No, because I wasn't sure you'd turn up.' He added, 'As you pointed out to me.'

'Oh well, I guess it will be an even bigger surprise for her.'

They crossed the road and walked through the dunes to the beach. The café was quiet on this early morning, only a couple of walkers sitting at the tables. Emma passed the spot where Arlo had been buried in the sand with a shudder. He'd been fine, in the end, and yet it could have been very different.

The beach was vast and empty on the falling tide, the waves a low rumble in the distance. She had a sense of being small and insignificant next to the power of nature. She thought of the sailors lost at sea: the ones who'd drowned on the wreck of the *Minerva*. The chaplain finding the coins they'd risked their lives to bring ashore — all in vain. And later, the lives that

120

had been wrecked by the finding of that 'treasure'.

Even though Silver Cove looked pristine from a distance, a closer inspection revealed some surprising finds. There were plastic buckets, spades and sand toys of every hue washed up, some faded and broken, others almost brand new. The waste was both sad and maddening.

Luke caught her grimace. 'People use them once and they break or the children get bored so they dump them on the beach and go home.'

'Who do they think will clear them up?' Emma asked, dropping a still shiny bucket in her sack. 'Do they care?'

He shrugged. 'God knows. Maybe they think it's like a festival and a professional clear-up team will come in after the party's over.'

There were more pieces of broken plastic along the tideline, however it was the tinier pieces that shocked Emma. They were everywhere, littering the shore amid the weed, shells and pebbles like a sinister invasive species. Luke explained how, over time, the plastic degraded into pieces so small they couldn't be seen with the naked eye — microplastics — and ended up in the water system so that humans, as well as animals, ingested them. It was a very sobering thought.

'To think, all these millions of feet tramping over beaches all over the world,' she said. 'All oblivious to this stuff or not caring.'

As well as ugliness, she had to admit there was great beauty too. Her eye became attuned to the shore life she used to be so familiar with, the names flowering in her mind as they searched the beach. They'd learned about the different tidal zones at school, though anyone living so close to the sea — as she once did — knew instinctively where to find the fauna and flora that lived there, from the colourful lichens in the splash zone, where only spray reached, to the pools exposed at rare low tides, where anemones studded the rocks like rubies.

It was such a unique environment that the line between plants and animals became blurred. There were creatures that looked like plant life and vice versa. Although Emma had visited the seaside a few times over the past years, she felt like she was seeing her native Cornwall through fresh eyes.

'Luke!'

A distant figure waved from the far side of the beach, the opposite one to the chapel. The flowing hair and garb was unmistakably Ursula.

Emma had secretly been hoping her ex-teacher wouldn't turn up at all.

'Hello!' Ursula's shout was carried by the breeze and she waved her arms in the air. She didn't move but beckoned them over with sweeping arm movements.

'Looks like she's found something.' Luke's voice was animated, and the excitement was infectious.

Intrigued, Emma hurried towards the rocks with Luke, leaving the other Beachcombers intent on their own patches of beach.

Ursula's sack was abandoned on the dry sand along with her litter-grabber. She clambered down from her rocky perch and met them a few metres from the rock pools.

'There's a wreck!' she cried, before glaring at Emma in amazement. 'You turned up then?'

Emma decided to call her bluff. 'As you can see. Hello,' she said as cheerily as she could muster.

Ursula nodded before addressing herself to Luke. 'Sorry I went AWOL. I had a message from one of my regular students late last night. She told me there was some gorgeous sea glass at this end of the beach. I thought I'd have a quick look before I joined you. The wreck debris must have been washed into the gully by the overnight squall. I wonder if it's from that fishing boat that went down last month?'

'Could be,' Luke said. 'Let's check it out.'

Leaving her bag on the sand, Emma followed them to the rocks.

'There are timbers and nails and some sharp plastic. Be careful,' Ursula warned before marching off to the rocks and scrambling up them. The rocky outcrops were charcoal grey, at right angles to the sea and worn smooth by the constant pounding of the waves.

'Over here,' Ursula barked.

The three of them stopped on a flat ledge and peered down into the gully. Several planks of wood, studded with rusty nails, lay in the water. Immediately a wave rolled in, lifting them up and smacking them against the end of the gully, with a crack that made Emma jump.

She peered down to see coloured pieces of plastic and fibreglass of varying sizes wedged in the back of the rock gully.

'We can't clear that out ourselves,' Luke said. 'But we ought to get the coastguard to put up a warning sign at the entrance of the beach, in case more of it washes up.'

'Do you know where they came from?' Emma asked.

The thought of the boat sinking to the sea bed gave her goosebumps.

'*The Lily Ann*?' Ursula glanced at Luke for confirmation.

'Could well be.' He turned to Emma. 'The skipper deliberately ran her aground here on the beach in March.'

'Deliberately ran it aground? That sounds pretty desperate. Why?'

'He was on board with his friend and his young son and it started to sink,' Luke stared down at the timbers as they rose and fell with the waves, slapping into the rocks. 'So he headed for Silver Cove.'

'The boy couldn't swim well,' Ursula explained. 'And so the skipper decided the only course of action was to run her onto shore.'

Emma shuddered. 'Why didn't they call the coastguard?'

'They did but apparently she was going down way too fast.' Luke climbed down onto a ledge below them for a better look. 'It's terrifying how fast a vessel can go down. They may only have had minutes.'

'What a horrible decision to have to make.' Her blood ran cold, thinking of the family on board the stricken vessel. 'They were OK, though?'

'Yes, thank goodness!' Ursula said. 'The waves smashed the boat up, though fortunately everyone on board was unhurt.' She stood with her hands on her hips.

Luke looked up at them from below. 'The owner cleared most of the wreckage off the beach but we keep seeing more debris from time to time. I'll have a word with Bryan and see if we can get rid of this too. I don't think it'll be washed back out now it's in this gully.'

The wreck had brought back memories of the

Minerva. Emma wondered if Luke was thinking the same as they made their way back down to the main cove.

'Nothing to be done with the wreck today,' Ursula said. 'How are you getting on?'

'OK. We haven't found anything exciting. Only plastic,' Emma said. 'How about you? Was there any sea glass?'

'A few interesting pieces I can use in my work,' Ursula said cautiously. 'I don't suppose you'd be interested in seeing them,' she added, her voice lifting hopefully all the same.

'Actually, I would,' Emma shot back.

Ursula treated her to a piercing glance. 'Then I'll show you, *after* we've done our job for the day.'

She scooped up her collecting bag and forged off ahead, leaving Luke and Emma in her wake.

Luke picked up his bag and handed Emma's to her. 'Better get on with it then,' he said with a mock serious frown.

'Hmm . . .' Emma watched Ursula march towards her patch of sand, brandishing her grabber like a warrior going into battle with her sword at the ready to repel anyone or anything that dared to invade her territory. Her old teacher hadn't changed much, if at all, although the invitation — more of a challenge, really — to look at some of her work had come as a surprise. She seemed to be hellbent on setting a series of tests for Emma, though goodness knew why.

Ursula soon vanished from her mind as Emma worked on her own patch of beach, clearing up plastic, the occasional tin can, fragments of nets and blue fishing ropes. It was surprisingly absorbing and addictive. Although she'd been born and brought up

125

at the cove, she'd forgotten how much life the sand supported, from the powdery edge of the dunes to the splash zones between the land and the highest tides.

Much of the life was either hidden away or almost too small to see with the naked eye. Insignificant to the hundreds of people tramping over it or lying on it and yet, forced to concentrate on it, Emma found it a magical world in miniature. There were hoppers, little crabs, mussels and limpets clinging to rocks, worm casts and shells that seemed empty but were home to tiny creatures.

Her 'job of the day' might be cleaning the beach but her day job was impossible to suppress. For every item she plucked from the sand to add to her bag, she stopped to take a picture of something else. Her mobile battery was almost drained by photos of shells, cuttlefish bones, and even some of the debris: tangled ropes encrusted with weed, driftwood and shiny pebbles striped with white and russet bands.

Despite her half-full bag, she guessed her haul was probably a bit pathetic compared to those of the regulars, but she couldn't pass up the opportunity to glean inspiration.

She crouched over a small pile of dried seaweed, taking a photo of its pistachio-coloured fronds. It was beautiful yet she guessed few people other than herself would have found it so fascinating.

'Emma?'

A figure shaded her from the sun: Luke was standing over her.

'We're done for the day,' he said.

'Already?' Shoving her phone in her shorts pocket, she straightened up. 'Sorry, I was in a world of my own. I'm afraid I probably haven't collected much rubbish.' She nodded at her bag.

'Doesn't matter. You helped.'

'A bit, though I spent most of the time getting ideas for my current commission. I think the others are waiting for us,' she said, spotting half-a-dozen faces turned in their direction, including Ursula's.

He glanced at them but seemed in no hurry to join the gang. 'You don't have to go back to the car park if you're enjoying yourself. I can take your bag back to the truck.'

'Thanks. I — I might stay a while. I've found some great references today. I've almost used up my phone battery, though.' She grimaced. 'I wish I'd brought my sketchbook.'

'I'm pleased you've not found it too awful.' His eyes were lit by amusement. Emma thought again how well he'd grown into his looks. His expression still held that quiet intensity that always gave her goosebumps.

'It was far from awful. Actually, I really enjoyed it, even if I didn't expect to.'

He smiled, not in the triumph some men would have shown, but with a genuine pleasure in her enjoyment. 'Shall I take your bag?'

'Thanks, but I'll come back to the group with you. I will stay but I promised I'd look at Ursula's sea glass first. If she still wants to show me.'

'I don't think she'll have changed her mind. She loves her work. Like you obviously do.'

With the briefest of smiles, Emma walked with him over to the group. There was a level of excitement and dismay with the Beachcombers showing interesting finds, while moaning about the general level of ignorance and behaviour of those who left litter on the beach.

'And the plastic. The bloody plastic! Look at this,' Ursula grumbled. 'If I'd wanted to spend my days collecting plastic bags, I'd have gone to bloody Tesco's. They should all be banned. All plastic bags. No exceptions.'

There were murmurings of agreement that made Emma think guiltily of the half-a-dozen bags for life lurking in the boot of her car.

'Too right, Ursula, and don't get me started on the wet wipes and paper masks,' said Marvin.

After sharing her own finds with the gang and dropping the bag in the back of Luke's truck, Emma hung around while Zoey, Marvin and the others drove off. She and Luke, who was making sure the bags were secure in the pickup, were the only ones left, apart from Ursula.

'Would you like to see this sea glass, then?' she asked, rather brusquely.

Emma resisted the urge to be sharp back, sensing Ursula's wariness might stem from fear that Emma would say no.

'I'd love to,' she said.

'Luke?' Ursula called. 'Do you want to have a look too?'

Luke came over. 'I always want to see what you've found,' he said cheerfully. 'But I have to call Ran back. There's something urgent that's come up at the dive centre. I'll join you in a minute, hopefully.'

Ursula's eyes glittered. 'I know you're only humouring an old fogey. You go and make your call.'

Luke walked off, already pushing buttons on his phone.

Ursula seemed relieved that Emma hadn't abandoned her too. 'Really, I do have some real beauties with me.'

She opened the boot of a battered yellow Citroën 2CV and laid out the pieces of glass from a fabric bag on a piece of black material. Even weathered and frosted, the colours were stunning.

'They're gorgeous. Like real gemstones,' Emma said in genuine wonder. She'd seen bits of glass on the beach many times, of course, but curated and collected together, they really did feel like precious treasure.

'I think so.' Ursula picked out a cobalt-blue piece about as big as her thumbnail and offered it to Emma. 'Today I was lucky.'

Emma held it up to the light, fascinated by the way the sun shone through it. 'It's stunning. What will you do with it?' she asked, intrigued to hear another artist's creative process. It was illuminating to see a different side to Ursula. When talking about her work, her sharp edges were softened, like the sea glass she worked with.

'I'll probably check if I have another similar piece of glass and turn it into earrings, or I could possibly make a pendant. Not sure until I get it home to the studio.'

'Your studio? Do you work from home?'

'Yes and no. I have a small workshop in the garden of my cottage in Falford. The gallery there sells a few of my pieces too, like a few of the gift shops and galleries roundabout. Of course, they want their pound of flesh for stocking it, but you'd know about that.'

'I do . . . or did,' Emma said, thinking of the fifty percent — or more — that retailers usually charged to display work in their galleries. They had rents and bills to pay, Emma appreciated that, but she could understand Ursula's frustration. 'I don't have my work in galleries. I tried it a few times but these days I work solely on commissions.'

'The horror of it is, I've had to resort to an online shop!' Ursula replied, as if she'd been forced to run a gambling den. 'Which is bloody hard work, but it keeps the wolf from the door. I'd far rather sell to customers in person, or work to a commission like yourself, even if some of the clients drive me insane.'

'I can appreciate that too.'

'Feel free to call in at the studio if you want to know more,' Ursula said. 'Only if you're round my way, of course. I wouldn't want to inconvenience you.'

'Thanks. I will.' Emma was amused — and strangely touched — at finally finding a patch of common ground with her old teacher.

Ursula glanced over her shoulder. Luke had finished his call but was still by the truck. 'I think Luke's ready to leave. I should be getting home too. I can't sell any work if I don't make any, now can I?'

'Same here,' Emma said, feeling she'd missed a chance to spend more time with Luke. She was surprised at her disappointment.

'The book with the tight deadline you mentioned at the market?'

Remembering her desperation to get away, Emma felt slightly guilty. 'That's the one. I have a magazine commission too.'

'Then farewell for now.'

Ursula tipped the sea glass gems back into the fabric bag and closed the boot while Emma returned to her own car.

Luke waved to Ursula and then came over to Emma. 'Everything OK at work?' she asked.

'Yes, crisis averted but I do need to drop this lot off

130

on my way. I'm leading a big dive session.'

'Oh, where's that to?'

'*The Carmarthen* off Kennack Sands.' His expression took on an almost dreamy look. 'The World War One wreck on the eastern side of the Lizard?'

Once again Emma thought of sailors sinking under the waves. Luke too . . . she wasn't sure she liked the idea.

'Have a good dive,' she said, almost adding, 'Stay safe.'

'Don't worry, I will.' There was a pause. 'Maybe you'll join us all again? For a beach-clean, I mean.'

'Maybe.' Emma nodded, surprised by the pleasure the invitation gave her. 'If I have time.'

'Of course. Your deadline . . .'

'I'll do my best,' she said, feeling that as a step on from 'maybe', it felt like a huge leap.

With an incline of his head and a 'Bye', he climbed into his pickup, unable to hear her whispered: 'Take care.'

Yet he didn't drive off immediately but sat in the seat, on his phone again. It didn't appear to be a happy call as he was frowning a lot and she caught the odd snatch of frustrated words through the open window.

It seemed early for a such a heated call on a Sunday morning. Perhaps it was more trouble at work.

She took her time getting into her own car, lingering by the open driver's door. Even when Luke had left, she watched the dust cloud signalling his exit from the car park and followed the cab of the truck up the twisting lane that led past the chapel and towards Falford.

Finally, the truck vanished, leaving her with feelings that ebbed back and forth like wavelets in a rock pool. She'd found inspiration and a brief moment of solace while searching the sand, yet it had also been a reminder of the treasures and misery it had brought for her father. She'd also enjoyed Luke's company far more than she'd expected — and that was the scariest thing of all.

13

'Another Beachcombing day? You'll be a regular soon.' Maxi's eyebrows shot up when Emma confessed she was joining the group again the following week.

This time, Emma responded with a wry smile and headed off to Silver Cove with a mix of excitement and apprehension. It had been a busy time, during which she'd been working hard to a deadline. She'd cooked dinner twice for Maxi and babysat the kids while she and Andy went to a play. That had been as exciting as it got, though, and she was surprised at how appealing the prospect of scouring the sands with the Beachcombers was.

Already on site, handing out bags and grabbers, Ursula greeted her with an amused expression. 'So you decided to join us again. I'm glad.'

For the first time, Emma felt Ursula meant her words. That must be progress.

'How could I keep away?' she said archly.

Ursula raised an eyebrow. 'Always ready with the smart answer. Do you want to work together today?'

Amazed, not entirely happy but not wanting to out-right refuse the invitation, Emma agreed. This time, she tried very hard not to be distracted by her finds, both natural and manmade, although she couldn't resist snapping a few pictures of a seaweed with leaves as pink and purple as a sunset. Nestling among one of the fronds was a small orange figure.

'Oh, wow!' she exclaimed.

'What?' Ursula asked.

'It's a plastic dinosaur.' She grinned. 'Kind of sad to find a T-rex on the beach.' She popped him into her bag along with the usual array of plastic bags, face masks, broken toys and balloons.

She also captured a few photos of jellyfish, consulting Ursula on their exact species. One was a compass, a perfect translucent circle with brown stripes radiating outwards to all points.

'Compass is the perfect word for it,' she said to Ursula. 'And, wow, look at this.' Emma pointed to a creature so fantastical it was hard to believe it was real, rather than the product of a sci-fi director's imagination. 'It's a by-the-wind-sailor. I haven't seen one of these for years.'

Ursula joined her, admiring the jellyfish with its own tiny 'sail.' Barely bigger than her thumb, it was exquisitely beautiful.

'I have to get some pictures. I must paint it. Look at those colours.' Emma discarded her bag on the sand to whip out her phone and capture the mini creature, which pulsated with intense blues from sapphire, cornflower and cobalt.

'Unusual to see them now. The storm must have brought it in,' Ursula said.

Emma snapped away.

'Of course, they aren't true jellyfish,' Ursula said. 'They're a colony of tiny individuals who travel together at the mercy of the winds, hence the romantic name.'

'Tiny but deadly collectively,' Emma said, clicking away. 'I remember our biology teacher bringing us out here to look at some. Some boy had to touch one to see if it still stung. Of course, it did!'

They attracted Luke's attention. 'What's all the

134

excitement about?'

'This,' Emma said. 'Isn't it amazing? I'm going to include one on my coastal book.'

'They are beautiful,' he said. 'Amazing to think they might have washed up from so far away.'

'From the far-flung corners of the earth,' Emma said in wonder, meeting eyes that were full of the same delight as her own. Not at the jellyfish, she thought: at her. At sharing her pleasure.

She held her phone but her attention was now on Luke. They were alone. Ursula had moved away and was now a figure at the far end of the beach by the rock pools.

'Oh no. Poor Ursula. I've abandoned her.'

'She won't mind. She knows what she's doing.'

'Still. I should go to her. Get on with the job in hand. Eh?'

Luke raised his bag. 'Me too.'

Forcing herself to turn away, Emma walked over to Ursula with fear in her heart. Her chat with Luke had felt almost friendly, but he had never been her friend, not at eighteen — not now. Friendship was cosy, measured and balanced. She felt none of those things towards him. Anger, resentment, physical desire, confusion, fascination . . .

It couldn't be sensible or wise.

She tried to laugh at herself. My God, she sounded like her mother.

'Where did you get to?' Ursula demanded, her old feistiness back.

'I could say the same about you,' Emma retorted then softened. 'Sorry, I was talking to Luke about the jellyfish.'

'I could see you were chattering away. Come on,

let's get on with it. There's so much rubbish, anyone would think people had been having one of those dreadful music festivals on this beach. Do you know, I've just seen a condom! A bloody condom! Can't people restrain their urges for five minutes?'

Ursula snorted in disgust and Emma had the greatest difficulty in not bursting out laughing. She was well aware that she herself had not been above some al fresco sex with Luke in the dunes of the cove.

The next half an hour sped by. There was nothing as unusual or exotic as the by-the-wind-sailor — or as disgusting as Ursula's 'find' — and soon Emma's bag was filling up with rusty cans, plastic bags and other rubbish. The other Beachcombers were stick figures in the distance, their reflections distorted in the sheets of water left by the retreating tide.

Emma was close to the rock pools where she'd done her sketching when she spotted the sun glinting off something in a damp patch of sand at the edge of the rock. A ring-pull or a shard of metal from a wreck. Metal hulls eventually broke up into thousands of tiny shards, which could be hazardous for people and wildlife. There was a beautiful beach in the far west that had only recently been made safe after a wreck from twenty years previously.

She walked over to investigate.

She bent down and saw the glint again. Lying on its side, the object wasn't silver or steel, it was gold.

'Oh!'

'What?'

Ursula's attention was caught and she glanced over.

Emma stood up. 'It's a ring. And I think it might be gold.'

Ursula swooped down on her. 'What? Let me see it.'

136

'I'm not sure, of course. It looks modern . . .'

Ursula snatched it from her fingers and stared at it.

'It's just a piece of old rubbish!' she cried and threw it back on the sand. It plopped into a shallow pool between the sand ripples.

Ursula marched off.

Astonished, Emma retrieved the ring. It wasn't rubbish, it looked like gold to her, though she was far more concerned for her old teacher.

What on earth was wrong?

Ursula was halfway across the beach towards the waves, her collecting bag and grabber abandoned. With the ring in her shorts pocket, Emma left her own bag beside the other and jogged after her.

'Ursula! Are you OK? I didn't mean to upset you.'

The older woman turned. To her horror, Emma saw tears on her cheeks.

'It's me who should be sorry,' Ursula muttered, dashing her hand across her eyes. 'Silly old fool.'

'I didn't realise — I don't understand.'

'You'd better get that ring back. It probably is gold and must have belonged to someone.'

'It's in my pocket.' Emma patted her jeans.

'Good . . . You must think I'm a mad old bat,' Ursula said brusquely. 'I probably am. Only you see, it was that ring . . . I thought it was . . .'

Inwardly, Emma held her breath. Ursula was clearly struggling whether to share something, and she sensed that it might be a precious nugget.

'Well, I thought it was mine.'

'Yours?' Emma burst out.

'Yes.' Ursula stabbed at the sand with her grabber, spraying up sand, as if berating herself. 'Damn it, I'm behaving like a stupid romantic teenager. Forget I

137

said anything.'

'Teenage feelings are powerful.'

Ursula glanced up sharply. 'Not when you're sixty-three, they're not.'

'Age doesn't come into it.' Emma spoke gently, 'Please tell me why you thought it was yours. I promise I won't think you're stupid.'

She waited patiently. It was shocking to see such a display of emotion from her teacher, even though she'd come to know her a little better over the past few weeks. It must have taken a lot for her to reveal a chink in her armour.

'That ring,' Ursula said. 'I thought it was one that I'd lost. You see, I do know how it feels to lose someone.'

The agonised expression on her face cut right to Emma's heart. Never could she imagine her old adversary looking so forlorn.

'I'm sorry. I'd no idea,' she said gently. 'Was this the person who gave you the ring?'

'Yes. I lost it on this beach.' Ursula gazed out over the sands to the horizon where the vast sky met the steely waves. 'I won't call it an engagement ring because neither of us were ever planning to do anything as . . .' she sighed. 'As boring as to get married. Yet it was a symbol, a pledge to each other.' Her voice became more urgent and she turned back to Emma. 'When Michael returned, he was leaving the services and we *were* going to settle down and have kids. We talked about it but we never did anything.'

Emma's heart went out to her, fearing what Ursula was going to say next.

'I fell for a soldier, even though what he did went against *everything* I believed in — everything I still do believe in. But you can't choose who you fall in love with, can you?'

Emma begged to differ yet said nothing. You could choose how you acted on that love. You could walk away. Sometimes you *had* to.

She still felt deeply sorry for Ursula. 'When did this happen?'

'Years ago. He was an army officer, fresh out of Sandhurst. He went to Iraq. I didn't want him to, of course.'

Emma shivered, dreading where the story was leading — almost not wanting to hear.

'He didn't come back and I never really got over it. It was difficult but I've had to face up to it. I tried to get over Michael. I failed. I also do what I love, and for a while I thought I had. I've had lovers, a few longer-term partners, but lately I've been feeling that it's harder to forget, not easier. I haven't come to terms with his loss. When I lost the ring too, that was the final blow.'

'When exactly did it happen?'

'While I was teaching at the school.'

'No wonder you were upset and unhappy.' Emma remembered the resentment that had festered between her and Ursula at school and regretted it. She'd been too young to imagine her teacher having a passionate romantic life . . . or any life outside the classroom.

'No excuse for taking it out on my students. I simply couldn't snap out of it. I suppose I was depressed though I refused to acknowledge that.'

'How did you lose the ring?'

'I used to wear it when I wasn't at school. I'd only put it on when I was on my own because I didn't want people asking about it. It was personal and I was worried I'd break down if anyone showed me any sympathy. One day, I decided to come down here for a swim. Stupidly, I forgot to take off the ring and leave it in the car. I went in the water — it was bitterly cold, I remember — and when I walked out, the ring had gone.'

'You must have been beside yourself.'

'I was. I ran back into the waves, I dived under until my eyes were raw and I almost had hypothermia. There was no sign of it of course. No chance of ever finding it. In all my time staring at this bloody beach, I've never had a glimpse of any precious metal.'

'Until today.'

'Yes.'

'I wish I hadn't seen it.'

'No. No! It belongs to someone. We could try and reunite it with its owner.'

'How do we do that?'

'Let's ask Luke. Please, though, don't share with him what I've told you. It's private. You and I are the only people on the planet who know.'

Emma crossed her heart, aware she had been trusted with something far more precious than gold. 'I won't say a word.'

14

'So, how was it this time, then?' Maxi said when Emma returned after the beach-clean.

'It was . . . not as bad as I was expecting.'

'Sounds promising. You'll be a regular soon, then?'

'I wouldn't say a regular! Although . . . the exercise is good for me and, of course, I keep finding fresh inspiration in the landscape and wildlife.' She was half-joking as she said it, hoping to put Maxi off the scent of thinking Luke was the sole reason she'd decided to join the Beachcombers a second time.

Maxi laughed. 'Nothing else?'

Emma was frustrated at being teased but if she carried on Maxi would surely trot out the line that she was protesting too much.

'Everyone was very welcoming.' She pictured Ursula's face when she'd turned up for a second time and thought of her secret. It was hers now, too, not to be shared even with Maxi. 'Even Ursula warmed up after the frosty start,' Emma went on. 'She showed me some of her sea glass finds. They're really very beautiful.'

Buzzing with ideas, Emma worked late and got up early to work as rain drummed on the roof of the lodge. Her photos and fresh perspective on Silver Cove had fired up her creative energy. Soon, she had a number of new illustrations completed for the coastal book. She looked back again at her sketches of Luke and Ursula. She wished they hadn't seen them but it was too late to fret about it now.

By early afternoon, she'd been sitting for so many

hours, her shoulders were stiff and her eyes were out on stalks. The sun had broken through and was heating up the lodge. It was high time she took a break. She borrowed some wellies from Maxi and stuffed her raincoat in her backpack.

A short walk through the woods behind the chalet led to Smuggler's Creek with the lone thatched cottage which was home to Ran Larsen, Luke's business partner. Emma paused for a moment and imagined Luke and Ran sitting on its terrace with a beer, before she splashed over the tiny stream at the head of the creek and reached the main path into Falford.

It took a good half-hour by the time she'd negotiated the muddy patches and stopped several times to admire the ferns, foxgloves and gunnera growing in abundance in the moist, shady spots. Sunlight dappled the path from time to time but largely it was a jungle of a place, reminding her of the landscape in *Jurassic Park*. The gunnera leaves were even bigger than she'd remembered, their undersides thick with snails. She wouldn't have been surprised to find a velociraptor appearing through the undergrowth.

She crossed the wooden footbridge across Falford Creek and walked the short distance down to the village, which straddled two banks of the River Fal. It was eye-wateringly pretty. Eye-wateringly expensive too, according to Maxi, and Emma could well believe it.

She recalled a few holiday cottages from her youth but in fifteen years almost every building had been whitewashed or painted in pastel colours. Many of the waterside properties had smart decking with glass balustrades and canvas sunshades. Sleek boats were moored at the marina and the boatyard was a hive of activity. Falford was sleek, a gleaming 'glossy maga-zine' version of the place she'd left.

The Ferryman was still there, now better main-tained with trendy furniture and a pizza oven on its terraces . . . the post office store too . . . and a quirky little shop called Cornish Magick.

Next to that was the gallery which had been a chic bistro when Emma had last set foot in Falford. Her father had looked down on it as 'pretentious', prob-ably because he couldn't afford to dine there. The thought brought a sharp pang of loss to Emma, think-ing of her father and the disappointed hopes that had turned him into a snob. Poor Dad . . . No wonder he'd been devastated when Harvey Kerr had found the treasure.

She took a deep breath and pushed the memory aside. It wasn't a bistro now, it had a new lease of life and she should focus on that, not bitter memories.

Emma wondered if Ursula had some pieces in it and was drawn inside. A young man reading a Daphne du Maurier novel sat behind the counter. He greeted her warmly with a 'Hello' and then allowed her to browse.

The gallery had paintings, of course, in all kinds of media from watercolour to pastel. Most were of Cornish scenes, though not all. There were also some ceramics, glass and a cabinet with jewellery, including a handful of Ursula's creations.

Some were in gold, some silver, at a range of prices. All exquisitely beautiful, and even more so to Emma now she knew their provenance. She thought of all those days and months spent combing the beach for the glass and, judging by the workmanship, they'd taken many hours in the studio. A pair of drop ear-rings in silver set with cornflower-blue glass gems was very tempting.

'Would you like me to get anything out of the case for you?' the assistant said, appearing at her side.

'Um. No, thanks. Not today,' Emma said. 'This artist's jewellery is gorgeous, though.'

'Isn't she just? Ursula Bowen. She's local, lives and works in the village. Very talented. She collects all the sea glass from beaches on the Lizard.'

'Really? How fascinating,' Emma said, slightly guilty about pretending she didn't know the artist.

'Oh yes. She's passionate about the provenance of the glass,' the man said.

'I can see how much work has gone into them. Thanks.'

'Well, if you change your mind and want me to get anything out, you only have to ask.'

With that, he returned to the desk. A family walked into the gallery and Emma took her chance to slip away. If she was going to buy any of Ursula's work, it would be direct from the artist.

Maxi had said that Ursula lived in a pink thatched cottage opposite the path to the ferry across the Falford estuary. Emma knew the house although she didn't remember Ursula living there when she'd been at school. Mind you, she hadn't really taken an interest in where her teacher lived back then.

She wondered if she dared visit the studio now. What kind of reception might she get? Would Ursula consider it an intrusion?

Then again, she was so close . . . literally five minutes away.

Deciding to be brave, Emma walked along the lane, enjoying the sweeping views over the estuary and the opposite side where the yacht club, boatyard and café were situated. The road turned sharply uphill at the top, but there was no access to the ferry path for vehicles other than residents. Fifty metres along the footpath, she spotted the white gate that led to the pink cottage a little further up the hill. A wooden sign on the gate read:

Ursula Bowen
Sea glass jewellery
Studio open

The public sign was encouraging. She'd hardly be disturbing Ursula if she was expecting visitors anyway. There were plenty of walkers and locals making their way up and down the steps to the ferry.

Emma opened the gate and walked up the steep path towards the cottage itself. The garden was glorious, full of allium, clematis and honeysuckle. Tubs of scarlet geraniums stood by the front door. The path to the front door was roped off with a plastic chain marked 'Private'.

A driftwood sign reading 'Studio this way' directed visitors round to the rear of the cottage and a large wooden shed. The door was open and Emma could hear a radio playing classical music. So far, so Ursula. Suddenly, she felt a little nervous. Should she have warned her?

Too late now. She went inside. The studio had several glass cabinets containing Ursula's work and the walls were lined with photographs of sea glass, some close-ups, some of the artist on the beach or at work.

Ursula herself was at the far end of the studio on the opposite side of a wooden counter. She was intent on her work, wiring up some earrings.

'Hello!' Emma raised her voice above the music.

As Ursula didn't hear at first, Emma went closer. 'Hi there,' she said.

Ursula's lips parted in an 'oo' of surprise. She removed her glasses and let them dangle from their chain. 'Hello.'

'I was passing — well I've been for a walk to see Falford — and I thought I'd drop by. I hope I'm not disturbing you.'

'You are but that doesn't mean the disturbance is unwelcome.' Standing up, she stretched her arms above her head and grimaced. 'I needed to get out of that chair anyway. I'd taken root.'

'What are you working on?' Emma took a step further inside.

'Earrings. With the cobalt blue we found the other day. I had another similar piece, so I went for it.'

'I'd love to see them.'

'You can. Come into my lair.'

After beckoning Emma behind the counter, Ursula showed her the earring in progress. She placed the finished one in her hand. The sea glass pieces were almost identical in size and colour, two fingernail-sized nuggets of frosted blue, as deep as a tropical sky.

'They're beautiful. Are they silver?'

'Yes, sterling silver. I also work in gold but mainly for commissions. I don't keep much stock. As you can imagine, it can be rather expensive.'

'Yes . . . Is this a commission?'

'No. It's going to go on sale.'

'Could I — could I buy them?'

'*You?*' Ursula sounded incredulous.

'Yes. To be honest, I almost went for a very similar pair in the gallery, but I'd rather buy them direct from you. And no, I don't want a discount. You should keep the gallery's cut.'

Ursula smiled. 'Thanks, but I'm more than happy to offer you twenty percent. That still leaves me thirty percent better off.'

'You don't have to do that.'

'I don't have to, but I want to. Is it a deal?'

'Yes.'

She shook Emma's hand. 'Would you like a cup of tea? It's too early for wine, I suppose. The sun's not over the yardarm yet.'

Emma had heard the church clock strike four a few minutes previously. 'I don't want to disturb your work.'

'I close at four-thirty after the last ferry spews out its hordes. I might have a few of them venture up here but it's still early in the season.'

Emma was torn. After getting off on the wrong foot with Ursula, she wanted to be kind and discover if her bark really was worse than her bite.

'Of course, if you have other places to be,' Ursula said briskly. 'You're a busy artist too.' Was that a twinkle in her eye?

'I've been working since seven a.m. My eyes are on stalks and the creative well is drained, which is why I came out for a break.'

'I'll put the kettle on, then. We can sit in the garden. The punters can ring the bell if they really need me.'

Ursula went into a small area at the rear of the workshop where she put an old-fashioned kettle on a gas ring. While they waited for it to boil, she showed Emma a dozen or more small plastic containers, each containing a different hue of sea glass. The white, green and brown boxes were almost full but the blue was half-empty.

Emma peered into them in awe. 'I'd no idea you could find so many different shades. Can you tell where each piece comes from?'

'Bottles mostly, of course, the neck lips and the stoppers, and windows — believe it or not — but also marbles and pottery shards.'

'How long does it take to weather like this?' Emma admired a piece worn to a frosted amber by the waves.

'At least twenty years but probably nearer forty. Some have been lying around for over a century, I should imagine,' Ursula said. 'The most recent are mostly clear, green or brown. But sometimes other colours, if you're very lucky, as you can see.'

Emma picked up a nugget from the blue box, which ranged from cornflower to sapphire.

'That blue piece in my earrings. Have you any idea what it might once have been?'

'Well, the colour probably comes from the cobalt oxide added to the molten glass so it could be Bristol Blue Glass.'

'What's that?' She felt she was holding a tiny piece of history in her hand.

'It was made in Bristol, surprisingly enough,' Ursula said with a wry smile. 'They produced it in the city for several hundred years until the 1920s. It was used for vases and glasses and tableware.'

'I love the idea of knowing the city it came from,' she said.

'It is rather romantic. Who knows what its exact story is or how it ended up in the sea and came to be here? It might be only a few miles from home, or thousands. Impossible to tell.'

'I like the mystery.' Emma nestled the glass into its

box as carefully as if it were a diamond.

'Me too,' Ursula said. There was a whistle from the rear of the workshop. 'Ah, kettle's boiling. Would you turn over the 'Closed' sign at the entrance to the workshop for me? I don't think we'll have any more customers today.'

Ursula placed a tray with a tea pot, two mugs and a milk jug on a metal bistro table in her back garden. She'd brought it up the stone steps from the workshop to a terraced area behind the cottage. Over the thatched roof, the Falford estuary was spread out in all its glory and on the opposite side were two other villages, with boats of all shapes and sizes moving to and fro between them.

'What a view,' she said.

'Oh, yes. It is. I should spend more time admiring it, I suppose. You grow used to it.'

'I think I took it for granted when I was young. It now seems incredible that I once lived here.'

'I can imagine. I could never leave.' Ursula poured the tea into mugs. 'Milk?'

'Thanks.'

What was more incredible was that she was taking tea in Ms Bowen's garden.

'Well, this is a turn-up, don't you think?' Ursula said, echoing Emma's thoughts.

'Just a bit.' Emma felt slightly wary again. She had a feeling Ursula was going to speak her mind and she wasn't wrong.

'I know you think I didn't like you at school, and that the feeling was mutual.'

Blindsided, Emma couldn't reply, and also didn't want to patronise her host by denying a truth, however uncomfortable.

'I was young,' she finally admitted. 'I had a lot of growing up to do, even if I didn't think so then.'

'Very generous of you, though I had no such excuse.' Ursula tutted. '*I* should have been more mature, made more of an effort to understand you. I realise your parents had high expectations.'

'Not of my art,' she said. 'They'd have been ecstatic if I'd dropped it.'

'Hmm. You never seemed to be able to make up your mind whether to go for it, or not.'

'It was difficult. Trying to please my parents and do what I really wanted.'

'I'm sorry. I didn't help but I *did* like you. Or not so much like but admire you. I saw myself in you, or a younger version with her whole life ahead of her. So much talent, so much drive and ambition. Someone who I hoped wouldn't make the same mistakes as me. Someone who would grab her opportunities and not be distracted by anything or anyone.'

'Really? I didn't know you thought about me at all.'

Ursula laughed. 'Well, I did and now, here you are, a renowned illustrator and artist, always in demand, your work in millions of books. Here I am, making trinkets out of glass for tourists.'

'No. No, it's not like that. Your work is beautiful. Mine isn't anywhere near as glamorous as you make out.'

Ursula shook her head. 'Ah, now you're being kind.'

'And you're not being the Ms Bowen I knew. Not that I ever really knew you.'

'You were my student. I didn't want my students to know the real me. Would you even have wanted to at that age?'

'No. No, I suppose not,' Emma said.

'Well, the fact that you're here means we can try to understand each other now. I'm sorry for your loss. I genuinely mean it. Had you seen much of your parents since you left Falford?'

'Yes and no. Obviously I was at uni doing my art degree for the first four years. After the coins were found, Mum and Dad had enough on their plate dealing with the fallout without having to obsess about me any longer. Dad became consumed by the fact Luke's father had discovered them on his land. I presume you've already worked this out or heard all the gossip?'

'It was the talk of the school and the village for a while. I never heard your side of the story though.'

'He blamed Harvey and Luke. He refused to accept the coins were on Roseberry Farm and he couldn't understand why they'd been found there.'

'I must admit I thought it was convenient for Harvey. I'm not trying to pry,' Ursula commented. 'However, what's done is done. I was only trying to work out why — why you and Luke aren't as friendly as you were.'

'His father found what my father had been looking for all his adult life. Dad couldn't take it. Not someone — someone like Harvey. There's nothing we can do about it now.'

'But how is it Luke's fault?'

'It isn't, technically . . .' Emma said sharply, feeling that Ursula was digging too deeply and half regretting being drawn in. 'Let's just say we didn't part on the best of terms.'

'Do you regret that?'

Wrong-footed, Emma hesitated, wincing at the final time she'd seen Luke alone. He'd tried to contact her

151

again a few days after he'd confessed to taking the journal. She'd agreed to meet him at the cove again but they'd only ended up wounding each other.

That conversation made her feel just as desolate now as it had when she was eighteen.

She found Ursula watching her shrewdly. 'I thought you two seemed to be getting on rather well these days.'

Emma snapped back into the present. She could never explain to Ursula the intensity of her feelings back then.

'Well, we're adults now. I can be civil. I'm going to be here for a while and Maxi's friendly with Luke. The children like him. He's a nice guy and I'm helping no one by avoiding him and being rude. As we said, we're grown-ups and it's up to us to behave that way.'

'Yes. Sometimes . . .' Ursula's voice quietened. 'Sometimes I wonder if being grown-up isn't about hiding our feelings, or pretending they're something else, but about having the courage to acknowledge them.'

Emma wasn't sure Ursula was referring to herself, or both of them. Nor was she comfortable with the conversation.

'Maybe,' she said. 'I really hadn't thought about it.'

Ursula replaced the cup carefully in the saucer. 'I expect it was a shock to find he'd bought the chapel?'

There was no point lying. Ursula was too astute for that. 'Yes, I'll admit it took me aback.'

'Well, if he hadn't it would have been completely gutted and turned into second homes. I shouldn't have been surprised if it had been demolished and replaced with some monstrous glass pile even if it had been listed.' She curled her lip. 'These listed places have a tendency to go up in smoke by accident. Especially when the developer is ruthless enough.'

Emma gasped at the vision of her home in flames. 'Burn down the chapel? I couldn't bear to see that!'

Ursula sighed. 'I thought not. Luke may not have been your ideal choice of purchaser, but it could have been a lot worse. He's a good man, you know. One of the best. Have you any idea of what he did in the navy?'

'The navy? No, what do you mean?'

'Why don't you can ask him?' Ursula said mysteriously.

'Oh no, I couldn't do that!'

'Fair enough, but if you do some digging around, you might be surprised.'

Emma was about to ask more when there was a noise outside and a call.

'Woo-hoo! Are you open?'

'If I was open, I wouldn't have a sign saying 'Closed', would I?' Ursula muttered.

'Hellooo!' Two figures in matching hiking shorts and fleeces appeared at the bottom of the garden by the studio. 'Bit of a cheek but we thought you wouldn't mind,' the man said. 'Didn't we, Val?'

'No. We saw one of your bracelets earlier this week and we're leaving tomorrow. We were gutted when we saw the 'Closed' sign, weren't we, Graham?'

'We were, Val. But we heard chattering and we thought, she won't mind as we're here to buy something.'

'You don't mind, do you?' Val said hopefully.

'As you're having a tea break,' Graham added.

Ursula dived in while she had a chance. 'Of course

153

not. I'll come down now. Do go inside. The studio's open.'

'Grand,' they chorused together and marched into the workshop.

'Give me strength,' Ursula said, easing herself from the chair.

Emma suppressed a giggle. 'Don't knock it. A sale's a sale.'

'I know . . . but I was enjoying our chat. Oh, before you go, will you be coming to the Beachcombers barbecue?' Ursula said.

'When's that?'

'Saturday after next. It's an annual thing, part social event, part fundraising.'

'I think I might have heard a few people talking about it, but I hadn't cottoned on to the details.'

'Don't get too excited,' Ursula rolled her eyes. 'We have a get-together, grill a few burgers and quaff some warm wine in the grounds of Falford vicarage. It's the one event where we're guaranteed a good turn-out. Even people who can't be bothered to pick up a Coke can mysteriously appear when food and booze are involved.'

Emma laughed. 'I can believe it.'

'The real purpose is to swell the coffers. Although we're volunteers, we need money for equipment and admin, and the damned health and safety courses and insurance. The idea is to make a small profit on the food and sell artwork we've created with our finds.'

'Oh, I love the idea of artwork made from beach finds.'

'Actually, it is rather fun. I'll be taking some of my jewellery, of course. You're supposed to offer a cut of your profits but most of us end up providing stuff for

154

free. Marvin makes driftwood sculptures and Zoey and her sister do hand-painted pebbles. One of the women makes some gorgeous collages from old pottery. Maxi usually comes too.'

'I'm surprised she hasn't mentioned it already, but I'll ask her about it.' Emma liked the sound of seeing what the other Beachcombers had created with their 'treasures'.

'I'd love it if you would . . .' Ursula hesitated then said, 'Look. This may sound a bit forward, but would you consider bringing along a couple of your paintings? I glimpsed a few in your sketchpad on the beach.'

'Me?' Emma shook her head, totally taken aback by the request. 'They're not created from beach finds, though.'

'However, they *have* been inspired by the Silver Cove,' Ursula declared. 'And from what I've seen of your other work online and in books, they're far better than anything we normally put on sale. I'm sure they'd go down very well.'

'Um. Wouldn't people think I was being — a bit presumptuous? I've only been here five minutes.'

'Original artwork from a renowned illustrator? My dear, they'd just be grateful you were helping to swell the coffers.'

'I suppose I have a couple of things I haven't used for commissions . . . but I'd have to get them mounted and framed . . .' Emma was already nervous at the idea of offering her work direct to the public, let alone muscling in on the Beachcombers' artistic efforts.

'Oh, anything you could offer would be brilliant,' Ursula declared, sweeping away further objections.

She gave in. 'OK. I'll see what I can do.'

15

'*How* many?' Emma said, horrified at the pile of Day-Glo plastic beach toys in the back of Luke's truck.

The Beachcombers were gathered in the car park, sipping from their water flasks and munching home-made saffron buns provided by Luke's mother.

'Around forty this week.' Luke picked up a broken bucket. 'Almost two hundred over the whole month.'

The midsummer sun beat down. Even at eight-thirty, it had been hot work scouring the sands.

'Don't forget, that lot's only from Silver Cove alone.' Ursula scowled beneath the rim of her straw hat. 'And it's not even the damn school holidays yet.'

Zoey planted her hands on her hips and eyed the buckets, spades and punctured lilos as if they were radioactive waste. 'You imagine what it'll be like by the end of the summer, with the crap abandoned on every beach in Cornwall!'

Emma pictured an Everest-sized mountain of broken plastic. 'That's unbelievable.'

'Sadly, it's all too true,' Luke said. 'And this is the stuff that's been left behind on the sand. Imagine how much is broken up and ends up in the sea or inside the marine life?'

'It's truly horrendous.'

'At least we've collected a tiny part of it and what we can't sell or repurpose will be off to the recycling centre,' Zoey piped up. 'So we're doing our bit!'

'Talking of repurposing, can we have a talk about the arrangements for the barbecue?' Ursula said.

156

'Marvin's bringing a couple of folding tables they were chucking out of the community hall.'

'There was an old wallpapering table at the chapel that'll do,' Luke said. 'It was in . . .' he checked himself. 'In one of the outhouses.'

Emma wondered if he'd been going to say it was in the attic, then decided she was being paranoid. Her dad cleared the place out from top to bottom when they moved, worried that anything else relating to the treasure might have been missed.

'Jermaine's got a table that he uses for craft fairs and I have one at the studio. He's bringing them in his car. They won't fit in my little jalopy,' Ursula said. 'I'm sharing my table with Emma.'

'Emma?' Luke was too late to disguise his amazement.

'Sorry, forgot to tell you,' Ursula said. 'Mind you, I only asked her a few days ago.'

'It's not much but I'd like to help. I'll frame a few of the watercolours I've done while I've been here.' His continued shock made her add, 'I hope that's OK?'

'It sounds fabulous,' Zoey said.

'Don't get too excited!' Emma protested, eager to dampen down expectations.

'She's too modest. From what I've seen her work is really very good,' Ursula said, which was high praise.

'They're more than good. I've seen some,' Luke said, unable to tear his eyes from Emma's face. She could see he was amazed and definitely pleased.

'So, what time should we rock up at the vicarage?' Zoey said, dragging Emma's attention away from Luke's gaze.

'Rock up?' Ursula laughed. 'You've made me think we should all turn up on Harley-Davidsons in

157

leathers with Black Sabbath blasting out. How wonderful that would be.'

Everyone laughed, including Luke. The event could be fun and a chance to build bridges in a relaxed setting.

'I've spoken to the vicar and she said we can set up anytime from ten-thirty as usual. We need to take our own barbecue equipment and keep it away from the orchard but otherwise she's pretty chilled about it. We can use the boot room entrance to access the cloakroom and kitchen.'

'Thanks, Ursula,' Luke said. 'I'll bring the barbecue stuff. We made an oil drum barbecue from stuff washed up on the beach,' he told Emma.

They were disturbed by a large family group arriving, lugging a wheeled trailer of beach toys and an inflatable flamingo.

With a curl of the lip, Ursula said: 'Back to the fray? Where next?'

'We haven't covered the western side yet and that wind we had is bound to have washed up some stuff in the rock pools. Shall we give it another half an hour?'

Heading for the rock pools as Luke suggested, the Beachcombers fanned out, scouring the shallow pools and rocky crevices for debris. Carrying her emptied collecting bag, Emma trailed along, trying not to be too distracted by the way the water rippled in the pools, and the reflections of sky and clouds. Discipline, she told herself in an Ursula-type voice. Don't get distracted.

She collected a few soft drinks bottles, trying not to think of the billions that were dumped every year. At least they weren't on her patch now. She went closer to the rocks and spotted a soggy blue item in one of the small pools. Closer inspection showed it to be a towel with a faded cartoon seagull.

Emma picked it out of the pool with her grabber, dripping water. 'Yuk!'

Luke came over. 'What have you got there?'

'A beach towel. Fancy leaving it here. It's clogged up that little pool.'

Luke shrugged. 'I've stopped trying to fathom out humans. They always disappoint you . . .' He looked at Emma. 'And occasionally amaze you.'

Emma melted under the intensity of his gaze.

Luke opened the bag. 'Pop it in here.'

She dropped it in. 'Will you bin it?'

'No, we'll wash it and dry it and find it a good home.'

'Who wants second-hand manky beach towels?'

'Actually, I know a place where the inhabitants are desperate for them.' He smiled at her incredulous face. 'The seal hospital. They're always delighted to have them.'

Emma burst out laughing. 'That's brilliant! I love the idea of the seals and their pups being swaddled in the towels we've found. I'd love to see them.'

Infected by his enthusiasm, and the understand-able desire to see baby seals, she realised what she'd said. Suddenly she noticed there was a cluster of peo-ple around Luke's truck in the car park.

'Oh! Everyone's gone back to their cars. They'll be wondering where we've got to.'

'Yeah . . .'

Toting their bags, they returned to the car park later than everyone else. They'd already begun sorting out their finds into a variety of containers, but Ursula was on her phone a few metres away. She didn't look happy.

'Oh dear,' she said. 'How terrifying. It sounds serious, Vicar.'

Luke emptied his finds into the plastic tub — recycled of course — in the truck flatbed. Emma hung back, as Ursula pulled a face.

'Oh no! That's such a shame. Are you sure it's not possible . . . oh, in that case, I see. Yes, health and safety must come first, Vicar . . . No, don't feel bad. It's not your fault . . . yes, He does certainly move in mysterious ways . . . Let us know if we can help . . . Bye . . .'

Ursula switched off her phone and let out a groan. 'Well, that's the end of the barbecue!' she declared.

'What do you mean?' Emma asked.

'Ursula?' Luke frowned. 'What's happened?'

'That was the vicar in a panic. Part of the vicarage chimney has collapsed! The builders and scaffolders are there now. Apparently, they're going to need the garden for the materials to make urgent repairs. It's not safe to hold the party in the grounds so it's off!'

'Oh no! Couldn't the chimney have waited to collapse after the barbecue?' Zoey's bottom lip trembled.

'At least it didn't fall off while we were there. Could have been carnage,' Marvin said gloomily.

'If it had, you'd certainly have been busy,' Ursula said wickedly.

'Can we find another venue?' Emma put in, feeling cheated. She hadn't realised how much she'd been looking forward to it.

'At this short notice?' Zoey laughed in derision. 'I doubt it. All the suitable places will have been booked up for fetes and summer shindigs months ago.' She heaved a huge sigh. 'It's such bad luck.'

Luke's expression was resigned too, though Emma could tell he was desperately trying to come up with a solution.

It crossed Emma's mind to ask Maxi for use of the garden at the house but it was a big imposition. She couldn't simply offer her friend's place.

'I wish the cottage was large enough, but I don't think I can accommodate fifty people,' Ursula said.

'Hold on!' Zoey piped up, eyes gleaming. 'I know somewhere perfect. What about the Old Chapel?'

The Old Chapel. Emma looked at Luke. He took a second to reply. She could see he was conflicted. 'Well . . .'

'It's big enough,' Ursula cut in. 'And right here on the cove, but it's a big ask for Luke . . . invading his home . . .'

The others clearly didn't think so. So many eager pairs of eyes drilled into him, willing him to say yes. Emma knew he couldn't possibly refuse.

'I guess so,' Luke replied. 'I can't think of a reason why not . . .'

Not one he would say out loud, Emma thought.

'Then, that's settled!' Zoey punched the air. 'Barbecue saved! Oh, it'll be brilliant at the chapel, with that amazing view of the sea. Much better than the vicarage.'

'Imagine setting up our stalls in the courtyard,' Marvin said.

'Maybe you could do tours, Luke?' Zoey added, jigging around. 'I've got to admit I've *longed* to see inside that place for years. I bet we all have. I'll need the kitchen anyway to prepare the salads. I *always* do the salads.'

'Of course, you can use the kitchen, Zoey. Everyone's welcome in my home.'

Luke answered Zoey with a warm smile but Emma knew him well enough to guess the turmoil behind the placid exterior. However, it was nothing to the tumult inside her mind at the prospect of returning to the place where every stone held a memory, of pleasure and pain.

16

'Hello, Mum.'

'Hello.' His mother's embrace was warm when Luke arrived at her home. Since she'd split from Luke's father and they'd had to sell Roseberry Farm, Sue had moved to a modern semi in Mullion, a village on the Lizard. It had shops, pubs and was home to the craft centre, where his mum managed the café. Today was her day off.

He arrived at coffee time and sat outside in her small courtyard garden. By now, he thought she must have heard that the barbecue was going to be at the Old Chapel. Luke dolloped jam and cream onto a scone and bit into it, while his mum brought out two mugs of coffee.

'Mmm. These scones are good,' he said after a delicious mouthful.

She sat beside him. 'Of course. They were your nan's recipe.'

He sipped from the mug, savouring the aroma. 'Nice coffee too. Is it fresh?'

She nodded in satisfaction at his compliment. 'A sample from the roastery at the craft centre. They supply the café.'

'You like working there,' he said. She was smiling and had seemed happier of late. She deserved it. She'd always worked very hard and it had been twelve years since she'd divorced his father, who now lived in Spain. After the treasure discovery, Harvey had urged her to give up her job as a school cook, which she hadn't wanted to do but had gone along with. When they'd divorced, and he'd emigrated with what was left of the money, Sue had gone back to cooking.

'I don't know what I'd do without my work at the café. Apart from the money, they're a great bunch, largely.' She smiled. 'Did I mention Angel Carrack has a unit at the centre now? Set up making trendy tea towels and the like and is doing very well and she's seeing Jake Trencrom. He used to work at the Country Stores but he's managing the centre now.'

'I heard about Angel from Ran and Bo,' Luke said, happy to see his mum upbeat and to chat about her close-knit group of friends. 'I've seen her in the Ferryman from time to time.'

'She deserves a change of luck.'

Luke finished his half scone.

'Another?' She held the plate inches from his nose.

'I shouldn't.'

'Rubbish! You need feeding up with all the diving you do. Carting those heavy tanks about. I bet they fed you well in the navy.'

'Ah, but they didn't make the best cream teas in Cornwall.'

'Flatterer.' With an eye-roll, she fetched another from the kitchen while Luke sat back in his chair and closed his eyes. The sun was hot in the sheltered courtyard. Summer was here and his mum was right. He was very busy, as more and more dive tours were booked. They'd taken on a couple of temporary instructors, a guy who'd been working in Grand Cayman and an Aussie.

'Have you heard from Dad lately?' his mum asked.

Luke thought back to the call he'd taken after he'd been beachcombing with Emma. Had he heard from

164

his father? Sure he had, but he wasn't going to let on the full content of the conversation to his mum. It would only hurt and upset her.

'As a matter of fact, he called me the other week.'

She sat down, her interest piqued. 'And?'

'He's still in Spain. He's sold the restaurant and bought a smaller bar on one of the Costas.'

She rolled her eyes. 'Another bar?'

'Yeah,' Luke said, filling his mouth with scone to avoid elaborating. The new bar was already in financial trouble, which was why his dad needed the loan.

She pursed her lips. 'Did he mention *her*?'

Luke wasn't surprised his mum had brought up his dad's latest girlfriend, one of many. He swallowed. 'No. It was just a catch-up.'

'Really?' She sounded dubious, as if she didn't quite believe Luke. 'Does he know you bought the Old Chapel?'

'Yeah. He knew a while ago. He must have found out from some old drinking pals.'

'And? How did he take it?'

'I think he was a bit surprised,' Luke said, skirting over the mix of amazement and gushing praise his father had heaped on him when he'd heard about the chapel. 'Never thought I'd see the day, son,' he'd said. 'You must have done well for yourself. I wish old Robin had lived to see it.'

Luke had cringed at his father's insensitivity and felt very uncomfortable, as Emma had still been in the car park. That's when he'd raised his voice and, shortly after, ended the call — right after his father had asked him for a loan. It had also set off some uneasy questions in Luke's own mind. Since Emma had come home he'd started to delve deeper into his motivations for buying the chapel. Had he, even sub-consciously, been hoping she'd one day reappear and he would be there waiting? It had never crossed his mind when he'd put in his offer, and yet he *had* been desperate to get it. *Why?*

'I'm pleased he's still enjoying himself,' his mum went on. 'I don't wish him ill. I loved him in my own way, despite everything, and I still do, I suppose, though I wouldn't wish him back. I don't mean to sound harsh, Luke, but you understand that?'

'Yes, of course I do.'

'You don't shake off your first love so easily, you know.' She clutched his wrist. 'You must also under-stand that.'

Luke shifted in his chair, seeking a means of escape from a conversation that had turned less than com-fortable. His mother wasn't about to let the subject go.

'I presume you've seen Emma?' she said. 'I heard she's joined the Beachcombers.'

'I've seen her a couple of times. She's joined us as research for the book illustrations she's working on. She's only staying with Maxi until her project's done.'

'Is she? Mmm. Well, I'm amazed she came back here at all. Mind you, Robin's passing might have had something to do with it. A blow like that must change your outlook. It shakes you up and makes you reas-sess everything.'

'It was very upsetting for Emma, obviously,' he said, keen to close down this line of conversation.

'I was very sorry to hear it. Poor Robin . . .' There was a break in his mum's voice that took Luke aback. 'I don't think he ever got over your dad finding the treasure. Still, there's nothing to be done now. No

166

use looking back and trying to undo what can't be undone.'

Luke was puzzled. His mother sounded far more upset about Robin's death than he'd have expected, considering their two families had been at war most of the time. He wondered if she was reflecting on the break-up of her own marriage to his dad, with all the regrets that must have brought.

'I presume Emma knows you've bought the chapel?' His mother's tone hardened again.

'Yes. Maxi told her.'

'And?'

'And . . . Does there need to be an 'and'?'

She shook her head in exasperation with him. 'Oh, come on, Luke. She must have had a shock when she found out.'

'I suppose so. We haven't really discussed it. We haven't discussed much at all.'

'Frosty between you, is it?'

'Like I say, she's just one of the . . .' Luke was going to say 'one of the gang' but that sounded way too pally. 'One of many.' He took the plunge. 'And she's going to have to get used to me being at the chapel because we're holding the annual barbecue there next month. Though of course you might have heard about it already on the village grapevine,' he added.

The expression on his mum's face told him she hadn't, which gave him a degree of satisfaction. 'I had no idea. How's that going to go down with Emma?'

'I don't know. Hadn't really thought about it.'

He tucked into the rest of his scone, hoping it would take a long time to swallow while he calmed his mind. The truth was he'd thought of little else in his spare moments. Emma's stunned expression when

167

he'd agreed to hold the event at the chapel had said everything. So many questions and doubts filled his mind. How would she react when she saw the place again? Would she be upset or angry? He'd thought they'd been getting along better lately. Would the visit ruin all that? And how would he react? He didn't want anyone to know the turmoil he'd be going through and it would be hard to act 'normally'.

'It'll be awkward,' his mum said, waiting for him to finish. 'Considering she thinks your father had a hand in ruining her dad's life, she's going to find it hard to go back to the place.'

Luke knew his mum hadn't wanted him to buy it at all. She'd told him it was 'a money pit' and that it would give her the creeps to live next to a graveyard, demanding why he had to buy a place 'with so many bad associations'.

'I can't do anything about that now,' he said firmly. 'The vicarage is closed for repairs and some of the other Beachcombers suggested the chapel so I had no choice but to volunteer. It is what it is,' Luke added, using a phrase he despised, but was handy in this case.

'Hmm. Well, like you say, I expect Emma will be off like a shot once this book thing's done and then you can *both* move on again. She won't want to hang round here with the likes of us.'

'I've no idea . . . but remember, Mum, I came home and I've made a life here. I can't control what other people do.'

'I suppose Hester's less than grief-stricken about Robin?'

He was a little shocked at his mother's harsh attitude to Emma's mum, especially given her own reaction to Robin's death.

'She's with a new partner now, but Emma mentioned they both went to the funeral. Robin was her husband even though they'd split up, so I expect she was upset. You said yourself that you don't get over your first love.'

'True, although I'm not sure it was that kind of love between Hester and Robin.'

'What do you mean?'

'Nothing.' She sighed. 'Ignore me. I'm probably being unkind to Hester, and you're right, I'm sure she was very upset about Robin.'

His mum had always been an unsentimental woman, devoted to Luke, but prone to speak her mind. However, he was taken aback by this glimpse into her feelings towards Hester, even though she'd tried to soften her remarks. He hadn't realised how deeply she resented the Pelistrys. He didn't quite understand why, either, since it was his own family who had profited from the find, or at least his father had.

Ding!

Phew, saved by the bell, Luke thought as his mum jumped up.

'That's the front door,' she said. 'It's probably Clive.'

'Clive?'

'The new postman. I say 'new' but he's been here in Cornwall a good four years. Only took up our round last summer though. He's from New Zealand, you know.'

While his mum answered the door, Luke had a discreet glance over the courtyard gate at this postman who'd managed to divert his mother's attention away from a very awkward conversation. The man was

169

sporting a bog-standard Royal Mail red polo shirt and blue shorts but there was nothing bog standard about the person inside the uniform. Clive wasn't the timid, late-fifties chap he'd imagined, but appeared to be barely out of his forties, Maori and an absolute unit at that.

In fact, Luke thought he wouldn't have been out of place on the front row of an All Blacks side.

'Mornin', Clive!' Luke's mum greeted the postie in a girlish way that had Luke open-mouthed in astonishment.

There was a warm greeting in return in a distinctive Kiwi accent. The window was open and, while Luke couldn't quite hear every word, he got the gist. Either his ears were deceiving him or the village postman was asking his mother out on a date.

Luke had just enough time to pretend he was admiring her tubs of geraniums by the kitchen door before his mum returned to the yard, clutching a couple of envelopes.

'It was the postman, then?'

'Yes. As you well know.' She gave him a stern glance. 'I saw you peeping over the gate.'

'Sorry, I was being nosey.' He smiled. 'That's Clive, then? He seems — um — very fit.'

'Oh yes, he is,' his mum said with a breathy sigh, her cheeks growing pinker by the minute. 'He coaches the Lizard's rugby team and, before you ask, he's only five years younger than me. He just looks great for his age.'

'I wasn't going to ask,' Luke protested, a little ashamed of his earlier assumption.

'I bet you thought it. I saw the look on your face when I walked back in. I presume you heard us arranging to go out at the weekend?'

'I couldn't hear every word so not exactly.'

'Then I'll put you out of your misery. We've been seeing each other for a few weeks,' his mum said. 'Nothing serious but we are getting on very well. He was asking me to the folk festival.'

'Sounds . . . nice,' Luke said, still reeling from the fact his mum was dating the postman. Or anyone. He hadn't been part of her life for so long. Not been present in so many ways to realise that she needed comfort, companionship — love — as much as he did.

He gave her a hug. 'Mum, I'm happy for you. Genuinely so happy for you. I'd like to meet Clive when you're ready.'

'You'll really like him too. He's lovely and we get on really well. He makes me laugh and I haven't met a man for a very long while who does that. Not from the heart, or because I felt I had to laugh to please him, or be polite.'

Her cheeks grew pink. 'I think it's time I put the past well and truly behind me. I do love your dad but he's part of history now, like the treasure. The here and now is what matters and we'd all do well to remember that.'

17

There was only a week to go until the barbecue, and Emma was still wondering if she should find some excuse not to go. The trouble was, it felt impossible to back out now she'd agreed to offer her paintings — which was why she was driving into Falmouth on her way to have the artwork framed and mounted.

Was it possible Ursula had lured her into agreeing to offer some pieces, knowing it would draw her more into the lives of the Beachcombers? She couldn't have known the event would be at the Old Chapel though. While it had felt comforting — the lifting of a burden — to make her peace with her old teacher, the new dilemmas the friendship had thrown up were anything but comforting. Emma was dreading going back to the house, yet also felt a compulsion to see it again.

After much agonising, she'd selected four watercolours of scenes and marine life at Silver Cove. She'd no idea what price to put on them, but was hoping Maxi and Ursula might help her decide. Anyway, pricing her work was the least of her worries.

Falmouth itself brought back bittersweet memories. There were new shops of course, more artisan bakeries and galleries. It had 'gone trendy' as Ursula might say, but several of the old high street favourites had closed, which felt like the end of an era.

In the past, Emma had enjoyed going into town on a Saturday, popping into the shops, with her mum at first then, when she was older, piling into the car of a friend. They'd buy clothes and make-up and indulge in milkshakes in the cafés. In the evening, they'd meet up with the lads of course, Luke included, arriving home in the small hours — and being told off by her parents the next day. She didn't blame them for that. Her dad had probably been right to worry.

Once, she'd had sex on the beach with Luke as darkness fell and the others were sitting around a fire drinking vodka.

How had she dared?

And yet it had been amazing. Lying on his jacket, sharing the warmth of their skin, sand everywhere afterwards, the inner glow, the sense that they were both invincible and could do anything, with the snap of a finger. Once again, the same questions occupied her mind — were they occupying his too? How would they both cope with her visiting her old home again, with all its associations?

She wasn't far from the dive centre now. Should she speak to him ahead of the barbecue? Ask him how he felt about her turning up? Actually talk like grown-ups? Would that be so scary?

Ahead of her, Emma saw a sign that read 'Falford Dive Centre — 500 yards'. A few moments later, she'd flicked on the indicator and was turning left off the road, down the short track to the centre. Even as she did so, she regretted it. The situation was so fragile, she could make things even worse, but it was too late now.

Emma parked and got out. The centre itself was a stone and wooden building, larger than she'd expected, with wetsuits hanging off rails at the front. A large dive boat was alongside the quay, with a couple of rigid inflatables, known as RIBs, moored at the pontoon.

There was no sign of Luke, so she still had the chance to make her escape, but even as she was thinking it, he appeared on the deck and started unloading air tanks from the vessel. He was in shorts and flip-flops, his chestnut hair brushing his collar.

Ruggedly sexy was how she'd have described him, if she'd had the breath to speak. Emma tried to dismiss the lightning bolt of desire, and failed miserably.

'Emma?'

Leaving an air tank on the quayside, Luke waved at her, a puzzled expression on his face. She lifted a hand in return and they met by the side of the dive centre building.

'You look busy,' she said.

'I've almost finished unloading and the dive's finished.' He frowned. 'Can I help you?'

'Oh. Um. I was passing . . . I've been to Falmouth to do some shopping. Actually, I went to get some pictures mounted and framed.'

He let her ramble on.

'Remember Ursula suggested I sell some of my work at the barbecue? Though if I'd known it was going to be at the chapel, I'd never have dreamed of coming.' Emma kicked herself. 'That sounds rude, and I didn't mean it to, but the way things have turned out, it might not be the best idea for both of us if I — invade your space.' Her outpouring left her short of breath.

'You won't be 'invading'. It's not a problem for me,' he said. 'Though I can see why it might be difficult for you.'

Emma wasn't sure she believed him. 'Yes . . . now I've offered to help, I don't feel I can back down. I

174

don't want to let the others down and I do want to raise some funds. I really like the Beachcombers. They've been so welcoming but I'm aware that it's your group. I don't want to blunder in and make things any more awkward than they already are.'

'It's not 'my' group. No one's in charge particularly and you wouldn't be butting in. You can turn up whenever you like.' He paused. 'The same as anyone else who wants to help.'

Emma's heart had lifted at the first part of his sentence, yet fell at the last. 'The same as anyone else.' Why did that caveat make her feel deflated? Her mind travelled to Zoey, who'd suggested the chapel in the first place and was so excited to be at the heart of the event. Luke hadn't seemed too upset about her asking him. For the first time, she experienced a pang of something horribly like jealousy. What if something developed between Luke and Zoey — or anyone? She almost felt sick . . . but why should she care?

'Well, I thought I should check anyway, now that the party's going to be at your place and as I was passing by anyway, well. Here I am . . .' She itched to be gone, wishing she'd never been tempted to call in at the centre. It had been a bad idea. 'Now, I'll leave you to it.'

Luke had other ideas. 'Wait, Emma. You really don't have to ask my permission to do anything.'

'I know, it's only that . . . I want to call a truce between us. I've done the same with Ursula.'

Maybe this was the instinct that had led her to turn off the road. She hadn't realised how much she wanted to make her peace with him.

'A truce?' he echoed, a frown on his face.

'For the short time I'm here. Ursula said something

about burying the past. Well, I don't think I can bury it, but I don't want to keep digging it up and turning it over and over. Not with other people involved. Maxi, Ursula . . . the others. I hate them sensing an atmosphere.'

'I don't think they do,' he said. 'And there's never been a battle between us as far as I'm concerned.'

'Not a battle, not now, but we didn't leave things on friendly terms,' Emma said, still wishing she'd never broached the subject.

'I agree it would be better if we were more comfortable in each other's company.'

Comfortable? Emma doubted she could ever be comfortable around Luke after all that had passed between them and the way she felt about him physically.

'I'd prefer it if we were friends,' he went on. 'While you're here, of course.'

'Friends? Of course.' Emma forced a smile. 'While I'm here.'

'I'll definitely see you at the barbecue, then?' His voice lifted hopefully.

'I'll be there,' she said. She left, thinking she ought to feel as if they'd taken a big step forward and cleared the air. She still wasn't sure. He'd made friendship sound anything but warm, more like colleagues or acquaintances. Could two people who'd been passionately in love ever be friends?

She'd begun to build bridges with Ursula but, with Luke, it wasn't going to be so simple — and the return to the chapel would be a huge test of her emotional resilience.

18

Wow. What a morning.

The sun was already hot on her skin when Emma stepped onto the deck. Mother Nature had pulled out all the stops for the barbecue, almost as if giving Emma no excuse to back out because of, say, a hurricane or unseasonal snow storm.

She'd lain awake long after dark, thinking about the day ahead and what she'd discovered on the Internet at Ursula's suggestion. Luke's naval record had stunned her. She'd no idea . . . and what she'd read was as terrifying as it was impressive.

With a pot of coffee and toast, she took advantage of the morning to work under the shade of the deck parasol. She was supposed to be doing pen and ink illustrations of mermaid's purses and bladder wrack for the coastal guide, though admittedly, her mind kept wandering.

Going back to the chapel seemed like even more of a momentous moment than she'd expected. So how must Luke feel about it despite his insistence that everyone — including Emma — was welcome?

She stopped, seeing the doodle she'd created, almost without realising it, on the edge of her sketchbook that morning.

It was of Luke, shirtless.

She ripped the page out of the book, screwed it up and threw it in the bin. Luke in person would not be erased so easily and she was glad when, at noon, Maxi messaged to meet up on the driveway.

She needed a distraction.

Grabbing her box of framed prints, Emma walked round the side of the house to find Maxi loading a box of beer and a basket of bread rolls into the car.

Her friend took the prints and gave Emma an admiring look. 'Well, you arrived in a suit. Now look at you.'

'Oh. Is this OK? Emma glanced down at her denim cut-offs and leather flip-flops, which showed off toe-nails the same colour of the violet sea snail that had captivated her. 'There's no dress code, is there?'

'A dress code for the Beachcombers' barbecue?' Maxi laughed. 'No way. I'd wear shorts myself if I had your legs.'

'You look great too. I love that dress.' Maxi was wearing a long, flowery sundress and had a large straw tote over her shoulder.

'It's comfy and cool. That's all I need. It's going to be a scorcher. I've chucked a bumper bottle of the kids' factor 50 in my bag.' Maxi opened the tote. 'At least I think I have. I also packed two folding hats, some wet wipes, plasters and aspirin. Once you have kids, you're always prepared for any eventuality.'

Emma laughed, her apprehension easing a mite. It was only a barbecue, not an ordeal by fire.

'If you think this is bad, you should see the amount of stuff Andy has taken with him.'

'I bet. They'll have a great time. It's been ages since I went to Newquay Zoo.'

'We've got annual passes. Bit of a trek, especially with holiday season here, but Andy owes me a day when I don't have to be a grown-up . . . Oh, hang on a minute! Is that a cloud? I'd better grab a brolly, just in case.'

178

After a final, *final* trip back to the hall for an umbrella, they were off on the ten-minute drive to the chapel, with Emma's stomach churning the whole way.

The nearby beach car park was already two-thirds full with holidaymakers and tradespeople's vans with surfboards on top. Novices were struggling into wet-suits and boots while the local pros jogged barefoot towards the dunes, their boards tucked under their arms.

En route, the talk had been about Maxi's week at school, and the approach of the busy end-of-term period, but Maxi hesitated before she locked the car.

'It'll be strange to be back.' She briefly touched Emma's arm. 'Will you be OK? It must have been a big shock to find the party had been switched to the chapel.'

'I'll have to be. I don't want anyone to know there was ever anything between me and Luke. The ones who don't remember won't realise and those who do will think we both moved on years ago.'

'Well done, but if you need to leave or talk, just say so. I must admit I half expected you to back out, even this morning. This can't be easy.'

'Nothing's been easy since Dad died but if you opt for the easy way every time, how will you ever move forward?'

'True. As long as this isn't tormenting yourself. No one expects anything of you.'

'Not tormenting . . . challenging myself. I suppose I've wanted to show I can behave normally around Luke. I'm trying to make sense of what happened. It was a long time ago.'

Maxi patted her shoulder. 'Come on, let's go for

it. You don't have to go inside the actual house if you don't want to.'

Emma had no intention of doing so, but even the suggestion made her butterflies take flight again.

With the sun toasting their bare skin, the two of them walked across the sandy car park and over the road, turning left towards the path that led to the chapel. The surf was up and the tide out, the frilly breakers a safe distance from the chapel. Strange to think that on a high spring tide those waves would toss spray and shingle high over the churchyard wall. She remembered one winter night when a tidal surge had even breached the wall and knocked over one of the older gravestones. At the time, it had seemed thrilling and dramatic; like something from a Gothic novel or painting, but today it made her shiver. Imagine being laid to rest after a shipwreck only for the sea to claim you again.

'Emma?' Maxi said. 'Need a hand with the box?'

'No. Sorry, I was on another planet.'

By this point they were only a few yards from the chapel and Emma had to stop to catch her breath. It seemed far bigger than she'd recalled. Her parents had moved in when she'd been a toddler, too young to remember any other home. She remembered Luke asking if it was weird to live next to dead people. She'd laughed at him. Having grown up living there, she knew no different and, anyway, she'd never been spooked by talk of . . . well, spooks.

Fantasy ghosts didn't bother her. It was the all too human regrets that did.

She'd been so angry with her father right up until his death. It had hurt that even though she'd been prepared to reach out to him, at least in the early days, he hadn't wanted to keep in touch. Perhaps she should have been more sympathetic. She still found it hard to forgive the affair but she could understand his disappointed dreams and thwarted hopes. He'd worked hard in a job that hadn't been his first love to try and keep his family financially secure. She knew how it felt to compromise. Even though her career had taken off, she'd never found anyone special in her life since . . . Since Luke.

Her chest tightened. The realisation was overwhelming. She stopped at the gates, metres from the pillars that guarded the entrance to the chapel. Luke's pickup was out of sight, parked around the back by her old bedroom, she presumed. The box of prints weighed a ton, the heat building by the minute. She felt almost light-headed.

'Emma?' Maxi's voice cut through the wooziness. 'Do you need a moment?'

She threw on a smile. 'No. I'm f-fine. The sun's so hot, isn't it?'

'It is. Why don't you give me that heavy box?'

'No, thanks . . . I can manage, though I'd love a cool drink.'

Before Maxi could reply, Ursula swooped on them from between the granite pillars that stood sentinel at the entrance. Zoey, beaming, and Marvin, almost looking excited, weren't far behind.

'Hello! You made it then,' Ursula said, sounding relieved.

'Finally!' Maxi laughed.

'Hello,' Emma said, as cheerily as she could manage.

Ursula might suspect it would be an ordeal for her to return to the chapel but she didn't want anyone

181

else to. 'Nice day for it.'

'Thank goodness,' Ursula said. 'Poured down last year, didn't it, Zoey?'

'Oh yes. The wind blew down the gazebo at the vicarage. Still, Luke soon had it up again.' She sighed with admiration. 'He's so good with his hands.'

'I can imagine,' Maxi said, deadpan. Emma wondered if her friend knew something she didn't. Surely not? Maxi would have told her.

'My sausages were soaked,' Marvin intoned gloomily.

'And no one likes a soggy sausage,' said Ursula.

Zoey jigged around. 'Come on, all the action's round the back. The barbie's lit and all the salads are in the kitchen. There's mountains of coleslaw and I rustled up a couple of pavlovas when I had a mo. Who doesn't love a pavlova?'

'No one,' Emma said, experiencing an irrational dislike for her favourite pudding.

'Oh, smell that! We've got sea bass this year as well as sausages. Must get back to the barbecue,' Zoey trilled. 'Can't leave Luke doing all the work, though he's brilliant at grilling!'

She scampered off, leaving Ursula to escort Maxi and Emma round to the chapel courtyard, not that Emma needed the slightest help to find her way.

'How many people are coming?' she asked, simply for something neutral to say to help tame her turbulent emotions.

'At least forty. Possibly more. Told you we're bound to see some folk who haven't picked up so much as a discarded cigarette butt in years.'

Maxi laughed. 'I'm hardly a regular.'

'Pish!' Ursula chided. 'You have your job and those

two to keep an eye on. We're only too happy to see you whenever we can. Let me take that box, from you.'

A few moments later, they'd reached the back door which served as the main entrance into the house. It was open and through the kitchen window Emma spotted Zoey standing at the sink.

The barbecue had been set up by the wall to the cemetery and was now being tended by Marvin who'd donned a stripey apron and was frowning at the coals. Only a low wall separated the graveyard from the sand and rocks of Silver Cove.

The smoke rising from the oil drum barbecue drifted across the courtyard, blown by the gentle breeze. People were milling about the yard and going in and out of the back door to the house, laughing and carrying food and drink.

A twinge of resentment took Emma by surprise. How could they all come and go as if they owned the place? It was so strange, as if she was living in a dream and an unpleasant one at that. Any moment, she might wake to find herself in her bed, the waves crashing against the wall of the graveyard.

She blinked and the house was there, basking in the sunshine, surrounded by chattering people.

Emma forced herself to take it in, determined to accept the chapel was no longer her home.

In essentials, of course, it was the same. However, the rather dilapidated stone outhouses at the rear — once outdoor toilets and a log store — had now been re-mortared and their peeling doors replaced with smart timber ones in a muted shade of grey-blue. Other doors had also been repainted and the windows seemed to have been repaired. The small open stable at the side was where Emma's parents had kept the cars, and was currently occupied by Luke's truck.

Her eyes were drawn to the round window in the attic gable, from which Luke had escaped after having found the journal.

That was closed, of course.

Her pulse quickened as Luke emerged from one of the outhouses, a bag of charcoal in his arms and a huge grin on his face.

'Found it!' he called to the knot of people by the barbecue. Dressed in a T-shirt, shorts and flip-flops, he was as gorgeous as she'd ever seen him and seemed perfectly at home. She clenched and unclenched her fingers. She had to act as if nothing had ever happened here, or between them.

Suddenly, he caught sight of her. The smile faded and her heart stopped.

He gave a nod and carried on to the barbecue, depositing the bag by the table.

It was done. She was here in his home. The worst was over.

If she believed that, she thought, she'd believe anything, but she had to carry on.

Several folding tables had been set up along the side of the garages, shaded by an assortment of gazebos, and she spotted Ursula's stall among them. Their curators were furnishing them with their wares: driftwood sculptures, painted pebbles and a table with some pottery on it.

'Is this OK?' Ursula said, ushering Emma to one nearest to the cemetery wall and putting the box on it. 'I've already made space for you.'

'Thanks. I only have four pictures. I'm not sure anyone will buy them.'

'Don't be silly,' Ursula said. 'Of course they will.'

'I admire your optimism.' Emma was buoyed by Ursula's praise.

'Let's get you set up,' she ordered. 'Come on.'

Happy to obey her old teacher's orders for once, Emma unloaded the prints. They were around A4 size, and she'd found a couple of small wooden crates, draped with dark blue cloth, to balance the pictures on. In a stroke of genius, Maxi had also 'borrowed' a toy easel from the kids' play box that was perfect for Emma's smaller painting of the violet sea snail.

The last painting was a watercolour, more elaborate than the rest. It showed the far end of the beach away from the chapel in the early evening light. Emma had felt compelled to paint the scene, but deliberately avoided a perspective that featured the chapel. It had taken ages and she'd dared to add a higher price tag. Finally. She added a photo of the location where she'd found the shell to demonstrate how her art had been inspired by the cove, along with some business cards, a book and a magazine showing some of her published work.

Maxi came to see her. 'Wow, that looks great.'

'Thanks. But I'm more nervous than when I'm pitching for a big commission.' She was worried she'd set the prices too high, even though they were original pieces of art.

'It'll be fine.' Maxi patted her arm. 'Don't worry, I'll buy one if no one else does.'

Emma laughed but her friend's joke didn't quite reassure her as much as it was meant to.

Ursula was far more chilled about the event. 'Now, you don't have to stand by your stall all day. We should enjoy some lunch first,' she said. 'The punters will spend more once they've had a few glasses of wine.'

She swept Maxi and Emma off towards the barbecue, where Zoey had laid out bowls of homemade salads. Emma presumed the puds were still in Luke's fridge.

More people drifted in, a few milling around the stalls, but mostly drawn to the food like bees around a honey pot. With the throng growing, Emma joined in the general laughter, determined to be pleasant, even towards Zoey — especially towards Zoey. The Beachcombers were a friendly bunch who'd welcomed her, even after her strange introduction to them.

Emma, Ursula and Maxi joined the queue at the barbecue where Luke and Marvin were dishing out the burgers with an older man Emma hadn't seen before. Emma was seriously impressed by his dreadlocks and he was sporting a pair of crimson Converses she'd have loved to own herself.

'That's Jermaine,' Ursula whispered. 'He's a potter. *Terribly* talented.'

They reached the front of the queue and, finally, Emma was face to face with Luke, in his home. For a second, her voice deserted her; she was a tongue-tied teenager once more.

'Hi there.' Luke's voice warm and steady.

'Hi.'

'There's a good turnout,' Ursula said.

Luke laughed. 'I think the free food helps.'

'I bet.' Maxi sniffed the air extravagantly. 'That smell is divine. Mind you, anything is gorgeous that I don't have to cook.'

'I have offered to cook dinner,' Emma burst out.

Luke seemed amused.

Maxi laughed too. 'You've bought three takeouts

already. I don't want you having to slave over a hot stove for us lot.'

'I wouldn't mind,' Emma said. 'In fact, I'm going to force you to let me cook Sunday lunch tomorrow. It's been ages since I made a roast.'

Luke smiled. 'Me too. Mum keeps inviting me round on Sundays.'

'Oh?' The mention of Sue Kerr made Emma think of her father again and the day she'd heard them at the chapel. Was it possible that Luke *did* have an idea about their affair? Had his mother ever told him in the years since?

Fortunately, Luke didn't seem to have noticed her discomfort, and carried on. 'Yes. She lives in a cottage in Mullion now. Mind you, we used to get roast dinners on board ship. Proper stuff: Yorkshire puds and the works. The food was very good. It had to be otherwise there'd have been mutiny.' He rolled his eyes. The way he was speaking, so cheerfully and without a trace of awkwardness, suggested he still had no idea of what had happened.

Unless he knew and thought *she* didn't.

Maxi let out a sigh of longing. 'You know, I might join the navy. Do you still get a rum ration?'

Luke grinned. 'Sadly, it was abolished in 1970.'

'In that case, I might have second thoughts.'

Everyone laughed, including Emma. Luke seemed determined to be welcoming and was not one to let any kind of secret slip out, today of all days.

'Don't worry, I can rustle up a tot of gin with your Sunday lunch,' she said, joining in the banter. 'I still have that strawberry clotted cream flavour I bought at the beach market.'

'Sounds like an offer you shouldn't refuse,' Luke

said. 'Now, I think the seabass looks ready. There's a mountain of rolls to put it in and Zoey's salads are irresistible.'

'Oh, yummy,' said Emma as if she were Daisy.

'They are,' Luke grinned. 'You can be first in the queue.'

Emma kept her smile in place. 'OK,' she said. 'Hand me a plate. I have no shame.'

With a beer, a fish roll and Zoey's yummy salads, Emma and Maxi perched on the wall that separated the chapel grounds from the cemetery. It still didn't seem weird to eat lunch next to the gravestones . . . after all, she'd done it before when she'd lived there. She began to think she'd make it through the day.

Someone put some music on, and as the beer, wine and Pimm's flowed, the volume of chatter grew louder. Jermaine and Ursula sat together, their heads almost touching. At one point, Luke was deep in conversation with Zoey, who'd batted him on the arm a few times. Emma tried very hard not to keep glancing over, wondering what they were talking about.

After lunch, she joined Ursula at the stall. A man called Bryan, a former graphic artist, chatted to her about her work and, to her amazement, bought one of her paintings of the rock pools at the cove.

'Well done, you made your first sale.' Ursula shook Emma's hand after Bryan had walked off with his painting in a recycled bag.

'I know and I still can't quite believe it,' Emma said.

'Oh, the punters will be over here like moths to a flame soon, now the booze is flowing.'

Ursula was right. Full of food, drink and bonhomie, the Beachcombers and their families started to visit the stalls. Ursula sold several items and Emma's violet sea snail was claimed by Marvin's auntie, who said it would go perfectly with the colour scheme in her redecorated bedroom.

Every so often though, Emma sneaked a glimpse at Luke, chatting easily at the barbecue with his friends. At one point he came out of the kitchen carrying a magnificent pavlova, followed by Zoey with a second, both piled high with whipped cream and strawberries. Emma was forcefully reminded that she was at the chapel only by invitation and that others were far more at home here. She dragged her attention back to the stall, hoping she'd make another sale soon.

Ursula took her aside. 'How are you doing?'

'OK. It's actually quite fun.'

'Despite it being here at the chapel?'

'Despite even that,' she said, catching sight of Zoey and Luke's heads almost touching as they uncovered platters of fresh fruit at the barbecue table.

After a bowl of pavlova, which was undeniably the best she'd ever tasted, Emma returned to her stall. Two pictures remained, and her hopes of selling them started to sink as the sun climbed higher.

By this point most of the guests were seeking the shade created by the yew tree planted by the cemetery gate and the wooded area at the side of the chapel. Luke was collecting dirty plates and bowls while Zoey and Marvin were browsing the other stands. Zoey had bought a dreamcatcher.

Emma was getting desperate — and for more than a sale.

Until now she'd actively avoided entering the chapel but, after all that wine and Pimm's, it was unavoidable. Even without the makeshift sign taped to the back door, she knew where it was: the cloakroom was through the hallway that led past the door to the sitting room that had been created from the main chapel area.

The contrast with the heat and dazzling light of the outside struck her physically. Inside, it was silent and cool, the thick walls keeping out the summer heat.

The cloakroom door was wide open, as some of the guests had been having a look around, probably curious to see the conversion and Luke's interior design skills.

After finishing in the bathroom, Emma paused in the open doorway to the main chapel living area. It was so surreal, yet so familiar: she'd watched TV in there, played board games, curled up on the sofa, laughed and cried and, occasionally, when her parents were out, done some sketching, though most of her art had been created in her own room.

The space itself was exactly as it had been before. She hadn't really expected anything different in that regard. She recognised a large clock on the wall, which the previous owners had bought from her parents. Luke had also kept a couple of the pews, a nod to the building's ecclesiastical heritage, now covered with scatter cushions similar to her day.

The rest of the furniture, she assumed, was pure Luke, unless he'd bought some of the vendor's stuff. That was possible, because the chapel was a cavernous space and not easy to fill or make cosy. Especially if previously you'd been living on board a ship or renting a flat.

Despite having expected a lack of homeliness, Emma thought the room was surprisingly comfortable and 'lived-in'. There were three large squishy sofas, and various chunky blond wood tables mixed with some older stuff. Several rugs were spread over the polished wooden floor. A wood burner with a shiny chimney had been placed on one wall, there was a huge TV and one of the sideboards had a serious-looking sound system. She smiled. It was very male, very Luke in that respect.

Emma turned away and wandered back down the hallway. To the right was the door to the study where she'd heard her father and Sue talking so intimately.

Don't go in there, don't stay any longer, she told herself, yet her footsteps seemed loud on the tiles. She stopped outside her old bedroom. The door was almost closed, yet a tantalising chink of light spilled out into the shadowy hallway.

Resting her palm on the wood, she listened. No one else was in the house. No footsteps, voices, only laughter from outside in the sun.

She couldn't resist. Magnetically drawn to her old room. A quick peek wouldn't do any harm. A very quick glimpse into the past while everyone was out.

Heart beating faster, Emma nudged the door a tiny bit with her finger, as if peering through the smallest crack didn't count as *actually* looking.

Had she expected it to be the same? Or for Luke to have moved in?

Neither was true.

Of course not.

She'd never seen it empty. Her parents had moved in the middle of a university term and, when she came home, her stuff was piled in boxes in the new house in Helston. So she had only ever seen it with books crammed onto shelves, her artwork on the wall, make-up all over the antique dressing table.

Like a moth to a flame, she was drawn inside.

This appeared to be a guest room now, judging by the double bed with unrumpled linen and the lack of any signs of occupation. There were two side tables on either side of the bed, each with a modern lamp, and a few large prints on the walls. One was a plan of a sailing ship while the others were canvas photos of underwater scenes. She presumed the divers in them were Luke . . . and her thoughts trailed back to Ursula's comments about his career in the navy. Typical Luke, he'd kept his achievements very quiet.

The largest canvas had pride of place above a chest of drawers. It showed him, in diving gear, in a turquoise sea, squaring up to a huge fish with bulging eyes, movie-star lips and a doleful expression that was almost human.

The fish was so comical, it brought a smile to her lips. Then, out of the corner of her eye, she saw another photo, a small unframed snap tucked into the edge of a larger framed photo. Her stomach did a somersault.

It was her and Luke, squinting into the sunshine in Dollar Cove. She was in a bikini and he was in board shorts. They were so young . . . so happy. The longing for that simpler time, before it had all gone wrong, was physical.

'Emma!' Luke's voice cut through the memories. 'What are you doing here?'

Standing in the gloom of the doorway, Emma didn't think she'd ever heard him sound so shocked.

19

'I didn't hear you!'

Her cry, half apology, half accusation, sprang from her horror at being caught in this most intimate of spaces.

Even if Luke had said that everyone should feel welcome, he could *never* have expected to find someone in one of the bedrooms, gawping at his personal possessions. She was no one special now, just another guest at the barbecue.

Another fear seized her. Had he seen her staring at the photo? Or would he assume she'd only been looking at the canvas?

'I was — the picture caught my eye. The one with the big fish,' she babbled, as he stepped out of the shadow of the doorway into a shaft of sunlight.

It was a big room but, somehow, he filled it with his presence. An image of him stretched out on the bed struck her. She was still mortified, but the fierce kick of desire shocked her even more.

Her pulse spiked as he walked over to the canvas.

The shock on his face had eased into puzzlement and then a nod. 'Oh, yes, the giant trevally.'

'Is it?' It could have been a giant goldfish for all she cared.

'You like the picture?' he said.

'Yes.' She looked again at his figure, dwarfed by the fish. 'I mean . . . it looks scary.'

'It's harmless actually, but pretty impressive up close.'

'I'll take your word for it. Luke, I'm *so* sorry. This is your house. I should never have come into your room.'

'Actually, it's not my room. I sleep in the mezzanine bedroom and I don't mind you wandering around. After all, it was where you grew up.' He turned his intense gaze on her. Emma felt she was melting under it. 'Though if you'd wanted a tour,' he added with an unexpected kindness that spoke deep to her heart. 'You only had to ask.'

She was painfully aware of the warmth of his body, the sweet tang of woodsmoke and the thrill of sharing this intimate space with him while the others were outside, unaware. She hadn't been so close to him for so long and the temptation was almost overwhelming. In a heartbeat, she could reach up, touch him, *kiss* him.

'Funny to think it started here, isn't it?' he said, his words resonating in her chest.

Emma's throat was dry. He must be feeling the emotions too, memories good and the bad. 'Yes . . . it is. It's like it all happened to someone else. Two other people.'

Her eye was drawn to the photo of the two of them again. Should she ask why he'd kept it? Should she even let on she'd seen it?

His brow furrowed. 'Are you sure you're OK? Coming back here today, I mean?'

The urge to blurt out the truth — 'Not really' and 'I'm so conflicted and confused' — was powerful. She wanted to shout out that she was torn between being angry with him and wanting to bury the past. That she was fighting the urge to either scream at him or kiss him.

194

'I'm . . . it's been a challenge. There are so many echoes of my dad, if you know what I mean and . . . and being here has brought back memories of the times we had. As a family, and . . .'

'I guessed it would be difficult for you and I wasn't sure you'd even come. I'd no expectations.'

Silently, Emma thanked him for saying it. 'I agonised about it but, as I told Maxi, I can't keep hiding from the past if . . .'

He waited for her to continue. It had been on the tip of her tongue to add, 'If I want to stay here.'

'If I want to move on,' she continued. 'Sorry. Terrible cliché.'

'Don't feel you have to leave on my account,' he said, as if he'd read her mind. 'If you want to take some quiet time here, there's no rush.'

'Thanks, but I've invaded your space for long enough.'

'You would never invade my space,' he replied. 'And it isn't my space. It's ours. Everyone who's ever lived here's space, if that doesn't sound crazy. From the chaplain to the people I bought it from. I've barely begun to make my own mark to add to all the others who've given it the atmosphere. We're all part of its history.'

What a change. The quiet young man of few words had gained self-assurance and emotional empathy over the years. Then again, after what she'd read about his service record, why was she surprised? He'd been willing to risk his own safety for others. That took a special kind of empathy.

'For what it's worth,' she began, mindful of Ursula's plea that she should build bridges to make peace with Luke and herself. 'I'm also very glad it didn't fall into the wrong hands. Now I'm back here, I realise I couldn't bear to have seen it broken up into flats. It needs to be kept as a whole, even if it's far too big. It would have been like dismembering the past.'

'I could never inflict that kind of damage on the old place. I did think twice when I saw it was on the market, even when I found out a developer was ready to pounce. The agent made no secret of the plans they had for it . . . I couldn't stand by and see it pulled apart either.'

'I hadn't realised when I first came back. I appreciate you saving it from a fate like that.'

'I'd no idea you'd ever see it again but I did think about how it might make you feel when you eventually found out I'd bought it. To be honest, I'm surprised it took so long.'

Emma knew what he meant. 'Maxi said she didn't want to upset me.'

Luke pressed his lips together and she realised what she'd said.

'Luke, I was shaken to start with but it was the shock,' she went on. 'But you've every right to be here; and the building's safe in your hands, I know that.'

'Thanks.'

'Don't thank me. I — I — shouldn't have been so hard on you that day at the beach. I wish I'd been more mature. Grown-up.'

He smiled. 'Being grown-up is overrated at times.'

'True!' Sharing his joke, she suddenly wondered what their lives might have been like if the treasure had never been found, if her parents had still been living here — if she'd never discovered the affair. Would she have stayed together with Luke when they'd left for the navy and uni, or would they have drifted apart anyway? The 'what ifs' were so powerful. She wanted to ask him if he'd ever wondered the same.

A shriek of laughter penetrated the stillness.

'Shall we go outside into the sun?' she said. 'You don't get that many days like this in Cornwall and the others will be wondering where we've got to.'

He followed her out. She was aware she was trembling a little, but the sun warmed her almost instantly and Maxi and Ursula found her back at the stall. Luke started talking to some of the other Beachcombers and making plans for the next beach-clean.

'Where have you got to? You've missed a sale!' Ursula said.

'Oh?' Amazed, Emma glanced at the empty easel. 'Who bought the picture?'

'Zoey. She's had to leave but she's left me the money.' Ursula patted her canvas bag.

'Zoey? I never thought . . .'

'She said she thinks you're incredibly talented.' Ursula grinned.

No one was more surprised than Emma. 'That's very kind of her. Thanks for sorting it for me and sorry I wasn't here. I — um — needed the bathroom.'

'It happens,' said Ursula with a twinkle in her eye as if she knew full well that Emma had been snooping around. 'The good news is you've only one picture left to sell.'

The remaining painting showed the full sweep of the beach, the breakers rolling in across pale sand, silvery rocks glinting. It was the most involved and expensive of the lot. She'd hoped it would sell but, if not, three out of four wasn't bad. Today had boosted her confidence that, perhaps, her art could stand on its own, not simply as part of a commercial project with no name attached to it.

Someone stuck another glass of wine in her hand and the afternoon sun became more intense. Emma bought a small jug from Jermaine's pottery stand, perfect for wildflowers, and a driftwood sculpture of a seal for the lodge. Ursula introduced her to a couple of the other artists and craftspeople. She hadn't really noticed that people had begun to drift off home when Maxi tapped her on the shoulder, an empty glass of Coke in her hand. Luke was chatting to Ran, who'd arrived late.

'Um. It's almost five. Andy texted. He's back and needs to get to the yacht club for an evening event.'

'Is it that late? Already?'

'I don't want to spoil the fun. You haven't finished your wine and you have a picture left to sell. Tell you what, if you want to stay longer, I'll pop home and come back to collect you in a little while with the kids.'

'I wouldn't put you to the trouble. I just need a few more minutes to help Ursula pack up.'

'OK. You've done well, selling three out of the four of your pictures.'

'I'm amazed, frankly, and thanks for all your help.'

Ursula began to pack away. Emma returned from helping her carry her unsold stock and equipment to the car to collect her own kit. The other painting would have to go home, but maybe she could sell it at the next beach market? She put the easel in her bag and had the final picture in her hands when a waving Luke dashed over.

'I'm not too late, am I?' he said.

'Too late?'

'To buy one of your pictures.'

'*You* want to buy one?' Emma burst out.

He laughed. 'Don't sound so surprised. I've had my eye on that one in particular all afternoon.'

Emma regarded him with suspicion. 'You're just being kind.'

'No. I'm not. I've wanted it all day, but I thought you'd react like this if I jumped in and bought it from the start.' He picked it up. 'It's my favourite view of the cove.'

Emma caught her breath. Luke was intent on the painting. It didn't show the chapel, but it did show the rocks at the end, glittering in a shaft of evening light breaking through the clouds. It was the place they'd crept away to, to have sex for the first time. The place where he'd told her he loved her. The spot where she'd said, 'Me too.' She hadn't even realised she'd chosen to paint that specific spot. It had chosen her.

'It's — it's yours,' she said, wanting to tell him: 'It could *only* be yours.' The idea of it being owned by anyone else, a stranger, filled her with horror.

'So, how do I pay?' he said.

Emma cringed. She didn't want to be paid anything by Luke. It felt so wrong.

'I — I — Ursula's taken the card reader. Can you — um — put the cash straight in the Beachcombers' funds?'

'If it's easier, I will, but remember you're only donating a cut of your fee. I can't put the whole cost in the funds.'

'I don't mind!' she protested. 'I enjoyed painting it. I know you'll look after it. I can't think of anyone else who should have it. So please, take it as a donation. Hold on, Maxi's calling me.'

Maxi was phoning to gently, but firmly, ask where

Emma was. Emma was torn, she wanted to stay so much and yet the events of the afternoon reminded her of how strong those youthful emotions had been. How strong they were *now*.

Luke lingered by her, obviously hearing the conversation from Emma's end.

'Maxi wants to know whether I need a lift. She's ready to go.'

'Do you have to leave?' he said, sounding disappointed.

'I — I ought to . . . Maxi's waiting in the car now.'

'I'd like to talk,' he said. 'I think we should.'

Goosebumps prickled her bare skin at his invitation. She hovered on the cusp of running away or putting her hand back in the fire and risking getting burned. It was a huge gamble so soon after Theo. If she fell for Luke again, it couldn't go anywhere and the disappointment would finish her — and she might be lured into revealing the secret she'd kept all these years.

Yet he *wanted* her to stay.

'Let me take this stuff to Maxi,' she said before she could change her mind. 'I'll tell her I'll walk home.'

20

Fizzing with nervous excitement, Emma hurried off to the car and explained the change of plan. 'Don't ask me anything else,' she said. 'Because I don't *know*.'

Maxi hesitated. 'If you're sure but you must call me if you need a lift later?'

'I will and I'll still cook you Sunday lunch tomorrow.'

Back at the chapel, Luke was waiting for her by the gates.

'Shall we go onto the beach?' he said. 'Neutral territory?'

Hardly neutral, she thought, but nodded. 'OK.'

They took a beer and a glass of wine out of the gate onto the sand. The steps were worn by age and storms and she almost spilled some wine as they made their way down the final drop onto the beach. They both laughed. The beach crowds were thinning but there were still plenty of families and groups enjoying the early evening sun. Some had set up barbecues and cricket stumps, while others splashed in shallows warmed by an afternoon of hot sun.

Emma and Luke sat on flat-topped rocks, both instinctively knowing which were comfortable.

'Best time of day.' Luke looked over the sea, aviators covering his eyes, a beer in his hand.

He still made her heart beat a little faster than she wanted it to. She was drawn to him after all these years, despite everything that had happened. It was as if they were connected by the most fragile of threads, stretched gossamer-thin. She thought it had snapped long ago — yet could it still be intact?

'It's a beautiful evening . . .' Emma was flustered by a rogue thought. 'Do you remember,' she said, resting her gaze on the horizon, 'when we all used to come here after dinner to swim after most of the emmets had gone home?'

He smiled, perhaps at her use of 'emmets' to describe the tourist hordes. 'Of course I do.'

'It seems a lifetime ago,' she said. 'Though today has reminded me how much I've missed Falford and the cove.'

'I said I wanted to talk to you and I do. We didn't part on good terms all those years ago and we've been dancing around each other since you came back, not always happily. I'd like us to get a few things straight. We said some pretty harsh stuff to each other.'

Emma felt heat rush to her face at the memory of the accusations she'd hurled at him when he'd come to confess about the journal. They'd been intended to hurt, and the words he'd flung back had stung like salt in a cut.

'You put your family before me! I should have known you'd side with them. You let your dad bully you into betraying us. Well, I might have known you'd cave in and give in to him,' she sneered. 'You're weak. A spineless coward!'

He'd visibly paled and even back then she'd known she'd hurt him. It seemed cruel now, but back then she'd wanted to wound him.

'I'm not a coward!' he cried. 'You're the one who was so ashamed to admit you loved me that you hid me away, so who's the one who can't stand up to her parents? I used to feel sorry for you, Emma, but now I know you're as much of snob as they are. You've been using me to amuse you

202

until you can go on to better things in the big wide world.'

'How dare you say that?' Emma was shocked at the way he'd turned. 'It's not like that, Luke. You're wrong.'

He shook his head in disgust as if he'd given up on her. 'You know, lately, I'd had the feeling you were only looking for an excuse for us to break up. This was it. And guess what? I'm glad. I could never have stayed with someone who only cares what other people think. Someone too frozen inside to ever make me happy.'

Emma couldn't say a thing. His words had seared her soul. She wasn't frozen and she did love him. She wasn't ashamed of him but she didn't know how she could carry on seeing him and pretend she didn't know about the affair. She was torn in two: desperate to stay together but not seeing how they could. So she'd given up on them too.

'You're right,' she said, a sneer in her voice. 'It was never going to work between us. We're too different. Goodbye, Luke. Don't try to see me again. I hope your family enjoy the money. Mine will never be the same again.'

'We were young,' she said, compressing so many emotions: guilt, regret, shock, anger at lost chances and profound sadness, into that short phrase. 'And I do understand how hurt you were when I accused you of stealing the journal. When I first came back here, I was so shocked to see you and mad about the chapel. I felt you'd done it to get back at me — which is ridiculous when you'd no idea I was going to come back. I know your reasons for buying it now.'

'Thanks,' he said, yet he didn't seem as happy with her apology as she'd hoped. In fact, it seemed to have darkened the mood between them. 'But you don't have to be happy about me living there, Emma. I'm not expecting that.'

'I'm still coming to terms with it. With the past

few months.' The whole fifteen years, she might have added.

He reached out and briefly touched her hand with his — only in sympathy, she thought — but withdrew it quickly. 'Give yourself time.'

She turned to him, suddenly feeling she could share more with him than she'd ever dreamed when she first arrived in Falford weeks before.

'I'll be honest with you. Losing the treasure broke my father. He wasn't perfect — he had a lot of faults — but I immediately knew that it would ruin his life. So when I thought you'd decided to show the journal to your dad, I was angry and hurt.' Emma paused before uttering the words she'd thought she'd never say to Luke. 'I'm sorry I blamed you for what happened.'

Luke wouldn't meet her eyes. He was either embarrassed or guilty. 'I did take it though . . .' he said.

'Yes, but not on purpose. You'd *never* have found it if I hadn't pushed you into the attic.'

'No, I suppose not.'

'Of course. I never told Dad about it obviously, or that you'd been in the house. I kept the secret because it would only have caused even more trouble for both our families and it wouldn't have made any difference.'

'Thank you.' His words were almost inaudible.

They spent a few moments in silence then Emma went on. 'Most of all, I'm sorry I called you . . . that I said you were 'a coward'. It was a horrible thing to say and I know it's not true. Not in any way and I want to get that straight.'

His lips parted in shock.

'You weren't a coward then. I know it was your

204

father's fault and he took the journal. You'd never have shown it to him. You're not a coward now and I am so ashamed I ever said it.'

'Emma . . .'

'No, please let me finish. There's something else I wanted to say. Something I only found out a few days ago. I know what you did in the navy. I know about the medal for finding that fisherman. I know what you did to earn it.'

He avoided her eyes, clearly uncomfortable with the praise. 'I did what had to be done in the moment. I was trained and I did it.'

'You went inside the wheelhouse of an upturned trawler in the pitch darkness to recover the skipper. Ursula told me so I went on the Internet and I've seen the news report on YouTube: the one about the accident and the one where you were awarded the gallantry medal.'

'The medal?' He shook his head. 'Won't bring back the skipper.'

'The report said you didn't *know* he was dead. It said you put your own life in danger to check and brought his body out anyway, through a tangle of netting in the dark.'

'I took a calculated risk.'

'I call that a very big risk.'

'Yeah . . . I thought that even if he hadn't made it, which was probable, the family deserved their loved one back, so they could mourn him. They're the ones who deserve our thoughts.'

Emma nodded and sipped her wine, wondering if she should have mentioned the award, thus revealing the fact she'd looked.

'Emma,' he said. 'I'm glad we've talked and . . .

there's something I've been meaning to say, too.'

She gave him space, waiting with bated breath to hear what he was struggling so hard to tell her.

'Yes?' she murmured, encouraging him with the lightest of touches.

'It's only that . . . that I — I'd like to . . .'

Pulse racing, she waited for him to speak. It must be something momentous, or at least important, for him to make such a big deal of it.

'That I'd like to tell you that I'd really like it if you'd come diving with me.'

'*Diving*?'

'Yes, diving. I realise that it's bad timing. After what we just discussed . . . the trawler, but I promise it isn't always dangerous and it can be incredible. It almost always is . . . You should come. See what it's like for yourself.'

From a fever pitch of expectation, Emma crashed down to earth. That was what he'd been meaning to say to her? She'd been expecting — well, she wasn't sure what she'd been expecting, but it wasn't *this*.

'I thought it would be a way of us — of us — doing something fun together,' Luke rushed on. 'I'm sure you'd love it and it would be good for your research. Your illustrations. You've no idea of how amazing the underwater landscape is and you seemed to like the photos.'

'I did but . . .'

'I can promise there's nothing scary in the seas off Cornwall. Apart from the rubbish that's been left there by humans, of course.'

'I believe you . . .' Emma said, still processing the fact he'd invited her out on a day out with him alone. 'I can't imagine actually going down into the deep.'

'Oh, there's no need to go too deep. A few metres down is enough to see some amazing sights. Coral reefs, seals.'

Her imagination went into overdrive. Imagine viewing the flora and fauna first-hand under the sea. Using all her senses. Luke was right; imagine how it could inspire her work.

'I'd never push you out of your comfort zone,' he said.

Too late for that, she thought, but his enthusiasm was infectious.

'I'll think about it,' she said, adding, 'Seriously,' when he gave her a sceptical look. 'Though, between Beachcombers and the business, won't you be too busy?'

'I'm never too busy to go diving.' He smiled shyly, back to the teenage Luke for a brief moment. 'Especially not with you.'

She was surprised to find that she was at the bottom of her wine glass. The sun was still very warm. Being with Luke was like being with an old friend and a brand-new one at the same time. Familiar yet exciting. Relaxing and yet somehow dangerous. Luke lifted his beer to his mouth and Emma noticed the chunky diving watch. There was something sexy about the way it wrapped around his wrist, and about his tanned forearms.

She also noticed the time.

'Oh God. It's almost seven! Maxi will be wondering if I've been captured by pirates on the way home. I'll probably have missed dinner.'

'I can walk with you if you like.'

'No. No, thanks. I'm sure you'll be busy clearing up.' Emma didn't trust herself to spend any more time with him and definitely wasn't keen to arrive back at Maxi's with Luke in tow.

'OK. I'll take the glass back to the chapel,' he said. 'Thanks for coming today. I know it wasn't easy.'

'For either of us. Thanks for hosting it.'

'It was a pleasure . . .' To her amazement, he leaned down and kissed her cheek. It was the most innocent of kisses yet it set off fireworks all over her body.

'Don't forget my offer about the dive,' he said. 'I promise we'll be safe.'

'OK. I'll text you,' she said, already in two minds about agreeing.

'Good. I'll check the forecast and we can arrange a time.'

Not until they'd walked off the beach, and she'd got out of view of the chapel, did she put her hand to her cheek in wonder at that kiss. It felt imprinted on her skin, an indelible mark. As for being safe, she'd no doubt he'd give his life for her if it came to it, but emotionally? Even though she still had secrets from him, she felt they'd made a giant leap forward and she was in more danger from him than she'd ever been before.

21

'So, what do you think about Penhallow Cove for a beginner dive?' Luke said, a few days later, as he helped Ran hang some wetsuits to dry outside the centre.

'Sounds good,' Ran said, 'But why are you asking me, mate?'

'I wanted to get your opinion.'

'You've taken scores of novices diving before. You know the best sites. Or is this more about the student than the location?'

Luke gave up trying to deny it. 'Yeah, I guess.'

Ran hooked a suit over the rail. 'Because Emma isn't just any newbie?'

'You could say that.'

Ran raised his eyebrows. 'Is this a dive lesson or a date? Because you need to decide.'

'She won't want to think it's a date. There's history between us. And when I say history, I mean *serious* history.' Literal history, thought Luke, though he wasn't going to even try explaining to Ran.

His stomach knotted. After the barbecue, they'd laid some of the past to rest, but not all. At the final moment, he'd chickened out of telling her the truth: that he had deliberately given the journal to his father. Her apology and generosity towards him had only made the situation far worse.

'*So when I thought you'd decided to show the journal to your dad, I was angry and hurt. I'm sorry I blamed you for what happened.*'

He'd asked her to stay behind, precisely so he could have everything out in the open, but then she'd dropped that on him. Finally, they'd been getting on so well, he'd sensed it was a big turning point for them, and when it had come to it, he simply hadn't dared to shatter the moment. The dive would be another opportunity to come clean, yet even now Luke wasn't sure he'd be able to. Should the whole truth stay buried? After all, only he and his father knew.

'To be honest,' he said, feeling slightly sick. 'I've been wondering ever since if I should have suggested it to her at all.'

Ran smiled. 'Mate, I'll let you into a secret. If there's all this 'history' between you, she's probably wondering exactly the same.'

'Yeah.' Luke had thought that very thing.

'Look, for what it's worth, I think Penhallow is fine. It's a nice safe shore dive. If the forecast is good, it'll look idyllic and won't put her off.'

'What if she hates it from the off?'

'There's always that danger but if you don't give it a go, you'll never know,' Ran replied. 'You're way more experienced than me: you'll know if it's going well or she's desperate to get back on dry land. Try and enjoy it. If you do, there's more chance of her liking it too.'

'I guess.'

Ran slapped him on the back. 'If there's anything I can do to help, you only have to ask. Good luck.'

Feeling slightly reassured, if only that he'd picked a good dive spot, Luke checked the forecast and rechecked the tides — even though he knew exactly when they were — for the next few days. He'd told Emma he'd confirm details with her once he'd made sure everything was set fair, and there was no point putting it off any longer.

He sent a brief message, saying the weather looked fine for the dive day and that he'd meet her at the dive centre at nine-thirty the following morning. As it was a shore dive he planned to drive her to the cove in the van. The boat was booked for a professional course but Luke wouldn't have risked seasickness anyway. Did Emma get seasick? He couldn't really remember. She'd never learned to sail, he knew that. He hadn't either, preferring to have the speed and convenience of the dive boat or a RIB.

He was still turning over every possible outcome — and not only in terms of the dive itself — when the day arrived.

He made sure he was at the centre early, sorting through wetsuits. Although he was almost certain of her size, he wanted to offer her the chance to choose one. It was all part of not making presumptions.

He stared at the rack of suits, as if they might have an answer.

Emma Pelistry was coming on a dive with him.

A few weeks ago, he'd have been astonished at the idea. A few years ago, he'd have found it completely incredible.

Now, they were going to spend several hours together, alone and focused on each other. Should he have invited her on a group dive, instead? Probably. Did he want to share his time with Emma with a bunch of strangers? Definitely not. He was also sure he didn't want to ruin the day with an ill-timed 'confession'.

He glanced at his watch. Five minutes late. All this agonising when there was a strong possibility she might not turn up at all. Even Ran had suggested that . . .

His phone rang.

Was this Emma calling to cancel? She'd taken a day to get back to him when he'd messaged her with suggested dates. However, the name that flashed on the screen wasn't Emma's and his heart sank. Should he switch off the phone? Deciding it was better to rearrange the conversation than risk being called while Emma was with him.

'Hello, son.'

Luke's heart sank to his boots. 'Dad.'

'Can we have a chat? Are you busy?'

'As a matter of fact, yes. I'm about to take the boat out on a course.' Luke had no compunction about his fib. His father would never believe him if he told the truth anyway.

'Right . . . well, I only wanted a quick word.'

Luke despaired. Nothing was ever a quick word where his father was concerned.

'Have you thought about my business proposition?'

'Business proposition?' Luke's dismay ballooned.

'Yes. I wondered if you'd got an answer for me because it's getting pretty urgent here. I need to know.'

'I'm sorry but I can't talk about this now. I've customers waiting on the quayside. I'll call you later.'

Luke ended the call, shaking his head in despair. His dad's 'business proposition' was his way of asking for a loan — another loan — that he'd no hope of repaying.

'Is this her, Luke?' Ran broke into his thoughts, pointing at a silver hatchback pulling into the car park.

His pulse shot up. He'd been on edge anyway and his father's call had wound him up further. 'Yes.

212

Thanks.'

'If you need me to help prep, you only have to ask. Otherwise, I'll keep out of your way, buddy.'

'Thanks, Ran.' He rolled his eyes. 'No need to hide, though.'

Ran grinned. 'OK . . . And, mate, relax and try to enjoy yourself.'

Luke's heart was still racing as he went to meet Emma at her car. Keep it light, keep it casual, he reminded himself. Act as if she's any beginner customer, wanting an intro to diving . . .

Oh, for God's sake. Who was he kidding?

Emma swung her legs out of the car. Clad in cropped skinny jeans, they were as shapely and coltish as they'd ever been. At one time, perhaps in Year 7, he remembered her being as tall as him until he'd shot up and was now a good six inches taller. She still seemed elegant and poised, making him feel awkward and too big for a space. He was still in awe of her, still never quite sure where he stood with her. Now more than ever.

'Morning!' His voice seemed to boom across the empty car park.

'Hello.' Emma's was more restrained. She must be nervous. 'Am I OK to park here?'

'Sure. Courses don't start for a while so you're the only one here. Apart from Ran, of course.'

'Are you sure you're not too busy?'

'It's fine. The course is Ran's thing and he has two other instructors with him. I'd only have been doing some boring admin if I'd stayed and, like I said, I never need any excuse to go diving rather than be stuck in the office. And it's the perfect morning: sunny and as calm as it ever gets in Cornwall.'

213

He'd said far too much, and hurriedly stopped himself.

She nodded. 'I'm relieved to hear it!'

She didn't look as glad as she made out. Luke could tell she was pretty apprehensive so he threw her a reassuring grin that also hid his own nerves.

'Come into the dive centre and we'll run through the paperwork and the basics before we take to the water.'

Still unable to quite process that Emma had actually arrived and they were going to spend the morning together, doing what he loved most, he took her into the small briefing room at the rear of the dive centre and offered her a drink and a breakfast muffin that Ran's partner, Bo, had baked. Bo ran the Boatyard Café in Falford and often supplied snacks for hungry divers before and after their dives.

Emma eyed the muffin as if it might bite her. 'They look lovely, but I don't think I can . . .'

'Have you had any breakfast?'

'A couple of coffees. Nothing else.'

Luke wasn't surprised she was jittery. 'We won't be going in the water for a couple of hours yet and diving needs lots of energy. If you can manage something, it would be a good idea. These are citrus and poppy seed and they taste even better than they look.'

She nodded. 'OK. Thanks. I'd better try to eat something.'

While he gave her medical and insurance forms to fill in, he made some decaf tea and then joined her, pleased to see she'd eaten most of the muffin. While he could understand her nervousness, he didn't want her keeling over before they'd even entered the water.

Even though a beginner dive like this held no

fear for him, he never forgot he was responsible for the safety of another person, whether it was hers or that of anyone else who came on the courses. Most dives went by with no problems at all but you had to remember scuba diving was a potentially very dangerous activity. Humans weren't designed to spend long periods underwater, especially not at any depth. Panic attacks, equipment malfunction, medical emergencies, the bends;

Luke had experienced and dealt with all of these issues in his time as a professional diver.

Safety came first, last and always, unless, he thought ruefully, there was a dire emergency. Even then you had to make an assessment of how far the risk was worth taking.

Hopefully, almost certainly, nothing like that would happen today.

'Great. These are OK, thanks,' Luke said, rather awkward that he'd had to check through Emma's answers to the questions on the insurance medical. Thankfully, they were all negative. 'Now we can go and take a look at the kit before we get the suits and head off.'

She hesitated. 'I still can't believe I'm doing this.'

He decided not to share that he felt exactly the same. 'I think lots of people feel like that on a first dive. I promise you, you'll wonder why you never tried it before. Diving, I mean,' he added hastily then scraped up his best 'confident instructor' grin. 'Come on. I promise you it won't be that bad. We're going to a great little spot: Penhallow Cove. We'll start off in shallow water and then go a little bit further when you feel comfortable.'

She laughed.

'What's funny?'

'You. Talking about 'feeling comfortable', as if we're off to lounge on the sofa or something.'

'You might surprise yourself,' he said, smiling back. He'd already got the fins, snorkels, masks, BCDs and regulators ready. 'It'll be fine.'

He ushered her towards his truck, chatting about how the visibility and conditions couldn't be more perfect. It was a good thing she couldn't see inside his head because it was safe to say he'd never been more nervous before a dive in his life.

22

'It might not be as bad as you think . . .'

As Luke drove her to the dive spot, Emma still wasn't feeling sure about that. The diving might turn out OK, but as for spending so much time alone with him? She'd agonised over whether she should have accepted the invite and had had to mention it to Maxi.

'It means spending hours together.'

'Looks like you were doing that at the barbecue,' Maxi said. 'I saw you creep in late.'

'I didn't creep in and it was only eight o clock!'

Maxi laughed. 'Fine by me. I'm not your mother. So if you admit to spending time with Luke after the barbecue, why would going diving with him be any different?'

'It feels more like a — a date.'

'Does Luke think that? Would it be so terrible if it was a date?'

'I don't know . . . I survived my visit to the chapel and we were getting along better after the barbecue. We talked — properly — about some of the stuff that happened when I left Falford. We cleared the air a bit.'

Not about *everything* though. Emma hadn't told him about the affair . . . He'd been hesitant and uncomfortable at times and she was still convinced he'd wanted to say more than he did. Then again, perhaps he'd just been nervous about asking her on the dive? He'd probably expected her to say no.

'That's great,' Maxi said. 'And it sounds to me like you've already made up your mind to go.'

Maxi was right. Emma hadn't been able to resist the chance to spend more time alone with Luke.

On their way to the dive spot, driving through Falford, she stared out of the window. They spoke about the village, how it had changed, and how it hadn't, the sights along the way, the Country Stores, the new housing developments, pubs that had been turned into homes.

Luke asked her about her work, and listened as she told him about her first job after art school working for a greetings card company and, later, how she'd taken the plunge to set up as a freelance illustrator. It struck her that they had something in common: as two independent spirits, it obviously suited them both to be their own boss.

'Oh, we're nearly at the cove!' she said, surprised when they turned off the road down a track hemmed in by tall Cornish hedges. There was grass growing out of the middle of the lane.

'Yes. It isn't far but still well off the tourist trail.'

'That's good to hear. Dad brought us sometimes to escape the summer crowds.' She stopped, aware of the memories she was bringing up. She'd been determined that today would be free of conflict, if not of tension. However, Luke didn't pick up on the reference to her father.

'I hadn't been either until recently. Ran and I came to check it out a couple of months ago. It's a little gem.'

A mile down the lane, he stopped at a rough parking spot barely big enough for three cars. No one else was there. There wasn't even a wooden sign saying where the beach was, and the stone stile was overgrown by weeds.

'It hasn't changed at all,' he said. 'No facilities. Nothing.'

'*No* facilities?'

'Um. Sorry. When I said it was the perfect dive spot, I should have said *almost* perfect. Sorry,' he said again, cringing. 'I didn't think.'

Emma couldn't help but smile at his face, which might possibly be turning a little red. 'Never mind. I'll make do with a discreet bush.'

They changed into wetsuits and carried the equipment down a short slope to a gap in a hedge. No wonder Luke was so fit, Emma thought. Even though she only had the fins, masks and breathing apparatus — Luke was carrying the full air tanks — her arms were aching. Suddenly, however, the cove opened up in all its glory and she forgot her screaming muscles.

The tiny cove on the southern tip of the Falford estuary was exquisite. A pocket of creamy sand surrounded by dark, low cliffs. The sand sloped gently into a sea of translucent turquoise, as inviting as any Caribbean spot — until you felt the temperature of it of course.

'Wow. It's even more gorgeous than I remembered,' Emma said, happy to unload the gear on the sand and take in the wonderful view.

'It's one of my favourite spots and, best of all, there's no one here but us.' Luke smiled. 'I'll fetch the rest of the gear and we can make a start.'

★ ★ ★

They waded into water so calm it barely kissed the shore, and so limpid that Emma could see every ripple of sand under her feet. Once they were chest-deep,

Luke showed her how to clear her mask if it filled with water. Taking it off below the surface was a bit scary, but she managed to empty it by holding the top and blowing and replace it without panicking. The next step was learning to retrieve the mouthpiece if it came out underwater. With his calm instruction, she went through a couple of drills and her anxieties started to ease.

Finally, with Emma neck-deep in water and Luke up to his chest, he grinned encouragingly.

'Right, you've done really well. I think we can venture further out. There aren't any currents here but, as you're a complete beginner, it would be better if I held your hand until we're out in the bay and you feel confident. Is that OK?'

Emma nodded. Even though she'd felt comfortable up to now, the thought of swimming off into the depths caused a flutter of panic. She didn't mind holding his hand at all.

'Are you ready?' he asked.

'As I'll ever be.'

'Good. I've brought the camera so I can take some photos. I thought they'd be useful for your work.'

'Th-thanks,' Emma said, the last thing on her mind being work.

They faced the horizon and she felt his fingers close around hers. Seconds later, they were finning beneath the waves, with the depths stretching out beneath them. Man-sized clumps of seaweed waved as fish weaved silently through their fronds. The sunlight shifted and moved with the gentle swell above them.

It was mind-blowing. Looking up, the surface was a blur of light, while below, the underwater forest glowed in a myriad of reds, greens and blues.

Luke let go of her hand and gave her the OK sign and she returned it. He let a little air out of her buoyancy jacket and they descended. The scary feeling of sinking deeper caused her to gulp in air, but she got her breathing back under control and tried to enjoy the incredible sights of the underwater world.

They finned towards a rocky outcrop, where giant sea plants and solemn fish glided to and fro. Underwater gullies were lined with kelp like the tresses of a giant's hair. Urchins and anemones studded the sides of the rocks and cuttlefish and a colony of sand eels darted around her.

Emma recognised many species from her work but to see them in their watery environment was amazing. Suddenly, Luke touched her arm and pointed ahead.

A large, grey shape with whiskers was barrelling towards them like a missile. Emma's breathing became fast and loud. Luke took her hand again and they hung in the water as the seal shot past a metre away.

Luke gave her the OK and Emma tried to calm herself. The seal was as big as Luke, and seemed curious to know what they were. It circled them, swam under Emma's legs and nibbled her fin.

Half afraid it would nibble *her*, she tried to stay still and breathe normally. She could tell Luke was excited too, from his eyes. The seal made a few more passes, so sleek and fast in its element. It was the closest she'd ever been to any wild creature in its natural habitat and it was almost overwhelming. Luke was snapping away with the camera.

Finally, bored with playing, it powered away into the deep and Luke indicated that it was time to ascend.

So soon? she thought. Surely they'd only been under-water for ten minutes?

However, he was already adding more air into her buoyancy jacket and telling her to fin towards the surface. A minute later they were making for shore and she found sand under her feet. Luke took out his mouthpiece and Emma pushed her mask off her face. She could barely speak for excitement and adrenaline.

'Oh m-my G-god, that was incredible!'

He broke into a grin. She couldn't help but think how at ease he'd been in the water, how confident and at home.

'I hoped you'd love it!'

Emma half stumbled out of the water and collapsed onto the sand to take off her fins. Luke sat beside her.

'I was so nervous at the start. I didn't know how I'd cope when we first descended but I soon forgot to be nervous. The vastness, the colours. It's incredible. I'm so glad we took the underwater camera. I can't wait to see the photos.' She was already thinking of how she could capture the marine life she'd seen.

'We were lucky to see the seal. I'd hoped there would be some but I didn't want to get your hopes up.'

'I know! It just shot out of nowhere. It was so big — so fast. When it nibbled my fin, I couldn't believe it.'

'Lucky it didn't nibble your suit.'

'Oh no! I don't fancy that!'

Luke helped her out of the tanks and breathing apparatus. In the water, she'd felt as if she were flying but their weight was so unwieldy on land.

She pulled her hair out of her eyes. 'Thank you. I wouldn't have missed that for the world.'

His eyes filled with delight. 'Let's go and get something to drink. Leave the kit here, I'll sort it.'

Feeling tired but exhilarated, they walked to the truck, still buzzing with the sights of the dive. Luke returned to collect the tanks, while she changed in the rear seats. Once back, he changed himself discreetly out of view of the truck. It was all so chaste . . . so different to the intimacy they'd once shared.

Yet she couldn't forget their connection underwater. Diving with a buddy was about trust, especially when she was a complete novice. It hadn't escaped her that, when they were young, she'd often felt in control in the relationship, and Luke had felt vulnerable. Today, the roles had been reversed, at least while they were underwater. It had been a joy to do something new where the past wasn't an issue: a new start for them both.

'Here you go,' he said, producing a flask of ginger tea and energy bars from the truck.

'Thanks,' she said as they finished eating. 'That was amazing. I really enjoyed that.'

'It was awesome,' Luke said, with almost childlike glee.

'You must have seen it all before, though?' Emma said, teasing him while they stood next to the truck, letting the sun dry her hair and warm her skin.

'I've only dived here once since I came back. Not seen a cuttlefish here or been that close to a seal in this cove. There's always something new to see, on every dive.'

Emma finished her tea and put the cup in the back of the truck. 'The diving might be great here but surely it can't compete with all these exotic places around the world?' she said.

'Ah, but it doesn't have to compete . . .' he said. 'Diving isn't only about the location. It's about the whole experience. Who you're with . . .' He looked at her intently. 'That's what makes it extraordinary.'

They were so close. His wet hair glistened in the light, and his blue eyes were full of fire. The fire of desire, the same as the longing that burned in her. It would be so easy to kiss him . . . she imagined his lips on hers, the tang of salt from the sea and the sweetness of ginger. Luke caught her intake of breath and matched it, leaning forward. It was actually going to happen, and Emma knew she wouldn't stop him, no matter how reckless it would be . . .

His phone rang.

'Damn it!' He jumped back, glaring at his mobile. His expression darkened and he strode away from her towards a hedge.

Emma felt as if she'd been snapped back from the brink of something amazing and dangerous. She was both relieved and frustrated.

Luke was pacing up and down, the phone clamped to his ear. She tried not to listen but it was impossible not to hear the irritation in his voice. She thought she heard him say: 'Dad, I can't talk to you now!' and something about money. It sounded as if Harvey was hassling Luke, though Emma had been sure he was living in Spain.

She tried to compose herself, still stunned at the crash to earth before the kiss had even happened. It seemed cruel and yet wasn't it for the best they hadn't taken things further? The whole day out had ventured into unknown territory that was both exciting and dangerous.

Luke's conversation ended abruptly and, when he

returned, it was with a brow furrowed with worry.

'Sorry. Had to take that. I—'

His phone rang again. He snatched it up. 'Dad! Stop calling me . . . Oh, sorry. Ran. Yes. It's gone well.' He listened and Emma heard him swear softly, and ask a lot of questions.

He broke off. 'That was Ran. He's in the Marine Wildlife Rescue, same as me, and they've had a report of a stranded dolphin up at the estuary. He's bringing the RIB round from the dive centre to try and move it.'

'Oh, the poor thing. That sounds awful.'

'It is, and I'm afraid I'm going to have to take you back to the centre and go and see what I can do.'

'Don't waste time doing that. I want to help too, if I won't be in the way?'

'You wouldn't. We need as many people as possible.'

'In that case,' Emma said. 'Let's go now.'

23

Emma could have wept. It was the most heartrending sight she'd ever seen. A few metres off shore, the dolphin was lying in a muddy channel, thrashing its tail. The animal must have been caught in one of the hollows scoured out by the currents. If not forgotten, her moment with Luke was pushed into the background — for now.

'Oh, the poor thing. It's stuck in the shallow water.'

'It looks like a common dolphin,' Luke said. 'Probably lost its way in the tidal creek. This is a well-known stranding trap.'

Emma winced at the dolphin's struggles. 'I remember it happening a couple of times when we were younger. Remember that time on your birthday?' she said. 'We were all drinking beers on the beach and the marine rescue people came by in their boat? It didn't end happily.'

'I do,' he said, adding gently: 'This one might not either.'

'We're going to try, though, aren't we?' Emma couldn't bear the thought of giving up. 'We *have* to try.'

'Of course. We're not going to leave it there.' Luke pulled out the radio in its waterproof pouch. 'I'll phone Ran now and see how long the RIB will be. We can't reach it by land. A boat's the best option by far, *if* it's not injured and we can get it refloated soon.'

Emma wanted to move heaven and earth to help it, but she was realistic. She hadn't needed Luke to remind her that many rescues of marine animals were doomed to failure. She had to set any sentimentality aside and accept the dolphin might not make it.

All they could do was wait on the shore until the boat arrived. It was too dangerous to wade out into the mud yet in case they got stuck themselves.

'What are its chances, do you think?' she asked.

Luke sighed. 'If we can transfer it onto the marine stretcher, and into the boat, we might be able to take it out to sea and hope it will swim off.'

'I feel so helpless but I know there's nothing any of us can do until the vet and divers arrive.'

'They'll be as quick as they can,' Luke said. 'In the meantime, I think we should get ready. I've got a couple of clean drysuits in the truck.'

Emma donned the drysuit, knowing they were in a race against time and tide.

The inflatable RIB arrived about half an hour later, with Ran at the helm and a woman in a drysuit. Ran anchored just off shore and the woman jumped off into the waist-deep water. Ran followed her, wading to the shore, and said hello.

'This is Shanthi, from Helston vet's,' Luke said. 'She's also one of our volunteer rescue vets.'

'Hi,' Shanthi said briskly. 'Let's have a look at our dolphin friend and see if we can get him back where he belongs.'

Ran, Luke and the vet waded out to the animal while Emma waited on the shore, wondering how she would be able to help, if at all.

Then Luke came back to her: 'Come on, then. Stick by us and you'll be fine.'

Thrilled to be asked, but still wary, Emma waded into the squelchy mud, her legs sinking up to her calves on her way to the dolphin.

She'd never been so close to such an animal. It was larger and far more majestic than she'd ever imagined, which made its plight all the more pitiful. It must be so distressed at being trapped, and relying on humans to save it. It seemed exhausted to Emma, possibly sick too.

Shanthi sighed. 'It looks like it's become detached from its pod, lost its way and been stranded here. I'll give it a good check over. Looks like it's a young one.'

'Is it sick?' Emma asked. 'It keeps flopping over on one side.'

'Not necessarily. Probably only exhausted. It could have been stuck here all night,' Shanthi said, gently examining the dolphin, which made clicking noises while she did so. 'Looks like it has a number of old injuries but they're all healed and not recent. It seems to be in moderate condition in terms of its nutrition.'

'What do you think?' Luke asked, after the vet had finished her examination.

'I think we've no choice but to try and move it,' Shanthi said. 'Ran?'

Ran scratched his head. 'I agree. We could take it out to the end of the estuary, give it a chance to rejoin its pod. Less chance of it trying to swim back up here from there. I'll fetch the stretcher.'

'I'll come with you.' Luke followed while Emma waited with Shanthi.

'Can I do anything?' Emma asked her.

'Plenty. We'll need you to help lift it into the stretcher and it's essential we keep its body cool and its skin moist so you'll need to keep pouring water over it. In the meantime, I'll mark its dorsal fin with a couple of stripes so we can identify it more easily in the future.'

Ran and Luke arrived back with the webbing stretcher, a green salvage sheet and a white bedsheet plus several plastic jugs. The dolphin kept trying to move and making plenty of clicking noises but it was obvious it couldn't possibly free itself.

They were all coated in mud as they tried to load the animal onto the stretcher and cover it with a sheet. It was incredibly heavy but together they lifted it into the boat. Breathing heavily and hot herself, Emma's only concern was for the dolphin. She clambered into the boat and filled her jug.

'Keep trickling water over it,' Shanthi urged. 'We'll go slowly, please, Ran. Don't want to stress it any more than it already has been.'

It was the strangest journey Emma had ever made; the dolphin wrapped in a sheet flicking its tail and making eerie cries, while she doused it with water and made soothing noises. Did it have any concept that they were trying to help or was it simply terrified?

She knew dolphins were incredibly intelligent. She'd read a lot about them when looking for references for artwork, but to be so close to one, to hear its plaintive cries, was an emotional experience. It must be going through what humans did: confused, out of its natural habitat, missing its social group.

It made Emma think about the first day she'd landed back in Falford and how out of place she'd felt. Even in her schooldays, she'd sometimes thought she didn't really belong and wasn't accepted. Some people had viewed her as the 'snooty Pelistrys' daughter' who thought she was better than everyone else. Her aloofness then had probably fed into that image. Ursula had made it clear she disliked Emma, even if her view had been coloured by personal reasons.

Luke himself had called her 'frozen' in the heat of their parting row. She hoped he didn't think so now.

Trying to refocus, she scooped up more seawater and trickled it over the dolphin, while the boat made its slow progress towards the open sea.

There was a discussion about the best place to try and release it. It had been a long time since Emma had seen the estuary from the water. Despite living on the very edge of the sea, her parents hadn't been boating enthusiasts and she felt she was viewing every headland and cove through fresh eyes. Fortunately, the swell was gentle, so the boat made good progress, albeit at a sedate pace.

'What about here?' Ran said.

Emma recognised the headland to the south, where the waters were calm, but the open sea lay ahead.

'As good a place as any,' Luke nodded in agreement. 'Shanthi's the boss, though.'

'I think we could try to release it now,' the vet said. 'OK, everyone, let's lower the stretcher overboard but keep it in place so the animal can get used to being in open water again.'

Emma helped lift the stretcher over the side of the RIB. Her arms were tired from the unexpected activity but she knew they had to hold on a while longer.

'It looks like it's trying to swim,' she said softly, encouraged by the creature's tail flicks.

Shanthi nodded. 'We'll give it a couple more minutes.'

The dolphin called and thrashed its tail, clearly trying to wriggle out of the stretcher.

'OK, I think we could try releasing it. Let go of the seaward side of the stretcher but try and keep hold of the other.'

Luke and the vet leaned over and opened one side of the stretcher, leaving the animal free to swim away — if it could. Yet it stayed in the webbing, as if it either didn't want to leave or couldn't. The dolphin tipped on its side as if about to roll over.

Emma's heart was in her mouth. What if it was now too exhausted to swim off?

'Give it a moment,' Shanthi said. 'Off you go,' she urged.

A few seconds later, the dolphin seemed to get its bearings and right itself.

'It's going!' Emma cried.

'Looks like it . . .' Shanthi was beaming.

Moments later it had slipped free of the stretcher and was on its way, its fin breaking the water.

'Excellent!' Luke cried.

Emma exchanged a look with him, sharing their pure delight.

'Woo-hoo!'

Everyone was buoyant with relief. They gathered up the stretcher while Ran motored gently behind the dolphin, which seemed to be growing stronger, breaching the waves and swimming faster.

'Can't believe it swam away after being stuck in that mud,' Emma said.

'It doesn't always end like that, so it's brilliant,' Luke said.

'Do you think it will be OK?' she asked.

Shanthi shrugged but was smiling too. 'Hopefully, it will find its pod. We've done everything we can so fingers crossed.'

Emma was bubbling over with adrenaline once Ran had taken them back to the shore in the RIB. By the time they'd got changed for the second time that day and driven to the dive centre, it was early evening. Ran was hosing down the stretcher and boat and Shanthi had stayed to help him.

'I dunno about you, but I'm starving,' Luke said. 'Anyone want to grab a bite to eat at the Ferryman?'

Emma's stomach rumbled. 'I could eat a horse!'

'Told you diving was hard work.'

'Hey. We have also rescued a dolphin.'

'True,' he said with a grin. 'Ferryman, then?'

'Normally I'd bite your hand off but I've got a lamb tagine waiting for me at home,' Shanthi said. 'I daren't miss that when my partner's cooked for me.'

Ran shook his head. 'I'd love to but I'm off to a Flingers rehearsal with Bo, or meant to be. I'm late so I'll have to grab something afterwards.'

'Flingers?' Emma was completely bemused.

'Falford Flingers. Rock and roll dance group,' Ran explained. 'I DJ and, for my sins, I also dance. We're doing a demo at Falford Summer Fete in August and, believe me, I need all the practice I can get.'

'Oh . . . OK. Better not keep you away from that,' Luke said. 'Looks like just the two of us then,' he added to Emma.

The two of them. During the rescue, thoughts of how close they had come to a kiss had been swept aside by the need to help the dolphin. Now, it came flooding back and Emma was still torn between relief and disappointment. She certainly hadn't meant to end up in a twosome at the pub, but she was starving and perhaps they'd have another chance to talk and cement the connection that was growing between them. She had no idea where it might go, if anywhere, yet she had to give it a chance.

She followed Luke in her car to the Ferryman, with

a sense of déjà vu that was hard to ignore. The pub had a cool new sign and had been recently white-washed, but its thatched roof and low beams were the same as they had always been. She and Luke and their mates used to pop in from time to time. They'd play pool and darts in the snug, laugh too loudly and cause some of the oldies to tut into their pints. However, her last memory of the village local wasn't so happy . . .

The inn was where Luke's father had gone to celebrate a few weeks after he'd found the hoard. Her own dad had been in there too, having a meal with her mum. When he came home to the chapel, Robin had been white with shock — and so angry. Emma still recalled every word.

'The arrogance of the man! Anyone would have thought he'd discovered DNA or something. Jesus Christ, he even had the bloody nerve to buy everyone a drink. He came up to me, you know. Held out his grimy paw and said: 'No hard feelings, Robin.' It was all I could do not to drag the man out and knock him into kingdom come. If your mother hadn't been there, I would have! I walked out, of course. With your mother. I thought he was lying . . . but he'd brought some of the coins with him. How could he? Damaging up a valuable archaeological site, destroying the context, looting artefacts as if they're souvenirs! Thumping all over it in his hobnailed boots. It's outrageous. It's disgusting. Though what do you expect from a man like him? A thug, a criminal, an uneducated liar. Him and his family!'

'Emma?'

'Sorry?'

Luke was frowning, clearly worried about her lack of enthusiasm. 'We can go somewhere else if you like.

The yacht club serves meals and it's only five minutes away?'

'No. No . . .' She struggled to regain her composure. 'The pub's fine. *Fine*. Honestly. It's only that I haven't been in here for years.' Taking a mental deep breath, she opened the door for him to walk through. 'Come on, before they run out of food.'

Though the beams and thick stone walls were obviously as they always had been, the Ferryman had been spruced up big time and there were now chairs, menu boards and sofas in its nooks and crannies. The 'snug', which had held the pool table and dartboard, was now turned over to additional dining tables, which brought in far more cash than a bunch of local youths drinking cider for hours. Indeed, Emma couldn't see a single free table; all were occupied by couples and groups tucking into fish, chips and steaks.

However when Luke approached the bar, the landlord greeted them warmly when they asked for a table.

'Bit short notice, mate. Guess you're heaving,' Luke said.

'I keep a couple of tables for walk-in regulars. There's one at the far end of the terrace if that's OK for you? It's a fine evening.'

'Great.'

After collecting drinks from the bar, they made their way down the steps to the waterside terrace, which was also buzzing with people. They ordered food at their table and Emma sat back to enjoy the evening sun on her face. More people arrived at the pub, some taking their drinks down to the pontoon. A few arrived in motor dinghies from yachts anchored in the estuary. With the warm rays on her skin and the light glinting off the water, she felt more relaxed than

234

at any time since she'd been back in Falford.

She could almost convince herself that the past was the past. She and Luke truly were different people now and today had shown that. They'd made fresh memories, diving and at the rescue — and as for afterwards, who knew where it might lead?

'This is lovely,' she said. It seemed like a momentous thing to say somehow. As if she'd made a giant leap forward.

'It's a beautiful evening. I'm glad you enjoyed yourself today.'

'I loved the diving and I'm so happy we were able to help the dolphin. I'm not sure I'm ready to do anything intrepid but the new perspective on marine life has been amazing. I'm itching to do some drawings.'

'I'll email the shots we took with the underwater camera as soon as I get home.'

'Thanks. You know, I couldn't believe it when that seal came so close to us, almost as if it was playing with us. To be honest I was a bit scared at first but it seemed friendly enough.'

'They're very curious creatures. As long as they're left well alone on land, and you wait for them to come to you in the water, there's nothing to fear.'

'Apart from it biting my fin! I was very grateful to have a thick layer of neoprene between me and its teeth.'

'He was only checking if you were edible.'

'I hope not!' She dissolved into laughter as Luke grinned. 'You're winding me up.' She had a moment when she longed to lean over the table and kiss him. They were dancing around each other, neither one wanting to mention the earlier moment. How long could they ignore it?

A waiter came to her rescue. 'Oh look, here's our dinner.'

There was a seafood platter for Luke and a 'Cornish paella' for Emma. The waiter put a bowl of chips with garlic mayo on the table along with a basket of bread.

'A feast. I'm not sure I can eat all this,' she said.

Half an hour later, however, there was barely a crumb left and the table looked as if seagulls had attacked it, with shells piled up in the near-empty chip bowl.

Emma added her final mussel shell to the pile. 'Wow. I'd forgotten the taste of seafood fresh off the boat.'

'I'd have thought Oxford was a gourmet city,' Luke said.

'This is gourmet enough for me.' Emma dipped the final chip in the mayo and sat back with a satisfied sigh. 'That was fabulous.'

He replied with a grin, 'In that case, do you fancy a pudding?'

Emma was stuffed but she didn't mind Luke having one. While he tucked into sticky toffee pudding with clotted cream, she cast an eye over her fellow diners, wondering if she would recognise any of them. One or two were vaguely familiar but it was an imposing middle-aged woman waiting on tables who drew her eye.

'Is that Lynne Stannard?' she said, amazed to see the first person she'd actually recognised. Lynne had barely changed since Emma's youth.

'Yeah. She helps out here when they're busy. That's Oriel, her niece — just getting off the motor boat at the pontoon.'

236

Lynne waved in the direction of the pontoon where Oriel was tying up. 'Really? Oriel was a little girl when I last saw her.'

'She runs the gift shop, Cornish Magick, now.'

'I saw it had had a makeover. Bit different to the dusty old place I remember. Dad used to laugh at the 'hippy-dippy crap' in there. He never found out I'd bought a crystal . . . I still have it, or did. I had to clear some of my stuff out of the flat. Most of it's in storage in a friend's shed.'

'Do you miss the city?'

'In some ways. Oxford's a beautiful place, even in the rain, and you can't say that about most cities. And I can't stay with Maxi forever. It's not fair.'

'No.'

Having polished off the pudding, Luke pushed his bowl away. Shortly afterwards, Lynne Stannard swooped on them, her eyes wide. Emma braced herself. Lynne had quite a loud voice that attracted attention.

'Oh, my word! I thought it was you! It's Emma, isn't it? Emma Pelistry?' she trilled. 'Bet you don't remember me!'

'Of course, I do. Hello, Mrs Stannard.'

'Oh, do call me Lynne. Everyone does.' She planted her hands on her hips and grinned at Luke.

'Evening, Lynne.'

'Well, how lovely to see you two lovebirds back together.'

'We're not!' Emma exclaimed.

Lynne held up a hand. 'Oh, my mistake. I am sorry. Only seeing the two of you cosied up here, I just assumed you were a thing.'

'No, we're not. We're in the Beachcombers' group

but we're here because we just rescued a dolphin,' she said, aware of Luke sitting opposite her. She didn't want to catch his eye for so many reasons.

'A dolphin? How exciting.'

'It was.'

'I see.' Lynne smiled. 'Well, if you've finished, I'll clear away, shall I? Would you like coffee?'

'No!' Emma said quickly. 'No, thank you. I'm full.' She patted her stomach, still unable to look at Luke. She regretted how vehemently she'd denied she and Luke were together. Even if they weren't and she didn't want anyone to think that.

'I think we'd better have the bill, please.' Luke spoke evenly enough but Emma was sure there was an edge to his voice. Annoyance? Disappointment?

'Good idea,' Emma said. 'Nice to see you, Lynne. Say hello to Oriel from us.'

'I will but you're sure to see her around, now you're back in Falford.'

'Oh, I'm not staying!' Emma shot back. 'I mean, not for long. I'm not sure yet. Haven't made any plans. Just here for a work project.'

Babbling again, Emma wished Lynne had never come to the table. She'd dug a hole it would take an age to climb out of.

'Oh, I see. What a shame,' Lynne said. 'Well, if you are around the village, Oriel's usually in the shop. She'd love you to say hello, I'm sure. I'll get your bill. Nice to see you both. Luke.'

'Thanks, Lynne,' Luke said warmly enough.

As soon as she left them, his tone became brisker. 'I'll get this,' he said.

'No. Absolutely not. After the free diving lesson, it's the least I can do to pay.'

'Fine, but you don't owe me anything.'

'I know but . . .'

'Why don't we go halves, if it makes you feel better?' he said curtly. 'And then, I'd better get off home. It's been a long day.'

Luke drove away first, leaving Emma sitting at the wheel of her car as the sun sank over the estuary. It had been a lovely day, yet it had ended sourly and she wasn't sure quite why. Either way, the warm glow left by their close encounter and cosy dinner had turned cold, and Luke hadn't even asked if she was going to the next Beachcombers event.

24

'Lynne Stannard tells me you've been out with Emma.'

'What?'

Luke's mum dished up the statement along with the apple crumble she'd just piled into his bowl on Sunday lunchtime a few days later. That was all he needed: his mother grilling him on top of the disappointing turn his day out with Emma had taken.

His mum held up a jug. 'Custard?' she said sweetly.

Wow, she'd waited her moment to drop her bombshell, knowing he was completely captive at the dinner table and softened up by a delicious roast.

'Thanks.' He waited for her to pass him the jug before answering. 'When did Lynne tell you this?' He was treading very carefully.

'I saw her this morning when I took some food to the cricket club ready for this afternoon's match. Lynne happened to mention she'd seen you together at the Ferryman the other night.'

'Bloody hell, Mum. The gossip in this place is worse than on board ship.' He attacked his crumble with the spoon, knowing he wasn't going to enjoy it anywhere near as much as he'd hoped.

'So, you *weren't* having dinner with her at the pub, then?'

'Yes, I was having dinner with Emma at the pub. We were starving after we'd rescued that dolphin, which you've doubtless heard about too.'

'A dolphin rescue? Lynne didn't mention that.'

'That's a miracle,' he muttered, angry with himself

for being drawn in.

'Don't be sarcastic. Who was on it?'

'Me, Shanthi, Ran and Emma.'

'Right . . . but *why* was Emma on a rescue with you? She's not in the wildlife group, is she? Unless there's something I've missed.'

Luke could have kicked himself. 'We'd been out on a dive and Ran called to say a dolphin was stranded in the estuary up the coast. I called the rescue team and we needed all the help we could muster.'

His mum pulled a face. 'This crumble's too sweet. Must leave out some of the sugar next time.'

'Really? It seems pretty tart to me.'

The sarcasm was lost on his mum. 'So. Was it an organised thing, this dive?' she probed.

'Mum! Why are you interrogating me?'

His mum frowned. 'I don't know what you mean by that . . . but Lynne says that Emma cut her dead when she asked if the two of you were going out together. Says she couldn't wait to let Lynne know she wasn't staying around.'

'Oh? Funny, but I didn't hear any of that and I was sitting opposite her.'

'Sorry if I got the wrong end of the stick, but that's what Lynne says. And she reckons Emma was very keen to let her know you and her weren't back together.'

Having thought the exact same thing himself, this was most definitely not what Luke wanted to hear — even second-hand.

'We're not,' he said firmly.

'OK. I only thought . . . I know you think I'm interfering but it's because I love you. I don't want you to be hurt again.'

241

Emma's words still rung in his ears. '*We're not together! I'm not staying.*' Even though he'd told himself she'd been caught off-guard by Lynne, those words had been on his mind far more than he'd wanted. The force behind her denial had surprised and disturbed him.

'I'm not hurt. I'm not a teenager. Neither is Emma.'

'I'm trying to help. I could say nothing but I'd never forgive myself if you ended up hurt. I've seen you growing closer and I don't need Lynne to tell me that. Emma's an attractive girl, clever . . . she may even think she likes you, but she'll go back to what she knows.'

'What's that supposed to mean?'

'That she hurt you badly. Treated you like dirt, just because your father got lucky!' His mother blew out an angry breath. 'She should have been happy for you that we'd had some good fortune.'

'But it wasn't 'good fortune', was it, Mum? Dad left us and spent all the money. It was a disaster for the Pelistrys. Emma was bound to be loyal to her parents.'

'Still no need to treat you like dirt. I know she blamed you for your dad finding it. That was totally unfair.'

'She saw it differently.' Luke felt slightly sick. He'd certainly gone off the crumble. His mother had no idea that he'd shown the journal to his dad.

'She'll always see things differently to us. Never think you're good enough. I wish she hadn't forced herself back into our lives. There are plenty of lovely young women out there who'd give their right arm to be with you. What about that nice Zoey? She's a lovely, caring girl.'

242

Luke knew it was hopeless to defend Emma further. His mother had made her mind up and was as immovable as granite.

'Yes, Zoey is a caring person,' he said wearily. 'But I'm not looking for a girlfriend and, Mum, I love you, but I don't need you to matchmake for me.'

'I'm only trying to look out for you. Why are you so teasy about it?'

Luke rolled his eyes. 'I am not teasy.'

'Yes, you are. Teasy as an adder.'

'I'm not teasy but I will be if you keep on at me. How would you feel if I interfered in your love life?' he cried in frustration.

'I don't have a love life!'

'What about the postman?'

'That's none of your—' She bit back the final word. 'It's different! Clive is a lovely, kind man. He's not a snob.'

Luke trod a narrow tightrope between reacting angrily and avoiding conflict. He believed his mother was trying to protect him, but he was long past the age of needing it.

'I think we should leave this, Mum,' he said firmly. 'Now, can I please get on with eating this crumble before it goes cold?'

They left the subject alone for a while. Luke pushed his half-full bowl away before his mother asked: 'Have you heard from your dad?'

'Yes. He's called a couple of times.'

'I suppose he wants money.'

Luke gasped. 'How on earth do you know that?'

'Because he *always* does. He's even sent me an email, saying he wanted a catch-up. He also mentioned that bar he bought and that he'd fallen on hard times.' She sneered. 'I've ignored it of course.'

'You should do! How dare he ask you for money,' Luke burst out, fired up with anger. 'It's bad enough him pestering me but he knows you're not flush with cash.'

'Don't worry, love, I won't be giving him a penny and neither should you. I know you've already bailed him out more than once.'

'I won't . . . but it's hard to ignore him. He is my dad.'

'It's emotional blackmail. Hard as it is, don't be taken in.' She hugged him. 'And let's not fall out over him or anyone else.'

'I've no intention of falling out for any reason.' He kissed her back. 'So, stop worrying about me, Mum.'

Knowing there was next to no chance of her not worrying, he drove home to the chapel along dusty lanes, with the window down and the tang of the sea on the breeze.

He was troubled by her comments about Emma and, no matter what her motives were, wished she hadn't interfered. Suggesting Emma didn't think he was 'good enough' was ridiculous. It had been crazy to think it fifteen years ago, and ludicrous now . . . Yet wasn't Luke himself still haunted by the same creeping fear that he could never live up to Emma's expectations?

What did it matter anyway? It wasn't as if he was looking to resume their relationship, was he? Even though they'd had a great time diving and, he'd thought, found a new connection at the rescue, it didn't mean they were going to pick up where they'd once left off. Emma had been very eager to let Lynne — and Luke himself? — know they weren't together.

244

As for Zoey, she was a nice, caring person, if a little full-on — he liked her and that was all. He couldn't choose who he fell in love with, that was the scariest thing about relationships. Emma seemed horrified by the idea of commitment, even if she'd made it clear she was still attracted to him physically.

He thought back to Emma's reaction: '*No! We're not together! I'm not staying.*'

Had she simply scared herself? Had she backed off because she felt too much — or too little? Or did his mother actually have a point?

Would she come through for him when the chips were down — and had she really learned to trust him again and forget the past? Would she ever?

Back at the chapel, Luke went through to the sitting room. It seemed huge and, even though the day was sunny, it felt cold. At the start, saving it from developers had felt noble, yet now he wondered if he had been right to ride in like some knight in shining armour. After all, it was way too big for one man and, for the first time since he'd bought it, he had a strange feeling that he had no right to be there.

25

'Morning.'

Emma threw open the doors of the chalet to Maxi. It was very bright outside but not as dazzling as her friend's smile.

'Ta-da! Happy school holidays! I brought some breakfast muffins. Kids helped me make them.' Maxi grinned. 'I made sure they washed their hands.'

Mirroring her friend's enthusiasm, Emma welcomed her inside. They'd had a quick chat about the dive but Maxi had been so busy at the close of the school term they'd had no chance for a proper catch-up. Emma had also had to mention she and Luke had a bite to eat at the pub, and let Maxi assume that Ran and Shanthi had been there too. She hadn't actually *lied*, simply not volunteered the information.

The almost-kiss — and the disappointment at the pub afterwards — were her and Luke's secret.

Emma put the muffins on the breakfast bar. 'These look great and smell even better but you can't keep spoiling me like this.'

'To be honest, it's great to have some adult company in the house now the school holidays are here.' Maxi spotted the paints and sketchpad covering the table. 'How's the project going?'

'Really well.' At least one thing was, Emma thought. 'Would you like to see some of the illustrations?'

'Love to!'

Emma opened the sketchbook. The dive and the rescue had left her bursting with ideas. She'd already

246

done several sketches and watercolours of dolphins, line drawings of seals, and painted the wavy kelp as the hair of a giant mermaid.

'Oh, Emma. These are gorgeous, just brilliant. I always love your work but these are something extra special.'

Maxi's praise gave Emma a quiet pride.

'It looks as if it was a really inspirational experience.'

'Well, I'd rather the dolphin hadn't been stranded but it was amazing to help it out. I've shown the illustrations to my agent and she was super pleased. We're going to send these latest ones to the publisher and add them to my website. My agent thinks I might get some more work off the back of them.'

'I'm not surprised. You look like you were in your element,' Maxi said, turning over a page with a diver — who might or might not have been Luke — up close with a seal.

'I wouldn't say *that*. I was very nervous at first but then I just got engrossed in all the wildlife and plants.'

'If you don't mind me saying, it suits you, being back here. Your cheeks are pinker and you look glowing.'

Emma's agent had said the same thing over their Zoom call, but Emma made light of it to Maxi.

'That's because I'm spending more time outdoors, not stuck in a city flat.'

'And stuck with Theo?'

'Yes. You know, I'm relieved we split up. I never thought I'd say that.'

'I think you had a very lucky escape,' Maxi said. 'Erm . . . will you be going diving again soon?'

'Oh, I don't know about that.' Emma recalled the

look on Luke's face at the pub when she'd denied they were an item. She'd panicked, not wanting any pressure on either of them. Not wanting a day that gone so well to be ruined by anyone else's assumptions or expectations. 'We're both really busy right now.'

Maxi nodded. 'I'll mind my own business.'

'I didn't mean it that way, Max.' She smiled. 'I had a good time; a much better time than I'd expected . . .' She thought back to Luke's face, so close to hers, their lips ready to meet. 'I don't know how and if I want anything to develop between us and I'm sure Luke doesn't know. I think it's all going well between us then something throws a spanner in the works.'

'OK. Well, I'll confess I didn't only come here to bring you muffins or solely to grill you about Luke. I've actually a favour to ask.'

'I might have guessed.' She laughed.

'Don't feel under any obligation at all, but I had coffee with one of my old antenatal club pals yesterday. She's a lecturer in the art school at Penryn Uni and they're running a summer school for the students the week after next. They'd only need you for a couple of hours one morning. I know it's short notice but she wondered if you'd mind going in and talking to the students about your work.'

This was most definitely not what Emma had been expecting. 'They want *me*?'

'Well, who else?'

'I don't know. I don't give talks and I don't do fine art. Some people can be a bit sniffy about commercial art.'

'Frida — my friend — isn't precious at all. I showed her your website and she was seriously impressed. It would really show the students some of the career paths they can take. If it will stress you out, or you're

248

too busy, of course, no problem.'

Bless Maxi, Emma thought. She'd given Emma a home for the summer and welcomed her so warmly. The least she could do was visit the university, surely?

'Do you want to think about it?' Maxi said. 'Though I do need to get back to her by the day after tomorrow, latest.'

'No. No. Tell her it's fine,' she said breezily. 'I'll do it. I need to get out of my cave.'

'Great! She'll be so thrilled and I think it will do you good, too. Will you be going to the next Beachcombers outing?'

'I'm hoping to.' Whether Luke wanted her to or not, Emma thought. 'What about you?'

'I can't. We're taking the kids back home for the weekend to see my mum and dad. Actually, that's one of the reasons for coming round. Will you be OK without us?'

Emma laughed. 'I'll miss you all but I think I can cope for a weekend.'

'Great. Please feel free to have the run of the house while we're away, though you know you're always welcome to drop in any time.'

'Thanks. You go and have a lovely weekend.'

'We'll try. The kids are already absolutely hyper at the idea of seeing Nana and Grandad. I don't think any of us will get much sleep.'

* * *

It was with trepidation that Emma went to the weekly Beachcombers clean, even though she hadn't been specifically invited. News of the dolphin rescue had

249

spread around Falford like wildfire and everyone wanted to know about it.

Ursula was on Emma the moment she arrived.

'That sounds exciting, though not for the poor creature, of course,' Ursula said. 'Still, all's well that ends well.'

'Fancy you and Luke being on the spot together to help out,' Zoey said.

'We'd been diving and were nearby,' Emma replied as levelly as she could. Ears were twitching and now everyone knew they'd been out together.

'Diving?' Zoey squeaked. 'Oh, you are brave. You wouldn't catch me taking the plunge, even if Luke is super-experienced. He's never been able to persuade me.'

'I didn't know he'd tried,' Ursula said curtly.

'He's invited me on a beginners' course a couple of times, *actually*, Ursula.' It was the first time Emma had heard Zoey sound frosty.

'Ah, a *course*. Now I see,' Ursula said. 'Not on your own.'

'No,' Zoey said haughtily. 'Why would he? Getting tangled up in all that seaweed?' She shuddered. 'I'm also allergic to neoprene.'

'Best you stay on dry land, then,' Ursula said. 'Oh, here's the man himself. Hello, Luke! I hear you and Emma have been helping the local wildlife again.'

Emma gasped in protest. 'No! I can't take the credit.'

'Nor me,' Luke said. 'It was a team effort and the vet made all the decisions.'

Zoey sidled up to him. 'Oh, I've been dying to hear about it first-hand. Why don't we pair up for the clean-up this morning and you can tell me all about it?'

250

She didn't actually take Luke's arm and waltz off with him, but Emma was sure she was trying to get him on her own. Luke seemed more than happy to go along with it and spent the next hour with Zoey, while Emma teamed up with Marvin.

Back at the beach, as they loaded their finds into his truck, Luke seemed normal enough, on the surface. He laughed politely at everyone's jokes, but Emma knew him too well. She sensed his wariness, and recognised that the camaraderie they'd developed during the dive and the dolphin rescue had vanished.

Later Luke drove off to the recycling centre with the day's finds, shortly followed by Zoey. The others made their way home but Ursula and Emma stayed chatting by the car.

'Luke seems . . . not quite himself today,' Ursula said.

Emma's mood darkened. So, Ursula had noticed too. 'Really? He seemed happy enough around Zoey.'

'Happy isn't the word I'd have used. Subdued and troubled are more like it.'

'What?' Had Ursula's antennae picked up the tension between Emma and Luke?

'Mmm. I only hope it hasn't got anything to do with his father.'

'Harvey?' Emma said. 'I thought he was in Spain.'

'He is, but that doesn't mean he's not bothering Luke.'

'Bothering him? How do you know?'

'Lynne Stannard happened to let it slip to me at the jewellery class. Luke's mother told her. They're thick as thieves, you know.'

'I didn't,' Emma said, wondering what other gossip had reached Sue via Lynne.

'Have been for years . . . and it's wrong of me to pass on the gossip to you. I suppose I'm as bad as Lynne for repeating it but I can't help mentioning it. Luke seems troubled, and if Harvey's hassling him for money, that could be why he's not been himself today.'

'Harvey hassling him for money? After all this time?'

Emma recalled the distress on Luke's face when he'd received the call after their dive. She hadn't misheard. It had been Harvey.

'Everything OK?' Ursula asked her.

'Yes, fine.' No wonder Luke was distant, Emma thought, feeling sorry for him but relieved that there might be a reason other than fresh conflict between her and him. 'Poor Luke.'

'Hmm. Last thing he needs . . . but nothing we can do. Now, on a happier note, I wanted to ask you something. How would you like to come on an adventure to Govenek Cove with me next week? There's a low spring tide on Wednesday and I'm sure we'll find some fabulous sea glass. I value your discerning eye.'

Emma laughed, flattered by Ursula's comments. 'Govenek' was the Cornish word for hope, and it was an undeniably beautiful spot, but she'd often thought it must be an ironic name as it was the place where many ships had come to grief, including fishing vessels, as well as a yacht in recent times.

'It sounds very tempting but I'm not sure. I'm giving a talk at a careers fair at the uni art department that morning.'

'Oh, I see. What a shame. Normally you can only get there by boat.' Ursula rolled her eyes. 'Some people try to swim but, frankly, I think it's a tomfool idea. Much better to wait for a chance to walk when the tide's right. Shame you can't make it; there won't be another chance for a couple of years.'

'Oh. I'm well out of touch. Hadn't even realised there was a spring tide next week.'

'One of the lowest for a decade. The gullies will be exposed for an hour or so around lunchtime. It'll be virgin territory as no one else will think of going. Certainly no emmets and hopefully none of the other sea glass amateurs.' Ursula grinned. 'It will be fresh inspiration for you too, Emma. Even more inspiration than you've obviously already been getting.'

It was true. Emma was entranced by the idea of capturing the cove on a sunny day. The cove rarely had any shore exposed so was never visited by tourists. It always looked tantalising from above, with rocky spurs and gullies running perpendicular to the beach that created shimmering pools. With luck, the colours — aquamarine, jade and turquoise — would be stunning. And the gullies would be studded with anemones and urchins that were almost never exposed. It would be like having a glimpse of the sea bed without having to put on a wetsuit.

The comment gave her a shivery reminder of Luke leaning in closer after the dive, and the tension after in the pub. She dragged herself back to the moment.

'Lunchtime, you say? Well, I should be done at the university by then and it does sound tempting if we're careful of the timing. A big spring tide like that will come in as fast as it goes out.'

'Of course,' Ursula said. 'Which is why we'll be there on the falling tide and wade round at the earliest possible moment. I know a way through the rocks that leads up into gullies.'

Emma made up her mind. 'OK, you're on.'

'I'm running a workshop myself in the late afternoon so we can't hang about even if we wanted to. I'll double-check the tide times and we'll set up a rendezvous. We can park in that little space at the end of the track to Govenek Farm. Prepare to get wet!'

26

While Emma didn't share Ursula's excitement at the prospect of getting wet, she was looking forward to the expedition, especially as the morning had started out so bright and warm. She'd double-checked the tides, though she'd never dream of letting on to Ursula, and they arranged to meet at twelve-thirty.

This gave her plenty of time to go to the careers fair. Despite her misgivings, it had been far better than she'd expected, with lots of the students asking her how she'd found her first job and gone freelance. They'd actually thought it was a cool job to have, and she'd left with gratitude that she'd stuck to her guns about making her art her career.

She'd taken some of her published portfolio along with samples of the more recent sketches and watercolours she'd produced in Cornwall. As she'd been trawling through her portfolio, she'd found her sketch of Luke. That one was definitely *not* going to be on display to the students.

The reaction to the illustrations inspired by her diving and dolphin adventure had really lifted her. Meeting and talking about her work to other creative people had also made her realise she'd been isolated for too long. Cornwall suited her, creatively. That still didn't mean it was the right place for her, or the right time to return.

Boosted by the students' reaction, she was looking forward to the adventure at Govenek as she bowled along the country lanes. Red lights ahead brought her to a halt. Unsurprising; it was the height of the school holidays and the roads were busy and, anyway, she'd left plenty of time.

Half an hour later, though, she still hadn't moved.

People had switched off their engines and were in the road muttering. Emma got out of the car to see the lorry driver ahead stepping down from his cab.

'Looks like we're stuck here for the next hour. A vegetable truck's run into a bin lorry and it won't be clear for an hour.'

With weary resolution, Emma pulled out her phone and leaned against the car.

'Ursula? I am so sorry but I'm stuck in traffic. There's no way I can make it in time and I don't want to stop you from going while you have the chance.'

'Oh, what a bloody shame. It would have been so much more fun with you.'

'I'm gutted but if you wait for me you'll miss the tide. You go and enjoy yourself.'

Ursula hesitated before replying. 'I'll miss you but I promise to take heaps of photos for you. Meet me after my workshop for a coffee and I'll tell you all about it. I'll be finished at the village hall at five. I'll need it after that!'

With a sigh, Emma switched off the mobile. Spending the afternoon sweltering and breathing in diesel fumes was hardly ideal, but it couldn't be helped. At least by phoning early, she hadn't prevented Ursula from the rare chance to hunt for her precious treasure.

* * *

Hot, frazzled and thoroughly fed up, Emma rocked up at the village hall at quarter past four intending to poke her head around the door so Ursula knew she'd arrived. Instead, she found a small group of women talking outside. One of them was Lynne Stannard, who swooped on her before she'd even got out of the car.

'Ah, Emma! Am I glad to see you. Do you know where Ursula is? She was meant to run a jewellery workshop at Falford village hall at four and she hasn't turned up.'

'Hasn't turned up? Hasn't she called?'

'No, and she's not answering her mobile. It's most unlike her to simply not turn up and we're getting concerned.'

Emma's skin prickled. 'Is she at her studio?'

'No, we went round to check and the place was locked up. Her neighbour said she saw her go out before lunch and doesn't think she's been back.'

'Oh no.' Her stomach turned over. 'We'd planned to go beachcombing at Govenek Cove at lunchtime but I was held up in traffic. She said she'd go on her own but she fully intended to be back in good time for the workshop.'

'Govenek?' Lynne flapped her hands over her bosom. 'Oh dear. That is worrying. Do you think she might have got into difficulty?'

'I hope not. I really hope there's another explanation but . . . Look, I think I should go down to the cove now.'

'I hope she isn't still there. It's a nasty place to be cut off.'

'I know . . .'

'Should we call the coastguard?' Lynne asked.

Emma did a rapid calculation of how annoyed Ursula would be if the emergency services were called out on a wild goose chase on her account.

'Not yet. I'm sure there's an explanation. Tell you what. I'll whizz down there now and if I see her car parked and no sign of her, I'll phone them myself and let you know.'

'I can make some calls to people to see if anyone's seen her in the village,' Lynne said.

'Good idea . . . and could you get in touch with Luke and tell him what's happened? He'll probably be at the dive centre. I don't want to waste any more time.'

'Of course. Oh, I hope she'll be OK.'

'Me too.' Growing cold with foreboding, Emma jumped in her car and headed off to the twisty lanes around the estuary to Govenek. She hoped she'd done the right thing in not alerting the coastguard yet. After all, there might still be an explanation for her friend's no-show at the workshop. However, the more she thought about Ursula's eagerness to visit the cove, the more she felt that something bad must have happened.

After the early sunshine, thick clouds had rolled in, bringing a strong breeze. The main Silver Cove car park was almost deserted. After checking that Ursula's car wasn't there, Emma drove on and turned into the 'not suitable for motor vehicles' track that followed a stream downhill towards the cove.

Every bump in the road jolted her churning stomach.

Please don't be here, Ursula. Please have gone somewhere, anywhere else. Please have lost your phone, or run out of battery, or been carried away with looking for sea glass and forgotten about the workshop.

Oh why hadn't she tried to persuade her not to go alone to the cove?

'Oh no . . .'

There, parked by the gate, was Ursula's yellow 2CV. It seemed such a jaunty vehicle, so vibrant and quirky. So much of a contrast to the fear swirling in Emma's belly, threatening to overwhelm her.

Snatching up her phone, Emma jumped out of the car.

'Shit.'

There was not a single bar of signal in the valley. She could only hope that Lynne wouldn't wait to hear from her before calling for help.

Turning back to the land, she scoured both sides of the path, wondering if her friend might have gone for a walk along the cliffs above. In that case, she should've stayed up above. Maybe Ursula had tripped and fallen on the coastal path, or perhaps she'd decided on a walk on her way back to her car. That decided Emma. She would make a very quick scan of the beach then return to the car. Meanwhile, she checked her phone again. One bar briefly appeared but then vanished.

She'd have to drive back up the track to find a signal. Or see if she could spot Ursula on the beach.

In her haste, she almost slipped on the path down to the beach. Every moment, she longed to meet Ursula, annoyed for having been so long. Maybe with a tale to tell of how she'd had to stay and help someone in trouble on the beach, the bloody idiots . . . Mizzle hung in the air, wetting Emma's face and hair. The stony path was wet and slippery but she refused to slow down.

The sense of panic made her heart race, and she

was breathing heavily.

She reached the top of the beach. Rocky gullies ran perpendicular to the shoreline, pointing like skeletal fingers at the advancing tide. No steps led down, only a pile of boulders eroded by storms. Gone was the vibrant palette of colours she'd imagined that morning, replaced by grey waves breaking over black rocks under a drab sky.

'Ursula!'

Why bother calling? No human voice would be heard above the surf pounding into the cove. The boulders glistened with rain and weed, but somehow Emma slithered her way down to the flatter section, which was still untouched by the surf. Searching for a clue, she tried to recall their conversation.

It was the rocky outcrops that Ursula had been so drawn to: the places where she'd hoped to find sea glass. Their spiky ridges reminded Emma of Arlo's model stegosaurus. On either side, the gullies in between the rocks were already filling with water. As each wave rolled in, it slapped against the openings before rumbling into the gully and retreating.

At first, she saw nothing but then — her heart thumped wildly — on the next spine of rocks, she spotted Ursula, sitting halfway along, staring out to sea.

'Oh, thank God.'

Flooded with relief, Emma waved at her. 'Hello! Ursula!'

Ursula didn't hear or turn towards her.

She picked her way along the rocks, aware that the waves were already being forced up the gully by the rocky walls. It was only thanks to some nifty footwork that she was able to clamber up the next spine and made her way to Ursula, who was sitting near the cliffs, a few yards away.

At first, Emma had thought her friend was wearing a cream and scarlet scarf but then she realised . . . and her stomach lurched violently. The red was blood. Ursula must have slipped and cut her head. The fact she seemed oblivious to the injury wasn't a good sign.

'Ursula!'

Ursula glanced up. 'Emma! Hello. What are you doing here?'

'Looking for you. I'm so sorry, I couldn't come but we hadn't heard from you and so I came to find you. We need to get off the beach because the tide's coming in.'

'Get off the beach?' Ursula frowned. 'But I saw it! I saw my ring!'

'Your ring? Where?'

'In a rock pool.' Ursula stood up and pointed down the spine of the rock, swaying.

She must be concussed. Why else would she be sitting staring at the sea and behaving in such a strange way?

'You've hurt your head,' Emma said gently. 'We should leave now and have it looked at.'

Ursula reached up and touched her hair with an expression of faint surprise. 'Oh . . . it's only a scratch. I wasn't knocked out. That ring is there in that pool and I'm getting it!'

Emma was horrified. 'There's not time. The tide's on the turn. We'll be stuck and there's no phone signal.'

'Now, come on, Emma Pelistry. I didn't have you down as a wuss.'

'I'm not being a wuss! I'm trying to be sensible for

once in my life.'

Ursula laughed and then winced. 'I'm going to find my ring. The sooner I do, the sooner we can go home.'

'No, Ursula. We have to leave.' Emma reached for her hand.

'No! I've come so close, I'm not giving up now.' Waving Emma away, Ursula tottered down the rocky spine like a drunken tightrope walker.

Oh God, this was the last thing she wanted. Emma was petrified, expecting Ursula to slip and fall into the sea at any moment. Should she follow and risk tripping herself?

Keeping an eye on her friend, she tried her mobile again but the terrain was continuing to stifle any mobile signal.

Ursula had tottered further down the rocks, within splashing distance of the tide. She sat down and shuffled towards the pool. A large wave broke on the other side of Emma, spraying her with droplets. She looked up at the cliffs, hoping someone would see them from above, but the weather would be keeping many walkers away. There was a lobster boat out, but the fisherman was intent on hauling up his pots.

All she could do was watch and hope and try.

'Please be careful!' she shouted, slithering down the jagged spine herself.

Ursula was kneeling on the edge, one hand steadying herself, the other reaching into the pool, her fingers outstretched.

'Watch out!' Emma shouted.

A wave rolled in, smashing into the rocks, throwing spray high into the air. Foam and water cascaded over Ursula. Emma was now soaked too and had to grab a rock to avoid falling.

Ursula yelled and when Emma looked again she was clinging to the side of the spine, her torso on the rocks, her legs scrabbling for purchase.

'Help!' she screamed. 'Emma!'

Emma's heart nearly leaped out of her chest. 'I'm coming! Hold on!'

She crawled down the rocks, ignoring the pain from their sharp edges.

'Wave!' she shouted, seeing another breaker rolling in. The rocks seemed to shiver from the force of the impact, and she gasped at the shock of the cold water. 'Oh my God.'

She expected to see Ursula dashed on the rocks or flailing in the sea. Relief flooded her when she saw her friend perched on a ledge a foot below, coughing and spluttering from swallowing water. Her clothes were plastered to her and stained pink from the cut on her head. Emma fought back panic. No one was coming to help. She was alone.

Just her and Ursula.

She sat down, her own feet dangling above the pool, and stretched out her hand as far as she could. 'Ursula. Take my hand and I'll help you climb up here.'

Ursula gazed up, a deep frown between her brows. 'You'll never get me up there. A slip of a girl like you.'

'I'm stronger than I look.'

'I know that, madam! I've seen the way you treat Luke Kerr.'

'What?'

'At school. He'd do anything for you. Anything and yet you don't appreciate him.'

'At school? Ursula, we're not at school now.'

'Ursula? You cheeky thing. It's Ms Bowen to you. Even if we aren't in school . . .' Ursula's eyes seemed to cloud over and she looked around her, in confusion. 'Why are we here at the beach?'

She must think they were still at school; the head injury had thrust her back fifteen years. How would Emma ever get her to do as she was told now?

'You slipped and fell, Urs— Ms Bowen. You hit your head but you're all right. It's time we went back to school. People will be looking for us and we don't want to cause a fuss, do we?'

'No . . .' Ursula pursed her lips.

'Then, please take my hand so we can go?'

Ursula grimaced. Emma almost wept in frustration. Then she nodded her head. 'Yes . . . I suppose that seems a sensible course of action.'

It was bizarre. Sometimes, Emma was Ursula's student. A moment later, Ursula was the child needing to coaxed home. The sooner she could get her some help, the better — but first she had to somehow help her from the ledge onto the rocky spine.

Emma inched a few inches further forward, her shoulders now overhanging the edge of the rocks.

'Wave!' she shouted, feeling the tremor and roar building as the next set of breakers approached.

She slid back and clung onto the rock as hard as she could as the wave broke only metres away, drenching her in cold water. The salt stung her eyes and the back of her throat.

She coughed and her voice was hoarse as she cried, 'Ursula!'

Peering over the edge, she wondered if it would be empty and Ursula in the sea, but she was still there, flattened against the rock.

'Come on! It has to be now.' Emma's fingers were outstretched, touching Ursula's shoulder.

Her friend's pale face stared up. 'Don't risk your-self . . . Not for me,' Ursula said quietly, suddenly herself again.

'Climb up now and we'll both be out of here in a minute,' Emma said, ignoring her.

'You go. It's too late,' Ursula said. 'Go and be with Luke.'

'Not without you.'

'You silly, stubborn girl.' Every word was weary.

'I am. You're right. If you don't come, we'll both be gone. Come now before another set of waves rolls in and washes us both away.'

A few moments passed then Ursula took Emma's hand. She held it then got hold of her other arm.

'Push off from the rock. Push!' Emma urged.

Emma's arms and shoulders burned. Both she and Ursula were wet and the rocks were slippery and rough.

Ursula groaned. 'I can't.'

'One more effort! Push with your feet. Kick.'

Emma pulled again and Ursula's feet scrabbled on the rock. Emma didn't know how long she could hold on but she gave one last heave and Ursula's head and torso were on top of the spine of rocks.

'Hang on!' Emma cried, hearing another wave bearing down like thunder.

With one lung-sapping effort, she dragged Ursula beside her and they flattened themselves to the rock. Emma put her arm tight around Ursula as the wave broke over them.

Water filled her mouth and she felt the retreating wave tug at her lower body. It was trying to drag them both back into the sea, like a giant claw. As she clung to the rock and Ursula, she thought of the *Minerva*

265

sailors floundering in the ocean, fighting for their lives, waves tossing them around. She coughed, spitting out the water, salty tears blurring her vision. Was this what it had been like? Clinging onto the ship, wondering if every moment was your last? Hoping to be saved but knowing you might not.

'Em-Emma P-Pelistry . . .' Ursula was face to face with her. 'This is my fault.'

'It's no one's fault,' Emma said, her throat hoarse from the salt and shouting above the waves. 'And we have to go.'

She helped Ursula to her feet and, holding her elbow, guided her along the rocky spine to the flatter area near the cliffs and furthest away from the waves.

She looked down at the sandy channel between the gullies that she'd walked along not ten minutes previously.

It was full of swirling water. The waves were being forced up the narrow channel and who knew how deep it was. There was no way she could climb into it and up the other side with an injured Ursula in tow.

Behind them, the rocky cliff was vertical. There was no escape that way either.

'I caused this. I've endangered us both.' Lucid again, Ursula held her cut head, fear in her eyes showing that she now recognised the danger they were in.

'You haven't and we'll be OK, I promise.' Emma patted her arm, wanting to cry but realising it wouldn't help either of them a jot.

She pulled her phone from her jeans pocket, praying for a glimmer of signal.

Her hopes sank into the depths. Not only was there no signal, there was nothing at all. The phone was dead.

27

'Dad, we've been through this before. I'm more than happy to find you some help to sort it out. You can pick up the phone to make an appointment with our business advisor right now on the number I sent you but I can't give you any more money.'

Luke paced the quayside at the dive centre, his phone clamped to his ear. He'd finally faced up to returning his dad's calls and now felt he was living in Groundhog Day.

His father wanted another bailout for his bar and Luke simply couldn't offer it. When Harvey had suggested he borrow more money against the Old Chapel — or even sell it to go into business with him — Luke had cracked.

'Now, I have to go. I'm at work. Call the advisor and then we'll discuss it.'

He cut off the call but he couldn't go back into the office immediately. He'd been thrust back fifteen years, to that afternoon when he'd had the journal hidden in his schoolbag. A time when his father had emotionally blackmailed him into revealing a secret he should have kept. Into *betraying* Emma.

Maturity and experience had made him accept that nothing would ever be enough for a man like Harvey. Harvey was the weak one — the coward — and the realisation made Luke desperately sad.

'Luke!' Ran hailed him from the door of the centre. 'Phone call for you.'

Luke jogged up to the door. He needed to get his

head together before he spoke to a customer. 'Can you get a name and I'll call them back?'

Ran grimaced. 'It's Lynne Stannard. I think you should take it. It sounds urgent.'

'So, can I make doubly sure, you said they'd gone to Govenek Cove?' Luke repeated a minute later.

Lynne's voice crackled again. The line wasn't great and Lynne was very agitated. His own stomach knotted as she relayed Emma's message to him.

'And Emma set off half an hour ago?' he said, slowly. 'And you haven't heard from her since?'

'It's probably been forty minutes because we were all talking about how late it was. I'd come out of the village hall to get a signal. We were all so surprised that Ursula hadn't turned up for the class. It's so not like her, Luke. And Emma said she might know where she'd gone and went to find her and told me to phone you.' Lynne's voice rose in pitch. 'And I have been trying, but you weren't answering your mobile and the phone at the dive centre was engaged . . . Oh, I wish I'd driven over myself or called the coastguard!'

'It's OK, I'll do that right now. Don't worry, I'll go to the cove myself. I'd better go. Thanks.'

Luke put the phone down, his troubles with his father swept aside.

Govenek Cove. Hope Cove. No-hope was more accurate, Luke thought with a shudder. The tide would be coming in fast and, being a spring tide, it would climb even higher up the beach than normal. Ursula must have got into difficulties there. Luke knew her too well and Lynne was right: she wouldn't simply miss a class without a very good reason — or barring an accident.

Clearly, Emma had thought the same or she

269

wouldn't have asked Lynne to call him if she wasn't worried. Now they both were in trouble.

Luke stared at the phone for a few seconds, before making a decision. He jogged over to Ran, who was hanging up wetsuits.

'Ran, is the RIB fuelled up?'

'Yeah. I filled it this morning. Why?'

'I need to get over to Govenek Cove fast. Emma and Ursula might be in trouble.'

Ran swore under his breath. 'Jesus. What can I do?'

'Call the coastguard for me. They might be fine but I'd rather get the lifeboat out on a false alarm than not call them at all. I'll launch the RIB.'

Five minutes later, Luke was on his way out of the estuary, opening up the throttle as he reached the open sea. Even at top speed, it would take twenty minutes to reach the cove. Emma and Ursula could have been on the beach for over an hour — if they were even there.

He sincerely hoped the RNLI would reach the cove well before he could.

The sea was only moderately choppy but the wind had freshened and the swell and the high tide would mean the cove would fill very quickly. He kept pushing aside visions of finding Emma and Ursula swept off the rocks. He could only pray he'd have a call from the women or Ran to say they were safe and it had all been a fuss over nothing.

The dark cliffs of the cove had come into view when Ran radioed. 'I've called the coastguard, but the helicopter's been scrambled for another job on Scilly. The Lizard in-shore lifeboat's on its way. ETA twenty minutes.'

'I'm almost there myself. No sign of them yet

but . . .'

Luke stopped. What he saw gave him brief hope yet immediately plunged him into despair.

'They're here,' he said. 'Tell the lifeboat to hurry. I don't think they have much longer.'

Emma and Ursula were pressed against the cliffs. Some of the larger waves were already breaking a few feet from them, having surged up the gullies, and pouring over the rocks at their feet.

'Shit.'

Luke had never taken dives to Govenek, access was far too tricky, and his knowledge of the underwater terrain was sketchy at best. All he knew for certain was that it was treacherous, with submerged rocks waiting to rip a hole in the hull. He steered the boat as close as he dared. The last thing he wanted was to wreck the propellor, putting them all in danger.

Emma had seen him and was waving wildly. He couldn't hear her words, only vague snatches of noise carried by the wind. She was holding onto Ursula, supporting her. Luke could see they were soaked through and Ursula seemed very weak. Something more must have happened other than them just being cut off, which raised the stakes even higher.

A large wave picked up the RIB and dumped it down again, perilously close to the rocks.

Keeping the boat as close as he could, he shouted to Emma to try and signal the lifeboat was on its way. She couldn't hear and started to walk along the rocks towards him but soon headed back when the spray broke over her.

Frantically, Luke looked for a way to manoeuvre the RIB near enough to attempt a rescue. It might be possible to slip through the deeper gully at the far side.

The lifeboat would have to do that, when it came, but they'd have an experienced helm in charge, and crew who could assist in a rescue.

'Hold on! Help's coming!' he shouted.

Emma seemed to reassure Ursula. They must be terrified, and they were right to be. They were in serious danger.

He grabbed the radio, while trying to keep the RIB steady. 'Any ETA on the lifeboat? Emma and Ursula are stuck on one of the gullies and they can't stay there much longer. The next big wave might wash them off and, anyway, the place they're standing will be underwater soon.'

'No ETA yet. I'll find out now.' Ran ended the call.

The next few minutes were agony and there was still no sign of the lifeboat. How much longer could he afford to wait? Luke couldn't watch them drown or be swept into the sea. He could never live with himself. He had to do something, yet it was a big gamble.

Surely that's what he'd been trained for though: to take calculated risks. This was as big a risk as he'd taken when he decided to rescue the skipper from that wheelhouse. Bigger, because it involved people he cared about, which was sure to affect his judgement.

Ursula screamed. Luke's heart almost leaped out of his chest. Emma was holding her tightly as seawater swirled around their ankles before pouring back into the gully.

'Hold on! I'm coming!' he called.

He steered the RIB towards the gully at the far side of Emma and Ursula. It was a little wider and deeper than some of the others and if he was very careful — and very lucky — he could slot the boat in

272

close so they could — hopefully — clamber aboard.

So many 'if's.

The radio flared into life. 'Ran?'

'Sorry. The lifeboat's been diverted to children in the water off Porthmellow beach. The helicopter's on its way but it'll be twenty minutes.'

'They haven't got twenty minutes. I'm going to try and get them.'

Luke waited for the next wave and rode the RIB into the gully. Its sides almost touched the rocks and it was bucking up and down on the swell.

'Wait!' He held up his hand to stop the women coming any closer.

'OK,' Emma called, her arm tight around Ursula's back.

Luke waited for the next set of waves to roll in, gentler this time though it took everything to keep the RIB steady. Was he making things worse? One slip and they could fall into the sea.

'Ready?' he shouted, hearing a grinding noise as a rock brushed the underside of the hull. He couldn't stay here more than half a minute tops.

Emma guided Ursula to the edge of the rocks.

'You'll have to help her in while I keep the boat steady!'

'Luke . . .' Ursula murmured.

'Get in the boat, Ursula,' Luke ordered. 'Now.'

'I — can't.'

'Go!' Emma ordered, shepherding Ursula towards the edge. As the boat rose, Emma manhandled her into the boat. She stumbled and slipped but landed on her feet. Luke breathed again but only for a moment.

'Jump!' he shouted.

The boat dipped on the falling swell as Emma

273

leaped from the rocks and into the RIB. The boat shook as she landed in the bottom. There was no time to see how she was. He put the throttle into reverse. The engine screamed as he fought the tide to power it backwards out of the gully.

Ursula was sitting in the boat, groaning.

'Emma! Are you OK?'

'Y-yes. A bit winded but I'm all right. It's Ursula I'm worried about.'

Out of immediate danger from the rocks, Luke had time to look at his old teacher. His relief at being in deeper water was swamped by her pale face. She was leaning against Emma, clearly in shock. What had he done? What if she had a spinal injury, he could have paralysed her — or worse. His only consolation was that Emma had a few grazes but seemed unhurt otherwise.

'Are you OK?' he asked. 'Stupid question.'

'I am but Ursula . . .'

'The lifeboat and helicopter are on their way . . . but I didn't think you could wait . . .'

Emma gazed up at him. 'We couldn't.'

As Ursula lay quietly in the boat, Emma stared at the cliff where they had been standing. A huge wave rolled in and crashed against it.

'I thought we'd be swept away,' she said.

'You're safe now,' Luke said, thinking Ursula was anything but. 'Proper help will be here soon. I'll radio the coastguard so they know where we are.'

As he steered the boat towards home, Luke could only pray he'd done the right thing.

274

28

Emma hadn't thought it was possible to be this cold.

Not even when she'd fallen in the sea, trying to find her bloody shoes. How ridiculous that seemed now . . . and funny.

This wasn't funny. It was the most terrifying thing that had ever happened to her in her life.

She sat in the bottom of the RIB with her arm around Ursula. The boat was almost at top speed, and the noise of wind, waves and engine was deafening. Her teeth were chattering and the wind cut through her like a knife. She'd refused to cover herself with Luke's waterproof coat, tucking it around Ursula instead.

'How long w-will it take?' She had to shout to Luke.

'Fifteen minutes,' he said.

She nodded, unwilling to voice her darkest fear: that Ursula didn't have fifteen minutes. She was slipping in and out of consciousness. Muttering one moment, then seeming as if she wanted to go to sleep the next.

They scudded over a wave and the boat bucked.

Ursula groaned and shook off Emma's arm, frowning. 'Emma Pelistry? What are you doing?'

'Trying to help you,' Emma said in desperation.

'Help me? I don't need help,' she said in disgust.

'You do today, Miss. You've hurt your head.'

'My head? Psshh. There's nothing wrong with me! I'm as strong as an ox.'

'You fell over,' Emma said. 'On the beach. Please try to keep still.'

Ursula shook her head. Fresh blood oozed out of

the cut. 'You never do as you're told. Always wanting to go your own way. Thinking you know best and I can't teach you anything.'

Luke glanced round. 'How is she?'

'Concussed, I think. She's gone back to our school days.'

'What are you saying?' Ursula demanded.

The radio made a noise. Luke picked it up and spoke into it but Emma couldn't hear what he was saying.

'The lifeboat's ten minutes away but we could be back in Falford by then.'

'I hope so.' Emma willed the boat to fly over the waves.

Ursula piped up. 'Is that Luke Kerr? That quiet boy from Roseberry Farm. He worships you. Are you treating him badly again?'

Worshipped her? 'It is Luke but we're not at school,' Emma said. 'We're trying to help you, Ursula.'

'It's Ms Bowen to you!' Ursula declared.

Luke glanced behind again, frowning.

'She thinks we're at school,' Emma called. 'She needs help.'

'I don't need help! I keep telling you. Let me go.'

To Emma's horror, Ursula tried to stand up, but collapsed back in the RIB immediately. She let out a whimper. 'My head is sore. What happened? Why are we in a boat?'

'You fell on the rocks, at Govenek Cove, Ms Bowen.'

'Govenek Cove? Why are we here? What's happening?' Her tone was suddenly childlike. She'd slipped from teacher to student in a moment.

'We'll soon be back in Falford. Help's on its way. Please, try to lie still and let us help you,' Emma

276

pleaded.

'I'm rather chilly . . .'

'She's getting very cold,' Emma called.

'Not long now, Ms Bowen,' Luke said. 'Look, there's the entrance to the Falford estuary.' He pointed ahead.

Ursula rested her head on Emma's shoulder. 'Good . . . I am a little tired . . .'

Emma's heart sank even further. She'd rather be told off by her old teacher a thousand times than have this subdued woman depending on her for life itself. It was a miracle they'd even made it this far, off the rocks and into a boat . . . on their way home. What if it was all too late? What if she, Emma, had failed Ursula when she needed her most?

'Lifeboat!' Luke shouted. 'But we're home now.'

Emma scanned the waves, and saw the orange boat approaching.

'I'm terribly weary,' Ursula murmured, her eyes fluttering.

'Don't go to sleep now,' Emma said with a brightness born of desperation, as she cradled Ursula in her arms. 'We're nearly home!'

Luke cut the engine as they slipped into the estuary and the dive boat centre came into view, an ambulance waiting on the quayside, its blue light flashing. In an instant, the relative quiet was shocking, just the slap of the waves on the hull audible.

'How is she?' Finally, Luke's calm had cracked, his voice betraying his concern.

'She keeps nodding off.' Emma exchanged a look with him, telegraphing all her fears.

He steered the boat to the quayside and cut the engine. Ran was waiting, taking the rope.

'Ursula,' Emma said gently. 'We're home. Help's

277

here. It's going to be OK.'

Ursula looked at her and smiled, suddenly herself again. Her adult, feisty self. 'Thank you . . . Emma. And Luke. I'd be a goner without you.'

'No, you wouldn't,' Luke said, finally able to turn to her, crouching low in the boat and holding her fingers. They seemed so small and fragile in his.

The paramedics were hurrying to the steps from the quay, led by Ran.

Ursula gripped Emma's hand. 'You and Luke. You shouldn't wait a moment. Don't make my mistake.'

'Come on,' Ran offered Emma his hand. 'Let's get you warm. Let the medics do their job.'

'Go,' Luke said. 'I'll stay with Ursula.'

'You'll be OK now, Ursula,' she said. 'Ms Bowen, it will all be all right . . .'

Aware she was shivering violently, Emma let go of Ursula's hand and took Ran's. He helped her out of the boat and put a coat around her shoulders as the paramedics climbed on board.

'Thank you,' Emma said to Luke. She longed to pull him close, hold him tightly and show him how grateful she was. Now she knew that he would risk anything for her.

Ursula's words came back to her:

'Is that Luke Kerr? That quiet boy from Roseberry Farm. He worships you. Are you treating him badly again?'

Luke had been deeply in love with her and she'd been in love with him, but she'd been young and unsure of what the future held, and scared of her parents' reaction. Then she'd discovered her father and Sue's affair and found it almost impossible to carry on seeing him, sleeping with him, hiding a terrible secret from him. Yet she'd still loved him and she felt the same now.

She struggled to stifle her tears of relief and gratitude. 'I don't dare think about what would have happened if you hadn't come for us,' she said.

Luke held back. He almost flinched and his reply cut her to the core.

'No need to thank me,' he said gruffly. 'I'd have done it for anyone.'

29

'I'm a silly old fool.'

These were Ursula's first words, the moment Emma walked through the door of the cottage the following afternoon. She looked tired and had an impressive bruise on her cheek and Steri-Strips on her temple but the eyes and mind were clearly as sharp as ever.

'No, you're not. It could have happened to anyone.' Emma's words echoed Luke's own after the rescue. They'd tumbled over and over in her mind ever since, like shingle in the surf. She knew they didn't stem from his natural modesty alone. The words had hurt and she could only pray he didn't mean them. She hoped he'd been trying to protect himself from her after she'd dismissed him in the pub — or was there something deeper behind the brusque comment?

The sitting room was dappled in sunlight. 'You're being kind. It's because I was obsessed with finding that bloody ring. I put you in terrible danger.'

'I was fine. I was worried about you.' Emma smiled. 'Can I make you a cup of tea?'

'Thanks, but I'm up to making a cuppa. It's a lovely day. Let's go through to the garden. That's an order from your old teacher.'

Emma sank onto a garden chair, breathing in the scene. The views over Falford were incredible on this bright July afternoon. The estuary sparkled as if it had been sprinkled with a million diamonds and the sky was that intense cobalt of a late afternoon at the height of summer. Flowers nodded in the breeze, their colours vibrant shades of pink, orange, purple, yellow, and the scent of honeysuckle filled her nostrils. Even the bees seemed loud as they buzzed from bloom to bloom.

It was good to be alive. It was a miracle.

Tears made her eyes scratchy so she got up, knowing it was the shock of the experience that was making her feel emotional. Ursula had been kept in overnight but released when she'd warmed up and a scan had shown nothing serious. Emma had been looked after in the dive centre by Ran and the staff. Shortly after, Maxi had arrived, horrified to hear about their ordeal yet hugely relieved they were OK. She'd insisted on taking Emma home and cosseting her while Luke followed Ursula to the hospital. He'd kept her updated on Ursula with a few brief texts, but Emma hadn't seen him since.

'Coffee for you. Chamomile tea for me.' Ursula put two mugs on the metal bistro table. 'You look on edge. Please try to relax.'

With a nod, Emma sat down again.

'Thank you.'

'I think I should be doing the thanking. You risked your life for me. I should tell you off...' Ursula smiled. 'And yet, out here with you on a beautiful day like this, how can I? I'm grateful to be alive.'

'Luke saved us both,' Emma said.

'Yes... you both did.'

'What have the doctors said about your head?'

'That I'm remarkably unscathed apart from mild concussion. Apparently, I'm out of danger of secondary drowning. I dodged a few bullets yesterday.'

'We both did.' Emma sipped her coffee, which tasted like the best she'd ever drunk. She wondered how long the wave of euphoria would last. When would she go back to taking life for granted? Would she ever?

'My memory of the events is hazy. It's like one of those damn TV recordings where you keep getting interference so you're only getting snatches of the story. I can't decide if that's a blessing or a curse.'

'I'd err on the side of blessing,' Emma said.

'Hmm. Yet you can remember it all. Luke too.'

'I'm not sure I can remember the details. I'm not sure I'm ready to. I think I'll have to let it drip-feed . . .' Emma said.

Ursula's keen eyes observed her over the rim of the mug. 'That scary?'

'In the moment, I could only think of what to do, how we could possibly get out of the situation, but yeah, it's not something I'd ever like to repeat.' Emma wasn't going to embarrass Ursula — or open up to any further comments about Luke — by reminding her.

'The medics said I was 'confused'.'

'You were cold and had a concussion.'

'Yes, but they said I kept going back to the past. I was treating them like children. The consultant in A&E had been at the school. He said I insisted on being called Ms Bowen.'

Emma had to smile. 'Really?'

'Yes. Was I doing this in the boat?'

Emma didn't know what to say. 'Um . . .'

Ursula lifted her eyes. 'Good God, I must have been talking some rubbish.'

'I wouldn't say it was rubbish.'

'Come on, girl. Spill. I need to know the full horror.'

'Well, I can't remember all of it. Not the exact

282

words. I was more concerned about making sure you were OK.'

'For which I am eternally grateful. Now let's have the truth.'

Not for the first time, Emma was thrust back onto the boat as Luke sped home to Falford, and she cradled Ursula in her arms.

'*Is that Luke Kerr? That quiet boy from Roseberry Farm. He worships you. Are you treating him badly again?*'

Ursula glared at her expectantly. Emma couldn't bear to repeat the words verbatim. They were too painful and hit too close to home. She gave an edited version.

'You asked if Luke was there, the boy from Roseberry Farm.'

'Is that all?'

'You said something about not wasting time and not making mistakes.'

'Oh . . .' Ursula heaved a sigh. Emma wondered if she'd set her up then Ursula's bright eyes pierced her. 'I wasn't babbling total nonsense. You should seize the day. You and Luke. Talk to him, be totally honest about how you both feel. I don't want anyone to live with the regrets I've endured by not marrying Michael before he went off to war. At least we'd have had more time together. Show you're committed. Commit.'

'It's not that simple. I want to stay but I can't live in Maxi's lodge forever, much as I love her and the family.'

Ursula shook her head, her voice laced with frustration. 'It's always later than you think. Hasn't yesterday shown you that?'

'That's the thing. It's complicated. I'm not sure . . .' Emma stopped, picturing Luke's momentary look of

283

horror as he'd found them on the rocks. The way he'd risked his own life to save them. His calm strength on the way home.

'I'm not totally sure about how I feel, and even if I were . . . I certainly have no idea what Luke's feelings about me are. It's been a long time, there's so much history, so much bad blood.'

'The only history that matters is *your* history. You and Luke: nothing your damn parents have done. Their mistakes are theirs. You and Luke should only be concerned about making your own story. The here and the now: the future. What is it with you and him?'

What is it? It's because I'll never forgive him for being my first love. For being the man that all others had to live up to. For leaving me incapable of loving any man with that intensity ever again. For leading me to think anyone else could make me feel the same. For coming into my life too soon. For being the right man at the wrong time. For our parents making life complicated . . .

None of it his fault. None of it mine.

'I — I — can't . . . it's . . . complicated.' Emma was overwhelmed by a maelstrom of emotions she wouldn't dream of voicing to Ursula. They were feelings she would share only with Luke and she couldn't see how she could ever be brave enough to tell him.

'I need to tell you something that I'm not proud of,' said Ursula. 'I didn't behave well towards you at school. It was two years after Michael was killed in action and I wasn't in a good place. You and Luke were close, I could see it. You — you seemed to dismiss him. Be reluctant to commit. He was besotted, deeply and hopelessly in love with you, and that made me angry. I wanted you both to have careers and adventures but I wondered if you'd ever find someone that perfect again. I knew you were too young but what if the person who's perfect comes along at the start of your life? What do you do then? You never found anyone else after Luke, did you?' Ursula said.

Emma thought of Theo, only her second remotely 'serious' relationship since she'd left school. Despite their new honesty, she certainly wasn't ready to tell Ursula about him. 'That was a very long time ago. We were eighteen and my parents were dead against it.'

'Yes, but when you've found someone — no matter how young you are — it's too late. You might dismiss it as youthful infatuation and move on — but you might also realise that they were the one. Too late, if you've married someone else who never lives up to that first flush of love.'

'Ah, but I've never married anyone else,' Emma shot back.

'Or found anyone who lived up to Luke?'

'Like I say, I was young. I still am. I've had a good career, good friends, I've travelled and I make a living doing what I love. Not many people can say that. I'm very lucky, even with what happened with Mum and Dad.'

'Forgive me for disagreeing but I have to say that work, friends — they're incredibly important, but if you've already loved and lost, there's always a gap in your life that can't be filled except by that person.'

'That's a bleak prospect.' Emma felt a shiver run down her spine. 'And things were — are complicated between me and Luke,' she added, desperately.

'Mmm. I've no doubt you feel they are . . . I've said my piece and I can do no more,' Ursula said briskly. 'I've no desire to make your life even more complicated, and I might not be able to solve your romantic dilemmas, but I think I can help with a more practical issue. I wanted to talk to you about it yesterday when we were meant to go on our beachcomb but circumstances and all that. Never mind, now will do.'

'What's that?' Emma said, relieved to be let off the hook but wary of what might come next.

'Jermaine popped round earlier. He's decided to move out of his place at the craft centre.'

'Oh no,' Emma said. 'Surely he's not thinking of leaving?'

'Well, he's getting on a bit and he wants to have more time to spend with his family up country so he doesn't need his working studio any longer . . .' Ursula pressed her lips together. 'It's a shame but people move on,' she said firmly.

'He's such a lovely man. He'll be missed.'

'Yes. But I'm not his keeper,' Ursula said sharply. 'Anyway, he's looking for a tenant. It's a studio with a flat above it, slightly away from the hustle and bustle of the main centre. You don't have to sell your work from the studio if you don't want to, but it's a lovely place to work. I've seen it and the light is beautiful and you can see the sea from it. You wouldn't be far from Maxi and Falford . . . and close to Silver Cove, of course.' Ursula paused. 'Or me. I'm not sure if you'd consider that a blessing or a curse.'

'It — it sounds ideal,' was all that Emma could reply.

'Ideal, perhaps, but is it right for you?' Ursula held up a hand. 'No, don't answer that. I realise I've dumped this on you with no warning but, as I say: seize the day is my motto. Jermaine is more than happy for you to view the studio. In fact, he's desperate for another 'true artist' as he calls it. When he

286

mentioned it a couple of days ago, I was in two minds whether to tell you and he said he'd give us — you — first refusal.'

'This is very kind of you, Ursula.'

'Kind? Pah! It's selfish. I enjoy your company, I want you to stay. Too many people are leaving.'

'I'll take that as a huge compliment,' Emma said, feeling a lump in her throat.

'It is.' Ursula laughed. 'Now, you have a think about it. Let me know if you want to view the place. No obligation whatsoever.'

'I will. I'll give it serious thought and I'll come back to you first thing.' Emma smiled. Giving the offer serious thought was the least she could do. Ursula had presented her with a huge opportunity: exciting and terrifying in equal measure. Like all unexpected offers of this nature, however, it also came with a huge side order of stress, of decisions to agonise over — and of consequences. Now was the moment when she had to decide to stay in Falford — or leave, with all the implications where Luke was concerned.

Finally, Emma thought her friend was looking tired so she got up.

'I promise I'll be in touch about the studio tomorrow,' she said.

Ursula's hug was warm, and went on longer than Emma expected, as if Ursula was scared that it might be their last. 'It's totally your decision. I won't pressure you at all.'

'I know. Thank you and . . .' Emma found herself on the verge of tears again. Even if she left Falford, she had an unbreakable bond with her friend, forged in their experience at the cove. Two people who'd thought they might not be here to even have this conversation would always have that powerful link.

'I'm glad at least, that we've rewritten our story,' Emma said.

Ursula patted her hand. 'So am I, my dear. So am I.'

★ ★ ★

Having messaged Ursula before breakfast to say she wanted to see Jermaine's unit, Emma jumped in her car for the ten-minute drive to the craft centre, which was in the opposite direction from Falford.

She knew the centre from her youth when it had been a small place converted from old farm buildings. In the past fifteen years, it had roughly doubled in size and was buzzing with high-season holidaymakers. The old units had been spruced up and some new ones built, though tastefully and in keeping with the character of the granite barns and outhouses. There was a small café, card shop, glass-maker, a unit selling soft furnishings and a chocolate-maker. The smell alone would be enough to lure her into work every day. She resolved to buy some chocs for Maxi and the kids.

Jermaine's two-storey flat was situated round the back of the more commercial units. It seemed to be an extension of the original farmhouse and was larger than she'd expected. She wondered if she could even afford it; she hadn't thought to ask Ursula about the rent.

The door was open and she could hear a faint whirr above a background of classical music.

The front half of the ground floor was a gallery space with jugs, pots and ceramics. There were some beautiful pottery seals, glazed in a dreamy blue. Again, Emma longed to buy one.

Emma glimpsed Jermaine through an open arch to the rear, sitting at the potter's wheel, intent on throwing a bowl.

It looked almost finished, so she waited until he'd stopped shaping it and slipped a wire under the base to remove it from the wheel before placing it on a board.

'Hello!'

He glanced up. 'Oh, hello, Emma. I'm so pleased to see you. I heard you had a lucky escape at the cove. Ursula made light of it, of course, but it sounded really scary.'

'I can't pretend it wasn't. I feel responsible for not going with her though I couldn't help it because I was stuck in a traffic jam. You can't help wondering 'what if?''

'Yes, though you know what she's like. If she makes her mind up, there's nothing you or anyone can do to change it.' He sighed. 'May as well try to hold back the tide.'

She nodded politely. 'That's true.'

'Anyway, I'm pleased you decided to take a look at the studio.' He wiped his hands on a rag. 'This is obviously the working part of the place. No prizes for guessing that!'

Emma laughed. 'It looks as if you've been busy.'

'Not as busy as I used to be. I can't produce stuff at the pace I did in my youth. I'm ready to wind down a bit. Obviously, I'll clean it up a bit for you, of course. The wheel and kiln will all be gone. I'm taking that with me when I move. Going to have a little shed at the bottom of the garden.'

'Ursula said you might move to be nearer your family.'

'Did she?' Jermaine frowned. 'Well, I *suppose* there's nothing to keep me here now and my daughter and her kids live near Bude. I'm ready to retire. Not from making pots. I'll never give that up!' He smiled, but seemed sad underneath it. 'I haven't quite decided where to move to yet. I might stay with my daughter for a while but one thing's for sure: I don't need all this space for one. Would you like a tour?'

'Yes, please. I'd love to.'

As Jermaine showed her round the unit, and the little 'cubbyhole' at the rear of the working area with its mini fridge, loo and gas ring, he became more animated. Emma was caught up in his enthusiasm. Even with the clutter, and clay, the pots and oven, largely covered in a fine white dust, it would be perfect.

'This is the business end, of course, but there's a small retail area at the front, if you want to sell direct to the public. Some of them make it down here to see the artist at work, and all that.' Jermaine rolled his eyes. 'I personally can't be doing with it but I'm friendly enough when I have to be.'

Emma laughed. 'I wouldn't be selling my work to the public. I work on commissions for publishers and design agencies.'

'Have you thought of doing your own thing too?' Jermaine said. 'That painting you sold at the barbecue is gorgeous. You'll see it upstairs in the flat. The public would love your work.'

'I hadn't but it's something to consider,' said Emma, thinking of Ursula's customers invading her working environment every day. Then again, her pictures had received a good reception at the barbecue. 'I'm not sure how good I'd be at dealing with the public,' she said with a smile.

'I think you'd be great but you don't have to worry about that. That's the beauty of this place. You can keep your doors closed if you want to, but still have the company of other artists. Pop up to the café for a chat or do your books over a coffee. Buy some chocolate or a cushion,' he added wickedly.

'I'd love to have other artists to chat to. It can get so lonely working in isolation.' Jermaine was really selling the lifestyle and it was very tempting to make a fresh start, but he had no idea of the other baggage it might bring. 'You make it sound great,' she said.

'It can be. There's the occasional country pong, of course, but Ursula tells me you're from round here anyway so that won't bother you.'

'She's right.'

'You play your cards close to your chest. Very wise.' Jermaine had a twinkle in his eye. 'Would you like to see the flat upstairs? There's a cracking view over the sea.'

'Yes, please,' Emma replied, half wishing the flat itself to be minging and tatty, but somehow knowing she was going to absolutely love it.

30

'You've changed,' Maxi said, bumping into Emma as she hurried across the garden early in the morning a couple of days later. Still in her dressing gown, Maxi had a large cup of coffee in one hand and a triangle of toast in the other. 'There was a time when I'd never have believed you would be up at the crack of dawn to go litter-picking.'

'We have to get to the beach early before it gets too busy,' Emma said.

'Yeah, but six-thirty? That's keen.'

'Some of the others have to go to work. Luke has a morning dive course scheduled and, anyway, I want to get back too. The book deadline's zooming up.'

'I admire your enthusiasm,' Maxi said. 'I wish I wasn't awake at this hour but Daisy decided to bring us breakfast in bed, which turned out to be a mug of cold water with a used teabag in it. I had to pretend it was delicious.'

Emma laughed out loud. With a wave, she checked her grabber was in the boot and jumped in the car. On her way, she couldn't help thinking Maxi was right. She *had* changed. Never in her wildest dreams could she have imagined she'd be almost enthusiastic at rising so early to clear up someone else's rubbish from Silver Cove.

The prospect of seeing her Beachcomber friends helped: it was Ursula's first time back after her accident. Part of her wanted Jermaine's unit. It really was perfect and opportunities like it were as rare as hen's teeth in Falford. She had to make a decision and soon.

As for Luke, she felt she was still on sands that shifted from one moment to the next. She might have expected them to have forged a closer bond since the rescue, but she'd barely heard from him apart from a message saying 'Good news' after she'd texted him to say Ursula had been in good spirits. She'd replied, saying 'See you at Beachcombers' and he'd sent a thumbs-up back. It felt as if he was using as few words as possible — or none at all.

Her pulse spiked when she saw him standing by the truck with Zoey and the others at the car park.

Ursula trundled up a moment later, in the 2CV.

'Oh my God!' Zoey shrieked. 'It's Ursula!'

She and the other Beachcombers flocked around Ursula like seagulls squabbling over a pack of chips.

'It's a miracle!' Zoey cried.

'Now, now. No fuss, please!' Ursula backed away. 'I can't bear it.'

'I don't care! I'm going to give you a great big hug, even if you'll hate it!' Zoey threw her arms around Ursula.

After Ursula had disentangled herself, Marvin insisted on shaking her hand. Zoey demanded an account of the rescue, but Ursula brushed off the calls for her to give the gory details.

'Look. I'm a tough old bird. It takes a lot to get rid of me,' she said. 'Now, please, can you stop reminding me that I was almost fish food and can we get on with the job? This beach looks like there's been a rock festival!'

Emma was in agreement. She didn't want to go over all the details of the incident. In fact, she had asked Ursula to downplay her and Luke's roles in it. She'd

293

already had one nightmare about it, and certainly didn't want to keep replaying it or have any thanks for helping Ursula. She sensed Luke felt the same.

They forged onto the beach, Ursula leading the way with her grabber held aloft like a warrior leading her army into battle. Zoey was by her side, taking her arm and declaring, 'We won't let you out of our sight.'

'Aren't I lucky?' Ursula replied. 'Come on, then, let's do the rock pools together. I can tell you all about my near-death experience.'

Ursula went off with Zoey, who was in transports of delight. Every so often, the air was punctured with a shriek of 'Oh my God, noooo!'

Amused, Emma hung back with Luke and Marvin. Silver Cove didn't quite look as if there'd been a festival, but after a busy weekend there was a lot of rubbish.

There were ripped bags for life, some stuffed with beer cans and soft drink bottles; punctured footballs, towels, broken flip-flops, odd clogs, and even a pair of swimming trunks.

'Who do they think will pick them up?' Marvin said in disgust. 'The bloody Wombles? I'll get the plastics if you collect the trunks.'

'Thanks a lot,' Emma said, laughing.

Marvin strode off but, to her surprise, Luke stayed with her.

'Yuk!' she said, picking up the tangerine 'budgie smugglers' in the jaws of her grabber. 'Not only no manners, but no taste either.'

She held them aloft.

'I dunno,' he said. 'I think they're pretty stylish.'

Emma blushed. 'I wouldn't have thought they're your colour.'

294

'You never know.' He gave a shrug of his broad shoulders and her heart skipped a beat. He came closer, his hair tousled by the breeze, his skin bronzed by the kiss of the sun. There was a hint of amusement in his voice that lifted her hopes. Perhaps peace could break between them out after all.

'Remember those pink board shorts you used to wear,' she said.

'I'd rather remember that yellow bikini of yours . . .'

'You still remember that?' she said in astonishment.

He arched his eyebrows. 'How could I forget?'

The years fell away as they shared a happy memory of their youth, when they were in the first flush of love. Even while she was holding a pair of old Speedos aloft, Emma still fancied him — more than ever. The urge to abandon the litter-picking, throw her arms around him and feel those lips on hers was almost overwhelming.

'Come on, you two. No slacking!' Marvin marched past them, on a mission.

'Better get on,' Luke muttered, the moment shattered.

Emma dumped the trunks in her bag, deflated as the abandoned football Luke had retrieved from the tideline.

As usual, the larger pieces of rubbish were the least of the beach's problems; it was the smaller bits, and the microplastics, ground into pieces so small that eventually they would be ingested by humans as well as animals.

By nine a.m., the beach was already filling up with early bird families and the Beachcombers retreated to their cars. Everyone had gathered at the car park, sipping from their water bottles and talking about their finds, when Ursula called them to attention.

'Right, you lot! Before you all go, I have some news,' she said, as if she was controlling an unruly class. 'We've been nominated for an award.'

'An award?' Zoey said. 'Oh my God.'

Emma glanced at Luke for a clue, but he seemed as nonplussed as she was.

'Don't get too excited,' Ursula said. 'It's only a 'green' community thing sponsored by the people who process our plastic recycling. I don't even know who nominated us. Might have been the parish council or an individual. All that matters is that we've won and it's being presented on Saturday night.'

'That's short notice,' Luke said.

'Apparently, they should have notified us last month but the email got lost.' Ursula gave an exaggerated sigh. 'What on earth happened to simply picking up a phone and talking to people?'

'Or sending a letter?' Marvin added.

'Ohh, what do we get?' Zoey cried. 'Black-tie event at the O2 Arena? Buckingham Palace garden party? A statue?'

Ursula laughed. 'Sorry. No. The email said the award will be presented at a hub of the local community on Saturday. As the village hall is booked for a Falford Flingers summer party, the only other place was the Ferryman. Looks like some PR person for the sponsors arranged it all. They've said they'll bring the award and also pay for a finger buffet.'

'I love a finger buffet,' Zoey said. 'I do a lovely mini quiche.'

'Ah, but you won't have to, Zoey. The Ferryman will be providing the catering and, as it's down the road from me, it means I can have a large gin and

296

totter home.'

'You're sounding more like your old self,' Zoey said. 'I might get a lift myself so I can have some prosecco.'

'I'll call for you if you like,' Marvin offered. 'I'm off the sauce because I've got to be up early on Sunday to take my girls to a trampolining competition in Exeter.'

While the others chattered and made arrangements to attend the 'ceremony', Ursula spoke to Emma. 'You'll be there,' she said, more a statement than a request.

'I'd love to though I'll feel like a fraud as I haven't really earned any right to an award. I only joined a couple of months ago.'

Ursula laughed. 'You've spent every week picking up other people's crap from a beach; I think that qualifies you.'

'If you put it like that, I will come, though only to celebrate with the rest of the gang. They deserve some recognition.'

'That's the spirit.' Ursula patted her shoulder. 'I'd expect nothing less.'

31

Luke had driven home from the beach, tasting salt on his lips and the memory of another kiss-that-never-was with Emma. Since the rescue, the thought of losing her had tormented him. He'd almost scooped her up in his arms and screamed at her in the boat: 'I might have lost you.' Lost her *again*.

He hadn't trusted himself to speak to her in case he cracked and told her exactly how much she meant to him. He'd ached to finish what they started after the dive, and whole a lot more. Every time he saw her on that beach, the memories snared him, wrapping their tentacles around him until he could barely breathe.

Except he didn't tell her because it would mean risking everything — again. He wasn't sure of her feelings and he never had been and she was leaving Falford sooner or later. Even if she stayed, would he be a part of that decision or her future? Because he didn't think he could remain in Falford, seeing her, talking to her and being so near and yet so far. It would drive him insane.

He was now on his way to his mum's to help her re-lay some of the flagstones on the rear patio. They were loose and rocking and one of them had already cracked. His mum was worried that one of her older friends might trip up.

Arriving at the house, he spotted her in the front garden, waiting for him, and a wave of guilt and responsibility swept over him. His mum had not been treated as well as she might have been by his dad or by life, and Luke had run off to the navy when she'd needed him most. Since he'd returned, he'd felt he should be making up for lost time, which was why he was making an effort to visit her more.

Getting out of the car, he put on a smile, determined to make this visit a happy one.

It was hot work lifting the old flagstones, putting fresh sand under them and bedding them in again. She'd helped him put the sand down and he was in the process of repositioning the slabs when she emerged with pint glasses of lemonade she'd made herself.

It was a childhood treat she knew he couldn't resist.

'Here you go,' she said. 'Bet you haven't had any of this for years.'

'Not since I left home.' He took the lemonade from the tray, enjoying the chill of the glass against his palms.

He drank half of the glass in two goes, savouring the lemony tang. 'Thanks. As good as ever, if not better.'

She beamed and they sipped the rest, while chatting about the garden and Clive, who was taking her to the Minack Theatre to see *Fisherman's Friends*. Seeing her happier than she had been for a long time, Luke began to relax.

Soon the job was done and they surveyed their joint handiwork with pride.

'Thanks, love,' his mum said. 'Looks so much better.'

'It was a joint effort,' he said, sharing with her a feeling of pride in their work. 'Oh, I meant to tell you,' he said. 'The Beachcombers have been given an award. Don't get too excited,' he added hastily, as her lips parted in surprise. 'It's no big deal, just a presentation by one of the sponsors at the Ferryman

299

on Saturday night.'

'That sounds exciting to me. You deserve it.' She lit up. 'I'm proud of you. For all you've done. You've been a good son to me.'

He smiled, though he wondered if he really had been good to her. Many times over the past few years, he'd thought he'd behaved selfishly, moving away for so long and leaving her to pick up the pieces with his father.

'I can even forgive you joining the navy now you've come back home,' she said. 'I hope you'll stay.'

'I'm happy here,' he said firmly and was rewarded with a flash of pure delight in his mum's eyes.

'Good. More lemonade?'

'Go on, then, it's thirsty work.'

She returned with another full glass for him and set it down on the table.

'Will Emma be at this ceremony?' she asked.

Luke was immediately wary. 'I . . . probably. All the Beachcombers are invited. Friends and family too, so if you want to come you'll be more than welcome.'

'Clive's taking me to Kev's Seafood Shack but we might call in the pub afterwards. I only asked about Emma because I heard she was looking round the craft centre the other day.'

'What?' Luke was wrong-footed. 'The Lizard Craft Centre?'

'That's the one. Angel Carrack mentioned it when I popped in to buy some of her new cushions. Did you know she does cushions now?'

Luke didn't, although cushions were the last thing on his mind right now.

'Oh?' He waited to get chapter and verse on what purchases Emma had looked at, bought or decided against.

'Well, Angel and I got chatting and she said Jermaine had told her that Emma was interested in his unit. The one at the back with the flat over it.'

'His unit?' Despite the heat of the day, the hairs on Luke's arms stood on end.

'It made me wonder if Emma was planning on becoming a permanent fixture, though I can't see it myself.'

'What makes you think that?' He spoke more sharply than he'd meant. He knew he was falling into a trap but was desperate to find out what his mum meant.

'Well, Angel reckons that Jermaine's not sure Emma will go for it. He said she made 'all the right noises' but wouldn't commit. He says it's the perfect place for an artist and the flat has a gorgeous view, but he told Angel he had a feeling she wasn't going to take it. Goodness knows why.' She shrugged. 'I think it's a lovely place but there you go.'

'I've no idea,' Luke said, reining in the emotions rampaging through his mind. Would she stay or would she go? Why did he care so very much? Was it because he *did* desperately want her to stay?

Here he was, pinning his happiness on Emma again. Waiting for her to make a decision.

History was repeating itself and he couldn't let that happen.

He had no control over what Emma did, but he could control how he reacted and he was determined not to care and show her and anyone else who was interested that he didn't.

'I'll take these glasses back in the kitchen, then,' he muttered.

'No, I'll do it. You relax out here.'

'I'm fine. I need to get home for a shower. I'm off out this evening.'

'Oh?' His mum's ears pricked up. 'Anyone I know?'

'As a matter of fact, yes.'

'Ohhh . . .'

'Ran and Bo and couple of the guys from the dive centre and their dance group. It's Ran's birthday.'

'Ah.' She wrinkled her nose. 'Thought you might have a date.'

'I do. With a bunch of mates.' With that, he scooped up the glasses and swept into the kitchen, leaving his mother outside.

She followed him in a moment later. He faced the window over the sink, readying himself for a conversation he hadn't sought.

'Look, son. I know you think I'm interfering and I should mind my own business. You may well be right but if I don't say what I think, I'll regret it even more. If you're pinning your hopes on Emma putting down roots in Falford, I think you'll be disappointed.'

He placed the glasses in the washing-up bowl.

'I had no idea she was even contemplating it until you told me about the craft unit, Mother, so how could I be expecting it?' he said, failing to keep the frustration out of his tone. He felt dark clouds had rolled in on a clear summer's day but he didn't want to argue with his mum. He loved and respected her, for all her interference, which came from her protective instincts. Maybe she felt she had to overcompensate for his dad's neglect.

She rested her hand on his arm. 'She'll keep you dangling again, love.'

Luke had his hand on the tap, about to turn it on.

Instead he left it and turned round. He was shocked at the fear in her eyes.

'What's your problem with Emma?' he said as gently as he could. 'Your *real* problem.'

'*My* problem? You've no idea, have you?' she said.

'No idea of what?'

'What went on between them and us.'

'Is this about dragging up the treasure again? I've buried that long ago. It belongs to the past.'

'It's not about the treasure. It started before that was ever found. Between Robin and Hester and your dad and me.'

Once again, goosebumps popped up on his arms. What the hell was his mum on about now? Stuff from the past that had nothing to do with him or Emma.

'Hester and Robin? You and Dad? What do you mean?'

'Personal things between us all. Painful memories that I'd rather not talk about, but I think I have to.'

His stomach knotted. She couldn't mean . . .

'Mum,' he said softly. 'Did Emma's mother have an affair with Dad? Is that what you're trying to tell me?'

'Hester and your dad? Them have an affair?' She laughed bitterly. 'God, no. No, you've got it all wrong. It was *me*. Me and Robin. We had a fling — more than a fling, I fell for him and I thought he felt the same. He was going to leave Hester for me because he knew I wasn't happy with your dad but he never did. When it came to it, he said he couldn't break up his marriage. Your dad found out. That's why he hated Robin and Robin loathed him.'

'I . . . I . . .' Luke kept shaking his head, unable to process what his mother was telling him and not trusting himself to reply. 'When was this?'

303

'It started while you were in the sixth form. It was still going on when your dad found the treasure.'

Still going on? Any reply stuck in Luke's throat.

'So you see why I worry for you. Emma's a chip off the old block. She's cold, the same as Robin! The ice queen who will never thaw.'

''Ice Queen'? Mum, I'm sorry that Robin treated you like that. I know Dad wasn't the best husband but to . . .'

She cut him off before he could defend Emma. 'That's an understatement! He was a womaniser. He hurt me too, and Robin knew it. He was sympathetic and offered me a shoulder to cry on. I thought he was being a sensitive, cultured man and he offered me a different way of life. Or so I thought. It was all lies.'

Though shocked and upset for his mother, he was determined to defend Emma to the hilt. 'I'm so sorry, but that's all in the past and I can't do anything about it. Emma isn't the same as her father. It's not fair to lay that guilt on her.'

His mother put on her best hurt expression. 'Maybe, maybe not, but you can't deny she blamed you for your dad finding the treasure. She was cold and she rejected you and I know she's doing the same now. It's only that I don't want you to be hurt. You do know the Pelistrys would never have settled for the likes of us.'

'This is the twenty-first century, not Victorian times. I'm not some tin miner who's fallen for the mine owner's daughter.'

His mother's eyebrows shot up. ''Fallen for' her?'

'*Fell* for her, in the past tense!'

With that, he marched outside and started tamping down a flagstone with his boot. With each thud, he tried to silence the shock he felt. His mother and Emma's father had been in love, having a relationship while he and Emma had been together; and while they'd been trying to deal with the fallout of the coins being found. His world, then and now, had been turned upside down.

He saw his mother staring through the kitchen window at him but Luke didn't want to speak to her. She must have felt the same because she moved out of the kitchen and didn't reappear. He raced through the rest of the job and left immediately, not even putting the tools away.

She came out and asked him to call her.

'Yeah. Bye, Mum,' was all he could manage.

On the way home, he found himself gripping the wheel until his knuckles were white. It had been such a shock to discover family secrets he'd never known about. More than the treasure had been unearthed all those years back; now he knew why there had been such ill-feeling between their families.

His mother was hurt and bitter and he could now understand his parents' hostility to the Pelistrys, but his mother accusing Emma of being cold and calculating went much too far.

Then again, Emma *was* known as the ice queen, and hadn't her aloofness been part of the attraction? Now, when they'd returned, older, wiser, bruised by life, he'd begun to believe they'd both changed. Could they? Or was he as deluded as ever?

The question was: did Emma know about the affair? If she did, why had she kept it from him? And if not, should he tell her?

32

'What time are you going to the Beachcombers Awards event on Saturday?' Maxi asked Emma, over coffee on the terrace.

'Beachcombers Awards?' Emma laughed. 'Sounds like a funky new music prize. I'll be there. I wish you could come with me.'

'I wish I could too but Andy's had this stag night in the diary for over a year and I couldn't get a sitter at such short notice. I'll put my feet up and think of you chugging fizz and basking in the glory.'

'I don't deserve to bask. All the glory is the rest of the group's. Ursula's, everyone. I'm such a newbie, I can't claim to have helped at all.'

'You're part of it now. You can't escape. Luke's bound to be there,' Maxi added mischievously.

'He was planning to, as far as I know, although he's not been around for a few days. Ran said he'd gone to Plymouth to visit some old diving buddies.'

'I'd begun to hope you two were growing closer lately, or at least had buried the hatchet. Am I wrong?'

Emma thought before she answered, unsure herself. 'No, you're not wrong . . . though it's early days. I can't tell whether Luke wants the hatchet to stay buried. I hope so but I can't say more than that. We're treading so warily around each other. Sometimes I think he's like a submerged mine that might or might not blow up in my face.'

'Maybe he's thinking the same about you,' Maxi said. 'Given the past.'

'Yes. That's a possibility.'

Emma went back to the lodge to work on the final few illustrations for the book. She tried hard but, every so often, her concentration would be disturbed. Focusing on beach flora and fauna reminded her of Luke. He'd pointed out that pale pink, almost translucent, shell she'd loved . . . and the dolphin she'd painted was an obvious reminder of their shared day rescuing the creature in the estuary. Even the seaweed she'd sketched brought him to mind, swimming beneath the waves on an idyllic summer's day.

Later that evening, Maxi called her in after dinner. Andy was working in his study so they congregated amid the toys in the conservatory, where the children were in their pyjamas ready for bed.

Daisy piped up, 'Mummy. I don't want to go back to school because, when we do, Auntie Emma will go home.'

'Daisy! Where did you hear that?'

Maxi winced. 'You said it to Daddy last night.'

'Oh God, I am sorry, Emma. They have ears like bats.'

'Bats have hairy ears.' Arlo grabbed his and waggled them. 'You have big, hairy ears, Daisy!'

'I don't. I don't!'

'Shh. Kids. No one has big hairy ears. I only meant that you can hear well. Not that you were meant to,' she said through gritted teeth to Emma. 'Sorry.'

'It's OK. I've almost finished my project so I do have to decide.'

'Are you staying, Auntie Emma?' Daisy slipped her hand in Emma's and Emma melted a little.

'I want you to stay.' Arlo sat next to her.

Maxi made an 'oo' of surprise over his head.

'I haven't decided yet. I might be . . .'

'Mummy always says 'might be' when she means no.' Arlo slid off the sofa and into the midst of his Lego. He started a fight between a triceratops and a T-rex that Maxi had bought from the Beachcombers' stall.

Daisy was more direct. 'Are you leaving us all on our own?' she said, her brown eyes huge and solemn.

Maxi gasped. 'No need to be quite so dramatic, darling.'

'It's OK,' Emma said. 'It's a good question. I might be. But if I do, maybe I won't be going far.' She felt someone else was saying the words.

'I'm not sure Auntie Emma can make an important decision just like that,' Maxi said to Daisy. She looked at Emma. 'Can you?'

Emma teetered . . . If she stayed, they'd all be able to spend as much time together as they liked. It was another powerful reason to take the unit.

'Well, you see, I — I might have already decided. I've been thinking what to do next for a while so, the other day, I went to see a live/work unit that's up for rent at the Lizard Craft Centre.'

Maxi's mouth opened again, her eyes as wide as Daisy's.

'Ursula mentioned it to me last week when I visited her. I didn't know if I was even going to check the place out but then I thought: what have I got to lose? So, I went and, I have to admit, I was impressed. In fact, it's perfect. All I have to do is decide to move wholesale back to Falford.' She threw on a bright smile, though her pulse rate had quickened at the momentousness of the decision.

'Simple, then,' Maxi said, with a half-smile.

'Yes.' Emma laughed.

'It goes without saying that we'd love to have you,' she said. 'But I know that it's not an easy choice.'

'No.' Maxi meant Luke. 'I think — I think — that whether he's here or not, it doesn't matter. It's how I feel, and what makes my heart sing that counts. I wouldn't be moving here for Luke. I'd be moving here for me. I love the landscape. I'd forgotten how much I missed the sea. I've found fresh inspiration and friendship here. With you, with the other Beach-combers. God knows, I never dreamed I'd say this, but I've grown fond of Ursula too.'

'I told you her bark is worse than her bite.'

'It is and I'm glad I found out. All in all, I'm glad I came home to Falford and I think I'm going to take the craft unit.'

Maxi blew out a breath. 'Wow.' Then she jumped up and hugged Emma. 'I am so happy to hear this. Selfishly of course I want you here, but, most of all, I want you to be happy.'

'That would be nice,' Emma said, thinking of her brave words about making the decision regardless of what happened between her and Luke. Too late now.

'I'm going to call Jermaine in the next few days and tell him I want to take over the tenancy. He'll carry on owning it, but I'll pay him rent. He wanted another craftsperson to take over and told me I came 'highly recommended' by Ursula, which he said must mean I'm a 'good egg'.'

'What's a good egg, Mummy?' Daisy piped up.

Arlo let out a chortle. 'A bad egg smells!'

He and Daisy descended into hysterics, rolling about the floor and singing about bad eggs and smells.

Their silliness was infectious and set off the grown-ups; though, watching them, Emma couldn't help wishing that life could be that simple enough that she could be distracted by silly jokes about smells.

Despite her bravado, she had no idea how Luke would feel about her moving back into his territory permanently. Would he see it as a new future for them both?

310

33

With a sigh of relief Emma laid down her paintbrush. The last illustration for the book was complete. Any more work on it and she'd spoil it.

Standing up, she stretched out her shoulders, stiff after bending over the paper for so long. The sun streamed onto the deck, creeping closer to the shaded area where she'd placed the table and chair. Seagulls cried above, and a blackbird pecked at the grass. Their chirps and the sigh of the breeze in the trees were the only sounds she could hear. She didn't miss the roar of traffic or distant sirens passing by her Oxford flat.

She was so relaxed that she jumped at a beep from her phone on the table.

Jermaine's name flashed up with a message asking for her answer on the craft unit.

It was crunch time. Emma picked up the phone and stood on the deck with it, watching the birds swoop down onto the feeder next to the lodge. The grass was dappled with the afternoon sunlight shining through the leaves. It was so beautiful here . . . she'd be mad to go back to the city.

She'd been resolved to accept the offer, had said as much to Maxi and the kids, yet something was holding her back.

Maybe a walk at Silver Cove would help clear her mind?

As she walked along the sand, the wind tossing her hair, she felt connected to the souls who'd tried to find answers there over the centuries before. Had the chaplain walked here, wondering what to do with the treasure he'd surely found on the sailors' bodies? Was it here that he'd wrestled with his conscience, torn in two whether to keep the money or declare it?

As she walked, squeals of delight and joyful barks filled the air, but she found no peace or solutions.

As she trudged over the sand back towards the car park, Luke himself trotted down the steps from the graveyard. He seemed to be on a mission, striding across the rippled sand towards the booming surf.

Despite the people around him, he looked lost and alone. Whatever place he was in, it wasn't Silver Cove, but somewhere more painful. His trip away hadn't done him any good, judging by the look on his face.

They could hardly avoid bumping into each other so Emma made the first move, walking over to him. Maybe she should tell him about the unit. Get his opinion.

'Hello there.'

His brief smile at recognising her soon melted away. 'Hi.'

'Are you OK? Only you didn't seem yourself at the last Beachcombers meet-up. What's the matter?'

'Nothing.'

'OK. If you don't want to talk about it, but you didn't answer my texts. I was worried. I'd thought we'd become friends.'

'*Friends*?' He sounded astonished.

'*More* than friends . . .' Emma said. 'But you seem upset about something. Is this about your dad?'

'Dad?' He frowned. 'What do you mean?'

'I couldn't help notice the call after we'd gone diving together. You sounded upset so I wondered if it was him.'

'Yes, it was Dad. I didn't think you could hear.'

'I didn't catch the actual words.' Emma squirmed. 'But I could tell you were upset and Ursula had mentioned something she'd heard in the village.'

'In the village?' He snorted in disbelief. 'The bloody Falford grapevine. Who told Ursula?'

'I'm not sure,' Emma said, fudging. 'I wouldn't have mentioned it but I don't like to see you unhappy. Is it anything I can help with?' she said.

'Not unless you want to give him every penny you've got and ruin yourself.'

He sounded so bitter, Emma felt sorry for him. 'I'm sorry he's hassling you,' she said, thinking that at least he'd shed a chink of light on what was bothering him.

'Me too but it's not your problem.'

'So, is that why you haven't answered my messages?'

Luke stared at her and the pain in his eyes was like a cold fire burning her. She'd stirred a hornets' nest and it was too late to back down.

'Luke, what's happened? I thought we'd made a fresh start but now something seems to have thrown us back to square one again.'

'Nothing. Forget it.' He hurried away, splashing through the shallow pools on the sand.

Angry at him for turning his back on her, she jogged after him and clutched his arm. 'Luke. Don't walk away and leave me hanging like this. Tell me what's made you shut down on me. If you care about me at all, please, share what's on your mind, whatever it is.'

He stopped. He looked down at her face. The torment in his eyes filled her with dread.

'You said we can't escape the past,' he said in the tone of a man who seemed completely defeated. 'Well, it's true. They had an affair,' he said. 'Your dad and my mum.'

It was as if a giant hand had scooped her up and flung her back to that day in the chapel when she'd seen her father and Sue in the chapel.

'How d-do you know?' she said, barely able to get the words out.

'I'm sorry to have to break it to you,' he said. 'But it was still going on when my dad found the treasure. My mother said it happened while we were in the sixth form.'

'When — when — did Sue let on about this?' Emma asked. Luke had obviously taken her shock as a sign she hadn't known and yet she was shocked because she *did*.

'She admitted it all the other day. She said your dad promised to leave your mother and said that they'd start a new life together. When it came to it, he changed his mind. My mum was devastated.' He reached for Emma, to pull her into his arms. 'I'm sorry. I didn't want to tell you. I never wanted to hurt you and I still don't . . .'

Emma backed away. 'Luke. I already knew.'

His eyes widened. 'You *knew* about it?'

'Not *knew*. Not for definite,' she said, trying to dig herself out of a hole that was growing deeper by the second. 'Only I saw them — heard them really — at the chapel. I'd come home from school early and they were arguing in his study and then — then — I think they made up.' Their words came back to her: her father's voice, the words more tender than she'd ever heard, soft and persuasive. '*Let's not argue, Sue. You mean too much to me.*' Then a silence which Emma had barely been able to bear, knowing what it signified.

314

'You knew and you didn't tell me?' Luke's voice rose.

'No. I didn't dare. I was in denial about what I'd seen and heard. I didn't want to believe it myself or risk sharing it with you. *Especially* not with you. I thought it would split us apart and if ever it had got back to my mother — or your father — God knows what might have happened. Yet also I didn't see how we could stay together after I'd found out. I wanted you so much and yet I was scared of the consequences. It's why I blew hot and cold with you, I was torn in two.'

'That's *why* Dad hated your father. Because he *did* know. He must have . . . The things he said about Robin. They make sense now!' Luke shouted the words at the sky, not at Emma. 'It's why my dad was so hellbent on finding that hoard. He wanted to punish your father, get his revenge. If I'd known that, back then, I — I would never have told him about the journal. Not for anything. Not for a bloody car . . .'

The *car.* Emma grabbed his arm and he whipped round to face her.

'What do you mean? You *told* him about the journal?'

'Yes. I told him,' Luke stated. 'I fetched it from where I'd hidden it and I showed it to him.'

'I — I always thought . . . you said he must have found it. You *swore* you didn't know how he'd seen it.'

'I'm sorry, Emma. I couldn't help it. You were so angry that I'd even *taken* it. I swear to God I didn't steal it intending to show him. You'd said we needed transport. I — I wanted to be independent and my dad — well, for fuck's sake, he showed me some attention. I was fooled, I was duped, I was stupid. I've

315

regretted it ever since. That's the truth!' he almost shouted.

'But how could you? How could you? My father was never the same. Ever.'

'How could I? I didn't plan to do it! I was bribed into telling him about the treasure. Lured into showing him the journal. I've told you I've felt bad about it ever since but I can't undo the past.'

'You kept this to yourself all these years, knowing how much it meant to me?' Emma said.

'I did and I've no excuses. I'm truly sorry but Emma, you kept your own secret. You never told me our parents were having an affair. If you had, I might have understood the seriousness more. The stakes. I might have understood why you were — why you never really seemed to make up your mind if you wanted me or not.'

'You're right!' She threw the words back at him. 'I should have told you about the affair but you lied too. You're — you're not who I thought you were.'

The man who looked back at her was full of pain and weariness but Emma was in too much tumult to care.

'Maybe I never was,' he said. 'Are either of us who we thought we were? Maybe we can never live up to the perfect lovers we want each other to be. Maybe we shouldn't even try. We've never been able to be honest with other and it's time to accept those secrets will always keep us apart.'

34

It was a blessing that Maxi, Andy and the kids were away visiting friends for a few days or else Emma would have found it impossible to hide how bad she felt from her best pal. Instead, she holed up in the lodge, allowing the grief to wash over her; not that she could have stopped it.

The past few days had been some of the bleakest of her life. It felt as if everything had collapsed on top of her: the grief over her father's death coming on the heels of the end of her relationship with Theo — and now the final blow: the shock of finding out Luke had lied and the finality of their parting at Silver Cove.

It was only because she cared for Ursula so much that she dragged herself out to the studio to deliver her news in person. Ursula was alone, concentrating hard on shaping the loop of an earring. Emma saw her burst into a smile when she walked in, which made her feel even guiltier.

'How lovely to see you.' She kissed Emma on the cheek. 'To what do I owe this honour?'

'I — I needed to talk to you face to face.'

'Oh dear.' Ursula frowned. 'That sounds terribly serious.'

'It's — I wanted to tell you in person that I can't take the craft unit.'

Ursula drew in a breath. 'You turned it down?'

'Yes, and I don't think I can come to the awards night.'

'What do you mean, you're not coming to the

317

awards night? What one earth are you saying?'

'I feel such a fraud. I haven't done anything to deserve an award.'

'Poppycock!'

Emma almost smiled. She hadn't heard anyone use that expression before yet it was so uniquely Ursula. Yet no smile would come.

'It wouldn't seem right to come to the party,' she said. 'As I'm leaving.'

'Leaving Falford?' Ursula sank into her chair. Rarely had Emma ever seen her so poleaxed.

'Emma Pelistry,' she said slowly. 'What's happened? You're not running away, are you? Is this about Luke?'

'Not exactly.'

'Are you sure?' Her eyes narrowed. 'What happened between you?'

'It's personal,' Emma said, unable to put into words the sense of shock and betrayal she was feeling.

'It always is . . . I can see it's painful so I won't push you, of course, but please come to the pub. You don't have to tell anyone you're leaving.'

'If I come, I do, and I might get upset and embarrass myself.' And be asked awkward questions to which she had no answer, Emma thought.

'There's nothing embarrassing about showing emotion. I've learned that. There's also nothing shameful about being sad to leave people you've grown to care about. Please come. It would mean a lot to me. Then you can slip away quietly.'

'I don't know.'

'You seem determined to make me say soppy things,' Ursula said. 'Which I always try to avoid. However, I'm going to. The past few months have meant a lot to me. I've loved your company. I feel invigorated. I've

318

even stopped looking for that ring. It's time to accept what's lost. I've plenty of life left, and loads to do. I've enjoyed seeing fresh blood injected into Falford, a new generation ready to take on the world . . . I'd hoped to see you and . . .' her voice trailed off.

'I've loved getting to know you better,' Emma said, though in her mind she was thinking: if you think Luke and I are going to pick up where we left off . . . we can't. It was never meant to be.

His final comments rang in her ears: that they'd never been able to be honest with each other and that secrets would always keep them apart. It was true.

'Emma? We'll be so sorry to see you go. You've become one of the gang. I think even Zoey will miss you.'

Finally, Ursula had drawn a smile from Emma. 'I'm not too sure about that.'

'Perhaps you're right but if she thinks she's going to step into your boots where Luke's concerned, she'll be very much mistaken.'

'Good luck to her if she does,' Emma said, although the idea of Zoey cosied up with Luke beside the chapel wood burner made her feel almost nauseous.

'You know you don't mean that. Are you absolutely certain you won't rethink your decision to leave us all?'

Ursula's voice was so full of warmth that Emma wavered, on the edge of tears again. Then she thought of Luke's harsh words as they'd parted.

'It's the right thing to do but I will come to the pub,' she said. 'Everyone's been so welcoming. It's not right to leave good friends without saying goodbye. I owe it to the Beachcombers and . . .' impulsively, she embraced Ursula, 'I owe it to you most of all.'

Emma packed away her paintbrushes. She'd spoken to her tenant, who was leaving at the end of the following week. It meant she had to stay in Falford for another few days after the awards night but it couldn't be helped. She planned to get off the Lizard and visit other parts of the county where she couldn't bump into Luke or any of the Beachcombers. She would pack in as much inspiration as she could before heading back to the landlocked city of Oxford.

Yet she also had unfinished business of another kind. It had been ages since she'd spoken to her mother and she felt that she needed to.

'Hello, Mum.'

'Oh, hello, Emma. How lovely to hear from you. It's been a while.'

'I've been busy with my deadline.' Emma felt bad that she hadn't rung sooner. 'It's done now, though.'

'I guessed you were so I didn't bother you. How's Falford treating you?'

'OK. Yes . . . it's been great to spend time with Maxi.' She took a breath. 'That's why I'm phoning, actually. I'm coming back to Oxford now this job is done so we'll be a bit closer to each other again, even if not exactly on the doorstep.'

'You're coming back to the flat? Oh, I see.'

'You sound surprised,' Emma said.

'I am, a little bit, though maybe I shouldn't be. I thought you might have decided to stay, you sounded so settled the last time we spoke.'

'I've had a good time but it's time to move on. There are a lot of memories here.'

There was silence from her mum's end of the phone

and Emma felt compelled to fill it. 'Luke's back here.'

'I see.'

Now Emma had started, she may as well tell her mother everything. 'And he's living in the Old Chapel. He bought it.'

The gasp was audible. 'He *bought* it — how? I mean, Luke Kerr? I don't understand.'

By which her mum meant: she didn't understand how Luke could have afforded the property.

'He served as a navy diver for a while and, afterwards, he did some salvage work,' Emma explained wearily. 'It's pretty lucrative apparently. He heard the chapel was going to be split up for flats by a developer and so he bought it. I think he wanted to come home to be nearer his mother.'

'His *mother*? Well, I suppose I can understand he felt he has to look out for her after Harvey left them in the lurch. Luke must have done very well for himself but I can't imagine him in our home. Thank God your father's not here to see it.'

So far, so predictable, Emma thought, although her own reaction had been exactly the same initially. Her mother's tone became sharper. 'Is Luke the reason you're not staying in Falford?'

'I — it's part of it, though not the only one. There are too many bad memories here for me to stay and that's partly why I'm calling you. When I come home next week, I'd really like to meet up and have a proper talk about everything that happened at the chapel when the treasure was found. There are so many things I want to say to you.'

'Oh? What about?'

'Everything. About my dad for one thing. I know he wasn't perfect but I've come to — to feel kinder

321

towards him since he died. There are things we should have out in the open and not allow to fester. I don't think it's healthy for either of us.'

The line was silent for a few seconds. Emma half wondered if her mother had rung off. Then she spoke again, in a brittle tone. 'If you mean that your father had affairs, then I know that.'

Emma almost dropped the phone. 'Affairs? You mean there were others as well as . . .'

'His fling with Sue Kerr. Oh yes, there were *others*.' The last word was laced with bitterness.

'B-but w-why didn't you tell me?' Emma stammered.

'For the obvious reason. I didn't want to hurt you, though you've found out about Sue. From her, I presume?' She sighed. 'Well, there was always the danger you might uncover old wounds when you went back to Falford. I accepted that when you told me you were going. These things have a way of rising up from the depths.'

They did. And how. Now one secret was out, Emma saw no point in not revealing another. The moment might never come again. Deep breath.

'Mum, I have something to say too. Something to do with Luke. That afternoon when Dad brought the Rolls home. Luke was with me in my room.'

'Luke?' Hester's exclamation pierced Emma. She was going to hit the roof but it was too late to back down now.

Emma held the phone tighter. 'Yes, I made him hide in the attic space because I was afraid you'd go mad. He was bored and he found an old journal written by the original chaplain. The vicar had come across the shipwrecked bodies at the cove after the

Minerva sank.'

'And?' her mother said tightly.

'And it held a clue to where the treasure was buried and Luke accidentally took it home and that's how Harvey realised . . .' Emma felt like she was confessing a great sin to her mother. She was a teenager again, fearing, dreading what her mother would say yet compelled to shift the burden from her shoulders even though it would create havoc. 'Harvey made Luke show it to him and that's how he found the hoard.'

'I should have known,' her mother said wearily. 'I should have known that someone might come across it one day.'

Emma was stopped dead in her tracks. 'What do you mean? You 'should have known someone might come across it'. No one knew it was up there.'

There was silence.

'Mum? Say something. What did you mean?'

'I can't tell you. Not here on the phone.'

'I can't wait until next week! I need to know what you mean *now*. Did you know about that journal?'

'I need to see you face to face. I'm coming to Cornwall and you won't have to wait until next week.'

'What? Now?'

'Yes. Greg's away on business so I'm on my own anyway. I'm packing a bag and I'm coming. I'll book a hotel right now.'

'But Mum . . .' Emma was terrified of news so awful that her mother was racing straight to Falford.

'No arguments. I'll see you this afternoon.'

35

Emma paced around the lodge, trudged around the garden, picked up her pencil and threw it down, made herself three cups of coffee that all went cold, then a sandwich that she ended up feeding to the seagulls.

Her mum called from a service station somewhere on the A30 and finally, as the shadows lengthened into early evening, Emma heard the crunch of car tyres on Maxi's gravel drive. The sound made her heart beat a little faster. In a matter of minutes, she'd hear what was so important that her mum had driven hundreds of miles to tell her.

Emma met her on the drive. Her mother was in a crumpled sundress and, for once, devoid of make-up. With flushed cheeks and hair escaping from a clip, she looked like she'd left in a rush.

She kissed Emma on the cheek.

'This is a lovely spot,' she said. 'You look very well. Glowing. Much better than the last time I saw you.'

All this was small talk, setting Emma on edge even more. 'I've been outdoors a lot,' she said.

'It's an inner glow, though you do seem a little tired?'

'I haven't been sleeping that well. Come round the back to the lodge. You must be knackered too after that long drive. Maxi and co are away.'

She led her mother onto the deck of the lodge.

'Tea? Something cold?'

'No thanks. I had a drink when I stopped.'

'Shall we sit out here in the shade rather than go

inside?' With the sigh of the breeze and the gentle gurgle of the stream, Emma hoped it might be a more soothing environment for them both.

'Yes. Good idea.' Her mother took a patio chair. She smoothed out her dress before she spoke. 'You must have been on tenterhooks since we spoke earlier.'

'You could say that.' Emma clenched her fingers.

'Firstly let me say that, while your father was no angel,' her mother went on, 'I've reasons to be ashamed of myself in this business. Things I've kept secret for a long time.'

Goosebumps prickled Emma's arms. 'Go on.'

'I'm not proud about it. I did know about that journal. In fact, I deliberately hid it inside another book jacket.'

'You did what?'

'I can see you're shocked. I don't blame you and part of me has I've regretted it ever since. I found it not long after we first moved in when I was sorting through the junk in the attic. God knows, some of it had been there for decades. The journal longer, obviously.'

'I'd worked that one out but why on earth did you hide it, Mum? Why didn't you tell Dad? You know how much he'd have loved to have seen it.'

'I did and that's why I never showed it to him. Your father bought the chapel partly because of its history. Not entirely because he wanted the place to show how important he was — we were — to the rest of the village, but he always hoped to find some clue to the treasure. I thought he was mad and the coins were long gone but he was right and ironically it was me who found the key. He'd never have been able to recover it of course, the coins were still on Harvey's land. Not that I had any idea of that when I discovered the journal.'

'Dad might have worked it out, though!' Emma shot back, incensed on her father's behalf.

'I'm sure he would have. I knew *exactly* how much he'd have loved to get his hands on it but — God forgive me — I'd recently found out he'd been sleeping with a sales girl from his office. He'd ended it and swore he'd never touch another woman again but it wasn't the first time, and so I decided not to tell him about the journal. I hid it inside a different jacket under the romance novels. I knew he'd never find it there.'

'Oh, Mum.' Emma gulped back a sob of shock. She'd known her parents' marriage hadn't been a happy one but it was devastating to find out that they had lied to each other and done such cruel things. 'This is horrible.'

'It is. I'm not proud and, at the funeral, I couldn't grieve properly. I felt it was hypocritical and that maybe I was in some way responsible.' She glanced up at her daughter, perhaps waiting for her to disagree but Emma couldn't. She was still too stunned.

'I still remember Robin's exact words when I came into the study. I still had cobwebs in my hair from that loft,' her mum went on. 'He asked me if I'd 'come across anything interesting'.' So I said no. I'd made sure that even if he decided to look in the crates, the book would look like any old novel.'

'You must have wanted to punish him very badly . . .'

'Not punish, more console myself and redress the balance. I thought I'd hold the journal back for a while. It wouldn't stop him straying but it gave me comfort — and a power when I felt powerless — to keep it to myself. Knowing that the thing he wanted almost more than anything, I held the key to.'

'Would you *ever* have shown it to him?' Emma was half afraid of the answer.

'I might have if things had turned out differently. I was waiting to see if he kept his promise to be faithful after this — woman — at work. I really began to hope he'd changed his ways but then I found out about Sue. That was when I decided I'd never utter a word about it. I did think of burning it but it gave me more satisfaction to leave it there. Knowing it was almost under his nose.'

Her poor dad, her poor mother. Slowly, Emma's anger was being replaced with desolation at the lives ruined. No one was the innocent party. She shook her head, unwilling to speak.

Her mother reached out and touched her hand. 'I can tell you're disgusted with me and, darling, I don't blame you.' Emma was sure there was an appeal for forgiveness in her eyes and in her voice.

'No, Mum, I'm not disgusted,' she said. 'I've done things I'm not proud of either but I am sad for you, and for Dad. He must have hurt you very badly for you to do that.'

'He did. People knew he was having affairs, you know. People in the village. I could tell from the way they looked at me, with pity. I think Harvey might have known about Sue too, which was why the man gloated so much when he got his hands on the treasure.'

'It was the ultimate revenge.' Emma said.

'I suppose so and I *do* regret what I did now, but mainly because of the effect it had on you — on our lives. I still loved your father, even if I was terribly angry with him. If I'd told him, Luke would never have come across that journal, would he?'

'No. But it's too late. Dad wouldn't have been able to get the treasure even if he'd worked out it was on Roseberry Farm.'

'And neither would Harvey,' her mum said. She sat up, defensively. 'There. You know the worst. You can tell Luke I hid the journal if you want to.'

Emma wasn't sure she could ever tell Luke. 'We're not really in contact at the moment,' she said, making the understatement of the year.

'That's a shame. Are you sure you can't patch it up?'

Patch it up. Patch up a rift that had gone on for years.

'We tried to be friends and — more, but it isn't going to happen.'

'You two . . . I am sorry. Your father and I only ever wanted to protect you but I've come to realise that we interfered too much. It was wrong to try and split you up. If you still care about him and he about you, nothing should stop you.'

'He's a good man. He's nothing like his father.'

'I'm sure he isn't. You're more mature and much kinder than me or your father. I deeply regret that I let all my anxieties and unhappiness affect you. I just wanted to make sure your life would be perfect but I'm afraid I never actually listened to what you really wanted or what made you happy. Instead of trying to split you and Luke up, I should have been delighted for you. I hope it isn't too late now? If you have that much faith in him — if you truly love him — then don't let anything stand in your way.'

'It's not that simple. He's upset and hurt at the moment because I knew what was going on and kept it a secret. He says he might have been more wary of his father. And I didn't know he'd shown the journal to Harvey deliberately. We said some hurtful things to each other and the trust between us has been shattered. I don't think it can ever be repaired.' Emma swallowed the lump in her throat. 'It's easier to simply leave the past here and move on to another fresh start.'

'*Easier*?' Again a hand was laid on Emma's, squeezing her fingers as if with an urgent need to make her understand. 'Will be it 'easy' to forget a man you love? To regret not being with him your whole life long? Ask yourself that.'

'Don't you think I haven't spent the past few months thinking about that? The past fifteen years trying to forget Luke Kerr?' Fighting back tears, Emma withdrew her hand. 'Whatever I do, it seems as if I can't win.'

Her mother left a short while afterwards to stay in a hotel in Helston. Emma paced around the garden. As for her mother's advice on making up with Luke, surely Hester should have been the last person to offer relationship advice. How could Emma possibly do that, without letting Luke know what her mum had done? He might not even believe Emma hadn't known. Either option — staying and telling him everything, or making a clean break — was a bleak prospect.

One thing was for sure, Emma had never felt less like going to a celebration in her life.

★ ★ ★

'What time do you want a lift to the pub tonight?' a beaming Maxi asked when she arrived back at the house the following morning, buzzing with excitement from their trip to see her old friends.

Maxi had no idea that Hester had been to the lodge and Emma couldn't possibly tell her. She hadn't yet come to terms with the revelation that her mother had hidden that book, and her father was a serial adulterer. That they were both more damaged and flawed than she'd ever realised.

'I dunno,' Emma said, dreading the news she had to give Maxi.

'Okayyy.'

'Sorry, Maxi, it's just that . . . there's no easy way of saying this. I am going to the party but I've decided to go home to Oxford afterwards.'

Maxi's intake of breath was audible. 'Wow. I wasn't expecting that. I thought you'd made up your mind to stay. I thought you were taking the unit. What's happened to change your mind, my love?'

'Nothing. I just don't think this is the right place for me long-term.'

'Is this anything to do with Luke?'

'No. Nothing at all. Maybe.' She couldn't lie to Maxi and yet she couldn't possibly share the truth. 'Just too many bad memories. I thought — for a while — I could make a fresh start here, but I was wrong.'

'So does this mean you'll miss the awards night?'

'No. Everyone's been so kind and welcoming. I really owe it to them to go along and say a proper goodbye, especially Ursula.'

'She'll be gutted you're leaving. Will you not reconsider?'

'My tenant's about to leave. If I don't go now, I'll

330

have to find someone else to rent the flat so I can afford Jermaine's unit and that's only the practical side of it. I've given this a lot of thought and I've decided it's best for everyone if I go home.'

Maxi frowned. 'Honey, are you really sure where 'home' is now? Is it a location? A pile of bricks and mortar like the flat in Oxford? Or is it where your heart truly lies?'

Caught off-guard, Emma had no immediate reply. Maxi was right. She wasn't sure. Falford was once her home and almost had been again this summer. Ursula had said she was 'one of the gang' after all.

'No matter where my heart lies,' she said carefully. 'I have to look at things with my head, and that tells me I should go back to Oxford.'

'OK. I get that but you said leaving Falford would be 'best for everyone',' Maxi added. 'It won't be best for me, or for Ursula, and what about Luke? Does he know yet?'

'No,' Emma said. 'And yes, he is part of the reason but please, Maxi, don't push me to say any more. Luke and I have said all there is to be said. There's too much history between us. Too much to ignore. You have to understand. The trust between us has been broken and it can't be mended. I promise you we've tried.'

'Have you?' Once more, Maxi questioned her.

Emma replied with a silent plea.

Maxi nodded. 'I can see how hard this has been for you. I won't push you but I'm gutted, I must say. The kids will be too, and a lot of other people I can think of, but if that's your decision then I respect it. It has to be right for you.'

With a hug that almost broke Emma's heart, Maxi

left. Emma had never felt more alone but the bitter-sweet memories were built into every grain of sand, every stone of the Old Chapel. Even as she dipped her brush into the water, trying to eclipse her troubles in her art, Maxi's question still nagged at her. Where was her real home? Where did her heart truly lie? And even if she knew the answer, how did that change things when the real question was: where did Luke's heart lie?

332

36

'Here we are, Cinders,' Maxi said when she dropped Emma off at the Ferryman in the evening sunlight.

'I want to go to the pub!' Arlo shouted from the rear seat.

'No, it's too late and it's very busy,' Maxi said.

'I want a pint. Daddy lets me!' Arlo bellowed. The windows were open and a couple who'd just arrived in a Porsche exchanged disgusted glances at the little boy in dinosaur pyjamas demanding beer.

'Daddy does not let you drink pints.' Maxi raised her voice. 'My children do *not* drink beer.'

Standing outside the open passenger door, Emma tried not to laugh at the kids, for Maxi's sake. She loved the children and all their quirks and she was going to miss them terribly. Arlo had made her sign in blood — a chip dipped in tomato ketchup — that she'd be back for visits.

'We want fizzy pop and crisps!' Daisy wailed.

'And I want a large gin but I can't, so we're going home where I can,' Maxi said in despair.

Emma leaned into the window. 'Be good for Mummy and I'll bring you to the pub for crisps when I'm next home.'

Daisy nodded. 'I don't want you to go.'

She looked so cute in her Peppa Pig onesie that Emma's heart broke a little.

'When *exactly*?' Arlo said rather menacingly.

'Soon. Cross my heart.'

'And we are leaving *now*,' Maxi said, starting up

the engine. 'Enjoy yourself, you lucky, lucky woman. Think of me when the authorities come to get me for letting my children down pints.'

And she was gone, leaving Emma in the car park. Below her, the terraces of the pub were thronged with drinkers enjoying the evening sun. The tide was in and the mooring jetty was full of dinghies which had ferried their owners from yachts, as well as probably a few locals. Emma recognised one of them as belonging to a Beachcomber who lived in a flat across the estuary.

The door of the pub was wide open and the sound of laughter and chatter filled the air. Luke's truck wasn't in the car park but Emma hadn't really expected it to be. He'd probably arrived on foot and intended to walk home too. Now, far from freeing herself of a burden, Emma had a new one. Luke knew nothing and she had to decide whether to tell him what her mother had done.

She braced herself. All she had to do was get through this evening. It's only a flipping plastic trophy and a sausage roll, she told herself. She took a few deep breaths then launched herself into the pub.

The Ferryman was already bustling with diners, though the main bar and snug had been taken over by the Beachcombers and their families and friends. Marvin and Bryan were chattering away by the bar. Lynne Stannard was talking to her niece Oriel and her partner Naomi.

There was a corner with plates laid out ready for a buffet and someone had hung a 'Congratulations' banner over the table, which had been decorated with shells and other bits and bobs found on the beach.

Over at the bar, with a pint in hand, Luke was talking with Ran, Bo and Zoey, until he caught sight of her. It was no more than a flicker of recognition, as if neither of them could bear to meet each other's gaze for more than a second.

'You made it!' Ursula swooped on her. 'Well done. I wasn't sure you'd come.'

'I wouldn't have missed it for the world.'

'Good.' Ursula squeezed her arm.

Emma scanned the room. 'Are the people from the recycling awards here yet?'

Ursula rolled her eyes. 'Not yet. They're running a bit late.'

A moment later, Lynne Stannard swept up. 'Emma! Hello. I've been telling Oriel all about your lovely pictures. She's dying to meet you.'

Emma was whisked off to chat to Oriel and half an hour flew by. At no point did she have the heart to tell anyone she was leaving Falford. There was no way she wanted to burst the bubble of excited Beachcombers chattering away about their finds, making plans for the future and wondering when the mysterious 'bloke from the recycling company' would turn up.

Zoey trotted back and forth to the car park like an excited spaniel, to see if the presenter had arrived, or couldn't find a space. She and the others were so excited, Emma felt more and more convinced that this wasn't the occasion to drop the bombshell of her own news. Maybe she should leave it until tomorrow.

'Oh, I hope the presenter hasn't had an accident!' Zoey squeaked, checking the time with Emma again. 'Maybe his satnav's not working and he's lost. It can happen.'

Emma let Marvin reply because she'd just seen another person enter the bar. Sue Kerr was followed by Clive the postman and, from the way he had a protective hand on Sue's back, he was doing more than delivering her mail. This was the woman who'd had an affair with her father, who'd almost broken up her parents' marriage. Did Sue have any idea that Emma knew?

'Sorry, I have to go to the bathroom,' Emma said to Marvin. In the cubicle, she took a few calming breaths before washing her hands and redoing her lipstick with unsteady fingers. Tonight was proving to be way more of an ordeal than she'd imagined.

'Emma?' Ursula found her at the basin. 'Everything OK?'

'Yes. I'm fine. I've decided not to tell everyone tonight.'

'Probably a good idea. Now, come on. It's time for the awards.'

'Has the presenter finally made it, then?'

'Oh yes. Now hurry along!'

Feeling as if she'd been ordered out of the school loos, Emma did as she was told. The best thing she could do was act as normally as possible and somehow get through the evening, hoping Sue wouldn't speak to her. Sue might well feel the same way.

With her fixed smile back in place as Ursula took the mic by the table, Emma wondered where the presenter was. Ursula had said he'd arrived but perhaps he was in the loo. Even so, Ursula had decided to start without him.

'Good evening, everyone, and thank you for coming. It falls to me to make a speech . . . and I'd like to say I was unaccustomed to public speaking but those of you who were taught by me know that's a big lie.'

Dutifully, Emma joined in the laughter. By the

336

sound of it there were a lot of Ursula's former pupils in the pub.

Someone called, 'Get on with it, Ms Bowen.'

Emma risked a glance at Luke. Leaning against the bar, a pint in his hand, he had a polite smile on his face but she sensed the tension in his body. His mother and Clive were sitting at a table, glasses of wine in front of them, happily watching Ursula.

'The first thing I'd like to do is thank my fellow Beachcombers for all the work they do trying to keep our beaches clean. They really do deserve an award.'

A ripple of applause.

'And the second thing I'd like to do is apologise. Because, as some of you know, there is no representative from the recycling company coming this evening.'

A groan went up.

'Oh no!' Zoey cried then laughed. 'What a surprise. *Not.*'

'What?' Emma mouthed. Who were the 'some' who knew? Zoey must be one of them, judging by her Cheshire cat grin.

Ursula held up her hand. 'That's because there is no actual award.'

She paused, her eyes sweeping over the faces, which were now growing puzzled. Marvin and Zoey and the other Beachcombers were looking unbearably smug, however, and not confused at all. Emma exchanged a glance with Luke. He had a deep frown on his face. He wasn't sure what was going on either.

'There's no actual award for the Beachcombers, wonderful though you all are. The real reason I've gathered you all here together to thank two very special people for their bravery in risking their own lives to save my old bones from a watery grave.'

Emma's stomach flipped. Surely Ursula didn't mean her and Luke?

Panicking, she glanced at him but he was now standing up straight, arms folded, staring directly ahead.

Ursula went on, 'Some of you may have heard that I was cut off by the tide at Govenek Cove recently. Were it not for these two, I'd have drowned before the lifeboat could rescue me. I owe my lives to them.'

There were gasps in the bar from the many people who'd had no idea of Ursula's escape, and every eye was now on Emma and Luke. She dug her nails in her palm. She was overwhelmed at Ursula's public gesture, and wanting to hide away from the glare. She'd never expected any public thanks. All she'd ever wanted was to keep her friend safe. Luke must be feeling the same. Ursula, however, wasn't going to stop now.

At the bar, Luke might have been frozen in time, his pint halfway to his mouth.

'Emma Pelistry. Luke Kerr. Please step up here!'

Beaming from the table, Ursula beckoned them to her, and a round of applause and cheers shook the rafters of the Ferryman.

Emma was stiff with embarrassment and Luke wasn't moving either.

'Gosh, you two look like you've been hauled up in front of the class!' Ursula said. 'Come on, you're grown-ups now. Bite the bullet and join me!'

Reluctantly, Luke peeled himself away from the bar and made his way to Ursula. Emma forced herself to move too, the smile on her face as rigid as concrete. A few people patted her on the back.

'Well done,' they said.

'Thanks,' she murmured. 'Really, I haven't done

338

anything.'

Luke was getting some banter too, and words like 'hero' bandied about. She cringed. She knew he'd be hating it.

They shuffled to the table, standing on either side of Ursula. A sea of beaming faces shone back at them as Ursula put her arms around each of them.

'You two look as if I've called you up for a detention. Try and enjoy this,' she said. 'I'll keep it brief for your sakes but I have to thank you for what you've done. Over the past few days, I've pieced together exactly what happened and remembered some of it. I've also heard how very brave you were from various people in the village.'

'Anyone would have done it,' Luke said.

'No, they wouldn't. You can't get away with that!' Ursula said. 'Even though you might not have believed it all those years ago, I always knew you'd turn into remarkable young people and I was right.'

Luke stared at his boots.

Emma longed to sink through the pub floor but realised that Ursula needed this public thank you, far more than she and Luke did.

'We were in the right place at the right time,' she said.

'You say that, if it makes you feel better, but I don't call hurtling along the lanes in your car and risking life and limb in a small boat to save an old bat like me 'being in the right place at the right time'. You actively put yourselves in danger to help me and I shall never forget it. On that note, I really wish I could give you a medal or an award or something, but I can't. So,' she paused. 'I've made you something.'

'There's no need . . .' Luke protested.

'There may be no need, apart from my need to do something. Call it selfish of me, but I want you to have these as a token of my gratitude.'

Ursula handed over two small paper gift bags. 'It's not much but I hope they're a keepsake.'

'Thank you,' Emma said. 'Thank you so much. You've been so kind to me. You've all been so kind to me.'

She clammed up in the nick of time. Another word would have been enough to make her crumble. The Beachcombers had welcomed her, pulled her into the fold, despite her reluctance at the start. She didn't deserve their kindness and she certainly didn't deserve an award. Now, here was Ursula, excited, a little nervous, waiting for Emma to open her gift and every eye glued to her, dying to see what it was.

She delved into the bag and drew out a small tissue-wrapped package. Luke made no attempt to open his.

Tearing the tissue open, she caught her breath. Inside was a sea glass bracelet made of silver, with nuggets of glass in stunning colours: orange, turquoise, pink and purple.

'They're the rarest colours,' Ursula said quietly. 'Only found once in a blue moon.'

Overcome with emotion, Emma had trouble not bawling on the spot.

'Oh's and 'Ah's and 'Aw's rang out from the crowd and a ripple of applause went around the pub.

'Luke?'

He nodded, a crooked smile on his face.

His gift was also a bracelet, but in black cord woven with chunky pieces of olive sea glass.

'I believe it's called a surfer bracelet,' Ursula said.

'Again, rare colours.'

'It's brilliant, Ursula, thanks.' Luke slipped it onto his wrist and tightened the knot. He held up his arm. Emma thought the knotted bracelet and colours looked great against his tanned skin. Once again, she had cause to marvel at his muscular arms.

As more applause and cheering rang out, Luke hugged Ursula.

She then embraced Emma, whispering, 'I hope you two will sort yourselves out . . .'

Turning to face the crowd, she declared, 'That's it, then. I'll let these people escape as I know they're longing to do. However, I do hope you'll join me in raising a glass to them. To Emma and Luke!'

'To Emma and Luke!'

Pints and Pimm's were raised high into the air and a chorus of 'To Emma and Luke!' shook the beams again.

Emma screwed up her courage. 'Luke. I want to talk to you,' she said.

He looked at her, his face full of such an intensity of emotions that Emma was silenced: fear, hope, regret. 'I'm not sure any more talking will help,' he said. 'It's too late for us.'

'What do you mean?'

'What I said. It's —' Suddenly he stopped speaking, and his eyes widened at something behind her. 'Not now,' he murmured.

'What?'

She never got a reply. Luke had turned away and was pushing through the crowd.

Emma craned her neck, desperate to see what had made him flee so quickly.

She heard, before she saw.

A voice from the past, laced with sarcasm, cutting through the buzz.

'Hello, son. It seems as if I've made it in the nick of time. Why didn't you tell me you and Emma were getting hitched?'

37

His dad. His dad was *here*. Like a ghost at the feast — a nightmare feast Luke hadn't anticipated and would have done anything to avoid.

Leaving Emma with Ursula, he marched out of the door to the terrace.

Then stopped.

Why was he running away from his own father? That was what Luke the boy would have done. He wasn't a boy, he was a man and he should face him.

He strode back inside, fired up and ready to challenge him. Harvey was in his sixties now but Luke was still unprepared for the way he'd aged in the past few years. He was jowly and florid in the face, his shirt button coming undone over his gut.

'What d'you want, Dad?'

Harvey feigned hurt. 'That's no way to greet your old man on such a happy occasion, is it? Congrats by the way.' He nodded at the banner. 'No wonder you kept it quiet. You and Emma . . . what a turn-up, eh? When's the wedding?'

Emma had joined them. 'There's no wedding,' she said, her voice high with strain. 'This isn't an engagement party.'

'Oh?' Harvey's eyes seemed glazed. 'What's all this fuss about, then? I came in to find everyone raising a glass to the pair of you.'

'It's a social evening for a bunch of friends,' Luke said, reining himself in with a massive effort.

'Looks like a party to me.'

'Just a get-together,' Emma cut in. 'We're all volunteers for the Beachcombers.'

'Beachcombers?' Harvey scoffed. 'Well, maybe that's just as well. I'd no idea you were back,' he went on, eyeing Emma as if she were rubbish washed up on the beach. 'And, son, I'm glad there's nothing between you. Don't want no Pelistrys in our family. No offence, love,' he said, with a smirk at Emma. 'Cold fishes and money grabbers. Like father, like daughter, I say.'

Emma had turned pale with shock, as if his father had struck her.

Luke was about to explode. All the hurt, the disappointment and sense of worthlessness he'd felt as a child rose up to the surface in an unstoppable wave. No training — even under the most extreme pressure — had prepared him to deal with this situation.

'Come on, why don't you buy your old man a pint?' Every word was a sneer, full of bitterness and self-pity. 'You can afford it.'

'I'm not buying you anything,' Luke said, barely keeping a lid on his anger. 'In fact, you should leave right now.'

Harvey snorted. 'Me? Leave? My own son is threatening to throw me out of my local?'

Out of the corner of his eye, Luke saw Emma slip out of the door. He panicked, thinking she might never come back. He had to take charge.

'I'm not threatening you. I'm asking you to leave. If you want to talk, we'll do it outside, not here in public.'

Harvey sneered. 'You just don't want people to know how you've treated me. You may be a do-gooder now, but I know the truth. Oh, look. Here's your mother, itching to give me a bollocking, I expect.'

Luke's mother was staring at them, shaking off Clive's hand on her arm. The last thing Luke wanted was his mum becoming involved in the situation. He caught her eye and mouthed: 'I'll deal with this.'

They were attracting an audience as people sneaked in through doorways to enjoy the entertainment. Behind the bar, the landlord was also watching with an eagle eye.

Luke took his father's elbow. 'Come on. We can have a proper talk outside.'

'Outside?' His dad shook off his hand. 'No, let's not go outside. Let's get this out in the open. I want everyone to know how you've treated me.'

'What do you mean?'

His dad snatched up the microphone. Static crackled then his voice boomed out. 'Hi folks! Sorry to spoil the party.'

Luke stopped dead. 'Don't!'

He found Ursula's hand on his arm. 'Luke . . .' she whispered. 'Don't cause a scene. Let him speak. Let everyone see the kind of man he is. You've nothing to fear.'

'Haven't I?' Luke said, aware of what his mother had told him and wondering if his father might be about to share their private business with the whole pub.

'Some of you know me of old. Some of you might be pleased to see me, but not all. Some of you don't know me from Adam. Those who don't, I'm Luke's dad. He's just told me he's in this Beachcombing bunch. I dunno what they do exactly but I'm sure it's good work. My son's always wanted to be helpful.'

Every face was turned in his direction. He had an

audience and he wasn't going to disappoint them.

Harvey was on a roll. 'Apart from helping me, of course,' he went on. 'I brought him up but when I needed a hand, well . . . the shoe was on the other foot. When I needed a bit of help to keep my business — my livelihood — afloat, Luke wasn't so keen.'

'Aw, why don't you button it, Harvey?' a man called from the back of the room.

A few people were heading for the terrace, embarrassed and disturbed at having their evening interrupted. Others were lapping it up.

'I see you've nothing to say now, son. Never have had much to say, have you?'

'No one can get a bleddy word in with you, Harv!' a local fisherman jeered, his comment met with approving sniggers.

Harvey curled his lip. 'See, he's not denying it. Because it's true. When I need him, he turns his back on me.'

A murmur of unease ran through the bar. Some people turned to look at Luke. There were frowns, whispers. Luke was frozen with indecision and hurt. He searched the room for Emma but she was nowhere to be seen. Was she listening? How must she feel about this? His father was drunk, but this was no excuse. He'd always tried to please him, always craved his attention, while knowing it was hopeless. The only real time Harvey had showed Luke attention was when he'd found the journal and now, when Luke had made his way in the world.

Emma was right. If he'd never said anything about the journal, Robin wouldn't have gone to pieces; maybe there might have been some slender hope his mother and father would have stayed together.

346

A woman shouted: 'Aw, pipe down, Harvey. That chip on your shoulder's the size of a bleddy trawler.'

Uneasy laughter. Some locals turned back to the bar, but others stared openly at Luke. They must be wondering if there was truth in the allegations.

Luke felt sick to his stomach. Each barb wounded him even though he knew it was unjust. It wasn't only the twisting of the truth that hurt; it was the active intention to wound. What kind of a father chose to hurt his son so publicly?

'What kind of son refuses to help his old man when he's on the ropes?' Harvey said, keen to keep his remaining audience while he could. 'What kind of son kicks him when he's down?'

The landlord appeared by Luke's side. 'I think we've heard enough. I'm sorry, Luke, but I'm going to chuck him out.'

'No, let him carry on.' Though Luke was horrified, his dad was still his dad and he didn't want him thrown out of a pub in front of half the village.

'He's clearing my pub. Upsetting people. Even if he is your old man, I can't have it. Sorry, mate.'

The landlord strode up to the table, towering over his dad. 'That's it, Harvey. You've had your time in the spotlight. Now, let these good people enjoy their evening. Take this somewhere else.'

His father stared at the landlord, seemed to be about to say more, then shrugged his shoulders. 'All right, mate. Keep your hair on.'

He handed over the mic and smirked at Luke.

'That's it. Show's over, folks!' the landlord said with an eye-roll and a grin. 'Let's all get back to normal.' He turned to Harvey. 'You. Outside.'

Luke stepped in. 'It's OK, I'll take him.'

'Got your attention now, haven't I?'

'You always did have my attention, Dad. The sad thing is you were never interested. Let's take this outside before you get yourself thrown out.'

Harvey hesitated a moment longer before laughing out loud. 'Can't have you shown up in front of your friends, can we? Or your girlfriend?'

'Out,' Luke growled.

Something in his tone resonated and his father shrugged and headed for the door. They had to run the gauntlet of mutters, smirks and disgusted glances but, to Luke's relief, they were finally out in the car park. A few folk pointed fingers but Luke shepherded his father to a far corner.

'Why did you come here, Dad?'

'Come to see you. Though I wish I hadn't bothered. I flew in yesterday and headed down here. Hoped we could spend some quality time together.' He snorted. 'Fat chance.'

'I would have talked to you if you'd come to the house.'

'Oh yes. The Old Chapel. How does it feel to be lord of the manor, now? Pillar of the community. Nothing to spare for your nearest and dearest though?'

'Don't be bloody stupid. We've been over this time and again. I've cleared your debts, I've taken an extra mortgage on the chapel to do it, but I can't help you again. Where's it all gone?'

'Businesses need investment. You should know that, now you're running one yourself.' Harvey laughed sarcastically.

'I do and I also know you can't run a business that's never going to pay. Cut your losses, get a job. With your experience, you're sure to find work.'

'Find work? Get a bleddy *job*? Is that all you can say?'

Luke struggled to keep a lid on his frustration. He felt as if he were the parent; his father the child.

'I've run out of suggestions. I've given you my advice. You've every right not to take it but I can't do any more.'

Harvey swore. 'I know where I stand then.'

'I'm always here to listen but I can't give you any more money.'

A deep sadness crept over Luke. Time and again, he'd hoped he could develop a meaningful relationship with his dad. Now, it seemed almost hopeless. He had to accept it was never going to happen.

'You know, it's not the money that bothers me, it's the lost opportunity. All my life, all I heard was that you were owed a break. That if you got a chance, nothing would stop you and you'd make a better life. You left us and wasted it. Let's end this now.'

Harvey grabbed his arm, wheedling. 'Wait, son . . . I admit I was a bit out of order in there. Emotions running high.'

'You're pissed.'

'Not pissed, though I did have a couple in the Falford Inn before I came. Dutch courage and all that. I just thought it would be better if I saw you face to face.'

'How did you know I'd be in the Ferryman?'

'Heard from an old mate there was a do going on here. I'm staying at the inn for a couple of days. Didn't realise it was an engagement party.'

'I've told you. It isn't.'

'No, but I came in to see the fancy banner and everyone toasting the pair of you and I assumed.'

349

'You insulted Emma. You hurt her. I can't forgive you for that.'

'Oh, come on. It's not a crime. She'll get over it. The Pelistrys have thick skins.'

Luke shook his head in disbelief. So many phrases filled his mind. *You'll never understand . . . Stop blaming everyone but yourself . . . Grow up . . .* and yet, seeing the contempt on his father's face, he realised none of them would hit home through the armour of denial and resentment his dad had built around him. It was sad and exhausting and Luke wasn't going to waste any more time on it.

The only person who deserved his time right now was Emma.

'That's it,' he said. 'I wash my hands of you. Don't come back inside or I *will* let the landlord throw you out, no matter who you are.'

He turned around and marched back into the pub. His only priority was to find Emma and make sure she was OK after the scene his father had caused. No matter what their differences, she didn't deserve to be dragged into his feud with his dad. Luke cared about her too much for that. Way too much . . . his heart squeezed. He'd never stopped caring about her. He never would. He'd probably never stop loving her either.

Brushing past people on his way back into the bar, he scanned the faces, desperate to find her.

There was no need.

Standing by the table, mic grasped in her hand, was Emma.

'Ladies and gentlemen!' she shouted. 'I need your attention!'

Luke stopped, in the middle of the floor, staring at

her.

She caught his eye and held his gaze, cutting through the hubbub in a voice as clear as a bell.

'Everyone, I've got something to say! It's important.'

The diners looked up from their meals again. Drinkers craned their necks. Faces peered around corners. All drawn to the woman standing at the table. His father appeared in the doorway, staring at Emma.

'You've heard from Harvey,' she said, her voice firm and steady. 'Now, I want to give you the real story. The truth as I see it. I want to say something, to you all, to Harvey — and most of all, to Luke.

'Harvey paints Luke as some kind of villain, and a selfish and uncaring son. Well, nothing could be further from the truth. You're wrong, Harvey. *You're* the lucky one. Lucky to have a son like Luke. Earlier, Ursula called me and Luke heroes. I'm not, absolutely not, but Luke is a real hero.'

'Emma . . .' Luke was dying in the blaze of the spotlight. He wanted her to stop and yet he didn't. Even though her words exposed him to attention he'd never have sought, he wouldn't stop her. He couldn't have, even if he'd tried.

He'd seen that expression before, saw it in the way she stood up straight and lifted her chin. When she set her mind to it, nothing could get in Emma Pelistry's way.

'For a start, I bet none of you know what he did in the navy?' she said. 'How he risked his life time and again defusing mines? That he won a commendation for bringing back the body of a skipper trapped in a trawler.'

The bar fell silent.

Luke spotted his mother and Clive at the door, mouths open. His father was leaning on the door frame, seeming to need its support.

'But that's not the truly heroic thing about Luke. Not only the extraordinary things he's done, but the ordinary ones too. He's a good, kind and unselfish man who puts others before himself without even thinking about it. He's always been that way, right from when he was a lad. The quiet one at the back of the class who no one notices but takes in everything. The man who's come back to his community and still wants to give back more and help those around him friend and stranger. Whether that's by taking on the dive centre, or joining the Beachcombers, with . . .'

Harvey stared at Luke in desperation, seeming to shrink in front of him.

'Yeah, that's your son, Harvey,' Emma declared. 'Not the selfish man you described who bears no resemblance to anyone but yourself. Luke's the man who's helped you out time and again and now, rightly, can't give you any more without risking his business and home.' Emma looked right at Luke. 'And — and,' she faltered. 'And that's it. I just wanted you all to know what kind of a man Luke really is and how — how—'

She held his gaze. Only the two of them now.

Emma lowered the mic. 'How I feel about him,' she mouthed, directly at Luke.

There was an agonising moment of silence then the pub erupted with cheering, applause and whistles.

Yet Luke was transfixed on one woman alone: the one who'd just declared her feelings for him in a way he'd never thought could be possible.

She replaced the mic on the table and walked towards the door. There was no sign of his father.

Luke tried to follow her but people kept detaining him with a hand on his arm, asking him if he was OK and what was going on.

He had to shrug them off, not always politely, desperate to get to Emma.

Ursula found him as he combed the room for her, and laid a hand on his arm.

'Luke? Are you OK?'

'No, but it's Emma I'm worried about. She's the only one who matters now and I *have* to find her.'

38

Emma stood on the jetty below the Ferryman, staring out over the water. It wasn't cold but she wrapped her arms around herself as the adrenaline ebbed from her body. Dusk was falling and the buzz of the pub had faded into the background. The water lapped softly against the jetty and a bird called as it settled into its roost. Lights shimmered in the water. What had she done? Shouted at the world — or at least at half of Falford — and told everyone how she felt about Luke.

'Emma!' His voice reached her as he jogged along the jetty. He was out of breath. 'What you said, back in there?' he demanded. 'Did you mean it?'

'I'm sorry I mouthed off in public but I was so angry with your dad,' she said. 'What he said about you was so unjust! I *had* to say how I feel.'

'I wasn't angry with him,' Luke said. 'Not for what he said about me because I know I've done all I can. I can't forgive the things he said to *you*.'

'That I'm cold-hearted?' she murmured. 'It *was* true when I was young and when I came back here. I was simmering with resentment. I was hurt and unjustly blamed you for what happened to our family.'

'You were grieving.' His hand rested on her arm and he spoke with such gentle firmness that she had to fight back fresh tears. 'And as for the crap he said about the money, ignore him. He's a loser. I'll never forgive him for that.'

'He was drunk and bitter,' Emma said, not wanting Luke to suffer because of Harvey's stupidity. 'And I have been hard on you. I should have listened more and tried to understand you . . . I should have trusted you.'

'Trust?' He laughed bitterly. 'I broke that trust a long time ago.'

'I should take some of the blame. I should have told you what I saw between our parents, and we could have tried to work things out together.'

'We were young . . . and none of that matters to me now. I'm sorry about the things I said the other day, about us never being honest with each other.'

'It *was* true though,' Emma said. 'Not now: I wanted to put it right and tell the truth in front of the whole world. What your father said about you was so unjust, and so cruel.'

'I don't care about me, I care about you. There, I'm being honest now too. No one has ever done anything like that for me. The way you stood up — in front of all those people — and said . . . you said that you felt . . .'

'I didn't finish my sentence because I wanted to tell you that part face to face, I'm still in love with you, Luke,' she said gazing up into his face. 'That's the absolute truth. No matter what I said before.'

His cry of relief made her heart sing. 'Me too. All my life I've tried to forget you. I tried to fall in love with other people and I failed. So, lately, I'd given up and built a shell around me.'

'Same,' she said, almost weeping with relief. 'And I refused to admit that it was because, sometimes, your first love is your last. How could I face up to that — admit it to anyone and myself — knowing, if it was true, how was I ever going to be happy again?'

'I've thought the same. In fact, I now realise that I

came back here trying to find what we'd lost,' he said. 'It was a crazy idea. I don't know how I thought that living in your house would bring me closer to you.'

'I didn't know you were here,' Emma said. 'The scary thing is that I wouldn't have come home if I had.'

'Yet you did come home.' There was such delight in his face, Emma almost cried.

'Even then,' she said. 'I was terrified that we'd get together and it would all fall apart again,' she said. 'And that this time, as adults, we'd have no excuses if it didn't work.'

'Then, we'll find a way to make it work,' he declared. 'Why wait until there's a right time for us? Let's make this the right time.'

'I want to. I want to so much. I don't want to go.'

'Then don't. Risk everything! We will make it this time. I love you, Emma. I always have deep down.'

Tears ran down her face. 'I feel the same. The moment you fished me out of the sea, I knew and I was terrified. I almost went straight back to Oxford. I almost ran there and then.'

'I knew too, but I couldn't run,' he said. 'I'd already made my home here again. I couldn't leave . . . though I talked about it when I went to see my mates in Plymouth. I thought about joining up again.'

'No!' Emma said. 'No, please don't.' She wiped her eyes with her hands, aware of people watching them though none dared to come near. 'I have no right to ask you that. Not after I was ready to walk out. Now it's too late. I want to be with you. I want to try again.' Suddenly she burst out laughing. 'I'm acting like a teenager.'

'There's nothing wrong with that.' His fingers

grazed her bare arm. 'Goosebumps . . .'

'It's cool.' It was but that wasn't the whole truth.

'You look beautiful,' he said, drawing a shiver from Emma; not due to any evening chill, but to the powerful pull of desire to this man. A desire she'd felt for so many years but spent so many denying.

'With goosebumps?'

'Always. Let's get away from here. I'm sick of being a spectator sport.'

She took his hand and they almost ran up the terraces and round the side of the pub.

'Where's your dad?' she asked. 'I hope I haven't made things worse.'

'I don't care. That's Dad's problem, not yours or mine. I'll message him but not yet. This is about us, not him.'

In the car park, Clive was comforting Sue Kerr.

'I'm sorry,' she said as Emma and Luke walked past. 'That took some guts.'

Emma nodded. 'I love Luke.'

'And I love Emma and now we're going,' Luke said firmly and, with his arm around her back, they left everyone behind. They didn't stop until they reached the bridge over the creek and the shelter of the willow trees.

'Thank God for that,' he said, pulling her into his arms. The cool evening melted into warmth as he threaded his fingers in her hair and kissed her. They were both greedy for each other, with a hunger born of so many long years.

So much time had passed, so much distance between them — all of it faded away into nothing against this moment: the present. Luke's mouth on hers, his arms around her. Luke: so gentle, so quiet, yet so strong. The teenage infatuation had been tempered in the fires of the trials they'd both been through and strengthened into a deep and long-lasting love.

On her side, at least.

On his, she could but hope and pray.

The kiss ended, but they stayed on the jetty as the stars began to twinkle in the darkening sky. A night bird called, startling her and causing her to hold him tightly.

They both laughed. 'Come home with me tonight,' he said.

Home. That meant the chapel. His home, her old home.

'I want to so much, but Luke, there's so much I need to tell you. Mum came to see me yesterday. I need you to tell you everything.'

'Does it have to be right now? Can't it wait until tomorrow?'

It took a nanosecond to decide. 'Yes.'

'Then let it. There are more important things now.'

He took her hand and led her away from the pub towards the head of the creek. It was almost two miles to the chapel, but the evening was so beautiful she might as well have flown there. They meandered around the estuary and through the deep shadow of the wooded banks, where owls hooted and the foliage rustled.

'Kweetures,' she said, the joy impossible to suppress.

'What are those?'

'What Daisy calls wildlife.'

Luke slipped his arm around her. 'I'll keep you safe.'

From creatures of the night, Emma thought, but

not from the powerful need to be with him, next to him, part of him . . . a need that had overwhelmed her. A feeling that made her completely vulnerable to him and which she could do nothing to resist any longer: love.

The dark woods gave way to the open skies of the dunes behind Silver Cove. Under the moon, the sea and rocks shimmered in the moonlight. The surf was running high up the beach with a low thunder that was majestic and soothing.

Emma rested at the top of the dunes, surveying the silvered beach.

'I've missed this so much,' Luke said.

'I've missed you.'

He took her in his arms and kissed her again before they walked down the lane and through the gates of the Old Chapel and up the stairs to his room. He had a new bed with a huge iron bedstead and they made good use of it until the first threads of dawn appeared in the sky over the cove.

39

Next morning, Emma sat on the wall, bare feet dangling above the sand. The stone was already warm under her palms and Luke's fingertips brushed hers. Behind them, the headstones stood as they always had, guarding the old sailors sleeping peacefully under the Cornish earth.

It was still early; barely eight o clock, yet promised to be a hot August day. Silver Cove would fill with people in the same way the tide had filled it last night. Today, it seemed golden in the sun, last night it had been deserted.

Luke gave her a puzzled look. 'What are you thinking?'

'That this is a funny old place to live.' She interlaced her fingers with his. 'That despite it being a graveyard, I've never felt more alive in my life.'

There was a glint in his eye as he replied. 'There's nothing like a night like we had to make you feel alive.'

She tingled with the memory of the hours in his bed. 'Yes, and no worrying that we're going to be interrupted this time.'

He slipped his arm around her, and she breathed in the sea air with a joy she hadn't felt for a long time. 'I still can't believe we're here. That I am and you are, after everything that's happened.'

'Believe it,' she said. 'I'm not going anywhere.'

'So, you're taking the unit?'

'If it's still available and Jermaine's not too pissed off with me after messing him around. If not, I'm staying in Falford. In the lodge if Maxi will have me. If not, I'll sort it.'

She waited for him to respond. It was a new dawn for them and so much still needed to be said, so much of their hearts needed to be opened.

'This is still your home. It can be both our homes. If you want it.'

She took a deep breath. Another momentous decision had been presented to her. So many in only a few weeks.

'I . . .'

'You don't have to tell me now. Everything is new for us. We can take it slowly.'

She brushed his lips with hers. 'Thank you.'

They walked back to the chapel through the graveyard and stopped in front of the chaplain's headstone.

'You still have the journal?' Luke asked.

'Yes, it's back in Oxford at the flat.'

'Strange to think that we're the only people who'll ever know what really happened. The whole truth, I mean.'

Her fingers tightened around his hand. She had plenty to say but he needed to speak first.

'I said Dad bribed me with the offer of a car,' he went on as the sun warmed their faces. 'Like I told you, I ran home in the rain and put it in the back of the airing cupboard to try and dry it out, then I went out to the yard. Dad was working in the barn. He started baiting me about where I'd been, guessing that I'd been with you and saying stuff . . .'

He hesitated.

'What stuff?' Emma said. 'About me?'

'Yeah, and your dad. About the fact I'd never be good enough. He wound me up and made me angry.

I thought he was just being his bitter, chippy self but now I think he must have known about the affair. He said a few things about your father that make more sense now.'

'I can imagine . . .' Emma said softly. 'Don't spare me. We said we'd be honest.'

'He said your father had no hope of finding the treasure. He was sneering at the idea, acting like he knew it all as usual and that I was just a foolish boy.' Luke sighed. 'That's when I hinted about the journal, to get back at him. I wanted him to realise that I knew more than him. Of course, I regretted saying it but it was too late.'

After Harvey's performance at the pub, Emma could picture Harvey manipulating his son, a young Luke desperate for a crumb of approval and genuine affection.

'Then he turned nice and started apologising and going on about the car. Saying Mum had been on at him and it was time I had my independence. I fell for it. I wanted his have his attention. God, I must have been so naïve.'

'No, you were normal,' she said. 'Like any child hoping for a kind or encouraging word. I spent a long time being disappointed and angry with my father but, since he died, I've tried to understand him more. The fact that, all the time, the clues were waiting in his own home drove him mad. Even if he'd found it, he could never have profited from it. Though I think he'd have tried to dig it up from the farm and bring it back to ours if he'd known.'

'I wish it had never existed,' Luke said. 'But once Dad saw the journal he worked it all out. That part about the coins having a Christian burial at the

362

farm . . . I didn't understand what the reverend meant at the time but Dad guessed: they were buried under the old Celtic cross at Roseberry.

'It was almost a week after I'd taken the journal that Dad had started mending the gate, saying it needed a new post, and that's when I connected the cross and the journal entry. Anyway, it was too late . . . The day after he started digging at the gate, Dad came into the kitchen, streaked with dirt, grinning like an idiot. I'll never forget his face.

'I *knew* then. I didn't want to believe it but I knew he must have read it. I was horrified and upset. I didn't know what to do. Come to you and your dad and tell you I'd taken it. Or keep quiet.' Luke searched her face for forgiveness he no longer needed. 'I wasn't sure if I'd committed a crime. It was theft, wasn't it?'

Her heart went out to him. 'It was accidental and I *would* have stood up for you. I'd have said I gave it to you. I locked you in there. It was my fault, really.'

'How could I put you in that position? I — I know I said some hard things to you earlier this summer. I thought you'd overreacted at the time. We rowed. I said I had no choice but to tell Dad about the journal.'

Emma winced. 'Forget it now. Let's put it behind us.'

He went quiet and Emma let him rest for a moment before she went on. 'I have something to say too. My mother came to see me the other day. She admitted that she'd found the journal when we first moved to the Old Chapel but she never said anything about it.'

Luke's eyes clouded in confusion. 'She already knew about it? Why didn't she tell your father?'

'Because she was angry with him. He'd recently had an affair with a woman at work.'

'Jesus Christ. Mum wasn't the first, then?'

Emma squirmed but she was determined to share everything with him. 'I'm afraid not. I think he'd made a habit of it and my mother was hurt and angry with him. She decided to keep the journal a secret; out of revenge, I suppose. She hid it inside the other dust jacket among the books in the crate. She said she might have shown it to him eventually if he hadn't . . .'

'Moved on to my mum?' His expression was grim.

'Yes. I'm sorry. If she'd revealed it immediately, you'd never have come across it. Things might have been different.'

He let go of her hand and turned away, causing her a moment of panic. He was rightly shocked and angry, even though it wasn't her fault. Heart racing, she waited.

His hand closed around hers and she could breathe again. 'You're right, things might have been different. We might have stayed together and with everyone living in blissful ignorance. Your parents might still be here now, mine too. We might have got married and returned to Falford.' He slipped his arm around her back and held her close. 'Somehow I doubt all of that.'

'Somehow, I do too,' she said, hope rising again. 'Maybe this is the only way things could have turned out, the only way we could have been together. Now we've lived other lives and grown up.'

'Yes. We've come back together and realised that we are the right people for each other. That it doesn't matter that we met when we were teenagers. What matters is who we are now and how we feel about each other.'

Emma brushed his lips with hers, a gentle reassurance. 'I think — I think — I gave the wrong impression

364

when I was young. People thought I was trying to be 'Miss Perfect' but it was all an act. I wanted to live up to Mum and Dad's expectations even though I kicked against them. I can't blame them though. I grew up and all my decisions since have been mine. None of us is perfect.'

'Possibly not,' he said, with a twinkle in his eye. 'Though that's not what I'm thinking at the moment.'

'No use looking at the tide and wishing it had never come in. It will come, no matter what we do. What matters is now.'

The biggest smile she'd ever seen spread over Luke's face as he murmured. 'And now is pretty bloody wonderful.'

'It is.'

They kissed again, holding each other, while joy flowed through Emma. Come hell or high water, in this moment she felt that she could never wish for anything more. Just her and Luke and Silver Cove.

Epilogue

A month later

'How many do you think will turn up to this thing?' Maxi asked Emma, unrolling a canvas banner that read: 'Beachcombers' Big Clean'.

'Could be anything from twenty to a hundred. Who knows? We've never organised a mass beach-clean like this before.' She laughed. 'What am I saying, 'we'? I'm acting as if I've been part of the Beachcombers forever!'

'You'll soon feel like it,' Maxi said.

She and Emma had gone along early to the car park so they could set up the stall with the equipment and refreshments for the volunteers. It had been Emma's idea to take part in the national initiative, which invited the general public to join the Beachcombers on a mega sweep of Silver Cove. The season was quietening down, leaving less visible litter to clear from the beaches. However, the days were shortening and a couple of storms had blown in over the past few days, bringing all manner of rubbish onto the beach.

'Hey, watch out. Here comes the cavalry.'

'Eek. Is it that time already?'

Andy had arrived with the children in his car and they sprang out of the doors, rocket-fuelled with excitement.

Daisy skipped around. 'We're going to find some treasure!'

366

Arlo took up the chant. 'Treasure. Treasure. Treasure.'

'Hey! Settle down, kids!' Andy tried to gather them in. 'This car park is going to get very busy and we don't want anyone *going missing*. I'll take them onto the beach now,' he added despairingly, as the kids wheeled round like mosquitoes.

'Good idea,' Maxi said, handing him a bag and three litter-pickers.

'Come on,' he said, taking their hands to cross the beach road.

'With any luck, they'll be knackered within an hour or two and he can take them home,' Maxi said, holding up crossed fingers.

Marvin and Zoey were the next to arrive by bike, sipping coffee from their flasks and complaining about the overflowing bins at the end of the car park.

Ursula's yellow car pulled up, but this time she wasn't alone. Jermaine emerged from the passenger seat.

'I've brought a new recruit,' she said.

'The more the merrier,' Emma said.

Jermaine grinned. 'Not sure what use I'll be, but Ursula's told me so much about you all, I thought why not. Might even give me some fresh inspiration.'

Emma gave him a hug. 'It's lovely to see you.'

'How's the unit suiting you?' he asked.

'It's brilliant. I've only been there a week but the view is fabulous and I love having my own space.' Emma's agent hadn't been as shocked as she'd expected when she'd first announced her permanent move to Cornwall. She knew it suited Emma creatively and Falford wasn't the other side of the world.

'Come on, let's get you a bag and litter-picker.'

367

Emma noticed Ursula rest her hand very briefly on Jermaine's back.

'I do as I'm told,' Jermaine said with a good-humoured eye-roll. While Maxi issued him with the equipment, Emma spoke to Ursula.

'Nice to see Jermaine here,' she said.

'It is . . . and I can see that look in your eye, Emma Pelistry.'

'What look? I've said nothing.'

'You don't have to. Suffice to say, I've found what I was looking for and it isn't a ring lost a lifetime ago. It's the hope and the strength to move on.'

'Does this mean you and Jermaine . . .'

'Have agreed to see where life takes us.' Ursula rolled her eyes. 'And don't you dare give it a name. We are not 'dating' or 'seeing each other'.' She curled her lip in disgust. 'We are simply . . . happening.'

It was all Emma could do not to burst out laughing but she contented herself with a small smile. 'Happening sounds good. I promise not to offer any advice.'

'Unlike I did to you? I'm well aware I've lectured you to death.'

'I'm glad you did even if I didn't seem grateful at the time.' Emma smiled. 'Now, Ms Bowen, shall we get on with the business in hand?'

Ursula gave a little bow. 'I think we'd better.'

Ursula and Jermaine started to walk to the beach. Soon, Emma became lost in the business of the day. More and more people arrived and needed briefing on what to look for and how to stay safe. Marvin, Zoey and Maxi joined her in handing out pickers, bags and safety advice.

Emma broke off to check her phone, but even as she was thinking that Luke was a little late, his truck rumbled into the car park, stirring up puffs of dust. She still hadn't got over the feeling of excitement that made her heart beat a little faster when he appeared. When she was young, she'd taken these feelings for granted, but they somehow seemed even more powerful and mysterious now she was older.

He greeted her with a kiss. 'Hello. Sorry I'm late.'

'I was getting worried you'd been captured by pirates!'

He laughed. 'Not this time but I did have a call from Mum and Clive, asking if they could join in.'

'Oh?'

'They should be here in a minute.'

A van arrived and two familiar faces approached. Emma hadn't seen that much of Luke's mother since the evening at the pub. Harvey Kerr had returned to Spain and, according to Luke, was in the process of selling the bar. She didn't know what he planned to do next.

'Is there room for two more?' Sue asked.

'Always,' said Emma and helped them find grabbers and bags, before following them onto the beach.

She paused for a moment, enjoying the breeze in her hair and the warmth of the early autumn sun on her face. Everyone was spread out across the sand, poking in rock pools or hunched over the tideline. Luke was helping to identify some 'kweetures' found by Arlo and Daisy.

Emma went over to Sue to see how the new recruits were getting on. She didn't think she'd ever been alone with Luke's mother before.

'Thanks for joining us,' she said cheerfully. 'How's it going?'

'Clive's hooked already. Seen stuff he never knew

existed.' Sue rolled her eyes good-humouredly.

The tension eased a mite, and Emma smiled. 'I still do.'

'I'm sure.' Sue became thoughtful. 'Emma . . . I want to say something. I'm sorry for not being as welcoming to you as I should have been in the past.'

'It was a long time ago,' Emma said, wondering what was coming next. This was the woman who'd had an affair with her father. Who still didn't know — possibly — that Luke had shared the secret with her.

'You're right and I can't put right the things I did wrong. I won't even try. But I want to say that I can see how much Luke means to you now and I know how much you mean to him. I'm so pleased you're back together. I've never seen him so happy.'

'I feel the same,' she said, filled with relief.

'He's told me that he loves you — several times,' Sue went on. 'It took huge guts to stand up and say what he meant to you in front of the pub and to face down Harvey. I should have done it myself. I'd like to think I would have but I'm glad you got there first.'

'I meant what I said. I love him. I always have.'

Sue's eyes glistened. 'I know . . . I should have realised years ago.'

'The important thing is that we all know it now,' Emma said, moved by Sue's admission. 'And we're not going to waste any more time.'

Clive bounded over. 'Sorry, I was distracted by a jellyfish. Bloody huge thing. Never seen anything like it.'

'Really? You're just like a big kid.' Sue linked arms with his. 'Come on, let's take a look.'

Hanging back, Emma watched them all, Luke, the children, Sue and Clive, surrounding the jellyfish before joining in the general excitement. Around them, dozens of people scoured the sand, each intent on finding their own treasure, whatever that might be. An hour had passed by in a heartbeat, and soon it would be time to round everyone back up and sort out their finds.

'I think it's going well,' Luke said.

'Better than I'd hoped. Everyone seems to be enjoying it. Being in charge for the first time, I was so nervous that no one would come or something disastrous would happen.'

He held her hand. 'It hasn't, so you can relax. Come on, let's do our bit.'

They meandered to the far end of the beach near the rock pools. The two of them were the only people at that side of the beach, apart from Ursula and Jermaine.

'Tide's going to turn soon,' Luke said. 'We should start to usher people back to the car park so we can sort out their finds.'

Emma nodded but, before they could turn back, they heard a shout from Ursula. She was running towards them, Jermaine in her wake.

'Emma! Luke!'

They jogged towards her, meeting her on the tideline. Her eyes were shining with joy and amazement. 'L-look!'

She held something between her fingers. It was small, grey and round.

For a second, Emma thought it was Ursula's lost ring.

'It's a coin,' Ursula said. 'And it looks like a silver dollar.'

'I found it,' Jermaine said proudly.

'You did, indeed!' Ursula slapped his back.

Luke was more circumspect. 'Surely it can't be from the *Minerva*?'

'Oh. I think it is. I'm almost certain. Take a closer look.'

He examined it, shaking his head. 'It could be. I think it is. Wow.'

'If it is, it's the first to be found since the hoard.' Emma eyed the small disc of metal in wonder, thinking of the way it and its companions had been fought over for so many years.

Luke handed it back to Ursula, nodding at a large man and a woman in pink wellies, who were observing them from a short distance away, like curious gulls.

The man trudged over to them.

'You lot look happy,' he boomed, beady eyes fixed on Ursula's hand. 'Found any treasure?'

Emma held her breath. The man's eyes were gleaming with interest.

Jermaine was about to open his mouth but Ursula cut him off.

'Sadly, no,' she said. 'Unless you count a Lego dinosaur as treasure.' She whipped a red stegosaurus out of her pocket. 'I was saving it for my friends' children, but of course you're welcome to it, if you feel the need.'

The man curled his lip in contempt then laughed. 'Naw, you're all right, love. Thanks all the same.'

'Actually, it's time we all went back to the car park with our finds,' Luke said to him. 'See you there?'

The man trundled off, laughing with the woman in the pink wellies, probably disgusted that grown adults were so excited about a stegosaurus.

'We must never tell anyone about this,' Ursula said

as soon as he was out of hearing. 'That means you too, Jermaine. I can't think of anything worse than seeing our beach swamped with treasure seekers and detectorists.' Ursula placed the coin in Luke's palm and closed his fist around it. 'Some secrets are best kept, don't you think?'

Jermaine crossed his heart. 'My lips are sealed.'

'Agreed, Ms Bowen,' Emma and Luke said solemnly.

'Good.' Ursula gave them a stern glare. 'Now, shall we gather up our other finds and go home?'

Lugging their bags, Jermaine and Ursula headed across the sand to the car park, leaving Emma and Luke alone on the beach.

Emma touched his arm. 'Is it really a dollar from the *Minerva*?'

'Who knows?' He shrugged. 'Could be. Does it really matter?'

'No. Not at all.'

Emma thought of the coin, tossed into the sea two centuries before and finally washed up at their feet. 'I've often wondered why the chaplain buried the coins at the farm. What do you think?'

Luke stared at the battered silver in his palm. 'I still can't work it out. The ship had been captured from Portuguese pirates by the Royal Navy when it went down in the storm. The Reverend Saul had obviously discovered one of its few lifeboats.'

'I think some of the officers and a few crew must have been sent ashore or escaped with part of the cargo but they didn't make it ashore alive,' Emma said. 'Whether they intended to return the coins to the Admiralty or make off with them, we'll never know. Either way, the chaplain must have taken the booty and hidden it on Roseberry Farm.'

Luke thought before answering. 'Judging by the guilt he felt, I wonder if he'd been blackmailed into handing over some or all of it by one of the locals who'd helped him move and bury the bodies,' he said. 'Maybe they planned on hiding it temporarily and then retrieving it later. Maybe he'd died before he could tell anyone and, for some reason, the treasure had never been found.'

'I guess we'll never know now,' Emma said.

'No, and . . . this is yours.' He took her hand and placed the coin on her palm. 'You keep it. I've got everything I need.'

She closed her fingers around the silver, still warm from his hand. 'So have I.'

Slipping it into her jeans pocket, she walked with him across the sand, certain she'd already found more than she'd ever need or hoped for.

Acknowledgements

I do hope you've enjoyed reading *A Golden Cornish Summer*. Like many novels, the story emerged from a conglomeration of ideas. That's the beauty of fiction!

The first seed was planted in my mind in 2009 after the Staffordshire Hoard — a trove of Anglo-Saxon treasure — was found on the outskirts of the village where I live. It fascinated me and I began to imagine what would happen if it was found on the land of two warring families. Like many people, I'd also become intrigued by the legend of the shipwrecked silver of Dollar Cove in Cornwall. When I started my Falford series, which is set on the Lizard, I decided I would finally write my 'sunken treasure' book.

Then, in 2020, during the pandemic, I started following a wonderful account on Twitter called @LegoLostAtSea by Tracey Williams, who has generously answered many of my research questions. After finding thousands of pieces of sea-themed Lego washed up on beaches in South Devon, Tracey became interested in the changing nature of beachcombing and began to research the age and origin of many of the manmade items she discovered. Tracey has now written a book called *Adrift — The Curious Tale of the Lego Lost at Sea*, which is published by Unicorn.

I got the idea for a group of beachcombers who are determined to clean up their local beach. Some of them are also interested in recycling their finds or using them as inspiration for art.

I must thank the hugely talented artist, Hannah George, who answered my research questions about Emma's job.

I also want to thank the friends who have supported me while writing this book: the Friday Floras, The Party People, the Coffee Crew and my bookseller buddy, Janice Hume. A big thank you to Milly Johnson, who has also been very supportive of my work.

While last year was very challenging in some respects, it also brought a lot of joy for me. More readers got in touch than ever and I was able to meet some of them face to face again. With their support, the first two novels in the Falford series became paperback and ebook bestsellers. None of this could have happened without the support of Team Avon including Cara Chimirri, Becci Mansell, Ellie Pilcher, copy editor Rhian McKay and the indefatigable sales team, who make sure my stories reach shelves and e-readers across the globe.

I also want to thank my agent, Broo Doherty, who has been with me throughout my career. It's great to be able to celebrate together in person once more.

Finally, my family have been amazing as always. Thank you Mum, Dad, John, Charlotte and James. ILY.